DRAGON'S CAPTIVE

CASSIE ALEXANDER
KARA LOCKHARTE

Whilst in my boundless world, I feel
both deathless and dead cold.
—Luceafărul, Mihai Eminescu

ABOUT DRAGON'S CAPTIVE

Sammy O'Connor didn't mean to steal a dragon's necklace... she just kind of did.

Little did she know that the viciously hot and muscled Rax Janvier would come to claim it—and her—would be willing to do anything to get it back. It's a fragment of a key that opens up a lock to his past—and hers.

Can she survive being kidnapped by a sea dragon who's obsessed with her? And what happens if she starts to want him back?

CHAPTER 1

"SO, DAMIAN DOESN'T KNOW ANY ELIGIBLE GUYS, LIKE AT ALL?" SAMMY was sitting across from her best friend and old roommate, Andi, at Jones and Shah Coffee. They were hanging out before their separate evening plans: Sammy, hostessing at a high-end restaurant down-town, and Andi, going in early to the hospital to work into a nightshift.

The small café was lightly crowded, full of the scent of strong coffee and the iced lemon scone Sammy'd bought to wolf down before work tonight. Other people's conversations wrapped around them, as spinning spoons clanked against glasses and the espresso machine hissed. One woman laughed loudly in a corner as she flirted too hard on a first date—Sammy recognized both the woman's tone and her date's slight expression of horror.

First dates always suck, Sammy thought.

"Sammy," Andi said flatly, giving her a maternal headshake, calling her attention back to the table. "No. You do not want this kind of hassle, trust me." Her best friend waved a hand over herself. Andi was dressed in purple scrubs and wearing Dansko shoes with a cute checkered print on them, and the blue streak in her black hair was barely visible in her 'I'm going to work' bun. Tearing off a bite of the scone to push into her mouth, Sammy had absolutely no idea what Andi was even talking about.

"The *hassle* of someone giving me a three-carat diamond ring?" Sammy licked icing off her finger and then mimed difficulty raising her coffee with her left hand, even though Andi wasn't wearing jewelry right now. "Oh yeah, I can see how that must be a really heavy arm workout," Sammy teased.

Andi laughed. "A ring that I can't wear to work because, while gorgeous, it's ridiculous. But no, really Sammy, you know what I mean." And Andi gave her that look that was all: *We've talked about this before. You know I'm engaged to a dragon-shifter, right?*

Which meant it was Sammy's turn to give her a meaningful, *But why can't I ever see him as a dragon?* stink-eye, back, until both of them grinned.

"Honestly, Sammy," Andi said, getting real, looking around the room they were in and leaning forward. "There are at least three security cameras in this coffee shop, ever since that attempted robbery. And I guarantee you that right now all of them are pointed at me."

Sammy pushed a wave of red hair out of her face as she glanced up to see the little plastic bulbs set in the coffee shop's ceiling, which were new. Andi was right. "Why?"

"Because I don't want to have a bodyguard. This is our compromise."

Sammy pretended to think. "So...you're kind of like Beyoncé, is what you're saying?"

Andi laughed again. "No. Although I do sing better than you do." She stuck out her tongue at Sammy. "Damian's people have better things to do than to watch over me personally—but there's a trade-off. If I get to pretend to have a normal life, then someone's going to be low level watching over me all the time. Or listening in," she said, tapping at her phone on the table between them. "So don't say anything lewd."

"Who? Me? I would fucking never." Sammy put an affronted hand to her chest, laughing as Andi laughed too, before taking a sober inhale. "It's...just hard to believe that your life's changed so much,

Andi. Don't get me wrong, I *do* believe you." Sammy knew the long term consequences of not being believed—she had known her best friend for too many years and they'd gone through too much stuff together for her not to. If Andi said her man was a dragon, well then, he really was. *Somehow.* "It's just different is all," she said with a half shrug. "I mean, who would've guessed a few months ago that Andi Ngo would become a dragon's most valuable possession?"

"Yeah," Andi said, giving Sammy one of those dreamy 'hopelessly-in-love' smiles that she'd been prone to, ever since she and Damian had become serious—the kind that made Sammy really happy for Andi, but a little sad for herself. Sammy knew it wasn't fair, but she was also only human, so she tried not to beat herself up about it. She shoved another tart bite of scone into her mouth.

"Although he doesn't treat me like a possession," Andi went on, in her man's defense. "He's not an asshole…. Well, actually, he is, just not to me."

Sammy laughed, then picked up Andi's phone to talk into it like it was a microphone. "Did you hear that? Damian's *not*, I repeat, *not* an asshole," she said loudly before setting it back down and grinning at her friend. "There. You're covered."

Andi snickered and pocketed her phone. "All right, girlie, so, enough about my relationship. Why are you asking about eligible men? What happened with the smart guy, Mr. Working-on-his-PhD?"

"Yeah," Sammy began slowly, sinking toward the table to massage her temples with the first two fingers of each hand, bringing her closer to the comforting scent of her coffee. "Remember the research project he was working on so hard? I guess you could say it was a 'group project.'"

"No!" Andi gasped, already knowing which way this story was going to go. "Don't tell me that! By which I mean, do tell me, so I can go and murder him!"

"I bet your phone caught that too," Sammy said with a headshake, although she and Andi had probably watched enough true crime shows on TV together in their time as roommates to get away with actual murders if they put their mind to it.

"How'd you find out?" Andi pressed.

"I drove over to pick him up from campus and because I miraculously found good parking I decided to surprise him—and caught him boning some other grad student on his desk."

"Ugh!" Andi said, furious on her behalf. "I mean, you're so much better off without him, obviously, but the gall!"

"Down girl, I know."

Andi's eyes narrowed and she frowned. "Sammy, why didn't you tell me?"

Sammy looked across the table at her best friend and couldn't really say what she was thinking: *Because. You look so happy—you make things look easy—why can't they be easy for me?* Andi reached across the table to grab her hand, reading a little of it on her anyhow, and Sammy squeezed her hand back.

"It just happened two days ago," Sammy said, blowing things off. "And I knew I was seeing you today—now that you're not living with me it's a lot harder for me to keep track of whether you're sleeping or not.. Plus, I'm not wrecked or anything. More just disgusted with the gender."

Andi let go of her hand but kept staring at her, and Sammy knew she was being *nursified*.

"I feel bad leaving you all alone, Sammy. What if…you get another roommate? Or—a cat? Or a puppy? I mean now that Damian's bought the building—"

"Don't think I don't appreciate that, Andi, because I do." Not having to pay rent, thanks to Andi's *bajillionaire* fiancé's largess was pretty damn amazing. "But a cat is not the same as a person—though it can't just be any person, you know?"

"No, it can't, can it," Andi said, agreeing with her—then getting a wicked gleam in her eye. "I mean, I probably am pretty irreplaceable as a roommate."

"Yeah, I'm not sure how that Craigslist ad would go: 'Roommate wanted, 20-something woman, must be into serial killer documentaries and cars.'"

"Hey now, I wasn't into cars."

"Well, if I'm going to bother replacing you, I might as well aim for perfection."

Andi laughed. "Actually? Yeah. You should. Hold out for the good stuff, always." She pulled out her phone to check the time and grumbled. "I'm sorry, Sammy, I've got to get going." Andi got up and navigated to the condiment bar to grab a to-go lid, while Sammy not so subtly tried to see if the security cameras really did watch as she returned. "Dress shopping? This weekend?" Andi asked.

"Wouldn't miss it for the world," Sammy said. "And you'd better wear your ring then."

"Why?" Andi questioned, picking up her bag.

"So if we get into trouble, without any bodyguards, you can punch somebody out with it," Sammy told her, pretending to give someone a left hook.

"I don't need bodyguards, Sammy, when I have you." Andi beamed and gave her a careful not-spilling-her-coffee hug. "Talk tomorrow?"

"For sure," Sammy said, and air-kissed her cheek.

SAMMY WAITED until Andi was off to the bus stop knowing that Andi wouldn't accept a ride into work unless she was going to be seriously late. Although maybe being on a bus was safer for her than being on the open road, because Sammy was going to have to break a few traffic laws to make it to her apartment in time to change and drive back downtown.

She parked outside her building, jogged up the stairs to the blue door of her apartment, let herself inside, and ran for her closet.

Andi was right—it was a little lonely here. Especially because Eumie wasn't downstairs in their bakery anymore—they were off doing God knew what. Sammy'd lost both her nearby best friends in the space of a few months.

Andi wasn't really *lost*-lost, but she was busy. Hanging out with Damian or letting him dote on her. Sammy had been over for a few awkward dinners at their place, and it wasn't the same as it had been —and it wasn't even Damian's fault. He was an excellent sport, and he played the host nicely. It was just that things were different now, what with Andi living there, was all. The last time she'd gone over and they'd tried to make a girls' night of it, watching the latest Netflix murder-show, some horrible sounding alarm had gone off in the middle of things. Sammy about peed her pants it was so loud, and Andi wouldn't tell her what was going on, "For your own safety, I mean it," and then had been tense until a few hours later when Damian had come back.

From…where? Doing…what?

Dragon-stuff?

Sammy supposed Andi knew, and she knew she didn't have a right to know. But now that they were keeping secrets from each other, things just weren't the same.

Then again, she'd been keeping a pretty big one from Andi—and everyone else she'd ever met, for the most part—her whole life.

Sammy sighed and tugged down the tight cream-colored dress she'd be wearing tonight, then de-sexed it with a loose pink silk scarf around her neck and a fitted navy blazer. She pushed her feet into matching navy flats—she was verging on stewardess, but that was okay, as long as she looked like she worked for a high-class airline.

It would just take time for their friendship to find a new normal, was all. Sammy knew that, and she could be patient. It wasn't like she had a ton of other friends besides. Acquaintances, maybe, and a string of disappointing men, for sure. But none of them were as solid as Andi, and Sammy just had to believe that if she waited out this phase in Andi's life—even if she wasn't sure of what it *was* or *how long it would last*—that they'd be strong again.

In a new way.

Eventually.

Right?

She looked at herself in her bathroom mirror, pulling her long curly red hair into a loose bun, swiped some lipstick on, poofed herself with blush, used the same blush for her eyeshadow, grabbed her purse, and ran for the door.

She swung it open to find a small box on her stoop—clearly labeled for their address, but not to anyone in particular.

Seeing as she hadn't ordered anything lately, it had to be for Andi.

She swiped her phone open and found Andi's contact in it as 'Lefty' because once upon a time when they'd still lived together, pre Damian, Andi had expressed a desire to date Vin Diesel and Lefty from the *Fast and the Furious* movies was as close as she could get. (Plus, it was kind of funny, since Andi didn't know how to drive.)

There's a mysterious box here for you, she texted using voice-to-text as she brought it inside. *Don't worry, it's too small to be a body part.*

Andi texted back an eye roll emoji, faster than Sammy would've thought—she must've still been on the bus. *D warned me this might happen. That people would send us stuff just because, to try to get in his good graces.*

Sammy snorted softly. *Well, it's not a toaster or a shoe rack, so I know they didn't get it off your registry—oh wait, you don't have a registry,* she said. Sammy had maintained that people would still want to buy them gifts, whereas Andi said that was silly because they already had everything.

Andi sent her back an emoji with its tongue sticking out. *If it's not ticking, and there's no loose powder, want to open it?*

Sammy hesitated—yes, she might be late, but.... What the hell would anyone send someone like Damian Blackwood's fiancée to try to get on his good side? As Andi's old roommate, she already knew that Andi's most useful possessions were an infinite number of pens and sharpies—there must've been some nurse version of the sock-eating dryer monster that lived in the hospital basement, subsisting entirely on black ink. Or maybe it was a small box of Vietnamese instant coffee packets....

She set it down on her kitchen counter and opened the packaging. Inside the shipping box was another box—fancy and old, made of very structurally sound black cardboard that was embossed with tiny ripples—and inside of that, she found a dark purple velvet jewelry box.

Sammy knew she probably should've slowed her roll, but she also felt the need to just confirm that it really wasn't any body part at this point, and her get-to-work-on-time clock was ticking. She flipped the lid and inside, cradled in more purple velvet, was a lovely teardrop-shaped red cabochon the size of her thumb, strung on a delicate gold chain.

She pulled it out of the box so it could swing freely. It looked old—and old-timey—because girls her age hardly ever wore jewelry like this.

Then again, could someone her age afford something like this? She honestly didn't think so.

She snapped a photo and sent it to Andi.

Oh God—gorgeous, but so not me. Who is it from?

Sammy investigated the rest of the box thoroughly. *No clue. No card.*

Well, I'll ask around, I guess? Although I don't think anyone in my contacts list sent that....

Me either. They both knew their friend group was more of the gift-card or booze set.

Your brother? Sammy guessed although she felt it extremely doubtful. The only jewelry Andi's brother had ever gotten Sammy when they'd dated was a little peridot solitaire ring for her birthday. She still wore it sometimes at work on her left ring finger to detour creepers.

No way, Andi agreed, and then went on: *Hey, so, don't hate me, but...I think I'm going to have to pass on dress shopping.*

Sammy stared at her phone, mysterious jewelry and upcoming job forgotten. *If you picked a dress out without me, I will not be your best friend anymore, so help me God,* she typed, followed quickly by: *joking-NOT-JOKING.*

It's not that! Andi protested. *We're taking a last-minute trip to Italy.*

But what about your job? Sammy asked, knowing full well that Andi only worked because she wanted to.

We just bought my hospital a new wing. They'll manage without me for a month just fine. And I've been thinking of going part-time, anyways.

Sammy huffed at her phone. That was the first she'd heard of it.

But just like she hadn't run straight to Andi to tell her about Mr. PhDickhead, maybe Andi was pulling back a little, too.

We'll dress shop the day I get back, I promise, okay? Andi sent her.

Sure. Love you, Sammy sent, with an emoji smooch.

Sammy put her phone in her blazer's pocket and stared at the necklace for a little bit longer. If no one knew who it was from...and Andi didn't like it...and if they'd shared clothes *all the time* back when Andi used to live with her—Sammy's hands rose, and she clasped the necklace around her neck quickly. The flat back of the cold stone warmed up quickly against her skin as she hid the gemstone with her scarf, and voila, no one would be the wiser.

CHAPTER 2

GETTING PAID TO BE NICE TO RICH PEOPLE WAS EXHAUSTING.

Andi had warned her about that—actually, she'd said, "Try sick, rich people, they're twice as bad" —but now that Sammy didn't have to pay rent, she'd decided to job hop a little. And when a friend of a friend had told her about an opening at Belissima's, she'd mentioned it to Andi, who'd almost certainly had Damian put a good word in, and the hostessing job there fell into her lap.

She circled the block in her Subaru WRX looking for parking, and Ernesto, working the restaurant's valet stand, took pity on her, flagging her down when she'd made her third loop.

"Need a hand?" he asked as she slowed and lowered her window.

"Yes, please!" She was already fifteen minutes late and who knew what mood Bastian was in tonight.

He whistled up the next valet and made a gimme-motion for her keys. She practically leaped out of the car and tossed them to him. "You're a life-saver!"

"Yeah, I know," he told her with a grin, handing her keys off to the next uniformed man.

She paused right outside the restaurant's tall glass doors to compose herself. At first, hostessing had seemed interesting and fun.

Challenging, even, to get used to a whole new workflow and way of being. And getting to dress up every night was nice—she had to admit that working downtown was a whole lot snazzier than the car shop. She could have manicures now that lasted even.

But over the past month, the dark reality of the situation had begun to settle in.

Because if the naysayers at the car shop talked to her long enough, they'd eventually realize she knew what she was saying. Sometimes it was like she could feel them finally acknowledge she was there after she talked about torque or turbo lag.

But at Belissima's…there was never going to be any equality. Not really. She was paid all right, but she saw the cars people brought up to the valet stand. (And not for the first time had she thought she might be happier out there, driving around other people's expensive vehicles, except for the fact that she knew she probably shouldn't be trusted with them. Just because she'd never gotten arrested when she'd done dumb shit with Danny didn't mean she hadn't deserved it….)

No, the people who came to Belissima's were just better than you, and they generally weren't afraid if you knew it. Most of them were pleasant…it was just that the ones that weren't, the ones who treated Sammy like surprise gum on a Jimmy Choo heel, were so tragically awful that it wiped the memories of the relatively decent vast majority away.

It felt like someone yelled at her at least once a night. The first week, she'd assumed the problem was with her; the second week, she realized the problem was with them.

Men would schedule their anniversary dinners on the wrong day and it suddenly became her fault, or a party would get upset that you couldn't accommodate an extra three people in the fancy room—which had limited seating! It was in a refurbished bank vault! You literally could not squish extra people in there, it was illegal! Or someone who she very clearly remembered double-checking their entire menu for their allergy considerations would still show up and, she didn't know, pull a shrimp from home out of their Birkin and pretend that it'd magically appeared in their salad. It was weird. *Rich people were weird.* And everyone was unhappy when they didn't get their way.

At the car shop when someone was an asshole, she could generally give as good as she got. Her old boss didn't mind and he'd never heard of Yelp. But Bastian was a restauranteur. He actually gave a shit, and Sammy knew he had a reputation to maintain. People weren't going to pay twenty-two dollars for shrimp-less salads at a one-star kind of place.

And he was also a yeller, which Sammy just didn't like. Camaraderie yelling was fine; like in the bleachers during sports games or checking in to see if everybody was getting their shit done, that was okay. But four drinks by the end of the night yelling…was not.

Which was probably why, subconsciously, she'd started running a little late to work each day this week. Like her feet were smarter than she was and just didn't want to put her body through the rest of the drama. Feet that she rewarded with flats, although Andi's Danskos were looking comfier by the day….

"You're late, again," Jeanine told her as she checked in. She was Bastian's floor manager and had a seemingly psychic ability to avoid getting yelled at. In fact, Sammy wasn't sure she could ever remember seeing Jeanine and Bastian together in the same room—maybe they had a Dr. Jekyll and Mr. Hyde situation going on.

"I couldn't find parking, I'm sorry," Sammy said, not really sorry at all. There was glassware to polish and a stack of menus to fold, and Sammy started in, dodging around Jeanine's disapproving presence for the menus Bastian had printed off for tonight.

"Look, if I could get paid to avoid all this crap, I would, but I can't, and neither can you, so, adjust your schedule to allow time for parking—or clsc your pretty little accent and your pretty little ass won't be able to save you."

Sammy bit back a retort and nodded. "Got it."

. . .

THE DOORS OPENED at 6 p.m. and the first wave of customers came in, older people who liked to eat early and go home to bed. It was easier then; no one had to wait for tables, so everyone got seated quickly and usually they just made small talk. It was nice and Sammy made sure to keep her Irish accent 'on' because she reminded them of past vacations, which led to fond memories and higher tips, even though at least once a shift someone would start to ask questions.

"What part of Ireland are you from, dear?" asked a woman with perfectly coiffed white-as-a-Q-tip hair.

Sammy smiled at her. "I'm not. I live in the Laurel district. My parents were from a small town in County Mayo."

"Oh, that's so nice! It's so beautiful there. We used to go there every few years, on vacation, didn't we, Charles?" the woman told her husband, expecting him to chime in.

He cupped a hand behind his ear where Sammy could see the tiny pigtail of a hearing aid. "What was that?"

"County Mayo. On vacation! Remember?"

"Oh! Yes. Lovely place! So many sheep everywhere!"

Sammy's smile ratcheted a few microns tighter. "So I hear," she said. But hearing's all she'd ever done. She'd never put a foot on Irish soil herself. Her parents had always planned to take her when she was older, but it was always easier for her grandparents to visit her in the US, since they didn't have jobs and her parents did, and then one by one they died and flying "back home" as a family for funerals was always too expensive and possibly too sad until everything went to hell and it was too late.

Because after one family trip to the beach, she and her parents had had a horrific encounter with a mysterious, violent stranger—and an eight-year-old Sammy was the only one who'd come back alive. She'd gotten a brief flash of notoriety and then been turned over to the foster system, where the kids had made fun of her until her accent had mostly faded away. And now that she was twenty-six, she only used her 'pretty little accent' because it felt like all she had of her past, but even then she knew it was a relic unless she was being silly, emotional, or drunk, or playing on the sympathies of elderly white people.

The woman who'd just sat down cleared her throat, waiting for Sammy to hand her a menu. "Thinking of the Bunratty Castle?"

No. Only castles made out of sand. "Yeah," Sammy said, with an apologetic headshake.

"No problem, dear," the woman said, putting a warm hand on Sammy's arm, as Sammy blinked herself back to the present and handed them their menus.

"I hear the salmon is really amazing today," she told them before quickly excusing herself.

AT EIGHT, THE 'GROWN-UPS' came in, people who might spend as much on alcohol as they did on the food, considering Belissima's vast wine cellar, and Sammy was glad she wasn't the sommelier, Salvatore, although she did find the man unbearably snooty.

She hadn't quite figured out how snoot adjacency worked. Like how long did one have to work here before you thought you were rich yourself and started looking down your nose at Applebee's and saying things like, "Two-thousand-seven was a great year for pinot?" She knew if she stayed here, it was coming for her; it seemed to have afflicted everyone else who worked here, with the exception of the valet team, and that, she thought, was because they were lucky enough to be working outdoors.

She had enough money to afford to look nice, but other hostesses definitely looked nicer and, what, did they do nothing but shop on Poshmark for deals on designer stuff all morning? Or did they just let more of the clientele hit on them and wind up dating people who could give them gifts?

Speaking of, she fished the little peridot ring out of her blazer's inside pocket and slid it on because here they came—guys from the financial towers downtown, maybe even some who worked for Damian, rolling in to visit the bar and bullshit about their days, raking her with their eyes. The ring was for them so that in addition to looking professionalish, she always looked a little bit taken.

And it helped with the attached women who came in for their

fancy dates, anniversaries, or birthdays—the fake engagement ring made her look safer to them, too. Samantha O'Connor was *not* lonely, and she was *not* here to steal your man, no-siree, she was just here to safely guide you to your table.

THERE WAS a brief lull for no good reason around eight-forty and a well-dressed couple came in, looking like they'd already pre-gamed a little down the street, giving her unreasonably expectant smiles. Sammy tensed. She knew that look.

"Do you have any tables open tonight?" the man asked.

"Just the bar," Sammy said, glancing back. "We can serve food there; there might be some seats, let me check?"

"No," the woman told her. "We need a table. It's important."

"I'm so sorry. All of our tables have been booked for weeks."

And this was where the snoot would've come in handy because if she just could've acted somehow like they belonged here less than she did, she might have been able to deflect them, but—

"I see one, right there," the woman said, pointing an exquisitely manicured nail through the semi-frosted glass behind Sammy.

"Yes, well, are you...." Sammy began, consulting the books, and then remembered what a bad idea that was, because people were not above lying sometimes, and once they were seated, it was impossible to gracefully kick them out, things were sure to end in tears. But then she saw an annotation in the reservation book in Bastian's thick, blocky handwriting.

Rax Janvier—single top. Give him anything he wants.

'Give him anything he wants' was underlined. She licked her lips as the man in front of her in the bespoke suit waited expectantly, perhaps hoping he could be a Smith.

"Mr. Janvier?" Sammy asked, trying to say the last name right and having no idea if she was accomplishing it or not. At this point, she was more curious to see if these people would just boldly lie.

"Yes, of course. And that's my table," the man said, giving the woman with him a look.

What was this to them—some kind of game?

"I'm sorry, but I'm going to need to see ID," Sammy said.

The man's eyes widened. "Who are you? Are you a cop? Are you carding me?" His voice stepped up in volume with each phrase, and Sammy knew it was only a matter of moments before it carried back to Bastian, who was surely hitting drink three by now.

Then, behind the couple, through the tall glass doors, she spotted a man getting out of a 1972 dark metallic blue E-type Jaguar at the valet stand—legitimately the world's sexiest car. Garrett, one of her foster brothers who'd gotten her into cars, would've wept to get to see one in person, and as it was, she was having a *moment*. And then the owner got out of it. He walked into the restaurant alone with the kind of stride that said he had places to be, and even through the glass, there was something about him. His hair was dark and wavy, barely tamed by whatever he'd put in it, his skin was the kind of brown that came naturally and stayed that way, and his eyes were—she looked away before she could see them, because if she saw them, then he'd catch her staring and—she returned her attention to the couple in front of her, even as her hands found one another and she slid the peridot ring from her left hand to her right hand quickly.

"I refuse to show you ID until you show me to my table," the man in front of her went on.

"Mr. Janvier?" Sammy guessed as the man from outside strode forward, giving him a look that said, *rescue me?* He frowned at her lightly, maybe not a frown, more of a pensive look like he was wondering if he'd ever seen her before. Sammy was very sure he hadn't. But now that she could stare a little, his eyes were a shade of rich amber.

"Yes," he said, coming up to the side of the host stand, looking impatient.

She glared at the two people who'd just lied to her, picked up a menu, and said, "Right this way."

Rax sat down at the table the woman directed him to, which had been conveniently set to face a nicer view toward the back of the room and the windows, and he didn't like that.

First off, because he wasn't comfortable not having his back against a wall—and the windows counted as a wall, more so than the rest of the space in the room did, and secondly, the hostess. Whom he didn't recognize. But he hardly ever ate out, although this was the only restaurant he went to when he did, on the rare occasions he had events to celebrate and felt like dipping into someone else's wine cellar. There was no reason for him to remember Bastian's prior hostess, or the one before that and so on.

Except—he rearranged his seat to be on the other side of the table, moving all of his place settings until the windows were at his back and he'd given himself a view of the hostess stand. The lightly frosted glass couldn't hide her from him; in fact, it made him feel freer to stare, as though she were an exotic animal trapped at a zoo. From his new position he could easily make out her disappointingly sensible flats, which led up to creamy calves dotted with light freckles, and those led up to her possibly pert ass—and as if hearing his mind's silent plea, she pulled off her blazer and folded it neatly, tucking it onto the shelf with the menus beneath the stand.

Pert indeed.

He drummed his fingers on the white tablecloth in front of him.

Who was she?

And—why did she radiate magic?

He didn't take his eyes off of the woman as the server took his order. He knew what he was having, the same thing he always did when he was here to remember the anniversary of his release from imprisonment. If it wasn't currently on the menu, he knew Bastian would make it for him.

He folded his hands in front of him, still considering the girl. Anyone wandering through life with that much magic on them should know better. Know to stay shielded. Hide it when they were out, lest they attract unwanted attention.

Like his, he thought darkly.

She was beautiful, yes, even though her dark blue eyes were set a little too wide, and her chin was a little too narrow. Freckles dusted her pale peachy skin, and her red hair was barely tamed by the bun she'd wrapped it up in; there were licks of curls springing free by her ears and against her neck. So he might have even found her entranc ing, regardless, despite the fact she smelled entirely human when she'd led him to his table—but the field of power practically pulsing off her guaranteed she'd intrigue him. And what was more, her magic had a familiar tinge to it. He licked his lips...he'd been alive a very, very, long time. He'd encountered all sorts of energies. Of course everything felt vaguely familiar. There wasn't much in this world that could surprise him anymore. Or in any of the others.

But she *seemed* familiar somehow, even though that was impossible.

"Can I interest you in a glass of wine, Mr. Janvier?"

Salvatore, Belissima's obsequious sommelier, came over with his hands folded behind his back and blocked his view. Rax's gaze flick ered up at him. Here was a man who made his living by recom mending rarified gastronomic experiences, which was in a way, Rax supposed, like what he offered at his casino, except the experiences he recommended there were more costly and occasionally violent.

Rarified nonetheless, though.

"I'll take a bottle of whatever you think pairs best with my order," Rax said, instead of asking for what he really wanted: *a bottle—and the woman.*

But he could just as easily drink and contemplate her from his table. She wasn't going anywhere else until close, and maybe between now and then he could figure out why it felt like he knew her.

SAMMY FELT Mr. Janvier's gaze on her, tracing down the back of her body like a lover's hand, and she hoped she was far enough away from him that he couldn't see the prickles of her gooseflesh.

19

Had he really just switched his place setting around to see her better?

No way.

But...*maybe?*

At first, she assumed she was just making it up for her pride's sake —he was the hottest man she'd seen in months, and she was bouncing back from being cheated on. She would've been lying if she'd said she hadn't wanted him to look.

But as she sat table after table of Belissima's patrons she realized her fever dream was, in fact, reality. His eyes had a dark amber fire as they narrowed, watching her with intent, his chiseled jaw that was shaded by just the right amount of stubble clenched periodically, and his lips were pursed in contemplation.

As he stared.

At her.

Unabashedly.

She wasn't sure how she felt about that. She'd taken off her blazer because it'd gotten hot—all right, she'd gotten a little hot and bothered there for a moment, right after he'd come in. *But that could have been because of his car!* And now she felt like she couldn't put it back on without....

What, being rude and interrupting his show?

A show that a tiny part of her was all too willing to give him?

In fact, right now, she found herself comprised of too many parts to count. There was the common sense part of her, fueled by her childhood, past bad decisions, and her obsession with serial killer documentaries, and it was all: *RUN GIRL RUN!* But some other parts —just as loud! —were remembering the shock of seeing her so-called-boyfriend railing some other chick over a desk a few days ago, and as unfeminist as it was to welcome male attention at work, it felt good to have someone be interested.

Especially someone who looked like *him* because *fucking hell.*

Oh, Andi, I'm going to have such a story for you—

But then she remembered Andi was off in Italy.

Which was possibly where Mr. Janvier was from.

Or was the name French?

"Sammy?" asked Jeanine.

"Yes!" Sammy said, snapping to, as the manager gave the group of people coming through the door a meaningful look—and then ditched her.

She realized why a moment too late, as the person in charge of the group—a waif of a girl, all smiles and cheer, not much younger than Sammy, although it was clear she'd led a very different life—leaned over and happily exclaimed, "We've got the vault for nine-thirty!"

"Is everyone here in your group?" Sammy asked, hoping her quick headcount was wrong.

"Yes! Some friends came in from out of town and—"

This was why her manager had run off. So that they could play good-cop bad-cop—forcing Sammy to be the bad one. "I'm sorry, but that room only has space for eighteen people." There were twenty-five tightly clustered people in the entryway right now, a group of swan-like young women and a few middle-aged-adults.

A ripple of horror moved through the group. Sammy could already feel the weight of their disappointment—and burgeoning anger.

"But my friends!" the girl protested with a pout as a man in a wool suit jacket trundled up, obviously the bad-cop of this group.

"Some of us flew all the way from Chicago for this!"

"That's very far, and I'm sorry—"

"We'll need another table then." He was gruff and Sammy could feel him looking for an excuse to yell.

"That's impossible, sir. We're fully booked. All night. Every night. You have a room here—but it can only seat eighteen."

"I won't eat!" the original girl volunteered.

Sammy winced apologetically. "That doesn't change things."

"Then we'll all go someplace else!" the man demanded and Sammy inhaled, bracing.

"You can do that. But—someone in your party," she said, looking at the books, "a Donna Breeland, reserved that room with a credit card. You'll be charged a thousand dollars for—"

21

"You'll charge my wife for a room we can't use? That's preposterous!" The man slammed his meaty fists on the stand. "It's my daughter's birthday—" he began, inhaling to go on.

She'd met less entitled people carrying guns, back in her chop-shop days. "Is your daughter in charge of fire codes?" Sammy said, with an 'I'm not even bothering to hide how fake this is' smile. "I'm just trying to keep us legal, sir."

The man's jaw clenched and his eyes widened. "Get Bastian, *now.*"

"It's not going to change anything—"

He planted a hand on either side of the hostess stand and leaned in. "Did you hear me?"

Yes. Unfortunately.

Jeanine chose that moment to swan in. "What's going on?" she asked, ever-so-innocent, and Sammy had that wood-chipper feeling in her stomach like she was about to be ground up and fed to the wolves.

"This woman here was telling us that we can't be accommodated!"

"Oh, no," Jeanine said, looking at the reservation book over Sammy's shoulder and then swinging her hips to get Sammy out of the way. "Mr. Breeland, there must've been some mistake, I'm so sorry!" Jeanine glared at Sammy for effect, and Sammy knew exactly what was going on.

She'd just become a human sacrifice.

"Let me go talk to Bastian right away and in the meantime, I'm sure Sammy can show eighteen of your guests to their tables." Jeanine snapped her fingers twice like Sammy was some kind of dog. "Menus!"

Rax watched the scene playing out in front of him with intense interest.

No one as magical as she was should've tolerated being treated so.

He watched the red-haired woman's spine straighten as she took a verbal jab at offense. He could tell by the way she held herself that she was pissed but she wasn't doing anything with it. He neither felt her energies swirl nor increase like they might if she were going to strike a magical blow.

She didn't use her magic to shield herself from their hassle, either.

Someone that radiated the kind of power she did shouldn't have to work here, much less put up with bullshit.

So what was going on? He circled an idle finger along the rim of his wineglass as the scene played out and the woman turned, ducking down beneath the stand to grab a stack of menus. Her scarf fell forward and a red stone on a necklace swung out behind it.

His finger stopped and he curled his hand into a fist rather than smash the glass on the table.

It couldn't be.

The red gemstone on her necklace...it was a third of the key to the Gate Below.

One of a set of gems created when he'd shattered the original key in its lock.

One was lost in the lock itself, he guarded one, and the other had been buried with his brother's wife, eight hundred years ago.

And now some human girl was just...wearing it. Out and about. Without any shielding, and apparently without any knowledge of what it was or why it existed.

Here, of all places.

Today.

It was on a human!

Rax stayed seated, thinking hard, as she took half the group downstairs, followed by a flock of women, and he knew as she disappeared around the corner that he shouldn't let her out of his sight. The necklace she was wearing was more valuable to him than the combined total of anything that'd ever been kept inside the decommissioned bank vault below.

He stared at the doorway she'd gone through as memories he thought he'd pushed down forever—as far away from him as his dragon now was—wracked through him like waves hitting rocks in a storm.

Summers spent going on adventures with his older brother, Tarian, sailing across the sea in grand loops under blue sky and golden sun. Stopping only to dive down to pull up ornate shells off the seafloor to gift their mother, laughing as they speared fish to eat raw over the side of the boat, both of them slicked with shiny scales until they swam again and knocked them free. Knowing that they were safe because they were both dragons, and that everyone else who sailed their Realm was safe because the Gate was locked.

If he could've ever traveled to any point in time, it would've been back to that impossibly perfect summer. Back when everything was simple and pure, and well before Tarian met Seris, the human girl that would go on to become his brother's mate and his family's downfall.

The woman reemerged—jogging, almost—at the top of the stairs, and he felt a visceral sense of relief at seeing her there. Her hand seemed to dive beneath her scarf without thinking, to grab hold of the stone for strength, and strong emotions flashed across her face. She was angry he could tell, and he read shame and embarrassment in the slope of her shoulders and the way she held her body, her blood pumping not just from the short run up the stairs but because she was seething. He shoved his memories away and returned to the present.

What had happened to piss her off so?

Who'd pushed this little human up to the edge and then over it?

How could he get back what was rightfully his?

She frowned and looked over, catching him staring, and he didn't look away as she stormed up.

"I know that face," he told her, rather than ask any of his questions.

Her light pink lips fell into a tiny pout. She had a smattering of freckles over her cheeks that she hadn't bothered to try to hide with makeup. "You do, do you?"

And she had the slightest hint of an accent. He'd noticed it all night. He nodded at her. "Yes. That's the kind of face an employee makes before she quits or does something to get fired."

She huffed, perhaps embarrassed to be so readable.

"I'm not wrong, am I?" he pressed.

She shook her head before she answered, "No."

24

The red stone peeked out from beneath her scarf, calling to him, just a few shades darker than her hair. There was no way she knew what it was or what it was worth. It had to have come into her possession by accident—all the better to let him steal it from her.

It was as if fate had shoved her into his path—on this day of all days.

Rax pushed himself back from the table. He no longer trusted in fate but he completely trusted in himself. She'd been alone all night, and what was more, she seemed lonely. And he...he knew exactly who he was. All he had to do was get her by herself. He kept his eyes on hers while moving to stand. He was taller than she was by over half-a-foot and while his greater size frightened some women, he knew others welcomed it. *Which was she?* She didn't step back. He had to stop himself from smiling. *So close, already, yes.* His dark brown eyes traveled her delicately boned face and watched her fathomless blue ones widen in curiosity, helpless and fearless in equal measure.

"Did you want to do something worth getting fired for?" he asked her in a suggestive tone.

She swallowed before her lips parted and asked, "Like...what?"

"Like meet me in the wine cellar in three minutes," he told her in a low voice, full of promises. He heard her gasp softly as he dropped his napkin on the table, turning to go down the stairs she'd just come up.

SAMMY WATCHED HIM GO. He didn't turn around to see if she'd follow or even give her a second look. It was like he knew that she would at least consider his offer.

Heavily.

Because right after she'd gotten that huge party seated downstairs, Bastian had torn her a new one, yelling at her for not recognizing Donna Breeland or her daughters and their friends, all of whom they were now shoving into the vault below, fire codes be damned. The only reason she hadn't quit at that moment was because he'd stormed away too fast, and the whole thing was bullshit. She didn't really *need-*

need this job right now, she had enough savings to coast a little, and even if her quitting would embarrass Damian, maybe, she knew Andi would totally understand.

She'd raced upstairs, ready to just go straight out the door and Bastian could mail her last check, two weeks' notice be damned, and then she caught Mr. Janvier staring at her, again, with his hot eyes, like someone was holding a piece of amber up to a bright flame, with his fucking perfectly fitted suit that showed off his wide shoulders, and his stupid handsome-like-an-ancient-statue face—she'd been pissed and had stomped over to see what the hell it was he wanted… only to find out that he wanted her.

Why?

Did it matter?

She stared at the path Mr. Janvier had taken. He'd already been downstairs for a minute, which gave her two minutes left to decide. She hugged herself, then saw Jeanine coming her way. She grabbed her blazer from the stand and went for the front door at a jog, flagging Ernesto down outside.

CHAPTER 3

THE WINE CELLAR WAS A CRISP FIFTY-FIVE DEGREES, AND MR. JANVIER had left the door open behind him. Sammy had avoided notice on her run back in, and now her flats were scuffing against the wine cellar's cement floor. She heard a throat clearing ahead of her, Mr. Janvier's way of calling her into the dimly lit depths.

She walked two racks back and found him standing in front of the most expensive reds the restaurant had.

"So you do want to get fired," he said as she turned the corner. The corners of his lips lifted wickedly and she felt her pulse jump. She knew she was five-six, so he was easily six-four, and as she looked up at him it seemed like his broad shoulders filled up most of the space between the narrow racks. One of his eyebrows rose in what seemed like amusement, and he had a strong, almost Roman nose. His chin had the slightest cleft in it, and his lips—*that might kiss her*—felt dangerously full up close. Sammy realized he looked like a *man*, which was not a thing she was used to really. She was used to dating *boys*.

Because boys were probably safer.

"Seems so," she admitted nervously, holding her blazer in front of her like a shield, like a scrap of cotton could somehow offer a thin layer of safety as he stepped closer.

"Two things," he said, spinning his hand, indicating that she should turn around. She did so slowly, fighting the urge to run. She felt him come nearer, wrapping his arms around her without touching her, taking the coat from her hands to cast it aside. "First," he said, near her ear, speaking with deliberate quietness, "the louder you are, the more likely Bastian is to fire you." She shivered as his breath brushed her shoulder. "Second," he began, undoing the scarf around her neck. "Don't worry. Anything we break, I'll buy."

He lifted the free scarf up and tied it around her eyes. She reached for it instantly, holding onto the fabric, but she didn't pull it down. *This wasn't safe, it wasn't safe, it wasn't safe.* Her heart began beating a familiar worried refrain but she ignored it, like she so often did, as his lips found her neck and started kissing.

Because what was safe, really, if you couldn't even just go to the beach and come back again?

What were the chances of something else really, truly, bad happening to her a second time?

More importantly, what were the chances of her giving a fuck if it did?

Her whole life, she'd veered between total compliance with the rules, like if she did everything right, it'd be a magic formula that would keep her safe, and absolutely not giving a lawless fuck, because enough bad things had happened to her already that she knew there were no rules and the world *owed* her.

And that's why she never told anybody about what'd happened to her parents, not even Eumie or Andi, because then they might expect her to act a certain way forever and be surprised—or disappointed—when she did not. All her childhood foster parents had expected a broken-winged angel or a tortured hellion—they could never handle that she was both.

It was always easier for them to think that she just needed more therapy.

"Red?" he whispered from the spot where her neck met her shoulder. His lips were hot compared to the wine cellar's chill, and the brush of his stubble against her skin made her prick up. She slowly let go of her scarf, deciding to throw caution and herself to the wind and see where she landed, reaching back one hand to run it through his wavy hair, scratching her nails against his scalp.

He rose up behind her like a cat and made a pleased sound as one of his hands wrapped around her just beneath her breasts, pulling her tight against his broad warm chest, while his other hand was on her thigh, slowly sliding down it for the edge of her dress. He smelled manly, like well-oiled leather, and even though she couldn't see him with the blindfold on—maybe that was better. Maybe it gave her more of an excuse—because most people needed excuses to be this reckless. Most people didn't spend all their free time learning about dangerous men and then walking the fuck toward them anyways.

She felt him press his body against hers, knowing so far that they were both safely, fully, clothed, and she put her hands out for the wine racks ahead of her, grabbing hold of the wooden edges to stop from swaying, and so she could push back.

"That's better," he growled, and the sound of it did shameful things to her lower body. He licked a long stripe above her dress's wide neckline and it made her sigh. His hand beneath her breast turned to cup it and began to stroke her nipple through the fabric of her dress and bra, and she listened to his breath get rough between kisses as he rubbed himself against her. She could feel his very large erection pressing through his slacks and against the cleft of her ass. She swallowed dry and arched up without thinking.

He made a satisfied noise at feeling her hips tilt and his hand that'd just been flirting with the hem of her dress started hitching it up in earnest, rolling the fabric up her body until it was around her waist and he could wrap his hand around her hips to dive his fingers beneath her underwear. They went straight between her legs, and she gasped at feeling him there, cupping her shamelessly, running through her lightly trimmed hair to play along her folds and stroke her open. Her hands tightened on the wooden racks in front of her as his fingertips rocked in to find her wetness and then drag it up to rub against her clit. His fingers made broad circles as the heel of his hand kept her hips pressed back, and his grinding, now against the lace of her underwear, became more insistent.

His mouth had gone from kisses to licks, trailing his tongue up her neck as if he owned her, and she moaned. All of this was dirty and reckless—*but then so was she*. And she leaned her forehead against the wine rack's smooth wood and panted as his fingers made her clench the hollow space between her legs where he should be. She heard herself whisper, "Condom?" from a million miles away.

He put his teeth where her shoulder met her neck as if to hold her there while releasing her with his hands to free something from a pocket or wallet. She heard the sound of foil tearing and a zipper being undone, then he was shoving her underwear down with one hand, and his mouth had released her, moving to her ear to whisper.

"You sure, Red?"

He didn't even know her name.

Good.

She nodded and whispered, "Yeah," and then felt him behind her, the thick head of his condomed cock swiping against her entrance. He hadn't pushed her underwear down far enough, her thighs were trapped tight, he was going to have to fight to get in, but that didn't stop him. He grunted and pushed up, and she went to her toes, jiggling the entire rack of wine she held onto.

"Remember, Red," he said, and she felt him sink a hand between them to position himself better before sliding it down to grab her knee and pull it up, putting her foot atop whatever undoubtedly priceless bottle was three rungs up from the floor, tearing the lace of her underwear away entirely. "The louder you are," he said and rocked up.

She cried out. She would've without his encouragement, God, he'd sunk himself so deep, and he was already thrusting again, and she could hear the bottles in front of her thump as their glass shifted against the wood. He made a satisfied sound again at filling her, and then he did it again. He started taking her in long, strong thrusts. He'd wrapped his hand around her to rub her clit, and his breath was hot on her neck as he kept kissing, and her nipples were tight from his touch and the cold. Everything that should've been wrong—getting fucked senseless at work by a stranger—were the same things that made it right. "Oh, God, yes, please," she begged in time with his thrusts, as he bit at her neck and moved his hand from over the top of her dress to down the front of it, reaching into her bra to grab her breasts, nearly tearing off her necklace, while growling in her ear.

"Louder, Red," he demanded, fucking her hard, plowing her into the wine rack, the bottles chiming with every thrust.

She knew what she wanted to do—same as she knew she shouldn't —which was kind of why she should. "Rax," she whispered.

His actual, real, first name. At least according to the reservation book.

He paused behind her. "That's Mr. Janvier, to you," he corrected her in her ear quietly. She quivered around him; she couldn't help it, so much had already been building up, and he chuckled darkly before ruthlessly redoubling his efforts.

She groaned and wrapped one hand back around his neck for balance, and it didn't matter what his name was—or hers for that matter—as long as he didn't stop, and she made sure he knew it, with the sounds she made and with her body. The angle they were at now, every time he pulled out she could feel the head of his cock dragging out of her, hitting all the right places before he slammed it back in, and his fingers were relentless, they kept stealing her juices to stay light and slick, rubbing her soft hood against the nub of her clit underneath. As she tensed she started to curl forward, but the heel of his hand pinned her back, all the better for him to fuck, so she had to let go of his neck and fall forward against the rack, feeling her stomach and ass clench at the same time everything inside her body did too, and she heard him growl behind her. She knew he was watching her, she could feel his eyes on her even if she couldn't see anything, ready to ride her, just waiting for her to come. Closer and closer and closer, and the rack was rattling, and she just needed one more stroke, one more rub, and she whined, begging for it, before calling out his name just like he'd told her too.

"Mr. Janvier," she shouted, feeling her orgasm grab her, feeling it make her grab him, as he plunged his cock inside her, and she shouted his name again.

"CHRIST, RED," Rax hissed from behind her, shifting himself to use short sharp thrusts up, not trusting himself to pull out and miss a wave. It was like her pussy had his dick in a vise, and he liked it, he wanted her to milk him till he came, and then he wanted to do it all the fuck over again. That wasn't why he was here—but did it matter?

Because—*fuck.* When was the last time he'd mounted anyone like this? If you asked anyone who worked for him, he knew they'd believe him mostly sexless, but it wasn't that at all. It was just after centuries of experiencing life, what joy could mere physicality hold?

Except he was hard enough now to fuck this young woman through a wall.

Because of the key, of course.

It had to be.

He brought a hand to her neck, intending to break the chain, and let the stone fall into his hand below, twisting the delicate gold in his fingers, while still thrusting—*he knew how to multitask.* But it didn't break.

He leaned over her and caught it in a kiss, bringing it up between his teeth to bite down on and it didn't give. In fact, if he kept going, he was sure that he'd chip a tooth before he dented the chain.

And he was a dragon.

He pulled his head back, the woman still pinned on him, whimpering as another aftershock rolled through her body; he felt her pulse and tremble, and it was as if his hips had a mind of their own.

"Hold on," he warned her, grabbing her waist tightly with both hands, and she instinctively braced against the rack as he thudded into her. He did it again, and again, feeling her swollen pussy grab the length of him, and he didn't know who this version of him was anymore, or why he needed to come inside her more than anything else, but if he couldn't take the stone that belonged to him back, he was going to fucking *have **her***.

She cried out his name again as he himself shouted, feeling himself cumming, pouring himself out inside her, and he cursed the condom that kept him from painting his life on her womb, because even if he never wanted children he suddenly wanted to claim this small human in every which way, and render her unable to think of another without closing her eyes and seeing him first.

He beat his hips against hers, making her take him until he finished himself off with a final grunt that came from deep inside and heard her give a breathy moan. He grabbed hold of himself to keep the condom on as he pulled out, found it every bit as full of cum as he thought it'd be, sliding it off with a practiced motion to discard. She pushed off the wine rack and slowly spun around, her face flush, as she shimmied her dress's skirt down and kicked her torn underwear away. She was so young—*everyone was, compared to him*—and despite her opting into what they'd just done and how heavy the scent of sex was now in the small room, he couldn't help but think her innocent.

Her hands went to untie the scarf he'd blindfolded her with, only to gasp and let it fall the second it was free.

"Salvatore!" she said, spotting someone standing behind him, side-stepping quickly. Rax whirled, he'd been so lost in contemplating her he'd dropped all his defenses. *What—how?*

"I'm telling Bastian!" the sommelier said.

"Do that!" The woman challenged him. "His very own note said to give this man anything he wants." She gave Rax a dazzlingly impudent smile before returning her attention to the other man. "And also? Tell Bastian I quit!" She bent down to sweep up her blazer and raced up the stairs, pushing past the sommelier, who fell towards Rax.

Rax shoved the man aside without thinking, finally breaking a bottle, the one the sommelier had been holding. He picked up the scarf she'd dropped and ran after her, flat out, but she was already through the front door and hopping into a waiting car. All he saw was a flash of red, the car more burgundy than her flame-colored hair, before she drove away.

Sammy had never felt more like she was driving a getaway car in her life, which was saying something, because she'd actually driven getaway cars before, back when she'd been dating Danny and 'working' at the chop shop. She caught three greens—*such luck!*—then raced up to a red before looking back over her shoulder.

Fuck Jeanine, fuck Salvatore, and fuck Bastian in the neck!

But not Mr. Janvier.

Because oh. My. God.

She grinned at herself in the rearview, then realized she looked like she'd been attacked by a bear. Her cheeks were red, her bun half fallen, and she was lucky he hadn't ripped her necklace off of her. He'd turned the neckline of her dress from boat to scoop, yanking it all out of proportion, it was never going to be the same, but did she care?

Not in the goddamned least!

She revved the accelerator, letting the engine roar, not caring what other people stopped at the same light thought of her. She felt alive again and it'd been a while.

Just like a car, sometimes somebody needed to ride her like she was meant to be *ridden*. She knew she accelerated quickly and cornered like a champ—and it'd been a long time since anyone had taken her out on the track.

She settled back into the driver seat, the light changed, and she sped the whole rest of her way home.

The second she got there, she went into the bathroom to take a shower and wash the day away. Shame, really, because she still looked mauled in the mirror—*in a good way*—and because she still smelled like a woman who'd just gotten fucked against a hundred grand rack of wine. She laughed at herself and decided to compromise, running herself a tub. No reason she had to wash her hair, really, and she didn't want to have to blow-dry it before sleeping anyhow. She poured in a liberal amount of bath salts into the water, sank in, and carefully texted Andi over the tub's edge, going into explicit detail about what'd just happened, and then groaned, realizing Andi was probably ten time zones away and on a whole different continent.

"Really?" Sammy complained, shaking her phone like that'd make her best friend text back faster, then set it on the ground and shrugged deeper into the tub; realizing she'd forgotten to take the necklace off, along with Danny's peridot.

The peridot she knew would hold up underwater, but she wasn't sure about the red gemstone—though it was stone, wasn't it? It had chunky square facets on the front and a flat back. She moved to take it off and then thought better of it because it was too late now. She straightened the chain and left it right where it was, between her breasts and slightly above, centered on her sternum, like a bright red drop of blood.

RAX WANDERED through the entryway of his home in a daze, throwing his keys aside and letting his coat drop next, then returning to his coat to fish out the scarf the woman had left behind. It still had her spicy aroma on it, her cinnamon mixed with their sex.

Rax had offered the valet a hundred dollars for her name, but he'd sensed Rax's interest in her was possibly untoward and clammed up, being a good man rather than a helpful one. Rax knew he could've just asked Bastian...but there was an element of pride, having been surprised by the sommelier, who'd no doubt told his boss all about what he'd been doing when they'd put the bottle of Domaine Leroy pinot on his bill.

Rax Janvier did not beg to find out a human woman's name. Not even when that woman was wearing an impossibly magical piece of jewelry and happened to be an exquisite lay.

No, his style was more unexpectedly appearing beside your bed at night, with a knife against your throat, demanding information, and it wouldn't take much effort for him to find out where Bastian lived.

He walked forward to the only thing currently lit in his improbable underground villa, a massive three-story high shark tank, with several creatures of the deep slowly circling inside. It was the main fixture of his home, and all of the rest of the rooms faced it, lit by its magical glowing lights. He placed a hand on the thick glass and his favorite bull shark swam up, expecting food, staring out at him with dead black eyes that Rax knew were every bit as unforgiving as his own.

"You're back early." Smoke leaped up to the top of his nearby piano and sniffed at him. The arctic fox had his summer coat on; he was the color of a heavy rain cloud, or smoke, just like his name.

"I am."

"You smell of woman."

"Yes."

Smoke jumped off the piano and sniffed directly at the scarf. "That...woman?"

Rax pushed the scarf into his pocket as he waved his other hand, and the coat he'd been wearing disappeared, just as his keys disappeared to inside his garage, the tunnel up from which was the only way into or out of his lair, and magically hidden on the exit side. "I saw the lost fragment of the key again, Smoke."

The last time he'd seen it, it had been in Seris's hand as she'd been lying in state in her coffin. His family had given her the elaborate funeral they couldn't give Tarian because his body was entombed behind the Gate Below. It'd been the last time he'd seen his father alive, right before he had been imprisoned to be punished for his brother's crime.

And by the time he'd been released, seven hundred years ago, today, everything that he knew or loved or cared about was gone. His father was dead of a broken heart. Seris's grave had been smashed open and ransacked. Tarian's mad grief was remembered only in songs that mocked him, and the people who Rax had sacrificed his dragon for spoke of him only in whispers—like he was an evil spirit—or didn't think of him at all.

It was as if everything true had been forgotten.

Smoke's tail bristled. "The key? After all this time?" he asked, and Rax nodded. "And, today? Of all days?"

"Indeed." In front of him, the shark got tired of waiting for food and swam off.

The fox whuffed his hand holding the scarf, then quickly wound around to breathe the other. "Well…where is it?"

The creature sensed his hesitation.

"It's not on you?"

"No. It's with the woman."

Smoke shook his head as though he had a flea in his ear. "You let her take it?"

Rax stared into the water, all the better to ignore his fox. "I didn't have a choice."

"You let her live," Smoke grumbled. "Life's a choice."

"It is, isn't it?" Rax agreed, without looking down. He knew it was because he'd wanted to die every day he'd been imprisoned, when he'd been chained to a rock as magicians slowly broke his body and pulled his dragon's form from him to wrap it around the Gate Below, reinforcing the lock his brother had almost broken with Rax's dragon's beastly strength.

He'd wanted to die under their ministrations for a hundred years…but he hadn't let himself go. The responsibility of keeping the Gate closed fell to him. And when they were done with him, he'd vowed to continue living, no matter what. To honor the rituals that would prolong his dragon's slumber, keeping his family's ancient pact.

It was just that the way he was living now didn't always feel like life.

He was split into two beings—half of him always at the bottom of the ocean, cold, deathless, sleeping. Whereas the half of him that got to walk the earth awake—no matter how many deals he made, how many games he played, how much money he stole—he wasn't so sure anymore that that made him alive.

Not as sure as he'd felt less than an hour ago, sinking into her.

"Did I hear you right?"

Rax felt the intrusion of Hachiro's mind pressing against his, as the first of the creature's tentacles appeared against the glass, crawling up from the darkness below. The tank went much, much deeper than the three floors his home occupied. The octopus slid up the inside of the tank, arm over arm, his suction-cups clearly visible, as it tilted to view him with one parenthesis-shaped pupil.

"You found the lost fragment of the key? And you let it go?"

It'd taken ages of training to hear Hachiro's mind in the first place and then to understand his tones, but even if he couldn't, he'd have understood the stripes of incredulous orange flashing across the creature's skin.

"I didn't *let* it go."

"But you didn't *bring* it here," Smoke said, giving Hachiro a meaningful look.

They were both magical, like himself. Creatures from a different place, a different time, who'd followed him out of his past into the present. The fox and the octopus didn't agree on much, and when they did, Rax knew he was in trouble.

Hachiro peeled himself off the inside of the tank, jetting water to hold himself aloft, looking like a parachute made of rippling muscle.

"When you have the mollusk in your grip, you ought not drop it," Hachiro counseled, gesturing for the glass, turning one tentacle into a knot.

"Yes, well, the next mollusk I see at a popular restaurant, I'll be sure to do just that," Rax said dourly.

Hachiro jetted up and then away from the glass wall, rolling his entire body because he couldn't roll his eyes.

Smoke put his paws on Rax's thigh and headbutted his hand. "I mark your anniversary of freedom."

He folded the fox's ears briefly and said, "Thank you," before taking the stairs up to the level that he lived on.

. . .

HIS PERSONAL CHAMBERS wrapped around the top of the tank, which created a four-foot-high boundary on the right side of his room so that he could feed his beasts and go swimming when he liked.

As for the dry side of his room, moving against the clock, a third of it acted as an open closet, stopped by a door to his luxurious bathroom, and then his bed and his altar occupied the rest of his space.

He tossed the scarf on his bed as he passed it, moving to the green coral altar where he would perform his nightly ritual. He kicked off his shoes and knelt down, unfolding the altar's top to reveal a shallow dish of sea salt, a dragon bone knife, and the chalice he used, a silver goblet encrusted with jewels, the inner cup inlaid with mother of pearl.

He spit into the cup, sprinkled in a pinch of salt, and ran the blade across his palm with a practiced hand. Three fat drops of green blood —dragon's blood—welled up, and he clenched his hand into a fist, adding them to the chalice, swirling the contents around while he said the words the magicians swore him to, in the language of his childhood:

LET all that is dragon in me slumber.

May my dragon lock the Gate Below in times of peace and in times of war,

That no one else's ears may hear a siren's terrible song.

It is my fate that I should do this, and no one else,

And I shall do it until the sirens die, or I do.

HE WALKED over to the edge of the shark tank and in doing so noticed the scarf against the darker colors of his bedding. It was the same soft pink that was hidden inside certain shells or in certain delicate places on women. He turned to the tank and added, "Or until I can find the key to free me," and plunged the chalice into the saltwater, emptying its contents out.

"ANDI, OH MY GOD, PICK UP!" Sammy stared at her phone while it rang. She'd been lying in bed in the middle of the night, not entirely sure what'd happened, until she'd felt it happening again—her whole bed had shimmied, and she'd watched the leaves of her houseplant sway.

"Sammy?" Andi's voice was incredulous but totally awake because it was lunchtime in Italy. "What time is it there?"

"It's three am!" Sammy said breathlessly.

"Is everything all right?" Sammy heard Damian ask in the background.

"Yes, well, no—but, we just had an earthquake!" Sammy was equal parts frightened and delighted. She was sitting in the middle of her bed, waiting to see if there'd be another one.

"No way, really?" Andi asked her.

"Yes, way!"

"How bad?" Damian asked, his voice picking up in volume.

"Just tiny for now. I mean, things moved and all, but mostly I just needed to call someone," Sammy said and laughed, now that the tension was releasing.

"Tell her she can go to my house if her apartment becomes unin-habitable," she heard Damian saying.

Andi laughed and said, "Shhh," and then there was a silence wherein Sammy knew she was walking away from him. "Was it fun?" she asked when she came back on, and Sammy could hear the grin in her voice.

"Crazy, kind of." Sammy put her on speakerphone and beamed at the word 'Lefty' on the screen in the darkness. "How's Italy?"

"Freaking gorgeous."

Sammy pretend groaned. "I know, you keep sending me photos."

"We're totally going to do this, Sammy, just you wait. I have so many things I want to show you now."

"Making a list, are you?" Sammy teased.

"Of everything. The art, the food, the eligible men—" Andi said.

Sammy heard Damian sharply say, "Hey!" distantly in the background as Andi giggled and Sammy laughed.

"Come on, I've seen you pack before. I know you can leave some clothes behind and just smuggle one home for me," Sammy said, falling back into her bed.

Andi laughed harder at that. "My fiancée might be displeased."

"Whatever. I've known you longer. I should get dibs."

Andi made an "Eeeeehhhh" noise. "He puts out though."

"Hey!" Damian said, from just as far, but twice as sharply, and Sammy cackled.

"What's up with Mr. Wine Cellar?" Andi asked.

"Uh, yeah, nothing," Sammy said with a sigh, flipping her sheets down and crawling back beneath them. She'd wondered every night since then if she'd made a mistake quitting Belissima's. Not because she wanted to ever see Bastian again in her life, but because it'd been her only connection to him. *Mr. Janvier.* Emphasis on the *Mister.* Even if anything happening between them afterward seemed improbable to the highest degree…it might've been nice to *know* that rather than just assume. But she hadn't really left herself any opportunities to figure things out, running away like she had. It'd been almost a week, so surely he'd moved on, just like she needed to.

"Boo," Andi said, and Sammy snorted.

"It's okay. Sometimes things are just like that. Good in the moment, but not meant for life, you know?"

"Yeah, I do. And? You'll always have me," Andi told her.

"Hmm. If you really loved me, you'd bring me back an Italian Stallion."

"Would you believe me if I told you I made this trip entirely with carry-on?"

"No." Sammy snorted hard. "But, I gotta get back to bed, now that the world's not shaking."

"I'm glad you're all right, and I'm glad you called. Go back to sleep, silly girl, love you."

"Love you too," Sammy said and hung up.

THE NEXT FEW days had passed in a regular rhythm as Rax considered his options. It was spring and everyone was happy to have longer, warmer days. His businesses were doing well. Ever since Damian's crew had gone to war against the hunters, magic-aware humans who killed shifters to steal their powers via wearing scraps of shifter skin and bone (or worse yet, via ingestion), their city had essentially become a hunter-free-zone. Word had gotten out, and his casino that served shifters and shifter-aware humans—ones that wanted to be fucked by, or fuck shifters, mostly—beneath a normal human night-club, had been full every night. In his more wry moments, he was tempted to send the other dragon a fruit basket with a card that said, "Thanks for the business."

And he'd easily gotten Bastian's home address. It would be nothing to demand information from the chef, although it might cut off his supply of Domaine Leroy forever, alas. Or he could stalk someone lesser—Salvatore or the chivalrous valet.

But the further he was out from having met the woman, the more that night at Belissima's seemed like a dream.

Because how could a silly, fragile human have gotten Tarian's fragment of the key? It'd been missing for centuries, lost in another Realm entirely. Why would it appear on earth?

No.

It just had to be him being haunted by his past. On the anniversary of his freedom, no less. When he'd been released from his chains to find out everything was lost.

He'd spent centuries afterward going on magnificent binges around the date, anything to erase the memories of his pain, trying to forget by swimming through an ocean of alcohol and into infinite number of willing women. Time had dulled the ache somewhat, but it seemed likely that his dalliance with that woman at the restaurant was just a throwback. His body performing again, out of instinct.

Another ritual.

Sheer habit.

And, several days out, the scarf was the only thing he had that'd proved it'd happened. Even then he'd doubt himself if the silk wasn't directly against his fingers. He'd taken to keeping it in his pocket, like any number of the fools on his casino floor who thought they held a good luck charm, not realizing that the magic he'd imbued his home-away-from-home with prevented them from working.

Whereas he knew the silk he held was plain silk. A reminder that he, too, could be susceptible to foibles and talk himself into believing something that couldn't possibly be real, on occasion. A timely warning to himself, to keep his emotions low and his walls high.

RAX'S OFFICE was a small and narrow affair. He didn't need it to be spacious when he was more interested in people having room to give him their money on the casino floor. His sizable desk was along one wall, made of dark wood with a different formidable magical lock for each of its many drawers. His walls had maps to the city that he'd acquired as it grew, so they appeared historical, though to him they were not, seeing as he'd lived through all of them. The far side of the office, opposite the door, was occupied by a massive mirror that took up almost all the space along the wall. It was in a gilt frame, and the currently quiet glass was fogged. And then he had several objects of power on display sheerly because he could, just as an arms dealer might have a few weapons on display, finding them pleasant.

He was running silk through his fingers and considering an offer a client had emailed for one of his objects of power; was he willing to part with it? Would they deserve it? More importantly, how much would they pay? He heard a heavy knocking on the far side of his office door, and he heard Namir's voice asking, "Boss? Can I come in?"

"Enter," Rax said, and Namir did so. The tiger-shifter-slash-archeologist, if stealing from museums counted as archeology, was his second in command and probably the only man he actually trusted on the casino floor.

So far.

Living as long as he had, Rax knew disappointment in other people was inevitable. People couldn't help themselves.

He put his hands on his desk. *Why had his hand been in his pocket again?* He watched Namir shift uneasily, taking up most of the space in the doorframe. The tiger-shifter was the same size as he was but had darker skin and wore a tightly trimmed beard, whereas Rax was clean-shaven most days. Namir's eyes were surprisingly hazel, and Rax knew they never missed anything.

"I have someone here I think you want to see."

Rax felt one of his eyebrows creep upward as he checked the corner of his laptop for the time. "I doubt that, Namir. It's four in the afternoon, and you and I both know nothing good happens until after sundown."

"I agree, but…" Namir tapped his slightly flattened nose meaningfully, and Rax knew what he meant. If he hadn't seen Namir change into a tiger several times now, he'd believe the man half-bloodhound.

"All right," Rax said, standing to sidle around his desk and walk out onto the casino floor with the other man. The casino wasn't open yet, but the lights were on. The chandelier over the extensive bar glittered and the green felt on the tables was brushed and ready. "Where?"

"The club floor. We're screening bartenders."

"Am I reduced to interviewing humans now?" Rax chided as they reached the secure hallway that led upstairs to the dance club that provided cover for Rax's much more illegal activities below.

"I have a hunch," Namir said.

"You mean your nose has a hunch," Rax corrected, blowing air through pursed lips as he pushed open the final set of doors.

There was a cluster of humans outside, sitting down on the chairs they'd pulled down from the tables, as the club was closed. They were chatting among themselves, and one woman among them had hair the red-orange of a cooling ember before it died out, and there was the slightest hint of cinnamon in the air.

"So?" Namir asked him.

"How did you know?" Rax whispered without taking a step further. He and the tiger-shifter were both hidden in the hallway.

"It's not often you smell like a woman, but this past week," Namir began, and Rax grunted to cut him off.

"I'll be sitting in on all your interviews today." He still didn't know the girl's name.

"I figured as much," Namir said in a rich baritone, pleased with himself.

CHAPTER 4

EACH TIME THE DOOR OPENED RAX GLANCED AT THE NAME ON THE resume in front of Namir and he'd try the name there on his tongue. Had the woman in the wine cellar been an 'Amanda' or a 'Kayleigh?' He didn't think so but he was willing to be wrong, just to see her and find out what'd happened to his gemstone. But the women walked in, one after another, and each time he found himself disappointed.

Nervous, even.

Because what if she'd somehow spotted him in the hallway and had run away again? It seemed impossible to consider. If fate had brought her to him once, it sure as fuck could bring her to him twice, but the longer he had to be patient, listening to why 'Britley' was going to bring her 'A-game' and be 'an excellent addition to the Lynx's hospitality team!' the more he wanted to crush his phone and throw it, instead of staring at its screen pretending to be coolly indifferent.

And then, just before he did that—or stormed outside to go grab her himself—Namir shuffled the resumes on his desk, pulling out one for Samantha O'Connor. An Irish surname would make sense, with the accent and the hair, but Rax skimmed it and didn't see Belissima's as a recent employer. His eyes were narrowed in contemplation when Namir went to the hallway to retrieve her, and as he heard her talking to Namir outside, he caught a hint of cinnamon in the air. He shoved Namir's chair over and took the center of the table they were using as a makeshift desk in the private room, waiting for Namir to escort her in.

The tiger-shifter, always able to sense a change in the wind, gave Rax a look at his having moved. "I'll let you handle this interview," he said, stepping aside to exit without complaint, revealing Samantha behind him.

She'd been totally eclipsed by the tiger-shifter's larger bulk but now that he could see her he didn't understand how. Her pale, freckled skin still had a luminescent glow to it, and her radiant hair was in loose curls around her shoulders. She was wearing jeans, a tight white top, probably the same blazer she'd had on that night, and last but not least—the red gemstone, a piece of the key, nestled right above her cleavage below the notch in her collarbone.

He stood up as her eyes widened. "Samantha," he said, trying out her name for the first time.

"Mr. Janvier," she whispered. *Good.* She hadn't forgotten his name, and her saying it brought back all the memories of the last time she had. His blood sank to answer her, but he controlled himself.

He would never let a woman be his master.

Not like his brother had.

"I'm sorry, I'll—" she said, wheeling to bolt out the door.

"Sit," he commanded her, half-a-turn-away already from him.

She looked back at him, swallowed, and then her eyes found the chair across from the table. She stepped over to it and sat down, as he did on his side. "I, uh, wasn't expecting to find you here."

"Nor I, you," he told her. "Yet here we are."

He fell into stillness then, watching her, as a flush crept up her throat. It was almost an affront to see her here in the flesh and find her exactly as beautiful as he remembered, which was exactly as beautiful as he'd been trying to forget. He wanted the key, yes, but there was so much of her he hadn't seen yet, nor touched or tasted, and now that he knew that she *was* real, well.... He watched her hands nervously play with one another in her lap, and he noted the ring he'd seen on her right hand at Belissima's, clenched around the wine rack as she'd moaned as he'd fucked her, was now on her left. Her gaze followed his, and she knew what he was looking at.

"It's complicated," she said, hiding the fist of her left hand in the palm of the other.

"And it's none of my business, besides," he granted like he ought to, despite the fact that he both thought and felt anything but. Was she truly engaged? Had she gone home, stinking like him, to fuck another man? An unfamiliar feeling twisted in his gut as he glanced down at her resume. "I see Bastian wasn't available for a reference?"

"No," she said, with a short laugh. "I...I do hope that bottle wasn't too expensive. I heard breaking glass—"

"It was." He cut her off. "But that was the deal we made, wasn't it?"

She nodded silently, and he—he wanted to storm the distance between them, to leap over the table, grab her throat and take the necklace from her.

Surely that was all.

He could restrain himself and forget the rest, undoubtedly. She was merely a human girl, and he had centuries of experience with control.

But what had changed from the prior night, when he'd tried to break the chain, first with fingers, then with his teeth? The key was a magical object, and he certainly knew magical objects had minds of their own.

"Look," she began slowly, then picked up steam. "If I'd have known you worked here, I wouldn't have applied for the job. I need a chance, but I don't need any favors if that makes sense. And I fear that...well, we've really set the wrong tone."

"I don't just 'work here.' This establishment is mine." *As is everyone in it. Including you,* he longed to add.

"Then it's an even worse idea, in that case, isn't it?" She scooted back bodily, making her chair scrape against the tile floor, and he had visions of her driving away again, slipping through his fingers like her scarf's silk.

"What job did you want?" he asked brusquely. He had to keep an eye on her until he could figure out how she'd gotten his necklace and how he could get it back.

She lightly frowned. "Bartender. But—I'll be honest, I've never done it before."

"Then you can be a bar back until you pick it up. It isn't rocket science." He folded her resume in half and tented it down in front of him.

"There are other people outside more qualified," she admitted. "I know, I just talked to them."

He shrugged. "Then perhaps Namir will hire one of them, as well."

"It's just that," she said, and he watched her waver. "I don't want you to hire me thinking I'm usually like *that,*" she said, as her cheeks pinked, knowing he'd know exactly what she meant.

He watched her hand rise to swipe her thumb against the gemstone. He wondered how used she was to making the motion. How long had she worn what was rightfully his?

What if she belonged to him, as much as it did?

The thought rose unbidden in his mind like a bubble from the depths rushing to the surface, and he popped it with a snort. "How are you usually like, then?" he asked, rocking back against his chair, surveying her coolly.

Her blue eyes traced the ground in thought. "I'm a hard worker. I'm punctual."

"Hmm. Those are things I think I know," he taunted, and her cheeks reddened even more. "So let me tell you how I am, Samantha, and then you can decide."

She swallowed and nodded, finally raising her eyes to meet his.

"In general, I am cold, I am precise, and I am demanding. I have no delusions about my employees liking me, nor do I feel a particular need to like them. If you choose to work here, you will work like everyone else. I will make no exceptions for you, nor have any additional expectations of you. In fact, in a perfect world, I would not think of you at all—nor you, me. If you find that tolerable, you may begin tonight. If you don't, then I'm sure you can find the door."

He stood, taking her folded resume, with her address and phone number on it, with him.

SAMMY REELED inside the small room, putting her elbows on her knees and her head in her hands. She had not been expecting to see Mr. Janvier here—not in the fucking least. Her heart was in her throat and now that she was in the room alone she needed some friendly advice. She pulled out her phone to text Andi and then remembered Andi was still asleep in Italy.

And?

She hadn't quite told Andi that she'd quit Belissima's. Not even on earthquake night. She'd told her all about the wine cellar tryst, but she'd skipped the quitting part because Andi had gotten her that job, and she hadn't wanted to disappoint her. So texting Andi that she was here at the Lynx, looking for a new job, working for Mr. Wine Cellar no less—just *no*. Andi didn't need to worry about her best friend being unemployed—or considering being employed by the man she'd desecrated a wine-rack with.

Did she?

Fuck.

There was a knock at the door Mr. Janvier had just walked through and Sammy glanced up to see the handsome gentlemen who'd led her into the room in the first place.

"I've still got a few interviews to go, but I spoke with Mr. Janvier." His hazel eyes looked her up and down, not in a lewd fashion, just trying to figure out why on earth she was special. *Good question,* she wanted to tell him. *Right place, right time, right vagina, maybe?* "Were you interested in being a bar back?" he asked her, sounding incredulous.

Sammy deleted the text she'd been about to send Andi and backed out of her text app entirely. "Yeah," she heard herself say. "I think so."

. . .

HER TRAINING STARTED THAT NIGHT. She barely had time to go home and change into what Namir had suggested. His precise words were, "Dark bottoms, light tops, and the more cleavage you show, the better tips you'll get, but you didn't hear that sexist shit from me."

When she returned, she was wearing a pink turtleneck crop top—a mullet of a shirt, Andi had teased her once, because it was business up top, with a party down below—and a swishy black skirt with a fun belt and heels that matched it. She'd gotten a whirlwind tour of the club from Namir, and then one of the main bar's three bartenders took her under her wing. Vanessa was dark-haired, gorgeous, and made sure that she knew they were a team. She explained how the tables worked, showed her where to come through the crowd with her orders, and made sure she noticed the VIP section at the back, which was set up on a raiser and cordoned off with gold chains.

Then the doors opened and they were off to the races.

Sammy was glad that so far it was slow. It gave her a chance to settle in and figure out how to roll from order to order. She'd done some waitressing in her prior life and she'd always had hustle, so running around came naturally to her. It was harder to hear the longer the night went on because there were more people and the music got louder, so she felt like she was practically lip-reading orders, but so far the biggest job hazard—other than Mr. Janvier himself, who she was sure was *somewhere* in the building even if she couldn't see him—was wanting to dance. Andi was right; she couldn't sing, but she loved dancing, and it was almost torture on a fairy-tale level to be listening to music all night and not get to do anything with it. But when Andi was finally back in town maybe she could get her comped and they could go out and have fun finally. Without Damian or even thinking about boys, just doing their own thing, like old times. She loaded up a table's worth of empty glasses onto her tray and spun with the music, thinking about being free, and that was when he struck.

The guy who'd been watching her for the past two hours, and not in an 'I need another drink' way. Her girl-radar was in full force— without Andi there as back-up, it had to be—so she'd known he'd been watching her all night. But she wasn't going to take on some rando when the ink was barely dry on her paperwork. She knew how to evade guys who couldn't take a hint or clock her fake-ring, but he'd bided his time, waiting for her hands to be full, so that his hand could reach out to grab her ass, and then Namir was there too.

Like he'd just *teleported* over. He appeared out of nowhere, grabbed the man's wrist so that she only gotten a ghost of his heat on her skin, and then made the man goose-step out of the club, his wrist twisted high above him. She couldn't hear him yelping in pain over the music, but she could see him howling it as he danced backward while Namir shoved him.

How...the fuck?

Not that she minded! Namir doing that made her feel a hundred times safer than she ever had at Belissima's, which was saying something. But she'd just made a tour of this room grabbing glasses and she would have bet money that Namir was nowhere in it. She scanned the edges of the room for alcoves she'd missed and then ran her eyes across the ceiling and spotted four tiny red dots among the dark eves above, sweeping back and forth.

Security cameras.

Maybe Andi wasn't the only Beyoncé. Sammy laughed at the thought and then hoisted her tray back up and walked for the bar.

At the end of the night, Vanessa cashed her out and gave her some tips for improvement but generally seemed pleased, and Sammy walked back to the employee breakroom to get her small purse out of her assigned locker. It was late, her feet hurt, and she might be going deaf now, but she hadn't felt alone. Not like she did at Belissima's...or her apartment if she were being honest. There was something about having the music cranked here that felt like having an extra heartbeat around. It was nice.

She walked out the back door to the employee parking lot and found Mr. Janvier looking like he was on his way back inside. She paused in the doorway—*like an idiot,* she told herself later—and then darted out as he backed up to let her exit first.

What had he been doing outside? He didn't smell like cigarette smoke as he waved her past himself. Just…clean man and oiled-leather. *Exactly like how he had at the wine cellar.* "And your first night?" he inquired, following her out into the dark. The back of the building just had one harsh LED light that was tinged blue. It made his skin look darker and his eyes almost black.

"It was fine." She held up her fistful of cash by way of illustration and finally shoved it into her purse as she pulled out her keys. "You know…Namir didn't have to kick that guy out for my sake. I can take care of myself."

His expression clouded briefly. "Namir kicked someone out?" he asked, and she sank in on herself for assuming.

Of course he didn't give a shit. Just like he'd told her. She'd been foolish to assume he would for even the teensiest of moments. "Yeah, but… forget I said anything."

One of his eyebrows crept up his forehead. "As you wish, then," he said and turned, angling around her, back into the building. She stood there as the door closed behind him, watching it for a little bit, feeling off, like *something* ought to have happened, but completely unable to place why. Like she was watching a movie where the soundtrack was just half a second slow. Tolerable, but eventually annoying. She frowned at him, herself, the night, and then went to her car.

RAX WAITED on the far side of the door, calculating the odds, something that he was very, very good at. Now that he'd found her —*Samantha*—and he liked the way her long name seemed sinuous on his tongue, he'd be damned if he let her—*or his necklace*—out of his sight again.

But she was a bright girl. He'd seen her look straight up at the security cameras after he'd told Namir to go rescue her from the creep that'd been encroaching. His actual phrase over the in-house system may have been: "kick him out of my club before I make you hide a corpse," which Namir had been surprised by but then had acted swiftly.

So he couldn't just go racing after her—although he had put a GPS tracker on her car. It would give him the ability to follow her from a distance which was good because if she spotted him, she'd startle and run, and then he wouldn't have the luxury of having her under his roof, under the gaze of his security cameras, for the working portion of her days.

It was hard to be patient, however. The entire reason he'd gone into the magical object trade was because he'd been searching for her fragment of the key. By the time the magicians had finished ripping his dragon from him and he'd been released from prison, Seris's tomb had been smashed, and everything of power inside it taken.

While the dance club above was closed, his casino would still be open for a few more hours. He walked down into it through the dual set of doors, all the better to delay intruders, then ignored the waves and attention from patrons and employees alike, until he found Namir again.

"Boss?" Namir asked, taking in his presence.

"Handle the floor," he told Namir. "Act with my authority. I won't be back tonight."

HE DROVE his Jaguar to the address listed on her resume, his phone informing him that it was an apartment located not that far from downtown, on the 'bad' side of downtown, which he didn't like, but he also knew that it was getting better. He'd seen waves of economic instability roll through, he'd seen the city high, and he'd seen the city low, and he knew now it was on an upswing. There was no point in hoping it would last, though—nothing ever did.

No, he'd lived long enough to know that his job was to take advantage of prosperity for as long as he could. To make as much money as possible—more because accruing cash was a game to him than because he actually liked to spend it. To operate his casino in such a way that it flew under the radar and under the law, bribing people who needed bribing, and killing the occasional person who stood in his way, be they human or shifter. To make his life as comfortable as possible for himself while knowing that he didn't need many comforts —and to take back the things that were rightfully *his.*

Many magic users had tried to anneal the broken key prior to his imprisonment, destroying more and more of the remnant of the key in the lock in the process until there was hardly any left. None of them had made any progress, including him. But he had been younger then. Less powerful, less knowledgeable. And if he could use the strength and skills he'd gained in the intervening hundreds of years, if he could make the key intact again, he could set the lock to the Gate Below and reclaim his sleeping dragon before he lost it forever.

He parked down the street from Samantha's apartment and got out of his car, knowing he was far too distant to be seen. There was a light on in a small curtained window, so he was sure she'd made it home, although all things considered he'd feel better if he had a tracking device implanted somewhere on her person.

How long would he be able to keep the pretense of her freedom up? Namir was still sourcing his knives for him. He didn't want to take her until he had to, but surely there would come a time....

Rax saw a shadow move inside of her apartment and the curtain pulled back briefly. She was looking out. *Why?*

He suddenly felt exposed, despite knowing the distance between them was more than mere human eyes could manage. His hand sank into his suit pocket, feeling the silk of her scarf still there, wishing it was her hair, while his hand was around her throat.

SAMMY WORKED the next three nights and didn't see Mr. Janvier again once, which was probably for the best; it made her new job far less awkward. And Vanessa had started looping her in earlier in the nights, showing her how to mix the club's themed drinks. She finally felt like she was getting into the flow, and that was when she realized there was a door at the back of the club, in a short, otherwise dead-end hall-way, that was always locked.

To her at least.

Other people seemed to have no problem getting in and out, and there were two security cameras stationed right above it.

She casually tried it early on in a shift and when that didn't work she tried it later, right after she could've sworn she saw somebody else using it, but it stayed locked.

After that, she kept an eye on it, marking people who got to go in and when—*and if!*—they came out again. They were always well dressed, although sometimes their clothing was strange, and not all of them looked like club-goers. She asked Vanessa about it once, but the other woman shrugged. "We don't talk about that. It's not our problem."

Which was one way you could think about things, yes.

But wasn't she even a little bit curious?

Sammy realized she probably wouldn't have cared if she had met Mr. Janvier under other circumstances. It would've been so much easier to give him the benefit of the doubt if he hadn't already been mysterious to her.

But because he was...she wanted to know.

What was he doing back there?

That had to be his lair, right? Wherever he was when he wasn't on the club floor. He didn't strike her as a hands-off kind of employer because, despite the fact that she hadn't seen him lately, it was like she could feel his presence. From the precise way that Vanessa knew to pour drinks, to the expertise with which Namir worked security, to how the DJs adroitly kept people dancing, drinking, partying. Everything at the Lynx had a particular way of being, and she felt sure it was because of him.

She was hovering near the door on her fourth night, clearing off a table to quickly wipe it down for the next group, as it swung open and a beautiful woman strode out. She was tall and lean, and she was wearing a shimmering silver evening gown, giving her four times as much hem as anyone else on the dance floor currently, and she had straight, ice-blonde hair that swept halfway down her back. Her brown eyes glittered over everything and everyone, and Sammy couldn't help but stare. First off, because she hadn't seen the woman go in and she'd been spying all night, and secondly, her beauty; there was no word for it but *otherworldly.*

And *she* was clearly Mr. Janvier's girlfriend. Who else could someone that beautiful be? Sammy could imagine the woman standing beside him easily, they would be a matched set. Tall, beautiful, cold.

When he'd seen Danny's ring on her left hand, he must've been relieved to be rid of her.

The woman neared, weaving through the tables, singling her out. She smiled at Sammy—rather smugly, Sammy thought—and reached out to tap her cheek, an intrusion which Sammy oddly stayed still for, like she was mesmerized.

"What a beautiful necklace," the woman told her, then drifted on.

Did...the woman know she'd slept with Janvier? Maybe if you dated him, you had to get used to infidelities.

Or maybe *she* was being remarkably stupid—*ugh*. Ever since Andi and Eumie had moved, Sammy had had way too much free time to get up in her own head. She needed to make some more friends—stat, as Andi would say.

"Sammy?" asked a loud voice from behind her.

She turned, and it was as if her prayers had been answered. "Ernesto!" She'd never seen him out of his valet uniform before. He was dressed sharply in black, he looked very handsome, and she would've run to hug him if she hadn't still been holding a tray of glasses. "Bastian set you free for the night?"

"Hey, that bastard doesn't control my entire life," he said, grinning.

She grinned back. "Are you sure he knows that, though?"

Ernesto laughed and looked around. "So is this where you've been hiding?"

"Yeah." She shifted the tray to her hips. "It beats being unemployed."

"Well, the eye candy here is much better," he said, giving her a look, before jerking his chin at the bar. "I bet the drinks are too."

"I don't know about that, although I'm sure they're cheaper."

"No doubt!" Ernesto shouted over the music overhead, following her over to her next table. She wasn't sure what, if anything, he'd heard about the circumstances under which she'd run off from Belissima's, but the whole time she'd worked with him, he'd always been cool, so hopefully that hadn't changed. "I'm here with friends," he hollered. "We're in the back. Come by when you have a bit?"

"Sure!" she promised, waving at him with her free hand.

THE REST of the night kept her busy, but she made it to his table later and got introduced as an old coworker. The people he was with were also hospitality, so they had working-class solidarity and tipped well, and then the club was winding down. Women were clinging to men and to each other to teeter out on tired feet, and guys were talking overly loud, too used to shouting now to change their volume.

She made another sweep, then she saw Ernesto wave her over. "Want to dance? Or are you too tired?"

Sammy weighed the tray in her hand. This would be her last round through the room and any second now the DJ would turn the music off.

"Yes!" she said, coming to a decision suddenly, setting the tray of glassware down on a nearby table. Her feet hurt just as badly as any of the women stumbling outside, but she still had some fight left in her.

He stood, coming to stand by her side, and she closed her eyes so she wouldn't feel embarrassed that they were the only people on the dancefloor. What was there to be embarrassed about anyhow? She was with a friend, she knew how to have a good time and, most importantly for dancing, she knew how to let the music move her. She didn't have to worry about getting in someone else's space even, she just had to let the beat ripple through her body and react to it, shifting her balance, swaying, raising her arms.

It felt good—like letting all her problems go—and just being in the now. The music made her feel like she was racing cars, with wind in her hair. It wanted her to be free.

"Am I paying you to dance with patrons, Samantha?"

The stern bass voice behind her stopped her cold. Her arms

dropped as she turned around and found Mr. Janvier there, as every bit displeased to see her as Ernesto had been happy to earlier.

"No," she admitted.

"No?" he asked her again. He wasn't wearing a suit jacket, and the top three buttons on his dress shirt were unbuttoned. His hands were in his slack's pockets as he stood loosely, eyeing her, waiting for something...more.

She gritted her teeth at his embarrassing her. *But she was on the clock.* "No, Mr. Janvier." She corrected herself with a spiteful tone, which she knew he registered because his eyes narrowed—then he nodded subtly, looking over her shoulder, addressing Ernesto and his group.

"The club is closed. Find the exit," he told them before turning on his heel and heading for the secret door.

"And you're sure this place is better?" Ernesto asked her as his friends all gathered their belongings to go.

She picked up her tray again and took a step toward the bar, shrugging her shoulders. "Not entirely."

SAMMY WAITED PATIENTLY for Vanessa to cash her out and then left quickly, doing all sorts of calculations in her head as she sped back to her apartment. If she didn't put Belissima's or the Lynx on her resume, it'd only look like there was a month-long gap in her employment history. She could totally tell people she had a sick aunt or had gotten to go on a vacation.

Because she wasn't getting paid enough to get treated like *that*. She should've dropped the tray at his feet, right there and then, or better yet, taken the glasses off of it and sent it sailing after him, like a Frisbee.

Even if he was ever so slightly—*the slightest of slightlys!*—right, that just wasn't cool.

Then again, maybe that's how normal places were? She'd lucked into the job at the car shop years ago. One of the mechanics there had gotten her in after she'd dumped Danny. He'd gotten out of the chop-shop life himself, he understood, and it'd been very mom and pop. So maybe everywhere else in the 'real world' was just run by condescending assholes....

She put her Subaru in park outside her apartment and walked over to her stairs, giving the darkened space beneath the stairs a healthy look just in case. *Nope, no ankle-slashers hiding there tonight, hooray,* then trotted up, pausing on her stoop to turn around. She'd had the strangest feeling she was being watched for a week now. She knew it was because she'd been watching too many Investigation Discovery shows, listening to too many true crime podcasts, and living too lonely.

She just couldn't help herself, really.

Paying attention to the darker side of life after what had happened to her parents seemed comforting when she was a kid, in a 'know thine enemy' sort of way. And she'd had the normal little kid hopes that she'd be the one to crack the case and figure things out. She did all her book reports on serial killers (and earned even more state-funded therapy.) She did her research. She knew the rules.

And at her age, she knew she ought to accept what had happened to her parents and let things go, but it was hard.

Maybe Andi was right, and she needed a cat.

She gave the parking lot outside one last long look before letting herself into her apartment and closing the door.

CHAPTER 5

BECAUSE THE CLUB DIDN'T CLOSE TILL FOUR, SAMMY HAD *JUST* GOTTEN to sleep when she heard the sound of someone running up the outside stairs. It was like, what, six in the morning? Sammy bolted upright and fell into Action Plan One. She reached under her bed and grabbed the metal bat Andi had left behind, seeing as Andi didn't need one anymore now that she was off purportedly living with a dragon.

A fist pounded against her door. "Samantha! Open up!"

Sammy jumped back in her bed, with the bat at the ready. Whoever was out there knew her name? But they weren't calling her Sammy, like everyone else in her entire life had?

"I mean it, Samantha—now!"

Whoever was out there hit the door again, sending it rattling in its hinges.

If only Eumie still worked below! They'd have heard this nonsense and come out to help Sammy put a stop to it.

Sammy grabbed her phone with her free hand and crept into the hall.

"I'm calling the police!" she shouted.

"Don't," growled the voice on her door's far side.

"It's too late!" Sammy called out, lying. "It's done! They're coming here, so you'd better go!"

A fist hit her door again. "I don't care! Show yourself!"

Now that the voice was more irritated than angry...it sounded familiar. Her door had three safety latches latched and a peephole besides. She peered out into the dawn and saw Mr. Janvier.

"What the fuck!" she shouted at him and undid all but the longest door chain, swinging the door five inches open to see him standing outside by the light of the oncoming dawn. He was still in the clothes she'd seen him in earlier at the club, a mostly unbuttoned dark blue dress shirt and slacks that clung to all the muscles of his thighs, but his hair was wet, and he smelled like...ocean? "What—why are you here?" she demanded.

His gaze looked her clinically up and down through the gap in the door. "Are you, or are you not, all right?"

"Jesus H," Sammy muttered, tossing her phone onto her kitchen counter. "No! Because now I need to call 911 for the heart attack you just gave me. What the hell are you doing here?"

He stood up straighter on the door's far side and she realized he was breathing hard. *Why?* And then he turned around like he was just going to go, without saying anything.

"What the," she began, in disbelief, then slammed her door shut to undo the final latch and run out onto her stoop in bare feet. She was in a pale pink t-shirt and striped boxers that tied at the waist and she knew her hair was wild, she didn't care. "What the fuck!" she shouted after him.

Mr. Janvier kept walking. "It's clear you're all right," he said loudly. He didn't even turn around.

"I know I am! I'm fucking fine—no thanks to you!" she shouted after him. She could see his sleek vintage Jaguar in the parking lot behind him and as she leaned over the railing Andi's erstwhile necklace swung out. "Hey!" she shouted, even louder, and he stopped. "You know, if you want to talk to me like a person sometime, you can!"

He slowly turned around to look up at her and she could see his jaw clenching. "Trust me, I do not," he said, and then continued walking to his Jag.

She rocked back onto her stoop like she'd been slapped. Her feelings were oddly...hurt? But what the fuck had she expected? He'd straight up told her she didn't matter to him. Repeatedly. Like he was a flagman atop an aircraft carrier, waving away planes.

Sammy watched him drive off in the car of her dreams, spitefully hoping he'd wreck it.

RAX HAD BEEN SWIMMING in his tank when someone—or *something*—had tripped the magical perimeter he'd set around Samantha's building. He'd felt the ripple of someone moving over his magic, just like he was a spider in the center of a web.

The necklace tripped it too; he felt it every time Samantha left her apartment building and every time she returned, so he knew she'd gotten home two hours ago, confirmed by the tracker he'd put on her car.

But twenty minutes ago, he'd felt something else brush up against his defenses and then break them.

He'd leaped out of his tank, pulled on the clothing he'd been wearing, and had disobeyed every traffic law on the way over. And as he'd parked outside her apartment, he'd pulscd out with his magic—but there was nothing there.

Only the necklace.

Which he knew was no promise she was still alive, because he'd already considered the fact he might have to decapitate her himself to free it. He'd run up her stairs, pounded on her door, and then gotten nothing in return but lip, and now he'd be lucky if she came back to work, between what'd just happened and their disagreement earlier in the night. He wrung the Jaguar's delicate steering wheel and cursed. There was no rational way to explain his interest in her, to her—it was one of the reasons he hadn't abducted her yet.

But if other elements were after the gemstone they would force his hand, and her freedom be damned.

He parked his car and returned on foot to realign his defenses, pacing around her block recharging the magical objects he'd created just for this purpose, a flyer for a lost dog stapled to a telephone pole, a brick he'd removed from a building and replaced with one that looked just like it, a glob of tar near a busy road, and a weed growing out of a crack in the asphalt. It was this last one that'd alerted him, and the weed itself wasn't looking well. He waved his hand in its direction discreetly and watched it renew, the blades of its leaves spiking up again.

Then he circled around, out from it, looking for clues, and found he wasn't the only thing out here that smelled like saltwater. He knew he smelled like open waves, but the thing he scented now was bracken and old, rotting and foul.

A drowned one.

He was sure of it.

More so when he found the wet discoloration it'd left on the cement sidewalk when it'd lost its integrity. *Fuck.* He would've preferred an actual enemy to this. He sank down to press a palm against the damp gray stain, feeling much like he'd been stabbed.

Drowned ones were exactly what they sounded like, bodies of people who'd died somewhere in the ocean. And if the Gate itself was sending out drowned ones as emissaries, trying to find the key to lock itself, it meant his sleeping dragon was no longer enough to contain the horrors behind its door.

Which meant that soon the only thing that would reinforce the door was him rejoining his dragon at the bottom of the sea. He stared up at the sun with his eyes closed and tried to imagine a life lived in total darkness.

IT TOOK Sammy hours to calm down after Mr. Janvier's intrusion. She'd crawled into bed and hugged her knees to her chest. She was still pissed off at how he'd ended it, but why had it begun?

Why would a man like that, 'cold and precise,' his own words, storm her apartment and bang on her door?

His concern had seemed genuine, if frightening. And after he'd realized she was all right he'd been relieved enough to leave.

But why wouldn't she be okay?

It was *weird*. Weird like the way she'd first met him, weird like him hiring her, and weird like his club's secret door.

On the scale between 'having parents murdered by a serial killer' and 'my best friend claims her fiancé is secretly a dragon,' though it felt pretty tame.

She was very aware that her scale was fucked.

Sammy held her phone loosely in her hands and wondered if she was at the part in the future documentary where she really Ought to Tell Someone, even if it made her sound crazy when she did. But she was fine and Mr. Janvier hadn't exactly been slavering outside with an ax, Jack Nicholson-style. So even though her fingers ached to tell Andi everything, instead of typing she just stared at her phone.

"I wish you were here," she whispered at it, then put it directly under her pillow and forced herself to go to sleep.

SHE WAS SUBDUED that night at the club, wondering if Janvier was going to come find her and make excuses for himself. Vanessa asked her if she was sick so she played it off as being tired, which wasn't entirely lying, whereupon Vanessa handed her a Red Bull and told her to "suck it up, buttercup." But as the night rolled on, she didn't see Mr. Janvier anywhere, and neither did anyone else that she asked. She haunted the strange door more than usual though because whatever had happened she needed...closure? Answers?

Something.

Around 3 am, just as the club was slowing down, she spotted him. She set down her tray and quickly followed him through the employee break room and outside into their private parking lot, not caring who saw. "So what was that really about?" she called after him in the hallway, chasing him outside, her heels clattering on the asphalt. "Be honest with me." She ran around to stand in front of him, blocking his path. "For once," she added.

The blue-tinged light cast his strong features in shadows as he bent his head in her direction, his expression flat and unbothered. He wasn't even staring at her, he was staring through her, like she didn't exist, and she may never have felt so inconsequential in her life—not even while seeing her boyfriend cheat on her. Sudden righteous anger rose up inside of her. There was no need for him to make her feel like that. He wasn't in charge of her—and she sure as shit didn't need him.

"No, you know what?" she shouted at his stupidly attractive yet implacable face. "Fuck you. I don't need this job."

It may not have been the best idea in the world to quit when her purse and car keys were still inside, behind him, but the second she started thinking the words they fell out of her mouth. "You're an asshole. And—I'm a person, goddammit." She thumped her chest with one hand, hitting Andi's necklace on accident, probably leaving a tear-drop shaped impression on her sternum. "If you want to pretend like I don't exist, it'll be a lot easier for you when I'm gone."

She stepped sideways to lunge around him and back into the building, to get her purse from her locker, when he grabbed her wrist, holding her outside like a thousand-pound anchor. "Let go of me," she demanded, wringing it in his grasp.

"I know you exist," he told her in a low tone she could barely hear. "I would rather not—but I do."

She stopped trying to free herself and he let her wrist go. She circled it with her free hand, massaging the blood back into it. "What is it that you want from me?" He'd wanted something from her ever since that night at Belissima's. It was why he'd been staring at her, why he'd fucked her, and why she now worked here.

"Will you try to believe me if I tell you the truth?" He tilted his head to look at her.

She frowned and braced but nodded.

He made a thoughtful sound. "Good. What I want is for you to come back here, tomorrow night, after midnight."

That...wasn't the answer she was expecting. Surely if he were going to murder her, here of all places, he'd just do it now, while they were still alone, outside.

Unless he needed to tape off a special room with plastic tarps first.

"It's my night off." She crossed her arms.

"You won't be working."

That sounded even worse. She tensed and snapped, "I won't sleep with you."

The corners of his lips quirked up, and a dark eyebrow rose. "Have I asked you to?"

"Just...the once," she admitted, still frowning.

"While I do not regret it, I will not cross that line again," he said, his voice a low rumble. "Just...come tomorrow, Samantha. Here. After midnight."

His words were almost cruel, because for the first time he sounded like the man she'd been with in the wine cellar. Decisive, certainly, but not uncaring, not like every other version of Mr. Janvier she'd met since.

She rose her eyes to meet his and found she had his full attention now. It was too much, she didn't want it anymore, she shook her head and looked away. "Why can't you just tell me now?"

He held up empty hands. "I can't."

"But that doesn't make any sense—"

"You're the person who wants the truth," he said, with a taunt in his voice.

She rocked back and muttered, "Fuck you, you fucking fucker."

He laughed harshly. "Is that a yes?"

"No." Sammy clenched her hands into fists. "It's most definitely not. You just want to play games. I've met so many men like you before—"

"I assure you, Samantha," he cut in, and she watched him lick his lips. "None of this is a game to me."

"But you can't tell me until tomorrow?" She rolled her eyes and started walking for the building behind them with intent.

"I see you on the security cameras," he called after her, and she felt herself flush. "You want to know what's behind the closed doors. I can tell you. Tomorrow night."

She shook her head and kept walking.

ONCE SHE HAD her purse and keys, Sammy walked out the front of the building and around the block to the back again, all in an effort to avoid running into him. She knew she was ditching Vanessa with a thousand glasses to wash, but she was also leaving her portion of the tips because *fuck this noise.*

She would quit on voicemail after she got home. Because no matter what he said, *it was a game.* Come back on her off night after midnight? She'd been with some strange men before, ones who had weird hang-ups or who tried to keep scores, she recognized the type. He was happier if she was off-balance, and just like that '80s film said, she knew the only way to win was not to play.

No, this would be the last time she'd knowingly set foot in a Mr. Janvier establishment. She still had savings, and her best friend hadn't married a billionaire for nothing because her pride was *not*, in any way, shape, or form, worth putting up with this level of bullshit.

She let herself into the employee parking lot, yanked her keys out of her purse, stomped to her car, and drove home, wired and angry.

SAMMY PARKED in front of her apartment and stormed inside, upset she'd wasted a week of her life and…for what? Stupid curiosity? And now she was going to have to find a new-new job that she also probably wouldn't like because working for a living largely sucked.

Her phone dinged. Andi, reporting in, with a view of her tan legs on the deck of a boat, toes pointing out at an impossibly blue sea. Andi was off swimming in the Mediterranean, absolutely living the dream, whereas Sammy was just…*not.*

Sammy's fingers ran over her screen, wanting to text her best friend everything, but she couldn't bring herself to even start. How on earth could she explain what she'd recently decided to put herself through...and for what?

Some strange man?

Hot—shit, yes—but also certifiable.

Was she really that desperate?

Sammy touched her phone to her forehead and wished she had telepathy so she could download everything to Andi rather than explain—or give up and shout: *I MISS YOU. STOP HAVING FUN. WHEN THE FUCK ARE YOU GOING TO BE HOME???* But in the end, she just typed, *Beautiful!!!!* like she always did and hit send.

Sammy pulled on her boxer shorts and t-shirt and went through her bedtime rituals even though it was five in the morning. She brushed her teeth, plugged in her phone, put in her earbuds, and turned on a murder podcast to listen to while she hunted down a cute goat .gif to send to Eumie, the more ridiculous, the better. She didn't know if Eumie even got them, if the new person who had their phone was just ridiculously tolerant or had her blocked, but just sending them made her feel a little less alone.

Then she lay in bed and stared at the ceiling as dawn rose through her curtains, listening to calm women talk about serial killers as she willed herself to sleep.

CHAPTER 6

SAMMY WOKE WITH THE FEELING THAT SOMEONE WAS IN HER ROOM WITH her, but there was nothing new about that, given what she went to sleep to every night.

Only…something smelled.

Bad. Very bad.

Like maybe there was a gas leak from Eumie's old bakery below.

She threw her arm in front of her face to breathe through the sheet and turned over and—there was a shadow standing right by her bed.

It was daylight and the window was opposite her so there was no reason she shouldn't be able to see what the fuck was just three feet to her left, only she couldn't; there was just a darkness there.

An unseemly black space.

Empty, with rippling edges. It stank, and it was reaching out for her.

Sammy screamed like a horror queen, jumping away from it before it could touch her, praying that this was some kind of night-mare she'd given herself by letting her podcasts run too long. But the longer she screamed, the more *there* it became, and it started making a horrible gurgling, breathless sound back out at her.

She couldn't get to her bat because the shadow was on that side of her bed, blocking her from both the bat and the room's exit, and the harder she tried to see what it was, the worse it became. Because it did have a face, it was just rippled like the rest of it, like it was in the process of being erased. No...like it was underwater. Like it was something, *someone*, trapped underwater too long; the thing you always were scared of seeing when you were swimming in a crisp, clear lake. The girl the older kids told you about at camp late at night, the one that'd died last summer, whose body had never been found.

Sammy scrabbled to the back of her bed, freed her top sheet, and flung it at the shadow. She wasn't sure what was worse, that it draped loosely around the shadow, making her very certain that the fucking thing was real, or that she'd turned it into some sort of paranormal-activity-slash-evil-Casper. She leaped off the foot of her bed and ran around it, racing for her bedroom door, feeling it come after her, still making its quiet, hideous gurgles.

She grabbed her keys off her kitchen counter and ran out the front door, barefoot, flying down the stairs, running straight for her car just as Janvier's Jaguar pulled into the apartment's lot and blocked her Subaru's exit. He leaned over and swung his passenger door open for her.

"This is what I was afraid of," he told her. "Get in."

Sammy stood there, panting, while her brain tried to figure out what the fuck was even real. Maybe this was all just a dream? A very, very real nightmare? That would explain why Mr. Janvier was in it. But she'd left her apartment door open behind herself and looking up she could see the fucking drowned-ghost-thing inside her doorjamb's empty square. That alone inspired movement. She leaped into the Jaguar and curled herself up into a ball on its tan leather seat, holding her knees to her chest, shivering with adrenaline and fear.

The second her door was closed, he drove off. He didn't even wait for her to put on her seatbelt. Instead, he reached across her for it, buckling her safely in, without even looking over as he went on to change lanes.

"Are you all right?" he asked, as she wiped her face with the back of one hand. It felt like fire where his arm had brushed against her, which was in its own way as worrisome as the ghost. "No." She twisted in the seat to look back at her receding apartment complex. *Had all that really happened?* Then she looked around herself, now in Mr. Janvier's exceptionally well-crafted car, and then at him. It was the first time she'd ever seen him in full daylight, she realized.

He was real. And he wasn't a monster, at least, she didn't think.

Would a monster want you to wear a seatbelt?

He spared a glance over at her and looked disappointed to have caught her staring. "I didn't want to have to do this," he said, more to himself than her, as they stopped at a red light—at the same time as he reached over for her throat. She screamed again, her hands scrabbling for the unfamiliar car's door latch, as she heard him intone: "Sleep."

"How long has this been your plan?" Smoke snaked around his feet, yipping his discontent at Rax adding another creature to his menagerie. Sammy was still passed out in his arms after he'd used his sleeping spell on her. He took her to his study on the villa's bottom floor, deep underground, that he'd turned into a bedchamber of sorts, where she could mostly be alone from him, and he wouldn't have to look at her.

"Long enough," Rax said, carrying her over to lay her down on the bed he'd made for her, out of two velvet couches pressed together. He'd known since he'd first hired her that this day would come, but he'd hoped to postpone it for her sake, or at least until Namir had gotten him his knives.

But another drowned one had tripped across his magic, and he couldn't take the risk of waiting anymore—nor had he had to, when she'd come flying down her stairs and practically into his car.

He had no doubt she'd be pissed when she woke up, though.

If he could've waited, if she'd shown up at the Lynx, and if she could've handled the truth, she would've jumped at the chance to be safe. But he should've known better than to leave so much to fate when a human was involved.

It'd have been one thing if she'd been shielding the necklace one whit, but no. The drowned ones were doomed to find her. They did the work of the Gate Below, they only longed to see it locked and closed. She was lucky she hadn't been attacked earlier, in the interim between when he'd fucked her and when he'd hired her. When he'd been wondering if she was even real.

He looked around the room after he'd settled her down. He'd tried to take everything personal out of it, except for his books, which he had nowhere else to keep—anything that would lead to her asking questions.

More questions.

Because the questions *were* coming.

There was no way to hide the shark tank unless he left her blindfolded the entire time, which seemed unnecessarily cruel. And he would likely have to explain at least some of the necklace's provenance to her when he started trying to remove it from her by magical means.

All the same, the less she knew, the better. He'd already seen how she'd reacted to the drowned one at her apartment. If her mind couldn't bend around that, showing her more things here would only break it, especially considering that when he was done he was going to have to deposit her back in the 'normal' world and disavow that any of this—that her, here, had ever happened, and if she ever approached him after this, he was going to have to make her seem unhinged.

And all of that was assuming she survived his attempts to remove the necklace. Hopefully, Namir's knives would do the trick.

But the obviously easiest tactic to take would be...the worst. He stood at the end of the mated couches, looking down at her sleeping form, her face relaxed, her orange-red hair loosely strewn over the velvet beneath her, watching the slight rise and fall of her chest, her loose t-shirt draped over her curves. The drowned one had done him a favor by scaring her into his grasp, so he hadn't had to abduct her himself. He could only hope she remembered its terror when she woke.

Until then, he had business to attend to.

"Have Hachiro summon me if she rouses," he told Smoke and left the room.

HE DROVE BACK by her apartment before heading into the casino. By some sort of miracle, no one else had noticed the open door on a morning weekday. Perhaps neighbors, if she had any, assumed she was home and was airing the place out. The weather was glorious, nice enough for even him to notice. He took her keys up with him and made a small circuit inside.

The floor of the living room was wet, and the stench of rot and saltwater was strong in the air. The drowned one must've lost integrity not long after she'd run away.

He stepped around a wet sheet and looked into her bedroom. It was open and airy, or would've been if it didn't currently smell like death. She'd painted it white with one light blue wall, almost the same color as the sky outside, and there was a framed car-themed movie poster on the wall. Her bed had ten pillows that she seemed to create a nest out of to sleep in; they lined its edges. There were little knick-knacks on a bookshelf and other surfaces, most of which seemed to be little resin sandcastles, but nothing magical, other than the residue of the drowned one's former presence.

There was nothing particularly familial, cither.

In fact, for all of its pleasantness, and apart from the bed, there wasn't much that seemed *of her* to it. Were it scentless, it could've been a background for a TV commercial or on a website. He went through the drawers on her desk, expecting to find more personalization, but no, just a few scattered bills. No handwritten notes. Nothing from friends or family.

He spotted her phone and pocketed it and its charger before moving back into the hall.

The bathroom smelled more like her, like the faint sweetness make-up had, and the hint of cinnamon that followed her—and there were little touches of her there. Earrings hung over the edge of a small silver cup with some necklaces nestled inside. Two kiss marks on the mirror, different colors, at different heights, different lip prints, perhaps left by friends.

But still, no magic.

All in all, she hadn't made much of a dent in life, not as exhibited by belongings or eccentric tastes. But he knew from the way she held herself and spoke that *something* had made a dent on her.

The apartment had another bedroom that was entirely empty, and he cruised through the kitchen, but there was nothing to explain how his necklace had come into her possession or anything else that was special about her.

He locked the door behind him, then he used her key fob to figure out which car in the lot was hers; the same burgundy Subaru WRX he'd seen her drive off in at Belissima's. He took a photo of its license plate and sent it to one of his contacts so that he could have it towed. He paused for a long moment, staring at the stains in its backseat, which had to be brown paint because they couldn't be blood. *Could they?* He snorted. Either way, he'd have it detailed before hiding it in his garage.

Finished with his rounds, he got back into his own car and drove to work.

THAT NIGHT, he sat behind his desk with an array of trinkets atop it, and a man sat across from him wearing a coat that had once been grand but was now fraying slightly at the edges. Namir loomed by the door. He only occasionally had Namir sit in on his deals, but he knew the tiger-shifter made Mathal, a rodent-shifter, anxious, and sure enough, Mathal was twitching in his seat. Rax wondered if the man changed into one very large mouse, and what was the point of that, if so? Or maybe one of those things swimming around in South America. *Capybaras.* A man who was half crocodile had once told him they were delicious.

Rax played with the items, killing time, after having first made sure that none of them were dangerous or cursed, while Mathal's impatience grew. One was a Rubik's cube that was already solved, although the colors on its stickers didn't match any of the ones on Earth he recognized. They were mesmerizingly iridescent, created from mother of pearl, and it was actually powerful—more than any other object he'd seen in quite some time. Someone had poured a lot of time and ability into crafting it, for all that it was otherwise made out of cheap plastic. He plinked it over with a flick of his fingers. Mathal's other items, a doll's head that had an evil look on its face, and a chunky statue of an apparently sleeping chameleon, made out of silver, with eyes that blinked periodically, were just so-so. This time last year, they would've been worth more, but not currently.

Rax pushed the cube and the doll forward, keeping the chameleon for himself. He knew Mathal had no innate knowledge of what his items were worth, only whether or not they were magical. For all that like all shifters he was made with magic, he was not a magic-user. "I'm sorry, Mathal. The market for magical objects is very soft right now. You know how much chaos there is in the Realms at the moment. Too many people are trying to liquidate assets and move into areas with more stability." He'd set up many refugees from the current war in the Realms with appropriate papers to exist on Earth, for a high price. He knew most of them would go back to the Realms the first chance they got, hardly anyone wanted to stay someplace that lacked any inherent magic.

Because most magic users, beyond shifters and other people trapped inside innately magical bodies, relied on absorbing it from their environment. A non-magical place like Earth provided no succor. Users could stave off normalcy for a time by imbuing objects with magical properties, to be drained later, rather like batteries, but that required both foresight and talent, and Rax had learned that foolishness was a universal constant, no matter the Realm.

He toyed with the blinking chameleon. "Where did you acquire these, anyhow?" He wouldn't put filching objects from graves past the beast, and despite how many deals they'd done before, Rax knew Mathal would stab him in an instant if given the opportunity. It was only fair, as the feeling was mutual.

"Like I'm going to tell you my sources with him standing here," Mathal said, gesturing with his head to Namir.

"Oh, I pay Namir very well," Rax said, because it was true. "He would never stray." Rax glanced over at the tiger-shifter, standing at attention behind the man, and watched him roll his eyes. "In any case," he began, hiding a smile. "This one—you need to get rid of." He tapped the Rubik's cubes side.

"Why?"

"That's unicorn horn," he lied fluidly. "A hunter creation. So I doubt it was ethically sourced."

"Which means it's powerful," Mathal said, narrowing beady eyes.

"True," Rax admitted. "But you try to sell it to the wrong person, or even show it to the wrong person, and you're likely to wind up with a unicorn horn in you."

Shifter retribution against hunters and anyone who helped them was sudden and violent, and Rax had met several unicorns before. They were assholes, the lot of them, and everyone knew it.

"Bah," Mathal said.

"I'll give you twenty chips for the chameleon," Rax said, holding up the living statue. It was a low figure, but he knew Mathal had a gambling problem, which he wasn't above using against him. "And as for the cube, you're better off just throwing it in the trash."

Mathal's hand pocketed the doll's head but wavered over the cube as the rodent-shifter tried to figure out his angle. "Twenty more chips, and you can keep the cube, too."

"And buy a hunter talisman?" Rax lifted his gaze wearily to Namir, who made a growling sound. "I think not. I have a reputation to uphold. I run a safe casino, Mathal. And while all shifters are equal here, any sign of me, or anyone I know, consorting with hunters—no." Rax laughed as though it were utterly impossible...even though he'd been forced to sell magical objects to hunters to ensure his own clientele's safety mere months ago.

Mathal banged his hand on Rax's desk in frustration and the cube rattled cheaply, just like Rax supposed Mathal's teeth would if he was hit hard enough.

"You're sure?" he asked dourly.

"Completely." Rax opened open a desk drawer, pulled out a stack of twenty chips, and slid them over. "Here you go then. Good luck, and don't forget to tip the staff."

"Starting with me," Namir growled, as he let the man out. Mathal cursed at him in some unknown tongue as Namir closed the door.

Rax picked up his phone and pulled up the name of the only unicorn he was currently on good terms with.

"Want me to follow him and shake him down?" Namir offered.

"There's no need. I'm calling in a favor from Prithia. When she gets here, make sure Mathal notices and then grab the cube when he tosses it." Rax considered things for a moment. "Although if he decides to run, use that as an excuse to beat him senseless and steal it from him for propriety's sake."

Namir looked bemused. "Is it actually horn?"

"No," Rax said. "Just mother of pearl." He remembered the vast vaults of the shimmering stuff from his childhood, mosaics inlaid by grand artisans who spent their entire lives decorating just one room inside the castle. "But magically, it's worth more than I need to be paying the likes of him, and you and I both know he didn't come into it with honor."

"Understood." Namir nodded, then opened up his coat. "By the way, these finally arrived for you earlier tonight." He handed a folded leather bundle over, and Rax didn't bother opening it up for inspection, perhaps the highest sign of trust he could ever give.

Rax stood, tucking the bundle under one arm. "Good. Cancel all the rest of my appointments. I won't be back until tomorrow evening."

Namir's eyes widened at that. "And what will I tell Prithia when she gets here?"

"Give her my love," Rax said with extreme sarcasm, "and say I had an emergency, or better yet, give her your love, seeing as she likes you better anyhow." He looked around his office. Everything important inside of it was magically warded, even his mirror. "In fact," he went on, "you can give her your love in here, Namir after you acquire the cube, and if you clean up after yourself."

Namir let out a low whistle. "I'd wonder why you're in a good mood tonight, but I don't want to jinx it."

"Then don't," Rax said on his way out the door.

SAMMY WOKE, slowly at first, then all in a rush, as she realized she had no idea where she was sleeping. It was like she was in a velvet playpen; there were soft red walls on either side of her that went two feet up.

She sat up quickly, looking around in front of herself. The room she was in was dimly lit, with bookcases lining one wall, a lectern with a particular book singled out upon it, and then a desk with more books on it besides.

Okay.

She was in between two velvet couches sandwiched together in a library, and someone was playing the piano, or the music was being piped in. Weird, but truth was she'd woken up in worse places before. She put her hand to her head and started thinking, trying to remember the last thing she'd seen—

The memory of the ghost was still imprinted on her mind, although it was like the longer she thought about it, the harder it tried to leave her, like her vision of it was just an oil stain, a residue of feelings left behind.

And then, after that...Mr. Janvier.

Saving her?

Or....

She put her hand to her throat and awkwardly got out of her strange bed.

A shadow moved in front of her. She was attuned to them now, seeing what she had—she leaped sideways before she realized it really was just a shadow. She turned back to see what'd cast it and found an enormous fish tank. It stretched from floor to ceiling, and she couldn't tell how deep it was in any dimension, and inside of it—she put her hand to her mouth and whispered, "Oh my God," as a ten-foot-long shark circled into view.

Another one, that'd already swum on, was what had cast the shadow on the floor here, backlit by some other light beyond. She was torn between running to the glass's edge to peer in and running away because *Jesus Fucking Christ!*

What the shit? Where the fuck was she?

The piano playing stopped and then restarted, allowing her to echolocate its source. Upstairs. There were stone stairs that wound around the tank's side because of course there were. She pressed the heels of her hands to her forehead, trying to keep her racing thoughts inside. What were they attached to? Why didn't they have a safety rail? If she started walking up them, where would they go?

Was there a chance they'd just reach to the top of the tank, and then some sort of comical mallet would push her in?

And why the hell did they have to be so close to the sharks?

She wasn't normally scared by aquariums, just beaches, and the open sea, but *come the fuck on!*

The music continued, and she slowly walked up the stairs to its meter. She was still in the clothes she normally slept in, for crying out loud; just tie-front boxers and a t-shirt and now one of the sharks was coming over to look at her, and she couldn't move too far away from the glass because the other side of the steps didn't have a railing and—she took the last five stairs in a burst, then went left out onto the next area, some sort of living-floor pavilion. There were more bookcases and objects of art from different time periods on the walls, some oil paintings of the ocean, couches to lounge on from which to view them, what looked like a very open-space kitchen, and—almost as improbable as the sharks—someone playing a grand piano.

His back was to her, but somehow she knew it was Mr. Janvier. It seemed ridiculous that someone his size could play piano so beautifully, but beautiful was the wrong word. It was haunting. Not because this place was like half-zoo, half-nightmare, but because there was something in the tones as they met and receded, in volume and duration. Whatever he was playing sounded like the ocean felt, when you were the only person on the beach, listening to the waves on a lonely day.

When you were all alone, and everything you'd ever known had just been taken from you.

Sammy opened up her mouth to say something but nothing squeaked out and then he stopped, and she knew on some instinctual level that he realized she was there. She swallowed and found her voice. "Your playing's lovely," she said, even if the song was not.

"Something here has to be." He pushed himself away from the piano and turned around. "What's the last thing you remember?" he asked. Her hand went to her throat without thinking. "Before that," he prompted.

She was going to pre-apologize for sounding stupid when she said she thought she'd seen a ghost, then she remembered where the fuck she was. "A ghost." Her voice was firm. She knew she might not have the right words for it, but whatever it was that'd been in her bedroom last night hadn't belonged there.

"Close," he said. "It was dead, but it wasn't a ghost, it was a drowned one."

He said the words with total authority. He wasn't worried about sounding weird at all. "Which is?" she asked him.

He shook his head. "It doesn't matter," he said and then considered her. "Where did you get that necklace, Red?"

She took a step back, remembering how the box had mysteriously appeared, presumably for Andi. "Why?"

"Because. It's why they're after you. And I know you didn't get it yourself, nor have you had it very long."

Sammy blinked. Andi's business with her fiancé, the dragon-shifter, was just that—*Andi's*. Sammy would never sell her best friend out.

"You might as well tell me now," he said. "Because you will be telling me, eventually."

She watched him stand and cross the room, arcing around her until he sat down on a couch in front of a low table. He kicked the table back a foot and jerked his chin at it. "Come. Sit." There was something folded up on the table; she wasn't sure what it was.

"And if I don't?"

"Do I seem like the kind of man you want to disobey?"

She heard the taunt in his voice. "If you wanted me dead by now, you'd already have killed me."

"Hmm. Is that so?" he asked dryly as one of his eyebrows lifted.

"Probably." She wrapped her arms around herself. There was a door behind him, she could—

"Locked, I assure you," he said. He was between her and the door. And just like when she'd seen him playing the piano, she felt like he'd be more agile than he looked.

Than was fair, really.

Because...what was this? "Have you kidnapped me?" She tried to keep her voice calm as she said the words, but a bullet of acid shot through her stomach. She didn't need his answer to know it was true.

He inhaled deeply. "You were in danger, Samantha—"

"Am I, or am I not, allowed to leave?"

She watched him for half a second too long, a vital moment, time she should have spent sprinting for the door. She raced in its direction, her bare feet slapping against the cement floor, jolts of pain running up her shins as she ran flat out. From the corner of her eye, she saw him leap over the couch he'd been sitting on and run after her, every bit as athletic as she feared. His shoes against the floor were loud, and he blindsided her on her left when she was ten feet from it, easily picking her up.

"LET GO OF ME!" she shouted at her highest volume, feeling her throat tear with the force of it. "HELP! HELP! FIRE!" She thrashed in his arms, feeling all the places he was clothed rubbing against all her naked skin where she was not. He crushed her against himself, as firm and unforgiving as the bite of any shark. "LET ME GO!" she howled, scrabbling against him wildly, throwing punches with elbows, trying to kick at his kneecaps, reaching up for the softer flesh of his throat and eyeballs, but nothing worked. It was like trying to wrestle steel.

She wriggled sideways all of a sudden and tried to bite the arm that held her.

"SAMANTHA, STOP!" he shouted, half-dropping, half-throwing her to the ground.

She caught herself, bruising a wrist, and then cleared the last few feet to the door in a scurry. She didn't see any locks on it, just a normal door handle. She twisted it and prayed. *Please, please, please!*

But the door didn't so much as tremble.

"See?" he said, behind her.

She tried the door handle again and again and then felt hot tears spring to her cheeks. She swallowed them back because fuck if this was it, there was no way that this man was going to make her cry. She let go of the door handle and beat her hands on the door, hurting her wrist further, and then swiped at her face with the collar of her t-shirt.

"Can you just settle down?" Mr. Janvier growled from behind her. At least he hadn't followed her.

He didn't need to. She was trapped.

"I know things are strange," he went on. "But I need you to be rational."

She turned to look over her shoulder at him, her hair flipping with the motion. "You fucking have pet sharks! I don't need to be rational!"

He was angry. He'd been angry almost every time she'd ever seen him, it seemed, so why should that change now? But then an unexpected emotion crossed his face.

Delight.

At what? Capturing her?

Before she could figure out how best to use it against him, his familiar expression returned. "Why am I here?" she whispered. Everything was cold here. Her feet on the cement she stood on, the water in the tank behind him, and the dark amber of his gaze. Cold and lifeless. Her eyes threatened to cry again, and she grit her teeth, blinking tears back.

"To keep you safe," he said, taking a step away from her without turning around. "The necklace you have on is more valuable than you know. If I am interested, others will be as well, like the thing that visited you earlier today. All I want to do is free you from the necklace and its curse. Which is precisely what I *was* going to tell you tonight."

Her hand reached for the red gemstone on her neck. "Why should I believe you?"

He shrugged lightly. "You don't really have a choice." He went back to where he'd been sitting on a couch and pointed to the table again. "Don't make me make you."

Sammy walked over to him as slowly as possible, holding her hurt wrist with her opposite hand. He was stronger than she was for sure, so if she wanted to survive, she was going to have to outsmart him.

In a very real, very horrible way, she'd been preparing for this moment her whole life.

She had a huge advantage. She'd already survived an attempted murder once before.

All she had to do was manage to do it again.

And she knew the first rule of surviving something like this was that if she ever had a chance to kill him, she shouldn't hesitate.

CHAPTER 7

HE SHOULDN'T HAVE RUN AFTER HER.

Rax knew in the moment he was making a mistake, but he hadn't been able to stop himself; it was a feral, predator thing. Then he wrapped his arms around her again, just like that night at Belissima's, breathing in the scent of her hair without thinking, and now it was too late—she hated him.

She would've hated him regardless, but he'd learned that people very rarely forgot when you made them feel anger mixed with fear.

It didn't matter, of course. She was human, so how could it? But watching her trudge defeatedly toward him, one foot in front of the other like she was marching to the gallows, he wished he could take that small part back.

Ah well.

She rounded the couch and sat on the table across from him, arms crossed beneath her breasts. He knew better than to assume her current compliance was a permanent state—he felt sure that the Samantha who'd just tried to bite him wasn't far away.

"Try to remove the necklace, Red."

There was no point in using any coddling phrases, like, "do me a favor" or "can you?" when he didn't mean anything of the sort. She would do as she was told, from here on out, or face consequences for it…once he'd figured out precisely what they were.

Her hands lifted and found the clasp behind her neck. He watched her fidget and then frown. "I can't."

"That's what I feared." He reached for the leather bundle on the table beside her, undid its tie, and opened it up, to reveal the magical knives he'd had Namir source for him inside. There were three of them, with different energies and different blades, gold, glass, and a blade made entirely of pressed rose petals, and this was where he'd begin. Either one of them would work, or he'd use his own magic to amplify them over the course of several days and imbue them with enough power—

"You're scaring her." Hachiro's voice rose in his mind as the creature did, hovering in the aquarium behind Samantha's shoulders.

He glanced at her face and saw her sheer terror. She was even paler than she naturally was, her eyes were wide, and her mouth had dropped open.

"They're not for you. They're for the chain." Something he probably should've mentioned prior to revealing them. "Tie your hair up, unless you want a haircut." Her shining eyes sought his, searching for any kindness, and he clenched his jaw. "Red," he warned. It was as close as he would come to saying please.

She swallowed as her hands rose a second time, sweeping her hair around itself and up into a bun like it'd been the night that he'd first seen her. She did have a lovely neck. *And there were so many freckles on it he hadn't kissed yet….* He growled at his own distraction and reached for the stone, plucking it up off of her chest, doing his best to not touch any of her skin.

"I'm not going to harm you," he said, picking up the gold blade.

Her eyes looked from his hand to him. "For how long?"

Rax took a deep breath. In general, he tried not to lie. And so, as comforting as it would've been for her to hear that he'd never hurt her, what were the chances of that, when he knew from just looking at her that he already had?

"That's what I thought," she whispered, closing her eyes and going still.

Making peace with her God? Preparing to die at his hand?

Rax knew he ought to bring the blade down to the necklace's chain and let his experiments begin, but how had his gem found her neck to encircle, among all the women in the world? He could see her pulse bounding at her throat. She was still terrified of him, but she was also so oddly brave, for a human. He'd seen every human emotion up close a million times over throughout his very long life, so he knew how rare real courage was.

Then the pulse at her neck slowed, and Hachiro warned, *"Watch out!"* at the same time as he saw her sweep up the glass blade and Smoke leaped. He batted Smoke off his trajectory for her throat as she rammed the blade into his stomach.

Smoke snarled, bouncing off the ground, rebounding quickly to Rax's side on the couch, making his strange cackling warning sound at her, as Samantha's eyes opened to see the sudden chaos she'd caused. She was breathing hard as his free hand went for his stomach. She'd given him a superficial wound and then the magical blade had shattered.

"You," he began slowly, raising his hand up between them. His blood was green, as was that of all dragons, and there were glass shards on his palm. He closed his hand quickly, but not fast enough.

"What are you?" she asked, her voice high.

He dropped the stone he still held and it thumped on her chest. "The worst thing that's ever happened to you," he growled. He slammed his unused gold blade into its leather case and folded it up before standing. Her eyes were locked on the green stain spreading on his dress shirt. There was no hiding it nor denying it now. *Fuck.* "There's food in the kitchen. The downstairs is yours. Come upstairs at your peril," he said, picking up the knives and heading to the stairs.

· · ·

"She stabbed you!" Smoke howled, following him up the stairs, running up a few at a time to look back down, making sure Rax wasn't followed.

"I know. I was there," he muttered quietly, so she wouldn't hear him. He and Hachiro could speak with their minds, but Smoke was unable to. He could speak his old tongue from the Realms with the beast, but it required sound. Smoke ran up the last set and stayed at the edge of the cement, growling.

"You should have let me bite her!"

"And then what?" Rax asked, stalking across his bedroom for the bathroom. He needed to make sure there were no glass shards left in his wound; magical wounds could fester. *A human girl had stabbed him!* It was wildly unbelievable, even though he'd watched it happen. He could've stopped her, or Smoke, but not both. What if the fox's sharp teeth had somehow hit her carotid? Just because he couldn't promise her no harm didn't mean he wanted her dead.

Although at the moment.... He yanked off his shirt, sending buttons ricocheting, and stood in front of his mirror, taking out the shards that were easiest to see. That knife had been expensive. It would be difficult for Namir to commission a second one so quickly. He ran water over a washcloth and then rubbed it over his stomach, wiping away blood and knocking more glass loose. Then he held his hand over the wound, summoning any remaining glass out. A scattering of tiny bits floated free and into his palm, where he carefully washed them down the sink.

How many people had tried to kill him before and failed? He ought to be inured to it, except that it was *her.* He was torn between being pissed off, amused, and mystified.

She had stabbed him, and what was more, he had let her.

He looked at himself in the mirror and frowned.

"You'd better come out here quickly, Rax, or I will bite her so hard!" Smoke warned, his yips sounding frantic at the top of the stair.

Rax washed his hands and then blotted his stomach again to make sure that there was absolutely no blood left on him. His body had already healed the physical part of his injury, but it would take longer to quiet his mind. "What is it that you want?" he shouted as he walked over to the aquarium's edge and stairs below.

She stood on the landing below him, hugging herself once more, looking disconsolate. "There's not a bathroom down here. Or if there is, it's locked."

Rax closed his eyes. His villa was not meant for visitors, and if he created a bathroom out of nothingness now, he'd be inviting even more unwanted questions.

"Did you want me to pee in your kitchen sink, Mister-The-Worst? Because I'll do that—" she threatened.

"Come up," he said, nudging Smoke aside with his shoe. The fox snarled, practically slavering at her as she took each step. "Stop that," he told the beast.

"I want to bite her."

"You've made that abundantly clear," Rax grumbled without thinking, and then saw her eyeing him warily, looking between him and the fox.

"Go," he told her, taking several steps back and pointing for the bathroom. She ran up the last few steps and then walked quickly where he pointed, occasionally looking back. Smoke made to chase after her. "Don't," he said, accidentally in English.

"Don't...what?" she asked from the door, hesitating.

He waved her on dismissively. "I wasn't talking to you. Hurry up."

Smoke looked between the now closed bathroom door and him. "And you're going to just allow this?"

"Which part?" Rax asked the beast with a snort.

"Her! Here! Invading your privacy! Not to mention mine!" The fox sniffed after the path she'd taken, nose wrinkling, tail perked up. Rax knelt down to be more on the fox's level.

"I'm going to need your help guarding her, Smoke. I still have business to attend to in the outside world."

The fox looked at him slyly, from the corner of one eye. "Am I allowed to bite her?"

"No."

Smoke sat back on his haunches abruptly. "Not now...or not ever? Because if it's not ever, dragon, I hardly see what's in it for me."

"Not now. We'll play the rest day by day." Rax ran a rough hand down the fox's back to calm it, and it shook itself in response.

"I'm not forgetting," Smoke warned him.

"I didn't expect you would."

The door to the bathroom reopened and Rax returned to standing. Samantha cast a quick look around his room and then at him, looking at his stomach where she'd stabbed him. She'd seen his blood earlier, and she saw that he was healed, now. He ran a hand over the muscles there, wishing he could brush her gaze away.

She didn't say anything about that, though. She edged nearer the stairs, and he backed up, parallel to the wall of water on his left. "People are going to be looking for me," she said.

"Hmm." He remembered the walls of her apartment. Empty, like a journal waiting to be written in. "I doubt that."

"I have friends," she said. She was trying to keep her voice firm, but he could still hear it quaver. "And a fiancée." She brought her left hand up to show him the gold band on her ring finger, with its tiny green stone. "He loves me. He'll find me. He'll get the police. I know he will."

So many lies. He took a step nearer her. "Would you like to know what I think about that, Samantha?" She didn't answer; she only licked her lips nervously as he said, "Give me your hand." Rax put his own hand out, waiting for hers.

Her pulse picked up again, and her breathing went rough.

"Give it to me," he growled at her, and she finally did, putting her left hand out while flinching. He held it up and folded her first two fingers and thumb in, then brought her ring-finger and pinkie to his mouth, sliding them inside of it, his tongue tasting the smooth-salt of her flesh until his teeth could catch at the ring on her ring-finger and tug it off. He sucked at her trembling fingers as he pulled them out of his mouth and then spat the ring into his shark tank casually. "That is what I think of that," he said, releasing her hand.

She gasped and her eyes went wide as she watched her ring tumble in the saltwater until it was out of view. Then she cradled the hand that'd been inside his mouth to her chest, like it was a tiny bird, her body shivering and shuddering in turns, and he could see her nipples were hard. From cold? Horror? Desire?

He ran his tongue across the back of his teeth, still tasting her there.

It didn't matter. Only getting the piece of the key did.

"Go below. Only come up here if you must, and do not talk to me if you do," he said, and she ran away from him, her hair a streak of red as she raced downstairs.

No place here was really safe for her.

Sammy dove back into the makeshift shelter of the two couches, and because she didn't have a pillow to scream into, she was forced to use her fist. She wedged it between her teeth—*much as he had!*—and howled silently, in a long hiss, getting everything out so that it would be over with, and she could move on with clarity.

She had to get it all out now because she didn't have long.

She knew the first forty-eight hours you were missing were the most important. And she didn't know how long had passed, or if anyone had even noticed she was gone yet. She and Andi had been texting back and forth, but because of the time delay, Andi might not realize she was gone for a full day.

So she was on her own and had to act accordingly.

She couldn't believe she'd stabbed him! She was equal parts proud of herself and disgusted and—why the fuck was his blood green?

She'd seen it. Legitimately green blood. Coming out of his body. She wasn't high, or drunk, or imagining things. *Green!*

Which meant that…. Sammy wedged herself even further into the couch cushions and shook her head. She knew that Andi's Damian had green blood and that he was a dragon. According to Andi, at least, because Sammy'd never laid eyes on him all scaled out, but Andi wasn't a liar and….

Did that mean that Mr. Janvier was a dragon, too?

It would explain a lot. In fact, if he was, then everything made a sort of horrific sense. Someone had sent a gift to Andi because she was going to be a dragon's wife, Sammy had intercepted it, and now a different dragon wanted her.

Not her, really, no, the necklace.

Her living felt fairly negotiable.

And that'd been the truth ever since that first evening in the wine cellar.

He hadn't wanted her, just the thing around her neck. He must've tried, and failed, to take it from her that night.

Her hands rose and she tried to unclasp it for real. She'd lied earlier sitting in front of him, too frightened to take it off and lose her worth to him while he was waiting with strange knives, but while there was a clasp, and she could catch it with her thumbnail repeatedly, she didn't feel it move. She tried to get it off until she made a spot beneath her thumbnail bleed and then brought it to her mouth to pinch between her teeth until the bleeding stopped. And what the fuck had been the deal with him and her ring? She could remember the hot way his mouth felt around her fingers, his teeth slowly pulling her ring free. How could something be so menacing and so carnal both at once?

Especially him standing there, shirtless, just an arm's length away. Covered in muscles, just as strong as she feared, and no sign of the wound she'd just given him.

Gone.

Healed.

Like it'd been imaginary.

But she'd seen the green stains on the washcloth when she'd used his bathroom, so she knew she wasn't insane.

And her intact mind was her current, best, defense. She was already leaps and bounds ahead of anyone else who might be in her situation, who might not even know that dragons existed, so there was that, although she'd never let on. It was far better for him to think that she didn't know anything at all. The more ignorant he thought she was, the better; the longer her leash might be.

Sammy took several cleansing inhales, then got up to the wall and started making rounds of the room.

RAX PACED on his upper level. It was clear he hadn't thought this through to the best of his capabilities. He was too used to thinking of humans as fragile and weak, especially compared to him, to have remembered that they were also often cunning.

Nothing she could do would have any effect on him, of course. She could stab him with anything in his house, and it wouldn't change things.

But if he didn't want her bound and gagged or magically sedated he was going to have to try a different tactic.

Maybe it wasn't too late to undo the effects of his chasing.

He went to his altar to center himself, ran quietly through his ritual, and came up with a plan.

SAMMY KNEW she should start with fingerprints.

She hadn't washed her face in, what, twelve hours? Maybe? She didn't have terrifically oily skin, but it would be enough to help. Sammy touched her fingertips to her face and then started at where the wall intersected with the aquarium on her far left, pressing them deliberately against the aquarium's glass and on the wall beside it.

Did police ever get to investigate crime scenes that happened inside of dragon's houses?

Maybe not. But if they did, she was going to do her damnedest to make it obvious that she'd been here. Once upon a time.

Just like a shitty fairy tale.

She heard Mr. Janvier muttering to himself up above. She didn't recognize the language, which wasn't comforting in the least, so she kept going. A broad stripe of fingerprints against the aquarium's glass, some high, some low. She was sure some would get cleaned away between now and whenever they were discovered, but she had hopes for the ones in the low corners. The sharks swam by but seemed disinterested, which was good. Maybe they were well fed.

After that, she turned to face the bookcases. They were floor-to-ceiling, same as the aquarium glass. Everything in Mr. Janvier's house had a looming sense of proportion to it, much like the man himself, and all of the titles were in languages she didn't understand.

She wanted to crack one open and start working through it, but first things first, she went through and touched every single binding. And then the wood of the bookcases they were in, the sides of the bookcases where she could reach them, whole palm prints, and finally she closed the books on the desk and placed her hands on it, leaning in repeatedly, wincing each time she pushed too hard into her right wrist.

Then and only then did she stop and turn back around.

She could still hear Mr. Janvier moving around above, which meant she didn't want to investigate the rest of the house just yet...so she might as well open a book.

She picked one at random. The words inside were written in silver ink and looked just as strange as the ones on the binding. The pages smelled old. She flipped through pages of words until she got to what she was looking for.

Pictures.

She flipped back and forth inside the book, finding more pictures to compare. This was obviously a history book, with maps of the same country she didn't recognize, changing over time, the borders being continuously redrawn.

A chopping sound began above her, followed by the scent of heating olive oil. Her stomach lurched and her mouth watered. She should've drunk water when she'd had the chance in the bathroom, but she'd been hurrying; she was too scared. She grit her teeth and opened another tome.

This one was full of architecture that was bizarre; buildings with flying buttresses off to nowhere or a spiraling stack of floors that in no way looked structurally sound. She snorted at the drawings.

None of them had shark tanks, but Mr. Janvier's home would fit right in.

And a third one she tried was a bestiary, with page after page of things that she didn't recognize or that she knew ought not exist. One chapter was dedicated to unicorns, another to a bird that was, if the height of the man next to it was to be used for scale, fifteen feet tall. Another had a strange creature that had too many mouths, wings, and eyes, all rolled together. She stared at it for a long moment, trying to figure out what it was that she was looking at, before giving up and finding the much larger part on dragons, in all sorts of slithery, scaled glory, painted in every color of the rainbow. Some had two legs, some had up to six, some had wings, some looked like worms, and whoever had painted them had put in painstaking detail.

Like he, or she, whoever it was…was doing portraits from real life.

And the very next page was torn out. She could see where it'd been ripped and feel the roughness of the paper at the binding's seam.

Was it just lost to time? Or ripped out intentionally?

The scents of cooking increased and her stomach growled. She snapped the book closed and found the fox hiding beneath it, not that far from her feet. It'd crept in while she'd been distracted, but now that they were looking at one another, it slowly lifted its lips and bared its white and needle-sharp teeth at her while making a strange hissing sound.

It was angry now and earlier it'd definitely run at her with intent. If Mr. Janvier hadn't swatted it from the air, the same teeth she saw now would've caught into the soft flesh of her neck or cheek.

Why was he fast enough to stop the fox, but not to stop her from stabbing him?

She frowned as the creature started to snarl, taking a step back and then another, as the fox pressed its advantage—maybe if she opened the book up again, she'd find a useful chapter on foxes. As it was, she waved the heavy book at the creature, which only made it snarl louder.

"Can you just not?" she whispered, standing firm at last. "Do you know what I've been through today?" She crouched down a little, using the book as a shield. "I don't even care if you give me rabies." Maybe if the thing bit her, Janvier would be forced to take her back to civilization. She waved the book again, and her sore right wrist made it bobble. "Fuck," she said, dropping the book with a thump to shake her wrist out.

The fox didn't move, it just put a paw atop the book to leverage its tiny black twitching nose even closer, and then Janvier shouted, "Smoke, dinner!" from somewhere up above. The creature squinted at her meaningfully, one last time, before bolting up the stairs.

She picked the book up again and put it back as he called for her, much the same. "Red, come eat!"

She was starving and dehydrated and everything smelled amazing but she shouted back, "I would rather die!"

Whatever objects he was clattering together above her stopped. "That can be arranged," she heard him mutter to himself, then say more loudly, "If you don't come up and eat, I'll spit in your food and throw it away."

She didn't honor that with a response.

Time passed, and she heard what sounded like him cleaning up after a meal, and then the sound of him going...outside.

She ran upstairs, hoping to catch the door before it locked, but by the time she got there, the door was shut. She investigated the handle but there was no space for a key. She tried to eye the mechanism where the latch met the door, then went into the kitchen, opening drawers until she found a strong paring knife and brought it back to leverage the blade between the door and the doorjamb, trying to find some combination of strength and movement that would wriggle the latch free.

Failing that, she realized she could just sit here and saw at it all night. She gave a bitter laugh and let herself collapse onto the ground.

Then, unexpectedly, the door swung back open, giving her a brief glimpse of a garage with the Jaguar beyond as she looked up and found *him* standing there. He'd changed clothing; he was wearing dark blue dress slacks and a crisp lighter blue dress shirt, like he was ready to go out to the Lynx.

What time was it?

"Just as I thought," he told her, closing the door behind himself. "Get up." Her hands clenched into fists, one of them around the knife she still held. "Or are you going to stab me again?" he asked, his narrowing with challenge.

"This one's metal," she threatened.

"The result would be the same," he said, stepping around her, fearlessly showing her his back. "You're welcome to work through all my cutlery." He walked toward a broad wooden table that was past the kitchen and sat down. There was a place setting across from him, along with a glass and a pitcher of water, and he gestured for it. "You recently asked me to treat you like a person. Don't make me regret it."

Sammy walked over. A perfectly cooked piece of steak sat beside a pile of greens and shaved radicchio, glistening with vinaigrette. She never cooked for herself anymore now that she was living alone, so it'd been a long time since she'd seen a salad that wasn't on someone else's plate.

She sat down, putting the knife in her lap. It was hers now, and she wasn't giving it back.

"Are you just going to watch me eat?" she asked him, pouring herself out a glass of water.

"I'm not sure yet." He tented his fingers in front of him, just below his chin. "I don't know if I can trust you to eat when I'm not around."

A surprisingly truthful answer. She took a sip of the water and fought not to gulp, but it tasted so good, and it'd only been what, twelve hours?

Or sixteen?

"How long have I been down here?"

"That information wouldn't be useful for you to have." His amber eyes watched her closely, and even though he wasn't lewd, she felt herself flush.

"Why not?"

"Because you seem prone to anxiety and paranoia."

She moved the knife in her lap to be on the table, slamming it down and jolting her wrist. "You kidnapped me!"

"For your own good," he said calmly. "Which is something you'll realize, eventually. In the fullness of time—and without a calendar."

She shoved the plate of food away from herself; she didn't care how good it smelled, how much the meat had the scent of being pan-seared in butter, or how fresh and crisp the greens looked.

"See?" he said, tilting his head.

She snaked her hand out to slap the plate across the table, but his hand was faster yet, catching her wrist to stop her. She yelped in surprise and in pain.

"If you won't eat it, my fox will," he growled, as her eyes watered. His grip lessened once he noticed. "Are you all right?"

He released her and she yanked back her hand. Her right wrist was puffy, but everything still moved, so she knew it was just a sprain.

"Answer me," he demanded.

She got up from the table. "It's a good thing you didn't promise not to hurt me," she said, then stopped, looking back before taking the first stair. "You know what, Mr. Janvier? You're right. You are the worst thing that's ever happened to me. The absolute *worst.*"

CHAPTER 8

Rax took his frustrations out on the things that he cleaned, the pots and pans he'd used making a meal *for her.* Yes, he had to eat too, but he had actually tried to make something nice after scaring her earlier, only to find he'd hurt her.

When?

Probably when he'd dropped her to the ground—*which is what she'd clearly wanted! And at the time, she'd been trying to bite him!*—and she'd caught herself wrong.

And then she hadn't told him she was hurt for half a day. He frowned at the pan he scrubbed, in danger of taking off a layer of its metal with his ferocity.

Why should she tell him though? It was clear she didn't trust him, nor would, for quite some time.

Possibly never.

But—his fists clenched around the edge of the pan that he held and bent it in his frustration—*she'd stabbed him!* So surely they were even if someone was keeping score.

Despite the fact that he was an almost thousand-year-old dragon-shifter that ought to know better, or at least remember that humans were inherently foolish—and fragile.

He dried off his dishes and put them away, and then went to hover at the top of the stair. If he asked if she was all right, she would likely lie to him, and if he made her show him that she was all right, he might wind up hurting her worse, so there was no point.

He ground his teeth together and left for work.

HE'D CALLED for Namir once he was settled in his office and presented the remains of the glass bladed knife to him; he'd saved the largest shards, just in case.

"Can they recover it? Or must I commission a new one?"

Namir reached over and picked up one of the glass fragments. "New one, for sure. Although this time, if they know you want one this badly, they're sure to charge twice as much."

"Try for less, claim shoddy workmanship on their part if you must. But be willing to pay up to three times more. Time is of more concern than money, currently."

"Understood." Namir nodded curtly and moved to stand. "I made an appointment for you tomorrow night. Someone claims to have an object that might interest you."

"Yes?" He folded the knife holder closed over the broken glass and placed it back on his desk. He'd left the other two knives at home, locked in his altar, until he'd have a chance to use them.

"It's related to the list you gave me."

He tensed. After he discovered that the key was roaming free, he'd wondered what other burial items from Seris's grave might be as well and had made a list for Namir. "Which ones?"

"I don't want to get your hopes up, and they haven't sent a picture, so there's a chance that they're merely lying to gain audience—"

"Skip to the end, Namir," Rax growled.

"It's a crystal ball. But they claim you can see the ocean in it. Which sounded a lot like—"

"A bubble of air, for times in the sea." It was a rough translation for the words, which sounded more melodious in his home tongue, a language he'd been avoiding speaking in public for centuries.

"Exactly so," Namir said and shrugged. "In any case, you'll know if it's real when you see it."

"Indeed." Rax tilted his head toward the large mirror he had on one wall. "Continue your search. And move Heaven and Earth to get a new glass knife for me."

"Your first appointment is in two hours," Namir reminded him, then left.

RAX WAITED until the door was closed, then waved his hand at the mirror on his wall. Perhaps the only thing that humans had gotten right, in their many depictions of the intersection of their world and magic, was their guess that mirrors were magical.

Even so, though his ability to use his magic to see his homeland was not always guaranteed. Mirrors talked from reflection to reflection, and anything shiny he remembered from his youth had been broken or scavenged long ago. All he could do now if he wanted to see the parapets he remembered, slowly grinding down to dust, was pray that the ocean in his Realm was calm.

Tonight it was, and a familiar image resolved slowly.

One of the moons of his old world lit up the sky overhead, providing enough light for him to see by, and the tide was in the pause between in and out, leaving the ocean still. The images it sent him were still marred by tiny ripples, but his ancient home still stood on a clifftop, looking out across the shore. Once, it had been gilded and would've shone as bright as the sun at noon in all directions. But now, it was a decrepit version of itself. It looked haunted to him, which was as it should be, given how the ghosts of his past from those days followed him relentlessly.

It'd been a long time since he'd gone home, but now he felt he had no choice. He took off all of his clothing, folded it neatly, and dove into the mirror's reflection, resurfacing in the ocean of his home. He took one last look at the castle above the waves and dove down, following the calling of his dragon's soul to find the Gate Below.

He swam through the slightly sweeter waters of his own Realm, following the floor of the ocean as it dove deep into darkness. Over the centuries, he had learned not to give his slumbering dragon much thought. When he was first released from imprisonment, it was all he could think of—the agonizing process the magicians had used to dissolve the connection between them had felt not like losing an arm but something more. One's skeleton. Or all one's skin. And the loss of his dragon had left him feeling weakened, naked, and exposed. In the beginning, his mind kept circling back to it, this part of him that *should* be there, and he was unable to let it go. If he had had the luxury of going mad, if him going mad wouldn't have condemned an entire countryside to the monsters trapped behind the Gate Below, he would have.

But he'd learned to do without. Somehow. Stumbling through life. Keeping himself safe and eventually sane.

And he could've gone on that way, indefinitely, except that his dragon—a chunk of him, excised from his very soul—could not. The magicians had been very clear. They'd been able to 'free' him from his dragon, and they would be able to live apart from one another, but only for a time.

Rax followed the bottom of a canyon, illuminating his path with several orbs he created with his magic, sinking until he saw the Gate Below's shadow.

The Gate was a carved door hewn into the side of a massive stone obelisk that stood alone on the seafloor. It was eighty feet tall, and halfway up the broken lock still looped through its latch. His dragon still circled the stone at its base, biting onto its own tail, sleeping, looking for all the world like a statue. His wings were sleek against his body, and his coal-like eyes remained closed.

Originally, his dragon looked like it'd been carved from obsidian without shine. His scales were so black they absorbed all light as if they were showing a void instead of where a dragon ought to be. But over time, the oceans above the Gate had acted like an hourglass, drifting millimeters of sediment down over his dragon's sleeping form, dimming his flat black scales with centuries of muck and decay.

The magicians had told him that once the beast was buried in drifting sediment it would die and the Gate would finally burst its lock and reopen, unless he rejoined it, becoming one with his dragon once again, spending the rest of his life here as the Gate's guardian.

Aware, yet trapped. Alive, but forgotten.

He stopped a hundred feet away, his soul could stand to come no closer, but even from his vantage point, he could tell that the beast was nearly covered. He could hear the thump of his dragon's heart echoing through the water like a slowing drum.

His choices were to join his dragon here and lose himself—or abandon his dragon, let the Gate open, and the monsters spill out and never be whole—or somehow make the lock work again, freeing his dragon and himself, if he could but wrest the key from Samantha's neck.

He closed his eyes and saw the gemstone in his mind, resting just above and between Samantha's two perfect breasts, almost like an arrow pointing downward, inviting him for more. The waters around him heated as he did with his thoughts.

She was so...*tempting*.

Too bad it seemed like he might have to kill her to get his portion of the key back. He didn't want to, but if he ever wanted his dragon free again, he might not have a choice.

Obviously, Sammy had lied to Janvier about him being 'the worst.' Crawling out of a car trunk and finding both her parents dead had sealed up that dubious honor and would keep it for all time. But he didn't need to know that—and it was better for her if he thought himself the apex of her horrors, rather than slightly-above-average.

She'd crawled back into her little velvet cave, listening to him move overhead without grace, on purpose, she thought, so she'd know he was angry, and then leave. She waited long enough so that he had to be truly gone and sat up to find the fox there, sitting on the lectern, watching her. The fucking thing was so silent she hadn't heard it, which was frightening, but on the upside, at least this time it wasn't hissing.

"Happy you got my steak, eh?"

She clambered out of the couches and considered her options. She didn't need to obey him, but she did need to eat. You couldn't escape on an empty stomach, or plant clues to your demise.

She quietly walked upstairs. The food he'd made her had to come from somewhere, and water, oh my God, she needed to drink so badly. She practically ran to the sink's faucet and put her head beneath it, turning it on. And then, after she'd drank so much she'd probably given herself a stomachache, she turned around to look through the rest of his kitchen, opening all the doors to his cabinets and pantry.

Everything here was sparse—because he lived alone too, she realized. The food he did have was high quality, Waygu beef, lobster tails, and scallops. It wasn't entirely a bachelor pad, not like the one guy she'd dated whose refrigerator had only been used to hold beer and ketchup, but it wasn't like there were snacks she could nibble on. If she cooked herself a steak he'd know, so she ate individual leaves of spinach, wishing she were Popeye while feeling like a rabbit.

Why couldn't he have just one jar of pickles?

The fox padded in and gave her a look.

"Did you have to eat the whole steak?" she asked it, snorting softly. It jumped up to the kitchen counter to be eye level with her. "Hey, are you allowed to do that?"

The fox spun its head almost upside down, like it was trying to make sense of her.

"Sure, okay. Whatever." She methodically went through all of the drawers and considered things as she did so. His oven had a range hood, the air from there had to go somewhere, right? So this facility did have some connection to the outdoors.

And plumbing.

Maybe she could put a note in a bottle and flush it. She rolled her eyes at the thought. Or, just toss it the fuck into his aquarium and hope it got taken out to sea. She turned to look back at the aquarium, something she'd been avoiding doing, ever since she realized there were sharks in it, and saw something unexpected, looking back.

A massive octopus, hovering, undulating its body to stay on a level with her.

She walked over to the tank, entranced. It swung and tilted its flexible body to look at her with its other eye.

"Don't run away," she whispered at it, while the fox caught up with her to pad beside her feet.

One of the foster homes she'd been at had taken all the kids to a local aquarium and she'd spent the whole time there in front of the octopus tank, ignoring all the other creatures. She'd sat in front of it for hours, watching it do its octopus things, slowly lacing itself through rock, wedging itself up into corners, playing its suckers along the glass, feeling the whole time like it was watching her as much as she was watching it.

Even though she'd never seen another one alive since then, she knew she could never eat one, even though Bastian liked to serve them often. They were too smart and too alien at the same time.

The closer she got, the bigger the octopus was, she realized. It was hovering at her eye level with its eyes, which meant that it was longer than she was tall because its mantle floated above her, and the tips of its tentacles drifted down further than she could see, below this level of the floor. It looked a healthy, vibrant red, and then it flashed slightly more orange.

The color of her hair!

She laughed and smiled and tears sprang to her eyes. There was something here that didn't hate her or want to hurt her, at least.

The octopus brought a tentacle-tip up as if to wipe away her tears, and she met it with a fingertip on her side of the glass, then used her whole palm. The octopus laced its tentacle against her palm-print on the other side, occupying an equal amount of space, like it was trying to hold her hand.

"What's your name?" she asked it, wishing that it could answer her.

CASSIE ALEXANDER & KARA LOCKHARTE

The fox sat at her feet, needle-teeth forgotten, looking disgusted at both of them in turns. "If he's Smoke, then surely you have a name, too."

The cold of the glass felt good on her sore wrist, and she moved to lean in with her entire forearm, peeking under her palm to see where the octopus had lined it with suckers on its side. "Inky?" she guessed, and the creature's skin went dark like it knew what she was saying. "No. Comet?"

Because it looked like an old-timey illustration of one, with its round head and streaming tentacles. As if pleased by her decision, it released the tank wall and zoomed around, staying on this level, propelling itself by using the skin between its tentacles like oars.

"Comet!" she shouted, as it showed off with delight, and then one of the sharks came over to investigate the commotion. "Comet, watch out!"

Comet spun in the water column, creating a pattern with its tentacles as it flashed its underbelly at the shark, and suddenly the shark had other places to be. It dove deeper to avoid the octopus, and the octopus slowly spun back around to regard Sammy again. She got a glimpse of the colors beneath its suckers and for a second they hurt her eyes like someone had just blinded her with a camera flash before they disappeared, leaving her with an afterimage of something she couldn't understand.

So strange, but what else was new here?

"Come on," she announced her intentions to the two creatures and then took the stairs up.

IF MR. JANVIER did not want her to touch all his things, he should have invested in actual doors.

Or an actual cage for her.

But that wasn't worth thinking on, not when Sammy still had a mission—Action Plan Spread Forensics.

One whole wall of Janvier's room was occupied by the top of his shark tank; it came up to mid-shoulder on her right after ascending the stairs. After that, the rest of it was divided into thirds, one part open plan closet, one part large bed with a door to his bathroom, and one part open space with a little low green table.

She walked to the low green table first. It looked like it might have a lid but when she tried to open it up she found it locked. She gave it a couple firm palm prints and then walked back to where his clothes were.

Mr. Janvier didn't have a literal closet, so much as a portion of his floor was a dressing room. All of his suits were hung along one curved wall, and below that were stacks of sweaters, t-shirts, and cedar-lined racks with shoes, above a final set of drawers.

Sammy ran her fingers through her hair, tugging out any loose strands, and she carefully threaded these in innocuous places on all of his clothing. She laced some underneath the collars of his suit jackets and dress shirts. Up close everything smelled like him, and she took a moment to inhale. It wasn't fair that someone so cruel smelled so good. She tucked a few strands of hair underneath the arms of his sweaters and then expertly folded them back how she'd found them —*how was he so precise with his own folding? Had he also once worked in a Gap?* She ran out of loose hairs and started pulling out a small fringe from the nape of her neck, one long orange-red strand at a time.

Comet watched her from his vantage point in the tank while Smoke followed her around, staring up with beady eyes. This was the part where, if she were in a fairy tale, some creature would arrive— other than an octopus or fox—to tell her that if she spun her hair just right, it would turn into the gold that would free her.

But instead, she only had real life...her stomach hurt, from too much water or not enough food, she couldn't tell which, and she was tired again. Plus, she was bone cold, without shoes or socks or anything but thin cotton on. Between the cement floor and the chill aquarium, there was nothing here that provided heat. How the hell did he live here?

The answer was, he was coldblooded. *Obviously.*

She forced herself to finish her circuit of the room, covering everything she could with fingerprints or hairs and hopefully follicle DNA. She then searched the whole strange house looking for anything resembling a thermostat. When she didn't find one, she considered her options—she could sit in front of the open oven. Or she could take a hot bath—there was a bizarre tub in his bathroom; she'd seen it when she'd used the restroom.

She went downstairs, retrieved the bestiary book she'd been looking at earlier, and returned to his level of the house.

THE ONLY PLUS side to Mr. Janvier's place—not including the pet octopus, which she was just going to assume liked her and was firmly in the good column for now—was that he had an infinite supply of scalding hot water.

His bathroom occupied the same footprint as his kitchen below. It was wide and curved, with a long sink so deep she could've probably taken a bath just in it alone. But the space where the kitchen held all of its appliances the next level down was occupied here by a massive tub.

The rest of Mr. Janvier's possessions had an old-world feel, mixed with modern restraint. Velvet couches, yes, but not too many of them. Ornately framed oil paintings of the ocean, big and heavy feeling, but they were graciously spread out.

All of that went out the window with the tub, though.

Sammy took one look at it and thought, *high-class brothel* or *too much goddamned money.*

Because who else but rich people—or people who wanted to pay to feel rich for the night—would want this monstrosity? It was a ten-by-ten clawfoot tub shaped like a seashell where the claw feet' were strongly carved animal legs from animals that she did not recognize. And not only did the outside of the tub look like a seashell, the inside did too. It was made of that shiny stuff on the inside of some shells, the kind you felt lucky to find at the beach as a kid because their opalescence felt precious in a way that nothing else you had did. The shine was shot through with veins of gold, like gilded lightning bolts shooting through opal clouds, and there were marble stairs on one side because how else were you supposed to get inside the contraption?

She set the book down and mounted the stairs, kicking off her clothing at the top, and then stepped in, feeling cold shell against the bottom of her feet. There was a bevel across from her with assorted soaps and products, and a chain hung down from the ceiling. She took a chance, pulled it, and hot rain poured down.

After that, she didn't care how ridiculous any of it was, as long as she was warm. She stood there, letting the water heat her and give her back her strength, and then she figured out how to twist the drain at the bottom of the tub to keep it so that she could fill it up.

She went through his glass bottles of scented soaps with abandon, cleaning herself off, washing her hair, rinsing away her panic, feeling human for the first time since she'd woken up here, and then when she was done, the tub was almost full.

She lay against its side, reached over its edge to blot her fingers off on a nearby towel, and picked up the bestiary she'd left on the second stair.

The silvery ink script was looping and beautiful, and every word in the book was still mysterious. She went through pages and pages— all of the pictures must've been in the back— and was getting ready to skip there when she realized her shoulders were catching a chill. She ducked down into the tub and then...the words on the page made sense.

Sammy hesitated, sure that half a second ago she was looking at pretty gibberish, only now it was sentences she could read:

...the casual observer will note that the scales on the lips seem perfunctory. However, these too serve a purpose...

She gasped, pushing herself up in the tub, and her ability to read the words went away. But in sinking back down....

The teeth should, in general, be avoided, because while not always poiso-

nous, it is difficult to tell the different specimens apart, and woe to the researcher who makes the wrong assumption.

Sammy looked around the room, in case there was any way that someone else was doing this—*to? for?*—her. But she was alone. She'd closed the bathroom door and even the fox was outside, something he was unhappy about, she could hear him scrabbling his paws beneath the door's bottom edge.

Then she looked down. She knew she hadn't changed. But the necklace that Mr. Janvier was interested in, the one she couldn't take off, was now underwater.

And as long as it was, she glanced back at the book—

These creatures are, essentially, untamable, despite numerous efforts having been performed to either crossbreed them with more malleable species or magically bind them.

Sammy laughed and would've splashed with joy, only she didn't want to get water on the pages.

If Mr. Janvier wouldn't tell her things she wanted to know, she was going to read his whole damn library, courtesy of her new magic necklace.

AN HOUR later her brain felt full, even if her stomach did not, and her wrist didn't hurt anymore. She felt like she'd gained a significant advantage. There were books about everything here; she'd have to start cataloging them tomorrow. Glance at the pictures first, see what they were for, and then sit down and learn everything she could behind his back. Either how to free herself from this stupid necklace, or something to use against him, to escape.

She got out of the water and dried herself off as completely as she could with the towel, then looked disconsolately at her clothes. She sighed and turned her underwear inside out before pulling them back on and then tugging her tie-front boxers on above them. Her shirt was okay for now, but how long until it smelled?

Whatever cleanliness she felt she'd gained from her shower and tub evaporated, and the depression that she was doing her best to stave off came back to lap at her heels, as cold as her wet hair against her neck.

She looked at his artistic sink...which didn't have a cabinet beneath it. And there wasn't really any in the room besides. He didn't have an electric shaver. He had a straight edge and one of those brushes in a bowl for his shaving cream, and a painful realization sank in.

Mr. Janvier didn't have a hairdryer.

Of course not, why should he? He had three inches of hair on his head, at most. He just had to slick product through it and go out the door, his hair was probably dry by the time he got to his car.

Whereas hers...Sammy looked at herself in the broad mirror above his sink. Water weight made her curls stretch halfway down her back and her hair was a dense thicket of a thing, the kind that'd made more than one foster parent give up on ever trying to comb it.

It would take hours of her freezing for it to dry, unless she stayed naked in his hot tub until he came home.

She put the heels of her hands over her eyes and contemplated just putting her head in the oven this time, rather than merely opening it.

What was she going to do? Hide in his bathroom forever? No.

He had warm things in his bedroom outside. She'd touched them....

She swept the door open and almost into the fox, who skittered back and then rounded it to stare at her. Comet was still waiting in the tank beyond and she waved at him before she looked around. *If she put on five of his sweaters,* she thought, but before she turned to that side of his bedroom, she looked at his bed, on her right. The frame was crafted out of the same dark wood as the rest of the furniture in the house, and it was unmade, the only thing really out of place in the whole building; the only thing that showed that someone lived here at all.

And it looked inestimably comfortable. The blankets were heavy; they rippled on top of the sheets like tiny mountains.

Tiny warm mountains.

Her feet, already freezing, started leading her toward it, picking up speed with her intent. She wouldn't have to be in it for very long—if she just curled up in it long enough for her hair to dry and no longer, maybe he wouldn't even know she'd been there.

It was a bad idea, it was reckless—and it was already too late. She dove in under the sheets just as her teeth started chattering.

CHAPTER 9

AFTER EXITING THROUGH HIS MIRROR, RAX DRIED OFF INSIDE HIS OFFICE and pulled his clothing back on, and no one else was the wiser.

It was a hot night outside and even hotter indoors. The casino was full to the brim of shifters enjoying their newfound freedoms.

Rax went through the motions, working in his office when appointments required him and walking the casino floor with a Boulevardier in hand otherwise, making the small talk he loathed and yet his patrons expected, all the while wondering what Samantha was doing back at his home, without him.

He was sure by now that she'd gone through all of his things. He would've done the same in her position, he supposed. Anything valuable or dangerous was locked up, excepting the sharks, and he very much doubted she'd opt to take a swim. He took a sip of his bitter drink, surveying his small yet very lucrative empire, and saw Namir, diagonal from him, make a subtle gesture before glancing at the roulette table.

Someone was cheating.

Rax was instantly intrigued. Not many people could manage a casino that actively encouraged magic users to participate. It was a testament to his skill that he could, and that they did, and that by and large, he didn't think he'd ever been scammed out of anything. He couldn't honestly say he was a hundred percent sure, but if he ever had, it'd been too low dollar to notice, although he did imagine there were a few out there who'd managed to take away a chip or two as trophy.

There was a crowd gathered at the roulette wheel, men and women leaning over as their dealer egged them on. His dealers were attractive, he encouraged them to be personable, and many of them had their own small cults of personality for working here.

Tonight's roulette dealer was Lily, usually a sassy slip of a girl, whose overly wide-set eyes gave away her swan-like nature. He knew Namir made her nervous, as her bird-side recognized Namir's beast, but tonight her eyes were telegraphing fear out to the both of them, looking quickly from Rax to the tiger-shifter quickly for saving, while the rest of her let nothing on.

Rax stepped up to the front of the table, while Namir circled the back.

She spun the wheel again, taunting the players a little breathlessly, as a thick man leaned over and placed his bet, a small fortune of chips on a black eight.

The ball danced as it spun, bouncing against the rail, until it finally coasted to a stop, hovering momentously between the red seven and the black eight before falling into the eight's divot with a plinking sound, like a water drop.

People surrounding the table clapped for the winner, sounding like a scattering of rain but the winner himself seemed resigned. His clothes were black, and they looked old, timewise. Rax couldn't place them from the back, but the outline of the man's face seemed vaguely familiar, as did the man's strange hat. Rax heard the water drop sound, again and again, like ice was melting from a great height.

His old Realm froze nearly solid every winter, and that was when the beasts beneath the sea roamed; from the castle's tallest parapet, you could see them searching underneath ten-foot deep ice as clear as glass. They were hungry, distant dangers, with jaws that could snap a boat's hull in two—but none of them compared to anything held back by the Gate. Trade ships threaded the needle between commerce, monsters, and ice, and not all of them always made it, no matter how good their magicians were….

He grabbed the nearest woman and moved her out of the way, using his arm to sweep the others on his side of the table back while giving Namir permission to do the same on the other side. Namir did so, pulling Lily away last, and the swan didn't fight the tiger once.

"Little Rax?" asked a voice Rax hadn't heard in almost a thousand years, voice soft and echoing, like he was being called from deep inside a cave. The sound of plinking water continued, and where the man's hand met the table a wet stain began spreading out.

"Rolm?" Rax asked as the man turned slowly to look at him. "Uncle?"

His uncle had died when he was eleven, off on a ship that didn't make it back in time, crushed to pieces by the ice and hollowed out by monsters from below. They'd given him a stately funeral, and as a child Rax had had nightmares for a hundred nights, imagining every way possible that Rolm could have died.

Rax raised his left hand, and Namir shouted, "Security procedures!" Dealers shut down their tables, and half of Rax's line of guards came up, while the other half funneled patrons toward the exits. Rax ignored the surprised screams and shouts of complaint while his well-trained people followed their containment plan.

"Why are you here?" Rax snarled, speaking in the creature's ancient tongue. He walked around to face the apparition that looked exactly like his uncle, but Rax knew it wasn't his uncle trapped inside. It was another drowned one, sent by the Gate Below. "I have given you most of myself for centuries. I have done everything my family promised."

"It is not enough anymore." The voice that spoke now wasn't Rolm's at all, and the eyes in his uncle's face turned to black. "The gate needs the lock; the lock needs the key."

"There is no key anymore," Rax said. "You know that. There's only the broken lock and my dragon."

The blackness inside his uncle's eyes started to pour out,

streaming down the drowned one's face like tears. "The gate needs the lock, the lock needs the key," it repeated.

"There is no key!" Rax shouted, bashing his hand down on the table, feeling the heavy wood crack beneath his fist. "The key is broken!"

The sickly blackness running out of the drowned one's eyes increased in volume as the rest of Rolm slowly became puffy and waterlogged, probably looking like Rolm had, before all the creatures of the Below had eaten him, bite by bite.

"The gate needs the lock!" the drowned one repeated, its voice a foul gurgle, and it didn't close its mouth. Murky water poured out of its mouth, and Rax could hear his guards behind him start to retch. "The lock needs the key!"

Rax flung an arm up. "No weapons," he shouted out for his remaining men. "And cover your eyes!"

The gurgling increased in intensity and the filthy water in volume until the shell of Rolm couldn't contain it anymore and it burst like a bubble, spattering everything in the casino with its sticky taint of death, leaving only Rolm's head intact, rolling into the dent Rax's fist had left on the table to stare up at him.

"When's the last time you heard the siren's song, little Rax?" his uncle's voice softly asked him before all the muscles on the face went slack.

Rax put out a hand to touch Rolm's face and felt the impossible chill coming off of it. He was covered in rank foulness, the sludge of death, peeled from the bottom of the sea, as was a good swath of his casino.

"What the fuck was that?" Namir asked, rushing up to his side.

"My Uncle."

Namir looked aghast. "I didn't know you had one."

"I don't. He's been dead for centuries." Rax took a step back to view the destruction; at least all of the patrons had gotten out in time. "Finish closing the books and spend the rest of the night cleaning." He wiped a hand across his forehead, knocking a sheen of slime away. "I need to go."

"Understood," Namir said, but as Rax turned toward his office to get his keys, the tiger-shifter called after him. "What was he saying?"

Rax knew no one else could understand his Uncle besides him. He'd spoken the language of the Realms, and not only that but an ancient tongue. "It's none of your business. Carry on."

RAX DROVE HOME QUICKLY, confident in his magic's ability to rescue his poor car's leather interior later, but the longer he had this stench of death on him the closer his own demise felt. Had the Gate known he'd swum down earlier in the night to see his dragon? Had he triggered its attention somehow, same as Samantha's key had?

He didn't know enough about the magic that went into the Gate, no one had, even in his own day. It was too strange and raw and distant. The Gate Below represented a pact one of his ancestors made, pulling all the sirens out of existence and shoving them into the Below with brute force, and no one had dared open it after that until his brother's all-too-human woman had died.

Tarian hadn't been able to accept her death and Rax had never understood why. After all, hadn't his brother known that falling in love with a human meant courting pain? Magic could make them live longer, but how long would ever be enough?

And how could you best keep them alive in the meantime?

They were attractive, yes. Beautiful, spirited, and warm as well, perhaps—but also frail. Damageable. In a way that natural magic users and shifters were not.

Humans could break. *And everyone knew it.*

When Seris had died, his brother had latched onto a philosophical line of thought in an ancient text, based off even older myths, postulating that the reason sirens knew how to drive you mad with lies was because they also knew the truth. That—combined with a perverse belief that the Seris that lay in state in their castle's antechamber was somehow not the actual girl herself—was enough to send Tarian to the bottom of the sea for answers.

Tarian was so certain his plan would work that he unlocked the

121

Gate to talk to the sirens inside. He was willing to withstand their insanity if only he could use their lies to somehow conversely triangulate the truth of where Seris was 'alive'. Rax had had to follow Tarian down there, wrestle the key from him, and then shut him inside the Gate because there'd been no other way to win. Rax wasn't strong enough to force his older brother to come back out with him, not even as a dragon. He bore the scars from their fight across his back, and he carried the terrible knowledge of what he'd done to his brother with him every day.

And when he'd locked the Gate...the key had broken. Most of it had flaked into dust, so only three pieces remained: one he owned, one hung from Samantha's neck, and the largest piece was still inside the lock itself, barely holding the lock shut.

How could the Gate ask for more from him? He had already given it his brother and his dragon.

What else of him was left?

Rax parked, walked into his villa, and found Smoke waiting for him just inside the door.

"What is that smell?" the fox demanded, dancing back.

"A drowned one," Rax said quietly. Hopefully the girl was asleep downstairs. He waved his arm so the animal would step aside. "I need to bathe."

"So did the girl, apparently," Smoke sniffed. Rax paused at that. She would have to wash, yes, although her using his tub to do so felt oddly intimate. But given that there wasn't a second one in his home....

"That was after she touched all of your things. I watched her. I didn't bite her. I wanted to. But you promised I could later, so—"

"I did not," Rax corrected him softly.

"As good as promised," the fox muttered, trotting alongside Rax as he went for the stairs to go up a level. "And then?" Smoke yipped with excitement, mounting the last three stairs. "This!" He pointed at Rax's bed with both his nose and tail-tip.

Rax saw his sheets were piled like he'd left them, only after a moment he realized something nestled inside his sheets was breathing.

"So can I bite her now?" Smoke asked, his copper eyes shining with hope.

"No," Rax said, walking over to his bed with a frown. If he thought her using his tub was intimate, then what was this? She was curled up in a tiny ball, her knees tucked up beneath her chin, her hair streaked along his pillow. She was sleeping peacefully, blissfully unaware of his presence. "What are you doing?" he asked at normal volume, of himself as much as her.

Her eyelids fluttered open and he saw her work through her surprise at her surroundings and then recognize him with a gasp. "You weren't supposed to…." she said in a rush before catching herself. "I just meant to nap. I didn't know what time it was. Oh my God, what is that smell?" She recoiled further into his sheets, putting a hand over her nose.

"It doesn't matter—why the hell are you in my bed?" He kept his voice just below a growl.

"Don't get any ideas!" she said, pushing herself to the bed's far side, taking all the sheets with her.

"You are human. I would never," he scoffed, then grabbed his sheets and yanked them back from her like a matador flipping a cape. "Explain yourself."

"You…you don't have a hairdryer."

What the fuck did that even mean?

She wrapped her arms around herself. To hide from him? No. To trap her heat in. He could see gooseflesh prickle all along her exposed skin. "Do you have any idea how cold your house is?" she went on, reaching out to grab the edge of his sheets and pull them back. He fought her once and then let her win. She quickly yanked the sheets up to her armpits. "I don't have blankets down there. Or pillows. Or anything warm to wear. You do."

Rax took a long inhale, realizing her point. *Human fragility, again.*

"Or clean clothes, or a toothbrush," she went on, building up steam as she clutched his sheets to herself. "Or any other indication that you don't mean to murder me tomorrow, basically."

He eyed her. "You do realize if I wanted to murder you, you'd already be feeding my sharks."

"If I don't get to brush my teeth soon, I might just jump in there myself." She crossed her arms beneath the blankets.

"Hmm. It might be easier to extract my necklace from a shark's belly than from around your neck," he said and watched her eyes widen briefly, not sure whether he was teasing or not. "Luckily for you, I value my sharks," he told her and snapped his fingers. "There's a piece of paper and a pen on the dining room table below. Make a list of things you need, and I will procure them for you tomorrow when things are open."

"It's...night...time?" she asked slowly. Her voice was soft and fearful. Not of him, necessarily, but the freefall of her current existence, totally dependent on him to even know the time.

He inhaled deeply and sighed. "It is. Take my sheets and go downstairs, Red. I need to shower and sleep myself."

He didn't wait for her to move, he just walked for his bathroom and shut the door.

By the time he emerged clean she was gone. She'd left him one blanket and taken the vast majority of everything else. He walked around his bed to the altar he had at the room's far side and performed his ritual out of habit, hoping it would calm him.

Hachiro's thoughts rose up in his mind. *"You are distressed. What happened?"*

He quietly recounted seeing his long-dead uncle for the octopus, who had also known the man. *"Poor Rolm, to be used so,"* Hachiro said.

"I know," Rax thought back at him, wondering if the nightmares of his childhood would come back. *"I just don't know how to stop it. I would relock the Gate right now if I could, but I can't. Not presently."*

"Perhaps things will work out in your favor," Hachiro said, his thoughts floating as calmly as he did.

"I hope," he said aloud, because he was more used to doing that than telepathy, in the safety of his own home.

"In any case, I healed the girl's wrist for you."

"Thank you."

Hachiro bobbed inside the tank. *"She seems more resourceful than you give her credit for."*

Rax got into his bed, which now smelled like her to him. He had extra sheets or he could've magically banished her scent away, but...he inhaled deeply. Her cinnamon scent was only fitting, considering the color of her hair or her freckles. Not such a terrible thing to fall asleep to, nor to wake up to, either.

"It doesn't matter," Rax thought with a shrug, bidding his friend goodnight. *"It doesn't change a thing."*

WHEN SAMMY WOKE UP SHE, as usual, wasn't sure what time it was. She blinked and pulled the sheets down— she'd taken him at his word and stolen all his pillows and blankets, so she finally felt warm and rested, having made a nest for herself on her strange couch-bed.

And then she realized she wasn't the only one awake.

Shadows crossed the light coming into her room from the aquarium. She peeked over the couches' edge to find Mr. Janvier swimming in the same tank as Comet and the sharks, swimming from wall to wall in an intricate pattern.

Totally naked.

Because of course he was.

Who needed clothes to swim with sharks? She fought the urge to let out an insane laugh and realized if she hadn't already known he was magical, this would've confirmed it. No mere mortal could be in water that cold with that much junk hanging out. And he was uncut, she noted with a little thrill of surprise, something she hadn't realized at Belissima's, what with him behind her.

She ducked down so he couldn't see her watching him as his body surged through the water, propelled by muscular arms and legs, slicing the water with fluid kicks. There wasn't a piece of him that wasn't made out of muscle, and all of his skin was the same olive-brown, except for lines of lighter colored scars across his back. Like a beast had slashed him, with a paw full of wide-set claws. She put her hand to her mouth in astonishment and winced without thinking.

What could scar a dragon?

She squinted, trying to see more—and that was when she realized he apparently didn't need to breathe. She tried to match him, inhaling a breath and holding onto it, and had to let it go. She'd just been sitting on the couch doing nothing and he was vigorously swimming. How was he managing it? Her level of his house was at least twenty feet deep, her ears hurt just watching him. Why didn't he need air?

His pattern took him slowly upwards until she couldn't see him anymore, and she rolled back onto the couches, looking up.

Not long after that, she heard splashing and then doors opening and closing as he presumably moved around, and then she felt like he was gone.

She went upstairs, tempted to go sit in his tub with a book, but then she realized he'd taken the list of things she'd left him on the table. It must be daylight then, for him to go out shopping, without her.

Sammy had put all sorts of things on the list, from toothbrushes to tampons—mostly just to see if he'd buy them for her—and wondered just how long it'd take him. While tempting, a bath probably wasn't safe.

He'd left his pen behind, though. She took it back downstairs and went to where the bookcases didn't quite line up with the aquarium's edge and drew two lines. Because it'd probably been two full days now that she'd been down here.

Maybe by now Andi had realized she was missing. But even if she had, she'd still have to come back all the way from Italy to look for her. So she needed to keep acting like she was on her own.

Sammy started pulling out books, looking for ones that had extra pages at the end of them, rearranging the bookcase so that no one would know she'd created a row of them—once she started learning things, she'd need a safe place to write them down.

And then she ran her fingers along the seam of the couches, looking for a loose spot in the upholstery. She found one wide enough that she could push her finger into it and shove stuffing around. She opened up a book, tore a blank page free, and began writing on it.

. . .

My name is Samantha O'Connor, and I am being held against my will.

I think it's been two days. I think my captor is a dragon. And if you're reading this, Andi—I'm probably dead.

SHE'D ALREADY FELT disposable enough before all of this. Would any of her friends notice if she didn't like their pictures on Instagram? Maybe in a week or two they might get suspicious if she didn't return their texts to go out on the weekend. But who would take it upon themselves to drop by? The guys at her old car shop were never her friends outside of work—they were all old and married and she'd never really made any friends at Belissima's or the Lynx.

She felt like she could disappear.

Part of that was her fault for not reaching out. It wasn't like she wasn't friendly, she just had learned that most times it was better not to try. Everything had been a mess after she'd lost her parents. Her foster parents either treated her like a pariah or with kid gloves—ostracizing her either way. When the other kids found out what had happened to her, she'd gotten locked in a trunk by bigger kids, more than once. And then everyone kept making her go to therapy, but none of her therapists ever really wanted to listen because when she told them her version of things, they kept telling her she was wrong.

But the worst part was that any time she'd meet good people, or made good friends, or even that one time she had a therapist that didn't think she was a liar—who believed her when she said it wasn't a man in a trenchcoat who'd come after her folks, it was something worse, something more, even if she could never wrap her mind around describing it—everything would get ripped away from her, and she'd be forced to move again. Once it was because her foster mom's mom got sick with cancer and they needed her room back. Another time it was because her foster mom became unexpectedly pregnant.

As an adult now, she knew that they were all trying hard and none of them meant to let her down, but after shit like that happens to you two or three times as a kid, you just stop trying. Stop hoping. Because you realize none of it counts.

So she knew she'd been blowing in the wind for years. It wasn't until she'd bonded with Andi over how much Danny sucked that she'd settled down. And then living with Andi had been so easy, and with Eumie living right below; she'd gotten spoiled. She'd kept up enough friends to have reasons to go out on the weekends when Andi was working and had met a rotating cast of friends-with-benefits guys, but she hadn't tried to make any real connections.

She wrote everything that'd happened to her since she'd met Janvier out in a sputtering attempt to feel like she had some presence —that she'd *mattered.* She understood now why prisoners counted days inside their cells. To mark that time had gone by, but also to just prove that they'd been there. She kept going until she heard the door open again upstairs and then she folded the note up tight and shoved it into the couch's stuffing.

The door above opened and closed two more times, and as she put the book away and hid the pen, Janvier bellowed: "Red! Come here!"

She kept the warmest blanket with her, coming upstairs with it wrapped around her like she was a queen. He saw her and his lips lifted, but he stopped himself from laughing.

"I got your things," he told her, gesturing at a pile of shopping bags on his side of the kitchen table before pointing at the empty chair on hers.

"Everything?" she asked him, her eyebrows arching.

He brought the list out of a pocket to consult it. "Crest toothpaste, check. Pickles, dill, and butter, check. Playtex regular unscented tampons, also check. Freedom though, however," he tsked, looking at the last thing she'd written on her list, shaking his head. "The grocery store was fresh out."

"Maybe next trip," she said, sitting down where he'd pointed.

"Don't get your hopes up," he told her before setting the list down and making a round in his kitchen. "I left you food." He opened up a slow cooker and the scent of oatmeal wafted out. He scooped some out into a bowl, sprinkled cinnamon and brown sugar on top, and brought it back with a spoon for her. "Before we play this game, you have to eat something," he said, sitting across from her again.

The oatmeal smelled *so good*. She stared at the bowl for a moment, ignoring whatever else he was saying as he went on.

"Red?" He asked while snapping his fingers for her attention.

She jolted up. "What?"

"Just eat already. We both know you want to."

"I'm good," she said and lightly shrugged. He closed his eyes and took a deep inhale. "I've been told I'm stubborn," she went on. "Just thought you should know."

"I had noticed," he said dryly. He gave her another patient sigh. "I want you to eat before your stomach shuts down and food makes you sick."

"Starved a lot of people before, have you, Mister Worst?" she asked, pushing the bowl away.

He let out a harsh laugh. "I spent years of my life imprisoned, chained head to toe against a stone wall, and my only sustenance was slop pressed to a sponge, which was then pressed to my lips, via a very long stick every other day." He was staring over her shoulder, lost in his past until he refocused on her. His spine straightened, and his lips curved cruelly. "So trust me when I say that you are neither starving now, Red, and also when I say that I promise I will not let you later. Even if that means me, eventually, holding you down and forcing broth into you through a straw."

Sammy gasped as he leaned across the table to stare at her. "Eat, Red. Now," he commanded before she could ask any questions. He picked up her bowl and slammed it back in front of her. "Do not force my hand. It is one thing for you to feel cold here, it would be something entirely else for me to *be* cold to *you.*"

She swallowed. Honesty shone in his amber eyes—his story was true, as was his threat. She pushed a spoon into the oatmeal then brought it up to her mouth.

As good as it'd smelled earlier, it tasted like chalk on her tongue now.

CHAPTER 10

Why had he told her that story?

He didn't owe her any words. He should've just skipped to the straw part of things. Just tie her down in a corner somewhere already, like it was clear she feared. Live up to her 'worst' expectations, like he'd already promised.

Rax ran a hand through his hair, watching her eat bite after bite of oatmeal without smiling—without any signs of life. He'd put cinnamon in it because it reminded him of her and of waking this morning, wrapped in her scent, with his cock so hard he could barely breathe.

So he'd jumped in his tank, swam to wash her away and cool himself down, and then gone to do as she'd asked last night.

Only to be repaid like this.

She was insolent. All of the time.

Tonight he'd change his sheets, and that would be that. Cinnamon would again be just a spice, and Samantha would again just be a depressed girl —no, worse, a depressed *human*—wearing something that was not hers.

He shifted his neck, stretching it until it popped, waiting for her to finish. She swallowed the last bite and showed the bottom of the empty bowl to him while staring at him blankly. Lifelessly. Like there were no batteries inside of her.

How come she could turn herself on and off like that?

"All right," he said, taking the bowl from her and moving it further down the table, then turning towards the many bags he had. "I'll give you certain essential items for free." He pulled out toothbrushes, toothpaste, tampons, soap, and a hairdryer, putting all of them into a bag and handing them over. "The others, you have to earn, by cooperating."

"With what?" she asked flatly.

"Me." He pulled out the leather bundle with the remaining two knives in it, setting it between them. "You trying to cut the chain on your own isn't actually a bad idea. So I figure we'll start with that." He opened up the tie and revealed the gold and rose petal blades still inside. "Try the gold blade first."

"What'll I get for it?" she asked, as her eyes narrowed.

He bit back a smile at feeling her come to life again. "What do you want for it?"

She surveyed the items in their opaque plastic bags. "Socks."

"An excellent choice." He pulled out a package of generic tube socks, tossed it on her side of the table, and gestured between her and the knives. She picked the gold one up. Hesitantly, in the exact opposite of the manner that she'd swept up the glass one to stab him with the other night, he noticed, and lifted her necklace, to saw at its chain.

He could feel the friction of magic hitting magic and he could see from the way the chain twisted in her hand that she really was trying, it just wasn't doing anything.

"From the inside out?" he suggested, and she changed grips, sawing it outwards like she was trying to cut through a rope. It didn't work.

"Let me try," he suggested.

"What do I get for letting you?" she asked, pushing her chair back, still holding the knife.

It was only fair, he supposed, plus he had bought her a lot of things. "Underwear, as requested."

"Do I get to see them first?" she asked.

"No."

She pouted up at him. "But what if you got the wrong kind?"

Rax inhaled and blinked, irritated and amused in equal measure. "Would it matter?"

"To me." She nodded fiercely.

"Is anyone else going to see them?" he asked while looking around. "Do you have a paramour down there that I don't know about?"

"Comet," she said definitively, her eyes challenging him as her nostrils flared. "The octopus."

Rax laughed and Smoke ran over quickly, jumping up on the table, knocking her spoon out of her bowl to clatter on the floor.

"Are you all right?" the fox asked, whining up at him, before glaring over at Samantha just in case.

"I'm fine," he told it, stroking back the short gray fur on its nose. And then he looked to her, finding her watching him with rapt attention—trying to understand what was going on between them.

And that was when he realized Hachiro was right, she was far more cunning than he was giving her credit for. She'd seen him swimming earlier, he knew, and she wasn't mystified by how come he could hold his breath that long. Or why his blood was green, or how come he could talk to a fox. She might wonder about those things, yes, but she wouldn't waste any time pondering her disbelief, nor let it hold her back. She was more mentally flexible than some magic-users he'd met before, and up until meeting him, he assumed she'd never seen true magic.

Or had she?

He gently scooted Smoke off the table and the fox jumped to the floor. "The octopus's name is Hachiro," he told her, reaching into the bags to find the underwear that she'd asked for. She'd been very precise to write down cotton and underline it and he had done as she asked, knowing that it would worry her if he brought back anything sexy. So he pulled two packages of very boring underwear out and handed them over to her and she took them with an embarrassed look, putting them out of sight, under the table, on the next chair over. "Now, may I?" he asked, holding his hand out for the knife.

She flipped it in her hand and offered the hilt out to him. As he took it his fingers brushed hers. She pulled her hand away like his touch burned.

"I like Comet better," she told him.

"You do, do you?" he asked, walking around to stand behind her. He bit the blade with his teeth to hold it and reached down to lift her hair, pulling it up with both hands, before moving it into one, keeping all of her strands safely out of the way. She gasped and sat up straighter with his motion, and he knew he'd surprised her...hell, he'd surprised himself. He could see the line of her spine stretching down from underneath the lowest orange-red curl at the nape of her neck, and it was all too easy to remember the last time he'd been behind her like this and then her hands came up, holding the chain of the necklace away from her neck for him so he wouldn't have to chance pricking her to lift it.

He slid the knife underneath it one-handed and pulled. She was holding the chain tightly, and he felt the friction of magic against magic closer now, but no give. "Damn."

"I don't know if I should say sorry or not, Mister Worst."

He hated that name and that he'd ever given her the idea to use it. His hand tightened in her hair without thinking. "You're the one who's trapped here with me until you're free."

"Then for that, I am sorry." Her head twisted away from him, showing him the delicate shell of her ear. "But only for me."

Rax made a low noise, deep in his throat. Her ignorance made him want to roar. She had no idea what the stakes were in this game for him, how long he'd already sacrificed his dragon for—and how much more sacrifice the Gate might require of him if he couldn't heal the key to fix its lock. Right now her slender neck was the only thing standing between him and his dragon's freedom. The alternatives were him reclaiming the beast and letting a flock of sirens fly out of the open Gate over an unsuspecting countryside—or him rejoining his dragon at the bottom of the sea and being horribly awake, for the rest of eternity, in the freezing, empty, endless dark.

"Hand me the other blade," he demanded.

She jumped but still asked, "In exchange for?"

"Letting you live," he growled. She did as she was told, fumbling in her fear, handing the other knife back to him with a shaking hand, as he cursed himself for scaring her. "Lift your own hair up, Red," he commanded, and she took it from him, bowing forward to put her elbows on the table, protecting her face with her arms like he might hit her.

Rather than fight with her on that fact—*fighting her about not fighting her, how droll*—he grimaced and yanked the chain up, trying to slice through it with the blade made out of rose petals forged together by magic.

The chain didn't budge. He made a dissatisfied sound and leaned over her, slamming the knife back in front of her on the table. "You try."

She did, letting her hair go as she took the knife up. She sawed against the chain to no avail. "It just won't," she said, her voice tinged with sorrow, as she held the blade out in front of herself. Her free hand reached for the dark blade as if it was magnetized. "It looks so soft," she whispered, right before he reached for her wrist, but it was too late; she'd sliced the tip of her finger and very red, very human, blood welled up as she yelped in surprise.

The scent of her blood hit Rax like a blow. *Humans—so fragile, and always in danger!* He rounded the table to reach into the bags and yank out another package of socks, tearing into it with his teeth to grab one and press it to her bleeding finger, winding it tight. "Hold it over your heart," he told her, lifting her hands with his to indicate how high it should be before letting go.

She did as she was told without fighting for once. "It didn't look like it could hurt me. It looked like velvet. How could it be so sharp?" she asked with all sincerity.

The sensation of him getting punched in the stomach hadn't lessened. If anything—it'd gotten worse. "Magic," he murmured. Their fates were tied, somehow—for as long as she had his necklace on.

Samantha looked between the fresh package of socks to him. "Were you...holding out on me?"

He glanced at her face, where he could very clearly read her thinking about teasing him—considering smiling at him. Attempting to be friendly. Because surely that was coming. When she realized there was no other way out of his home for her, eventually, she'd try to cozy up to him. Whether she meant it or not, it didn't matter. *Because her blood was red.* "Yes," he said, stepping away from the table and shaking his head. "It doesn't matter. I'll feed you again in several hours, and you will eat," he threatened, sweeping the knives up to take upstairs with him to empower them at his altar while leaving her with all of the rest of the bags below.

SAMANTHA WATCHED HIM GO. Something had happened, but she wasn't sure what. They'd been getting along, and she'd even made him laugh, and then everything had fallen apart again. They never showed this part in the serial killer documentaries, here the eventual victim tried to get on their good side, trying to dance a dance they didn't know the steps to.

Maybe because hardly anyone ever survived.

Once her finger had stopped bleeding, she'd made three trips downstairs with everything he'd purchased her. Fleece leggings just like she'd asked, and they'd probably been a pain in the ass to get, too, because it was almost summer. Several sports bras because that was easier than sending him *actual* bra shopping—*God, having him get her underwear had been weird enough*— and some sweaters and long-sleeved tops and flannel pajamas and....

Everything was really nice. Expensive. She bit the tags off with her teeth and started pulling stuff on, sighing as soft things cradled her, finally feeling warm, and as she pulled on a dark purple cashmere sweater all of a sudden she thought she understood how Stockholm Syndrome worked.

She spent the rest of her alone time working through the bookcases while the fox watched. She was trying to figure out which ones she'd take into the bath with her and in what order, organizing them into three piles of interest: information about dragons, historical books, and anything that looked like it had to do with magic.

A few hours later she heard the sounds of him above cooking again. In between stages of whatever it was he was doing he would play the piano. She knew it wasn't for her—*why would it be? it was clear that he hated her*—but it was still lovely, and she found herself lingering closer and closer to the stairs.

Then he stopped playing entirely and she heard more sounds of him moving before calling, "Red," though not as loudly as before.

She came up the stairs, feeling like half a new woman because she was finally dressed. "You rang?" she said with a tease.

The more he thought of her as a person, the safer she was, right? *Hopefully.*

"Sit," he said from his kitchen, without looking her direction. He was dressed in clothes to go out again, the uniform of his dark slacks and jewel-toned dress shirts for the Lynx. The current one was so purple it was almost black, and he'd cuffed both the sleeves up so they'd be out of his way as he cooked. The table was full of food; more steak, salad, and if her nose was right, there was something sweet still baking. He brought over a warm loaf of bread and she caught him giving her a once over. She wondered if he was pleased with what she'd chosen to wear and wondered how far she was willing to go to use that when he frowned. "Show me your finger."

She flipped him off, and he blinked at her—but half of his cruel lips lifted into a smile. "Your injured finger," he corrected himself.

"Oh, well, you should've said so," she said blithely, holding her forefinger out for inspection. There was a fine cut across the meat of her fingertip, but she'd avoided catching it on the books she flipped through downstairs. "I'm fine now." She rocked her wrist around as well. "Even my sprain's better."

"You have Hachiro to thank for that," he said, using salad tongs to serve her.

"Uh, I can serve myself," she said, swatting at his hands without touching him. "And, his name is Comet."

He sat back and watched her get her own salad. "You're not in awe that my magical octopus has healed you?"

She looked around the room pointedly, then gestured at herself with her knife and fork before stabbing a piece of steak for herself. "My body only contains so much adrenaline. I've decided to start rationing it for when it counts. Magical octopuses don't rate currently, no offense, Comet," she said, with a nod towards the aquarium. "I've gotta save what little I have left for strange men with strange knives."

His eyes narrowed on hers as he cracked into the loaf of bread with his hands. "He says none taken. Because he's also telepathic."

"Oh, so, then you know he prefers Comet as a name to Hachiro then," she said, smiling, as she shoveled food into her mouth. It tasted better now and she needed to eat a lot, because after he left tonight….

"No, he definitely prefers Hachiro," Mr. Janvier said, tapping his temple with a finger.

She frowned and shook her head. "Not possible. We're taking this to the tank. Otherwise, you could totally be lying." She got out of her chair and went to the aquarium. Sure enough, the massive octopus propelled itself up from the depths. She looked back at Janvier. "Well?"

His eyes traveled over her like he wasn't sure what to make of her. *Good.* She could dance this dance, at least. If he wanted a Manic Pixie Dream Girl, she could so do that and then knife him in his sleep.

Once she figured out what would kill him and all.

She gave him a serene smile as he joined her in front of the glass, taking a stand six feet away from her.

"Okay, Comet. You go and float in front of whoever calls you the name you like best." She cupped her hands around her lips and stage-whispered, "That name is Comet," at him, and she heard Janvier snort.

The octopus wavered in between them, stretching out tentacles to either side, but then decided, grabbing hold of the glass in front of Sammy and pulling himself in her direction.

"See?" She turned toward Janvier in triumph.

"He's only doing this to get on your good side," Janvier grumbled.

"Maybe because he's bored of your side," she said, putting her hands in her pockets, pleased to actually have pockets again. "Maybe because your side is," she began, about to mouth off—having real clothes was making her cocky. She'd been ready to say *mean* and *cruel* but bit her lips just in time, remembering that taunting one's prison guard wasn't exactly a great idea.

"My side is what?" he asked her, turning, framed in blue light.

She swallowed. "You're telepathic, Worst. You tell me."

He took a great inhale and let it out very slowly. "The only kind of telepathy I have in regard to you is when you're considering doing something to annoy me. Which appears to be all the time," he told her, and then took a step back toward the table. "Come eat before your food gets cold, Red."

THEY ATE IN SILENCE.

Everything he'd made her was beautiful and delicious. The kind of meal she used to photograph and send to Andi or Eumie for bragging rights.

Only she couldn't because she didn't have her phone, and who the hell knew if she would even have service if she did? She cut off another piece of steak and put it in her mouth to chew. Too bad she couldn't pretend that this whole adventure was some sort of 'social media detox spa' like she knew rich people got to do. She saw their Instagram posts. *Oh, I can't wait to get offline and reconnect! Not having social media makes your skin glow!*

BITCH, WHAT IS THE POINT OF HAVING GLOWING SKIN IF NO ONE IS AROUND TO SEE IT?

And, conversely, what was the point of being kidnapped by a dragon if you couldn't tell anyone? She stared down at the rest of her steak. She really needed to eat it because—

"Do you not like it?" Janvier asked her. She looked up and caught him looking at her with a furrowed brow.

"It's not that. I mean you could give Bastian a run for his money if you wanted to. A-plus-plus-food, amazing ambiance, but...." She let her voice drift and her shoulders drop.

"I couldn't buy you any freedom at the grocery store," he finished for her.

"Yeah." *Just that one, small, vastly important thing.*

He leaned forward on the table with both forearms. "I promise you're here for your own good, Samantha."

She rolled her eyes. "Because of this necklace that you can't tell me anything about?" She picked the stone up off her chest to look at it.

"You mean the one where you can't tell me where you got it from?" he asked her.

"Touché," she admitted. "But you must see that you have the advantage here. Like…literally every advantage."

He nodded, slowly.

"So what's your end game?" she asked him. "What the hell is the plan here?"

"I'll try to get the necklace off of you with the knives. Once or twice a day. Every day, until it works."

"What's going to change in the meantime?" she asked while frowning. "You gonna go work out a lot? Swim some more, maybe?" She put her silverware down and pushed her plate out of the way. "Just say it, Worst. If the octopus is magic, then who the hell cares if you are, too?"

He considered her closely. "I neither need to confess nor deny things to you."

He didn't, true, but if he never would—how the fuck long would she be down here? She let her shoulders slump and gave an exasperated sigh. "Just tell me one more true thing," she begged him. He moved to stand, ignoring her, and she sent her hand across the table to keep him there on instinct, catching his wrist as he had so often caught hers. "What the fuck are you? Just tell me," she pleaded. She could feel the light wiry give of the dark hairs on his arm, and she was surprised to find his skin hot to the touch; he only seemed cold all the time, but he really wasn't.

All those times, it'd felt like his touch had burned her—*maybe it had.*

He rocked his wrist free as she let it go with a gasp, realizing too late she was still touching him. She scooted herself back from the table to create more space between them, knowing she'd gone too far, even if it was on accident. Touching him set up a bad precedent—it was tantamount to giving him permission to touch her. She twisted away and wiped her hand on her leggings, biting her lips, nervous to look up.

But eventually, she did and found him still waiting. His eyes narrowed on her with curiosity and distrust. "Why are you taking this so well?" he asked her, his voice rough.

She blinked at him, completely taken aback. *Where 'well' equaled roughly forty-eight hours of a sub-clinical panic attack?* "Oh, fuck you, Mister Worst," she told him and then laughed in his face. His head pulled back in surprise and she knew she'd landed the first blow of her entire captivity. "The only reason you think that 'I'm taking this so well' is because you have no idea how women work." She stood and pushed her chair in as he began to frown deeply. There was a line of tension across his shoulders, and she wondered if she'd pushed her luck too far but if she had, fuck it. At least she'd die with a full stomach and some pride. "That's right. You heard me. Fuck. You."

His freshly shaved jaw clenched and she watched his chest heave as his fox growled from somewhere in the kitchen. "You should go back downstairs, Red," he warned her.

Sammy strode for the stairs. "Don't mind if I do."

SHE HALF EXPECTED him to follow her down and take all her new warm things, but he didn't. She dove into the nest she'd made of the couches and listened to him roughly clear the table above her. The sheets she'd stolen from his bed still smelled like him and she regretted not asking for new ones, but it was too late now; she doubted he'd go out of his way for her again. She hid inside of them, waiting for things to blow over, hating that she remembered so vividly how it felt to be helpless like this so many times in her past. How much of her life had been wasted waiting for things that she had absolutely no control over to change? She'd had to be half-weathervane in so many strange homes after she lost her parents, able to sense minute changes in moods and tempers to survive.

She was good at it, but she also hated everything about it, and it made the food inside her stomach sour. When it was quieter up above she got out of her bed as quietly as she could and went back to arranging books.

The answer to her getting her freedom was in one of them.

It had to be.

RAX KNELT in front of his closed altar with closed eyes while Smoke paced back and forth in front of him.

"Just say it," he murmured. "You know I've got to concentrate." It was hard enough to already, remembering the way he'd felt when her hand had grabbed his arm. Her action he understood; she was human, prone to fits of emotions, of course, she couldn't control herself—but his response to it surprised him. He'd been suffused with longing immediately afterward to grab her wrist in return and use it to reel the rest of her in...to...*what?*

He tamped down his lust with a lengthy exhale. He knew *what*, his entire body knew *what*. Taking her at Belissima's had been a terrible mistake, given that he could remember how any point of her body felt against his now, not the least of which was his hard cock buried inside her.

It gave her a power over him that he didn't like.

He heard the tick-tack of Smoke's claws against the floor again. "Spit it out," he commanded the fox quietly, finally opening his eyes.

The fox tilted its angular head in his direction. "She knows more than she's telling you."

"Yes," Rax readily agreed. For all that she thought he didn't know women, he did know humans, and most of them did not have her fortitude. By and large normal humans would be in a corner crying to themselves, next to useless....

"Doesn't that bother you?" Smoke asked him.

"Of course it does," Rax quietly snapped. "But as of yet, I'm unwilling to—" He didn't want to say the words aloud....

"Torture her," Smoke finished for him. "But don't you see? That's how I can help!" the fox offered, gnashing its teeth by example. "You can't bite her but I can!"

"Smoke," Rax said, sighing. "No."

The fox made a snarling sound, chased its tail in a fast circle, then accosted him when he stopped. "Has it occurred to you that there's some sort of subterfuge going on? That's she's a part of some plot?"

"A plot to do what?" Rax asked with a hiss. "No one even remembers the Gate anymore. Just you and I and Hachiro." And the Gate itself...which would hopefully not send anymore drowned emissaries to his casino tonight.

Smoke wrinkled his snout. "There's something more to her. And if you're not willing to bite her to find out, I will."

Rax unlocked his altar and pulled his knives out and caught a glimpse of her phone below, beneath her scarf, where he'd hidden both items. He pulled it out and showed it to the fox. "I'll look into things this evening," he said. "No biting."

Then he took a knife into each hand and started pouring his power into them, hoping that tomorrow they'd be strong enough to cut the chain and free him.

CHAPTER 11

"Do you know someone who can unlock this for me?" he asked Namir, holding out Samantha's phone as he surveyed the casino before they opened the doors. He had no idea how long it'd taken them to get the funk of death off of the tables last night, but somehow they'd managed, and replaced the roulette table as well. Namir did look a little tired, though.

"I do," Namir said, taking the phone from him for inspection. "It's not...magical, is it?"

"Not to my knowledge, no," Rax said with a snort. "Any information on it is mine, however. Tell whomever you trust to open it and not look any further, lest they risk my anger."

"Do they need to be subtle?" Namir asked.

Rax considered this. Did he have any intention of ever giving Samantha her phone back? "No. All of the data on a thumb drive will do."

Namir nodded. "Fair enough. I'll work on it tonight." He pocketed the phone and then made a pained expression. "By the way, the glassmith said to tell you his work was exceptional, asked quote-unquote, 'How the hell did he break it?' and told me to tell you there's no way he can make you another knife unless you comp him and ten of his closest friends a hundred chips each for one night next month."

Rax gave Namir a look he usually reserved for daft drunks being forcibly removed.

"His wife is turning sixty; he's been looking for ways to surprise her apparently." Namir raised his hands to the heavens. "It's a Tuesday night at least."

Rax rolled his eyes. "Fine. That's almost cheaper than a new one—I'm not comping him drinks though—and I need the knife in hand by tomorrow evening."

"I'll let him know." Namir paused outside the bar while Rax went in to make himself a drink. The tiger-shifter needed to seem perpetually on his toes, whereas it suited Rax to occasionally seem more louche to put people off their guard. "That woman you had me hire; she didn't show up to her last shift."

Rax paused from where he'd been adding whiskey to sweet vermouth and Campari. "So?" He'd been magically wiping Samantha's scent from himself on his way in every day.

"Did you want me to...look for her?" Namir asked, eyebrows raised.

"No," Rax said curtly.

The tiger-shifter's lips pursed. "Are you seeing her?"

If seeing her meant having his eyes on her, then yes. In all other senses of the word, though, no. His life would be much easier if he didn't have to see her, honestly, watching Samantha veer from hope to hatred, her moods bouncing like a ball on a roulette wheel, when she didn't entirely turn them off. What would she be up to tonight without him? *Probably hanging out with Hachiro, the traitor.* He ran the fingertips of his opposite hand over where hers had been on his wrist earlier in the day, like a cuff. "Unfortunately."

Namir made an appraising sound. "I wouldn't have—"

"I don't pay you to consider my personal matters, Namir," Rax cut him off.

"True, and I appreciate that. But...Delphine is coming in tonight, all the same." Rax groaned as Namir continued. "She's the one with the crystal ball for you. I knew it was related to the selkies and I pressed my contact there, who admitted it to me for a low price." Namir gave him a dour look. "Would you like to reimburse me, or should the joy of me kicking her out a second time in as many weeks be recompense enough?"

Rax snorted and took a sip of his drink, considering. Delphine had been pressuring him to take her colony's side in an upcoming territory fight last week, and despite their extensive history, he neither cared to support her nor did he currently have the time. "If it is not what she's promised, don't worry, I'll kick her out myself."

"Works for me," Namir said, nodding a little as he backed up. "Your first appointment is in two hours. I'll go open the doors."

RAX WAS ALREADY EMPLOYING a fleet of forgers and hackers and at the rate inhabitants of the Realms were abandoning their homeland, he would have to hire more.

"I want to experience the best this world has to offer." The couple sitting across from him were dressed in Earthly clothing with a Realms sensibility, which meant they looked eccentric on Earth, verging towards ridiculous. The man was in purple leggings splashed with gold paint and a tie-dyed t-shirt, while the woman was wearing a tight blue-silk sheath dress, with crystals liberally applied on her face, and a tiara. Good thing for them it was almost festival season, and non-royal women wearing crowns were 'in.'

"Alas, I am not its tourist board," Rax said. He finished what he was doing on his laptop and then closed the lid, handing the valuable piece of equipment to Namir, who was standing behind him. "You're welcome to do whatever it is that you like with the funds I've transferred into your accounts but be aware that I cannot add more unless you trade me something else of value."

The man of the pair, who was handling his phone with increasing confidence since Rax had seen him last, Rax noted, squinted at his screen until the transaction processed. "I believe a million dollars will be enough to start with."

"It *should* last you for quite some time. But funds on Earth are not as replenishable as those that you're used to. You don't have any peasants here to tax, for one."

The woman laughed. "Not yet, at least."

Rax grit his teeth together. "In any case, congratulations on your new world. Earth is now your oyster," he said, pointing at his door. The couple gathered up their paperwork from him: social security cards, drivers licenses', bills to former addresses they'd never lived at, and stepped out. "And I hope you choke on it," he muttered once the door was shut behind them.

"I liked it better when we were just a casino," Namir said.

Rax twisted to look back at him. "You enjoy hunting down things to trade."

"Yes. I just like it when they're not attached to—whatever that was." He glared meaningfully at the door.

"People who've never had to work hard in their life?" Rax guessed, and Namir grunted. "But it's more fun to steal from them."

A wicked smile played across Namir's face, showing a line of even teeth. "Agreed."

The couple had traded him ten magical objects, each one more powerful than the last, although neither of them had seemed strong enough to create more. Rax supposed between them they had a cache of magical generational wealth and wondered what they'd set aside to live off of and also what they'd left behind. Good guards were hard to find in the Realms, and no matter who they'd paid or bribed ahead of time, it was likely their now empty ancestral home was being plundered—just as Rax's had been—and items taken from it might also come to Rax in time, via people like Mathal.

Or people like Delphine bringing him an object from Seris's grave.

There were other Sea Bubbles still in existence, most likely, but he did find it odd that now two things buried with his dead sister-in-law had come to light. He would have to wonder on it later, though, work called.

· · ·

RAX MADE sure to top off his drink and center himself before Delphine's arrival. She was tall and pale, with straight blonde hair. No matter what she wore, it was always gray or silver; like a fabric version of her sealskin, which he knew she kept safe in a chest somewhere so that no man would ever be her master.

Not that many people would volunteer to try if they truly knew how dangerous she could be. He'd been involved with her years ago, mostly because of their unspoken mutual agreement not to impinge on the other in any way, shape, or form, both of them knowing the other was essentially untamable. They'd wandered into and out of each other's lives like cats, which was why her coming to him for help had surprised him, as had her very venomous subsequent anger at having been denied.

But of course she'd found another way to come beseech him, and this time she actually had leverage.

Rax stood politely as Delphine strode into his office like she belonged there, because once upon a time she had, and he waved Namir away. The tiger-shifter gave him a look and closed the door, as the both of them sat down on opposite sides of his desk. "Are you tired of your little human yet?" Delphine asked him, watching him with her large brown eyes, the only thing that might give any of her true nature away.

How had she known of Samantha? He didn't let his curiosity show. "Namir said you claimed to have something of interest to me."

"I do. And it would behoove you to be more polite to me for it." She tilted her head, sending her hair cascading over one shoulder. She was wearing skintight white leather pants and a shimmering top, covered in reflective beads on short tassels. "I need you to come and fight on our behalf, Rax."

Rax ran a finger around the rim of his drink. "And, as I told you earlier, I am currently unable to. I have my own matters to handle, and my casino is neutral territory. Taking sides during shifter conflicts invites conflict here—it's a bad look."

"Then I guess you don't need this," she said, giving him an icy smile. Her hand disappeared into the shimmer of her dress, and she pulled an object out, almost like she was offering him an organ. "Because this is what you seek, isn't it?" She held a clear globe over his desk, twisting it in the light.

Rax had a sudden memory of being a child and visiting a room full of such bubbles with his cousins, not all of whom could breathe underwater like he could, and then running as a group, shrieking with delight, for the shore.

"Where did you get it?" he asked softly.

"The bottom of the ocean. Where else?" Delphine snaked her arm back toward herself, hiding the orb inside the shimmer of her shirt again, using the mirrors of the beads for magic, stashing the orb someplace else on their reflection's far side. "Now that you know what I possess, we should discuss terms."

"You may take all of these." He gestured to the objects the wealthy couple had left behind. He'd given them a million dollars for them, and they were easily worth three times as much. "But I cannot fight in your war."

"Rax," she said, in a disappointed tone. "I know last time I was here I might have come on too strong because, let's be fair here, you and I have been good together in the past, and I so rarely am told no. But now, let's let bygones be bygones." She licked her lips and slowly pushed the objects on his desk out of her way and then moved to crawl over it toward him, with intent in her gaze. "There are so few men I can stand, Rax, and fewer still that can satisfy me. So let's fuck like we used to, and then see how you feel about fighting."

Rax surveyed her. Delphine was beautiful, yes, and she was as coldhearted as the waters her seal-self swam in, which matched him well. And now that Samantha was safely locked away and he knew exactly where she was, he had time…. He dipped his fingers into his bitter drink and then reached out to swipe them across Delphine's lips, pushing two fingers into her mouth, pulling her head down, and forcing her to look up at him like he had speared a fishhook through her jaw. "You think I'll come in you once, and all my obligations will be forgotten?"

She didn't nod, but her wide brown eyes made him promises his dick wished he'd let her keep. But even as her teeth grazed his knuckles and her mouth sucked at him, something still felt wrong. Perhaps it was the fact that her pale skin was too perfect—it didn't have a single freckle. "I respect the lengths you're willing to go to help your people, Delphine. But I have my own people to think of."

She bit his fingers, hard, and then rocked back. "Don't lie. You care for no one, Rax."

"Fine," he agreed. "But so what if I only care for me? I cannot help you, regardless. And you should appreciate the fact I'm telling you now and not after I came in your mouth."

Her upper lip curled in a snarl. "I would bite off your dick if you had."

"Hmm. Dragon scale is hard to bite through. And it's always just lying underneath, isn't it?" He jerked his chin at the objects on the table. "Take these in trade. Use them in your fight. It's more than fair, and we both know it."

"I don't want the objects," she said, dismounting his desk. "I want you, by my side, in this battle."

"I cannot," he began, then Hachiro's mind rushed his and latched on.

"RAX!" It was like he felt the octopus's suckers grab hold inside his skull, and a migraine was imminent. *"The girl—Smoke says she's bleeding!"*

A strength Rax had almost forgotten ran through his veins in an instant, as he quickly thought back to Hachiro. *"Is it her period?"* Samantha had had him buy tampons for her, and it wasn't like his animals were used to women.

"He says she used a knife!" There was a pause while the octopus and fox conferred. *"And now she's in the bathroom! Smoke says he hears running water—"*

"Cannot deny me?" Delphine guessed, with a wickedly hopeful smile.

"The opposite, in fact," he growled, ripping his mind away from Hachiro and back to his office. "I'm going to buy it from whomever else you sell it to."

Delphine gave a harsh laugh. "Then I'll keep it just to spite you."

He stared at Delphine's perfectly structured face and through it as he thought.

How much blood was in a human? How badly had the girl cut herself? Why was she in his tub again...did she truly hate him that much?

How much time did he have?

And at the thought of wasting a moment more negotiating with Delphine when he needed to check on Samantha; he put his hand out and spoke calmly. "Delphine, if you do not give me the orb immediately, in a very reasonable exchange for these magical objects I have offered—I will peel your current skin off of you, and we will see together what new magical creature waits underneath."

Delphine's head pulled back like he'd slapped her, then her eyes narrowed, and she dove her hand into the shimmer of her beads again and retrieved it. "You have made an enemy today, Rax," she said, throwing the orb at his chest, hard.

He caught it deftly and set it carefully down. "If that is the case, so be it. Take your objects in trade and go."

She started lunging for the objects the couple had left, pushing them into the shimmer of her dress one by one. "The bottom of the ocean is not the same place you remember."

"Luckily for me, I have no intention of ever visiting again," he said and pressed a button beneath his desk to summon Namir.

SAMANTHA WAITED until she was sure Mr. Janvier had left for the evening, no games. She assumed he was really gone once the fox started following her around again. She brought the books she was interested in up to the second floor and looked in the fridge.

She *had* smelled a dessert earlier, some kind of pie.

But he hadn't taken a single bite of it for himself. She reached in and broke off a fraction of the crust and popped it into her mouth.

Perfect and flaky, and when was the last time she'd had homemade pie? She continued her investigations, pulling the pie from the fridge and working her way into a piece.

What were these…blueberries?

Her mouth watered, and she groaned. This was totally unfair. *Fuck him.* She went and found a plate and cut herself out the tiniest sliver while realizing that he'd know she had when he came home.

But maybe this was a pre-reward for keeping her strength up.

Maybe she should eat the whole pie and not leave any for him.

Did foxes or octopi like pie? She broke off a piece of the crust and tossed it down to the fox, who only growled at her in response.

Seems not.

Sammy ate her piece and then got herself a glass of water. She'd come up with several ideas for things to do since she'd been alone last and started with the easiest. If the necklace's stone let her read when it was underwater in the tub…the tub's water wasn't special, surely? She opened a book and leaned forward, dipping the stone into her water glass.

Sure enough, that worked, too.

Excellent…now….

She tugged the stone up and flipped it so that it was in her mouth. Its roughly carved surface lay against her tongue and she looked at the book in front of her—which she could still read.

Water was water, no matter where!

She would've squealed with delight but she knew it'd startle the fox.

Round two—she opened up a book that had a few empty pages at the back, carefully pulled them out, and then took them over to the stove. The fox hadn't really stopped growling the entire time. It'd gotten louder when she'd damaged the book, but if growling was all it did she was fine with that.

She paced the kitchen again, staring up. She hadn't made out any fire alarms anywhere overhead. Either his entire home wasn't up to code—*and how the hell with a three-story aquarium could it be?*—or they were hidden from her, magically.

She was hoping the latter and that if they went off they'd trigger something, like a 911 call to the fire department.

Past that and the range hood—*which went where? not up to the third floor!*—she hadn't seen any heating or air conditioning vents in Janvier's home either, but she knew there had to be, so he was hiding those, too? And if there were vents and ductwork, maybe there was something she could send a signal through, or if she was lucky enough, climb out of.

So she was killing two birds with one stone, really.

She twisted on the gas burner and then fed the paper into it, watching it catch fire, and then she used that to catch alight a dish-towel she'd wrapped around the end of a wooden spoon, creating a makeshift torch. It burned slowly enough that she could take it up to Janvier's level, which was where she assumed any alarms or air vents would be. His bed was still unmade with only the sheets she'd left for him the prior night. Acrid smoke curled to the ceiling, and she followed the smoke's path with her eyes, looking for anything that would help her.

"Please," she whispered to the smoke, waving it slowly overhead, as Janvier's fox snapped at her heels and she ignored him.

But the smoke just sat there.

No alarms—and no air movement.

"That's impossible," she muttered to herself, then realized how ridiculous she sounded, given everything else that'd happened to her.

A wet slithering sound began from behind her. She turned and saw Comet hauling himself over the aquarium's edge and then down it, moving much less fluidly out of the water than he had in it, extending suckered tentacle after tentacle, pulling himself toward her on the floor.

Sammy stood, rather stunned that an octopus was crawling towards her, as it maneuvered itself to look at her with one baleful eye and then squirt a jet of water out to quench the torch she held.

"Oh, come *on!*" she complained, as Comet turned back to crawl back to return himself to his aquatic environment. "That's so not fair!"

But nothing down here was.

Which was why she didn't really have a choice in things.

It was drastic, yes, but...she ran downstairs with the ruined torch and picked up Janvier's sharpest paring knife.

RAX DROVE HOME at reckless speeds, his own blood thundering in his veins. He could have reached out to Hachiro again, but it was clear the girl had locked herself away. To do what? Grim images floated through his mind, and he couldn't quantify how the thought of her hurting himself made him feel. Angry, yes. *Because all things considered, he hadn't even been that cruel!*

But underneath the anger, there was a bud of fear that felt unseemly as it blossomed in his chest. If he had been responsible for her injuring herself—and there was no doubt he had been, she wouldn't have been cutting herself if he was entirely absent from her life—what did that say about him? If he couldn't even keep one delicate human alive? He, who had sacrificed his dragon to save a nation, but let some girl slip through his fingers?

And not just any girl.

The one who the key had chosen for some reason.

It would be like failing the Gate all over again in the deep dark with Tarian, screaming for his brother to come out from the other side.

He parked his car and ran inside without shutting the door behind himself, shouting her name as loudly as he could. "SAMANTHA!"

Hachiro was right, his home did smell like blood, and Smoke bounded down the stairs yipping with worry at the same time as he raced up.

"SAMANTHA!"

"Leave me alone!" He heard her voice from the far side of his bathroom's door, and it sounded tiny. He crossed his room in a rush and tried the handle, knowing there were no locks as he was the only one who lived in his home, and barged inside.

She was lounging in a tub so hot his mirror was steamed. Her red hair was dark beneath the water, flowing around her like she was some kind of goddamned mermaid, with one of his books spread out on the tub's stairs as she leaned over to read it. At seeing him, she screamed in surprise, and didn't stop as he stormed to the tub's side to peer in at her.

"Let me see all of you," he demanded.

"What? No!" Her arms fluttered down and he caught sight of a bandage on one palm, but he grabbed both her wrists and hoisted her up as she shrieked and tried to thrash away.

SAMMY WAS LOUNGING in the tub. She'd finished reading the chapter on unicorns and was now idly flipping through the bestiary's pages, trying to figure out what she'd read next, when she saw something that scratched an itch at the edge of her mind.

She flipped back to the page she'd stumbled over earlier, the strange flying creature made of wings and eyes and mouths. The wings spun every which way, the eyes pointed in all directions, and the mouths…she could almost hear their howls, like wind ripping down the beach on a lonely day.

Why did it seem so familiar?

And then Janvier had burst into his home, shouting her name.

She slammed the book shut to hide it from him and heard him running up the stairs. She hadn't even thought of locking the door. Did it even lock? Then he was inside the room with her, staring at her, *reaching for her*—and she was scrambling, trying to get away. "Stop looking at me!" she howled, as he half-suspended her in mid-air, trying to fight with him and losing. Why the fuck was he so strong? She knew why—and she knew it wasn't fair. There was nothing she could do to change anything and she was on the verge of crying out in terror as she felt him catch his breath and lower her back down so that her feet touched the bottom of the tub again. His eyes traveled over her naked body in the rhythm of his breathing—fast—as if he'd just run a race here or like he'd actually been afraid.

Of what? the remaining rational part of her mind demanded.

"Leave me alone!" she shouted, embarrassed by the way her voice trembled, twisting her head away from him. Her wet hair was slicked against her skin, offering no protection. "I fucking hate you!"

Janvier's hands tightened on her wrists and then he dropped one. "Who did that to you?" he demanded, keeping her right arm up.

She grit her teeth and knew what he was asking about; the line of three cigarette burns a foster 'brother' had left on the inside of her upper arm years ago when she was a teenager. They were shallow scars now, and she made sure no one ever saw them. "You don't get to ask!" she snarled at him with so much venom that he released her and took a step back. She covered herself with her hands. The hand that she'd cut earlier started throbbing and she really fucking wanted to cry now, but she would *never* give him the satisfaction.

He stared straight into her eyes, still breathing hard, but at least his gaze didn't stray. She wondered if he was trying to read her mind and if he could, what he would see there—then he turned and started walking away. He paused in the doorway and she dropped back down into the water because she didn't know if he was going to come rushing back at her or not and she wanted to hide from him. He inhaled the steaming air in deeply and it was her turn to hold her breath, wondering what his next mood would bring.

He twisted his head down to speak to her without turning around again and said, "A scar is how you know you escaped," before closing the door behind himself.

Sammy gave up then and sank into the tub entirely beneath the water and safely sobbed.

RAX WENT DOWNSTAIRS and closed the door with Smoke at his heels. *Little did Samantha know how easily she could have had her precious freedom.* "After you left, she burned things! And then she sliced her hand open and painted on that wall!" Smoke tattled.

The fox ran over to the darkest wall on his living floor, between a

J.M.W. Turner no one else had ever seen, seeing as Rax had bought it from the man himself—the man could paint what the ocean felt like—and a Winslow Homer, whose ocean was just as beautiful but slightly more literal on the canvas.

He summoned magic to himself, cast out with his hand, and found where she'd written her name and a message between the two in blood: SAMMY O'CONNOR IS HERE—PLEASE HELP ME!

Rax sat on his coffee table and sank down, putting his elbows on his knees and his head in his hands. He was aghast, both at her ingenuity, because he knew how hard blood was to remove—even magically it was easy to sense long term—and that she felt she needed to go that far.

Who did things like this?

But it was easy for him to answer his own question; someone who had been hurt before.

One burn scar could be an accident, but three, in a precise row? Someone had held her down and done that to her. And at the thought of anyone else mistreating her—*no matter what the fuck she thought was happening right now*—something unholy moved in him, and he wished for violence on the scale of which he hadn't felt in a very long time.

Smoke, who had gone back upstairs, raced down to report, "I think she's crying," and then made to run back upstairs to listen in again.

Rax kept staring at the ground, seethingly angry in turns at something unknown in her past and himself, as he whistled Smoke back to his side. "Leave her be."

SAMMY WAITED in the bathroom until she'd gathered herself up as much as she was able, painfully aware that it wasn't as much as she'd been able to do the day before or the day before that.

The longer she was here the more she felt like an unsolved puzzle. Each day took away another piece and she wasn't sure what picture she was going to be left with when everything was done. She could keep herself focused on trying to escape, or reading, or hoping to find answers, but not having a plan that would work soon was going to break her. Her brain was going to run itself ragged, trying to think of ways out, like a cartoon coyote, forever running into brick walls.

She pulled on her clothes, dried off her hair as best she could, pulling it into a thick damp braid, and picked up her books, hoping that he wouldn't be waiting just outside for her while knowing that there was nowhere she could go to escape him.

Not really.

No matter how hard she tried.

There were no trunks to hide in here.

And sure enough, he was sitting at the dining room table just one floor down. "We need to talk," he told her.

She spared him a glance. He'd put out two slices of pie, one for each of them. "Sure, yeah, let's talk about pies," she said and ignored him, continuing downstairs.

"I mean it, Samantha," he said, standing. She rushed down the stairs as he moved to the landing. "I want you to feel safe down there, so come up. This isn't the kind of conversation I want to corner you for."

She moved away so he wouldn't be able to see her, setting her books down on his desk. The cut on her hand had reopened when she'd put it underwater, so she pressed a clean tube sock against it now.

"Samantha," he said again, at a reasonable volume. He didn't even sound frustrated with her. *Hooray.* "Please."

She blinked at that, her hands hovering over the books she'd just sat down. It was the first time she'd ever heard him say that word.

Which didn't mean he wasn't luring her upstairs for his own benefit, but better he do whatever he wanted up there then down here. "I'll come up...if you back away."

"Done," he said, and she heard him walk over to his table and the sound of his chair moving as he sat down.

She knotted the clean sock around her hand with her teeth and kept it clenched, coming up the stairs to sit across from him.

"I saw you already had some," he said in an even tone, nodding at the pie.

Her eyes flashed across the table at him and she snorted. "Did you really want to have a discussion about pies with me? Well, okay then." She held up her whole hand and started ticking down. "My favorite kinds, in order: pumpkin, cherry, apple, pecan, key lime. Blueberry doesn't even make the top five—"

"Samantha," he cut in.

She crossed her arms. "Just say it. Whatever you want to say—stop pretending any of this is normal."

"I know it's not normal. I just wish you wouldn't treat it...like this," he said, giving her hand a meaningful glance.

"What, you want me to pretend this is an extended sleepover where someone threatens me a lot?" Her panic became a square thing in her throat, rising higher like a temperature gauge on an over-heating car. And more than that—her anger.

How dare the world do this to her for a second fucking time.

She might have gone and played with metaphorical fire some, and gotten burned—but the chances of getting hit by fucking lightning like this, twice? In one lifetime?

She wanted to tear everything to pieces.

Starting with him.

"I do not want you to pretend anything," he answered simply, and she blinked at him as some of the wind fell from her sails.

"Good," she snapped. "Because I can't, okay? I don't like you, and I don't want to be here."

He clenched his jaw and nodded slowly. "That's fair."

Her eyes narrowed, refusing to hope until she heard him say the words. "So...you're...letting me go?"

"I can't, Samantha. I wish I had a better plan or a way to make you truly happy."

You do! She thought at full volume. *You just won't give my freedom back to me!*

"I just know I need to keep you safe," he went on. "And this is the only safe place for you, whether you believe me or not. But I can't have you hurting yourself again. And I don't want to tie you down or install cameras to watch your every move and deprive you of your privacy." He took a deep inhale and steadied himself against the edge of the table with both his hands, bringing his gaze down to bore into her with his fiery eyes. "Do not make me."

"Do you even realize what you're asking, Mister Worst?" she asked him, her voice just above a whisper. He shook his head, lightly frowning. "You're asking for me to give up." She bit her lips together, knowing she knew she shouldn't admit what she wanted to next, but completely unable to stop herself. "Every time I go to sleep, I don't know whether or not I'm going to wake up and you want me to make things *easier* on you?"

He closed his eyes and then opened them with an exhale. "I'm not going to kill you, Samantha."

"Yeah, I can't tell you how comforting that is to hear," she said, as sarcastically as possible, and then put her hands to her face, trying to keep everything inside. Her emotions were a jumble right now, she wanted to yell, and spit, and cry, all at once, but none of that was going to get her through this.

It was just that she didn't know what *was*.

"I'm not," he repeated.

"Why should I believe you?" she asked him through her fingers.

"Because," he told her like that was an answer.

She started shaking her head and couldn't stop shaking it. "No. You can't just say that like it means something. There's nothing between us. No reason for me to trust you in the least. My entire relationship with you—*if it can even be called one*—was built on a lie! You never wanted me at Belissima's, you only wanted the necklace. And everything from then on has been downhill."

He made a low sound, half-a-growl, and then he surveyed the table between them like he was looking for something, getting pissed for not finding it. She made herself small across from him, waiting for him to take it out on her.

"Give me your hand," he demanded when he was done. She looked between her hands. "The injured one," he specified, shaking his hand across the table for hers, pushing his piece of pie aside and then moving hers as well.

She shrank back even further. "No thanks, I'll have my magic octopus friend heal it if it's all the same to you."

"Your 'Comet' is the same friend who ratted your bleeding out to me. I wasn't lying about the telepathy." He shook his hand for hers. "Please," he said for the second time. She could tell by the way he said it he was utterly unfamiliar with the word.

She hesitated, then realized if she fought him again—she had nowhere to go, so what did it matter? She shoved her hand out at him and he quickly undid the sock she'd tied around it. She'd given herself a deeper gash than she'd meant to. His knives were as sharp as he was cruel and the edges of the cut were still oozy post-accidental soaking.

He squeezed her hand hard, making the wound weep, as he pulled her arm forward. She gasped in pain and surprise and watched him bite his own thumb to blood—*green blood!* Then he swiped it across the fresh blood of her palm.

"I swear that I will not kill Samantha O'Connor, with my blood and my life," he said, leaning across the table to draw a line across her forehead with their blood combined.

She felt a frisson of electricity at his touch that she'd never felt before from anyone, ever. It rippled over her body, standing all of her hair on end from her scalp down, then it raced beneath her skin, pulling her nipples tight, making her core ache, and the line between her legs throb. She wanted him—oh God, she *needed* him—and if he'd just stop being an asshole for long enough and also free her, she would give him the ride of his life.

"There," he said, releasing her hand as he sat back down. "I just swore."

She swallowed and caught her breath, sure that all her thoughts were written on her face. "I heard you," she murmured, but realized she hadn't. He'd been speaking some other language, with her name thrown in, only her brain had made sense of it.

Because of the necklace! It didn't even need to be wet now to work for her.

Smoke sprung up on the table. "You can't possibly mean that!" the fox said, as Samantha gasped.

"Of course not. But I need to give her some hope," he told the fox— only in a different tongue—and she heard that too.

Sammy felt herself turning beet red. She'd been so turned on and... for what? *For nothing.* He was still him—the kind of man who would lie to her to get his way. She bowed her head quickly, both in shame and to buy herself time to think. He'd acknowledged that he was lying, while he was talking to a fox. She was still slightly ahead of where she'd been just moments ago. She could listen in on him now, thanks to the stone, and she knew where she stood with him.

No matter what he claimed he'd told her.

It was something.

"Are you all right?" he asked her.

"Sometimes the fox scares me," she admitted, both because it was true and to cover her reaction.

"He can be intense. I will tell him to calm down."

Janvier gently pushed it off the table and she heard it mutter, "Just wait till I bite you," and she tried not to flinch. Maybe she was better off not knowing what the thing thought of her. She clenched her hand, hissed in pain, and then moved to knot it up again.

"Did you want help?" he offered, as she retied the tube sock with her teeth.

"No," she told him. She didn't want him to touch her ever again.

TOUCHING her with even pretend magic had been a bad idea.

He'd wanted to give her the sensation of *something* happening so that she'd trust him more, at long fucking last, but it'd meant opening himself up to her, just a little, and her to him, and he hadn't expected her to react so strongly. Most humans were mute to magic and actively fought any in their lives. It was how rifts between Realms could go unnoticed, as stubborn human minds discounted anything that came out of them.

But while Samantha wasn't magical...she was receptive to it. And when he'd drawn his finger across her forehead, he'd felt a wave off of her.

Not of magic—but potential.

There was something latent inside of her that wanted to be used, like the strike pad on a matchbox might long for a match to light, and the thought of *him* using her, in any capacity, made him rock hard. Exceptionally long term practice at gambling made it easy to keep his face straight and his breathing even as he watched her rewrap her hand, and he trusted in the table to hide his erection.

In his mind, though, *the things he wanted to do to her*. His bed was just one floor up, but if she gave herself to him, they wouldn't make it there. He'd wind up eating her out here on the table, surely as fine as any meal he'd ever cooked, and drink her juices, surely as potent as any wine he'd ever tasted. Then his dessert would be fucking her until her nails clawed gashes into the table's wooden surface, making her scream out his name until even his thoughtless sharks knew what it was.

But.

She wasn't *like* him.

Which was part of the allure, yes, and he'd fucked hundreds of humans before, how could he help himself when they were so plentiful and willing?

But this place, and the way they were trapped together, here; he still had some modicum of honor. Probably the size of a grain of sand at this point, seeing as he'd spent centuries grinding it down, but it was still present, rattling around somewhere inside of his cold soul.

And watching her tie her sock around her hand, she looked much like a wounded animal might, because that's exactly what she was. He'd spent almost a millennia watching people— friends, humans, shifters, enemies—aging and dying and leaving him. He'd had to harden the remnants of his heart against getting too attached to anyone, and so he knew he had more reasons than most to avoid her.

For one, she couldn't seem to stop hurting herself, it seemed.

And he'd be damned if he let her hurt him.

Or stand in his way of relocking the Gate.

No, he didn't need to fuck her to get the key. That was not the answer to any of his problems and was almost certain to cause more if he did.

"How do you know of magic, Samantha?" He reached out across the table to push her pie back in front of her. "And you should eat. I already know you like it, or you wouldn't have eaten any earlier."

She gave him a wary frown but still picked up her fork. "I can't tell you."

"Why not?"

"Why would I sign anyone else up for this?" She gave him an incredulous look as she spun the fork around at her surroundings, and he snorted.

"Fair enough. Where did you get the stone?"

"Same answer." Her gaze fell to the pie and she stabbed it a few times without taking any bites, then she looked up at him. "Where did you learn to cook?"

He tilted his head to look at her. "Why do you ask?"

"Because the question game seems fairer if I get to participate."

He pulled his piece of pie back in front of himself. "When might be the better question then."

Her eyes lit up a little. "All right then, when?"

"In my free time. Of which I have a lot." He took a bite and waited for her to do the same.

She followed his lead, chewed, swallowed, and asked, "Is there a TV with baking shows down here somewhere? Can Comet and I watch...what does he watch...National Geographic?"

"There could be a television if you wanted one." *Anything to keep her out of trouble.*

She considered it for a moment then nodded. "I'd like that."

"So would I, if it would keep you out of my books." He'd noticed the stack of them near her in the tub. She'd been reading them over the side and then carried them back down below. "I don't remember them having that many pictures in them," he murmured to himself.

"What's that supposed to mean?" she asked, squinting at him, talking around her fork.

"Nothing. Just that they're written in a language you can't possibly understand."

Her eyes narrowed even further. "I don't like how you treat me like I'm not very smart."

He held his hands up. "No. There's a sign on my wall in blood that says you are. Smart, devious, and apparently willing to escalate."

"You found it?" she asked, frowning.

"And read it," he told her. *No reason not to be honest.*

"Did you...wash it off?" Her voice was small. It was like he could feel her fading, and he didn't like that one bit.

"Of course not. It's my very own modern art piece. A Samantha O'Connor original."

Her eyes flashed up at him. "You're making fun of me. Again."

"No," he told her again, definitively. "I'm trying to make you laugh, for some strange reason."

She shrugged and looked away. "Why?"

"Probably so you won't burn things again while I'm gone." He bowed his head and leaned over slightly, so she would be forced to see him. "I do have some objects here I'm attached to."

She gave him a look then, just as sly as his fox could be. "Care to point them out?"

Rax laughed before answering. "All of the books. Please don't burn them."

She picked up her fork again. "And what if I only burn the pages with words?" she asked with casual menace.

"I'll teach you how to read them if it stops you."

The words were out of his mouth before he could assess whether or not he truly meant them. It just felt right to say at the time. But then the look she gave him then, open-eyed, open-mouthed, as she breathed, "Really?" and he knew he couldn't take it back.

Nor did he want to.

"Certainly. If it keeps you even vaguely compliant."

"When do we start?"

The majority of the night was left. Rax knew it wasn't too late for him to go back to his casino, but he also knew he needed to spend time here with her if he was going to stop her from further harm. "Now, I suppose," he told her. "Go pick the book from below you're most interested in."

She got up to do as she was told. He moved to be on her side of the table in her absence, wondering what she'd bring back, and he wasn't surprised when it was a bestiary. She sat back down beside him, placed the book between them, and opened it to a chapter on unicorns, another unsurprising choice. He watched her flip the key into her mouth to suck on like it was some kind of pacifier and he fought not to frown. "Do you want me to teach you, or just want me to read it to you?" he asked.

She looked concerned. "Mostly...I think I just want to know if everything in here is real."

"It's a big book."

She twisted to look at him. "Don't deflect, Worst, it's unbecoming."

"Fine," he said with a snort. "Everything in here is real. Somewhere else though. Not here." That was safe enough to tell her.

She frowned then, and he didn't know why. He was doing exactly what she wanted, wasn't he?

He leaned her direction slightly without touching her and started reading the words aloud, translating them into English, something about unicorns not really caring about virginity, then glanced at her. Her eyes were following as he read, from right to left.

The opposite of books in English on Earth.

He grabbed her chin and made her look at him. In the light of his kitchen, her eyes were fathomless blue, the kind of blue that started off light and then got darker as the shore dove away.

Have you always been able to understand me? he asked in his home tongue. She seemed appropriately confused, but he knew how smart she was. He changed tacks: *Your eyes are the color of a sea I want to swim in.*

She let out a little gasp at that, and he felt her heartrate bound beneath her chin where his fingers held her.

"You understood me," he said.

She yanked her chin away. "Don't flirt with me," she complained around the stone.

"Would you rather I threaten to strangle you to watch your pupils dilate?" he asked, tucking a finger beneath the curve of her lower lip to pull the key out of her mouth by its chain, watching her soft pink lips open to let it part, wishing he could push other things between them instead. "How long?"

She swallowed as he set it on her chest. "From my first bath. I realized when it was underwater I could read."

"Which progressed to this," he murmured, looking at the stone, shiny from her saliva. *What about now?* He asked her since the key was safely out of her mouth.

She tried for confusion again—emphasis on tried.

Earlier in the water, you looked like a mermaid I once fucked, he said aloud with a smirk, and watched her flush, shrugging her head and shoulders away from him. He rocked back, thinking of all of her perfect peachy skin he'd seen earlier, dusted with freckles like constellations, marred only by the three small scars someone else had given her. *Someone he wanted to find and kill.*

"You are a very smart girl, but only a so-so actress."

She crossed her arms. "Well, at least I'm not a mermaid fucker."

"You shouldn't knock things till you've tried them," he taunted, then jerked his chin at her neck. "Why didn't you tell me you understood?"

She gave him a baffled look and then guffawed. "I'm sorry, did I miss where we were on the same side? Like when you were telling your fox you lied to me when you pretended to swear?" He groaned as she continued, swiping an angry hand across her forehead where their blood had been comingled. "Yeah, I know exactly what you think of me." She shrank away from him even further. "Probably better hide your books and tie me down."

He watched her try to erase herself right in front of him, making herself small, bowing her head, and he felt like if he tried hard enough, he could watch her hopes rise like the smoke she'd made earlier, to try and disappear.

It was all utterly foolish.

He was going to be obsessed with her—and there was nothing she could do about it—until she returned his key.

He made a thoughtful noise and knew he only had himself to blame. Pretending to swear anything to a human as a dragon, how absurd. And now that that bridge was broken, there'd be no way to cross it with her again.

Did he even want to? *No.*

"There's more at stake than just your life, Red. Which is why I can't promise you a thing."

Her fingers found the chain around her neck and wrapped it, lifting it so that the stone swung freely. "It doesn't matter. Nothing here is real."

He found those words coming from her mouth strangely disappointing. He'd been so worried about keeping her body intact when perhaps he should've been more concerned about her mind. "I am."

She pointed at the book between them. "What page of that book are you on then?"

Rax stared at the bestiary and swallowed. At the rate he was going, it would be hopeless to try to reassimilate her into polite society, and things might be easier for the both of them if he confessed.

All the same, he found his hands hesitant to flip a few chapters back and show her. What if she didn't believe? He had no way to prove he was a dragon, seeing as his had been ripped away from him forcibly with magic, and was now living at the bottom of the ocean in a different world.

"That's what I thought," she whispered, shaking her head, putting a leg down, getting ready to walk away.

Four hundred seventy-three, he told her in his old tongue, to keep her there.

She hesitated. "That's very precise of you."

"You would be surprised at all the things I remember, and these books have been in my possession for a very long time."

She kept her eyes on his as she flipped to the back of the book, turning over thick and heavy pages, with scrawled text framed neatly around pictures until she found the chapter about dragons. She put the stone into her mouth again, and he watched her read, her eyes scanning from right to left, until she reached the section he'd torn out long ago, one that'd previously had a portrait of him.

"Do you believe me?" he asked, feeling an odd upwelling of concern than she might not.

"If you're real...and unicorns are real," she murmured around the stone, putting her head into her hands, "I don't know what to believe anymore."

He wanted to move toward her but it seemed wiser to give her space, so he pulled back. "I don't think I can help with that."

"Actually? You can." Her eyes dared him to leave her. Then he watched her flip through the book with alacrity, looking for something and finally finding it. "What is this?" She stared at a page for a moment and then tilted the book to show him.

A siren.

A single piece of the monster that was behind the Gate Below. The creatures that had cost him both his brother and his dragon. He shook his head quickly. "That's not what was in your apartment. You were haunted by a drowned one," he corrected her.

She pointed a finger at the illustration. "No, I want to know what this is," she repeated.

"Why?" She stared at the image, with its too many mouths, stricken by something, he couldn't tell what, and he wished he had a corollary to the key on him, something magical he could wear that would allow him to read her moods. "Are you all right?"

She shook the book at him, making it jump on the table with a thump. "Is it real? I need to know!"

He took the book from her and snapped it closed. "Reading about that will only give you nightmares."

"More nightmares," she corrected him softly. She took the book away from him. He didn't fight her for it as she moved to stand. He would never envy a human at the best of times, but he particularly would not now. She looked as fragile as the sandcastles she collected at her apartment. "I'm tired. I need to sleep."

"Of course," he told her, also standing, making sure to stay well out of her way. "Other than perhaps a television and pie—pumpkin this time—what else can I do?"

She took a long time to consider this, like her thoughts were hard to follow, and then shrugged, holding out her cloth-wrapped hand. "Probably more socks."

"Yes. And I'll get you an actual first aid kit. Though I hope you won't require it." She nodded and walked over to the stairs, and he called after her. "If I practice my piano, will it bother you?"

She shook her head subtly. "No."

He wanted to know what was wrong with her, what had changed, but why ask? She had more moods inside of her than there were waves in the sea. He pushed in his chair and headed to his piano. "All right then, Samantha. Good night."

SAMMY CLAMBERED into her bed and pulled the sheets up around herself, leaving the bestiary at the end of the couches. She wasn't ready to read the entry yet, even though she could.

Because it was real.

For years everyone had told her that she hadn't seen something terrible rise out of the sea to kill her parents; that the flapping things she'd seen in the wind must've been a long coat, like a trench coat, and that the reason she'd never seen the killer's face was that he'd been wearing a hood.

But what if all this time, she'd been right, and the reason she couldn't have seen it was because he didn't have one?

Or, he had too many faces to count? Too many mouths to count?

All of them screaming?

Sammy cupped her hands over her mouth to hold in a scream of her own, wincing as her chin hit the cut on her palm.

The thing that haunted her nightmares, the thing she'd taught herself to never talk about because no one would ever believe, that other kids mocked her for, and therapists deflected until she gave up on her own memories and nodded, yes, my parents were murdered by the Sandcastle Killer, a stupid name for a life-destroying crime, was in this book.

Why?

HOW?

She held his sheets up to her cheeks, trying to hold everything in, as waves of emotion crashed through her. It'd been bad enough when she'd finally 'accepted' that her parents died because of a serial killer, but to find out that their deaths had been caused by a monster from some other reality? She would've run upstairs to the bathroom and puked, only that would've invited more of Janvier's questions, and she didn't want to talk to him.

She just wanted to be alone with her sorrow. She'd lost her parents and then everyone else had told little eight year old her that she'd lost her mind, and what was worse was that she'd believed them. She'd told herself she had to, to survive, to just tell everyone what they wanted to hear, but every time she'd told them she hadn't seen the killer, she felt like a liar, and more and more of her soul had died inside until she wasn't sure how much of it she even had left.

Mr. Janvier started playing piano up above, a soft song, probably for her sake, if he believed her sleeping—but what she wanted was a loud, crashing piece. Something that would feel like chunks of sky falling from overhead, showing a world behind this one, where monsters roamed free and sometimes came over and killed little girl's families.

She dove under the covers like she had so many times as a child, like a cotton barrier could protect her from all evil, and quietly sobbed her heart out.

An hour or so later—*who the fuck knew?*—she felt like just a shell of herself. Her eyes were dry, and she hadn't moved, but she'd emerged from beneath the sheet to stare at the aquarium, watching the sharks swim inside of it, solitary and strong.

She wished she were one of them. A creature that nothing could hurt anymore. Able to fend for herself, to ignore things that didn't matter, and to handle things that did. Feared, loathed—she wouldn't mind that either. Other people's expectations would just slide off of her, washed away by endless sea.

Janvier stopped playing and she heard him take the stairs up to his level. It was clear from the way he acted that he was used to living here alone—from the fact that his bathroom door didn't have a lock, to the way he didn't feel a need to be quiet in his own home, even with her there. Maybe he didn't realize how easily sound traveled in this zoo exhibit of cement and glass. And then she heard him repeat the same phrases to himself as he had before, only now she could understand him:

Let all that is dragon in me slumber.

May my dragon lock the Gate Below in times of peace and in times of war,

That no one else's ears may hear a siren's terrible song.

It is my fate that I should do this, and no one else,

And I shall do it until the sirens die, or I do.

HER JAW DROPPED and she reached for the end of her bed to grab the bestiary and yank it open.

CHAPTER 12

AFTER THAT, SHE READ FOR THE REST OF THE NIGHT. EVERYTHING ABOUT the sirens that she could find, flipping through the pages of book after book like it was her job. She brought all the history books over to the aquarium's edge and placed her back against it, using its strange blue light to read by.

Comet floated overhead, peering down at her, using his suckers to gently tether him to the inside wall.

"I'm not burning anything," she whispered—except for the proverbial candle, at both ends—but this was the first time in her entire life that she felt like she'd ever had a lead.

The bestiary only mentioned sirens in passing but there had been other events in other books' historical pasts; monsters flying out of the sea, with too many wings and mouths, shrieking songs of terrible lies until the people listening died in horrible ways, killing themselves and others to escape the madness. Hunting through the books reminded her of being forced to read the Bible as a child. Each historian had their own slightly different version of events, but the one constant in all of them was that sirens were devastating. Killing solo travelers, taking out trade caravans, murdering entire small villages and towns, making ears bleed and skulls shatter.

She found that part all too easy to believe. She'd spent so long suppressing what'd happened to her parents, but now that she'd opened up the vault to her memories, images kept pouring out. Her parents running with her between them on the beach, her father shouting at her to *get in and lock the doors!* and the monster that no one would believe existed making her mother bleed out from her ears, right before she opened the door to their Buick and shoved Sammy inside.

Sammy had been screaming the entire time, traumatized, splashed with blood, and she remembered the moment that probably saved her life—when she'd crawled into the backseat, popped the seats down, and hidden in the trunk. She'd pulled the seat closed after her, listening to the thing howl outside—*you're not worth dying for, dying for, not worth, you're dying*—until it'd finally gone away.

And then just sitting there, believing what it'd told her. She wasn't worth dying for, yet her parents had, and now she was trapped.

Because there was no one else at the beach that morning.

She'd gotten the courage to go outside and grab the car keys from her father, risking the monster's return, indelibly scarred by the mess of his face, but it didn't help.

She could start the car but she didn't know what to do next, how to hit any of the pedals—she could barely reach them! All she could do was lean on the horn and hope someone heard her.

Eventually someone did and the rest was history. A horrible story, splashed across the front page and on the news for three weeks straight, until the next bad thing happened and she was forgotten. Her only mercy was that her name was common enough no one could get anything about her from a google search.

She closed her eyes from exhaustion and emotion.

She hadn't borne witness to her parent's final moments. They'd died alone. They didn't even get to know they'd saved her.

And she'd been saved...for what?

For this?

She rocked her head back against the aquarium glass behind her.

Comet was still there, watching down. He'd slowly lowered

himself to be on her level, draped around her shoulders on his side of the glass, reading along with her.

She looked at the mess of books she'd made around herself, using books on top of or inside other books for bookmarks, which was another thing she should probably ask Janvier for. She didn't think he'd want her dog-earing any of his precious pages.

But somebody had already desecrated these books ahead of her. Any time she got close to the end of the story, to what happened, how they stopped them, all the pages were ripped out.

Why?

"What happened?" she asked Comet in a whisper. His colors flashed in soothing tones, but he couldn't answer her.

She stood, exhausted and woozy, worn out from too many emotions, and she desperately had to pee. She snuck upstairs and thoroughly considered peeing in the kitchen sink before sneaking up one more floor. She stood at the landing, listening to the steady sound of Janvier's breath. He was shirtless and turned away from her, with the single sheet she'd left him wrapped around his hips, and she could see the ragged lines of the scars down his back even in the near-dark. She tip-toed past him, but he still stirred. "Red?"

"Shhh," she said, heading for the bathroom door.

"Are you all right?"

It was a good thing he was facing away from her. "Yes," she lied.

SAMANTHA WAS STILL SLEEPING when Rax got up the next day. He knew both because he didn't hear her and because the first thing he did was go swimming in the cold tank to get rid of his inconvenient hard-on. Doing so let him see straight into her room, where she'd made a jumble of all of his books. It was hard to concentrate on swimming after that.

"*She seeks knowledge,*" Hachiro told him, rippling up to his side. "*She only went to sleep an hour ago.*"

"Any knowledge in particular? Or is she just dismantling my rigorous organizational system to irritate me?"

"I believe she is interested in learning about sirens."

The exact thing he'd told her not to research, of course. Underneath the water, Rax groaned. Human minds weren't meant to understand the Realms, not without magical abilities. The sirens from the Odyssey were an interesting comparison, but visually the closest description he'd found was when he'd bothered to read the Bible a few decades back and recognized the creatures in Isiah that humans called Seraphim. Only instead of singing "holy, holy, holy," sirens from the Realms sang words that sounded true but inspired madness. There were myths of people besting them and learning actual truths, but that's all they were. The only reason Tarian had believed them was because he was desperate.

Rax frowned. He'd purchased swim trunks for the first time this century and had put them on for her because he'd expected to catch her staring again, and he wanted her to know that he respected her boundaries; more so than he had yesterday at least. And now he was swimming in the cumbersome things for nothing, while she was sleeping, probably having the selfsame nightmares he'd warned her about.

He made his way up in the tank until he finished and stepped out and found Smoke guarding his phone, his personal cell service in his home provided by his magic.

"It beeped without you," Smoke informed him, batting at it with a paw. Rax picked it up and found a text from Namir.

I have the phone and the knife at the Lynx now, if you want to pick them up.

I'll be right over, he texted back, then showered, dressed, and set oatmeal into the slow cooker.

"Be gentle with her," he warned Smoke before heading out the door to work.

· · ·

"It's an old enough phone that they didn't have to hurt it much," Namir said, sliding the phone and glass-bladed knife his way over his desk. There was a passcode taped to the phone's case. "You can use that to get into it now."

"Thanks," Rax said, fighting the temptation to open it up in front of the other man.

"Do I want to know whose that is?" Namir asked.

"You could probably guess," he said as he pocketed it.

Namir shook his head. "No, I can't, because I can't begin to wrap my head around the thought of you giving a shit about some human."

"I do not 'give a shit' about her," Rax said, quoting the other man's tone. "I merely want to make sure my path is clear."

"A path to…." Namir began, trying to lead him.

"I'm not sure yet," Rax told him. *Just hopefully not down to the bottom of the sea.*

The tiger-shifter squinted at him, then shrugged. "Well as happy as I was to kick Delphine out a second time and to run the casino myself, if you keep flaking out on me, I'm going to need to get a raise."

"Oh, and here I thought my warm companionship was reward enough," Rax told him with a snort, and Namir laughed. Rax opened up one of his desk drawers and pulled out a sheaf of cash, tossing it to the other shifter. "I need you to buy me a very large, very nice television, but you can keep the change as a bonus for your recent efforts."

Namir caught the envelope, and his eyes brightened. "Are we going to start sports betting now?"

"No. It's for personal use," Rax said.

Namir inhaled to speak but then hesitated.

"What?" Rax said, growling lightly.

"Most girls would prefer jewelry. Just saying."

"Not this particular one," Rax informed him.

Rax managed to wait until he was in the parking lot and his car doors were locked before he typed in Samantha's passcode, opening her phone up.

She'd missed thirty texts from a friend, someone named Lefty.

A drug dealer's name if he'd ever heard one. He then hopped into things to find he was wrong. 'Lefty' was clearly another woman around Samantha's age, who had known Samantha for a long time.

Yo, Sammy-bo-bammy, where are you???
I didn't really get a dress without you, I swear!
TEXT ME BACK OR ELSE!

ABOVE THAT WERE MORE protestations of innocence, a photo of a flowing white dress, and assorted shots of what had to be the Italian countryside.

He went through the rest of her phone. Other texts included Samantha sending movies of baby goats to someone who apparently never responded and not too much else. A series of podcasts that appeared to be all about strangely violent fascinations. It was clear those had given her the idea with all the blood.

This 'Lefty' person was the only person he had to worry about, clearly, and they were currently in another country. *Good.* He put his thumbs on the keyboard and tried to imitate Samantha.

I'm so sorry! I was busy, and then I lost my phone for days! he typed out and then added, *I'm not mad, don't worry—we'll talk when you get back!*

He hit send and tossed the phone into his glove box.

WHEN HE RETURNED, Samantha was still sleeping, and the oatmeal was stuck to the bottom of the slow cooker. He pushed it around with a wooden spoon, one she hadn't burned, and then decided to go down to check on her.

She was nestled inside all of his sheets, sleeping hard. She hadn't even washed off the mark he'd made on her forehead the prior night, she'd been too tired or too distraught. It'd been easy to scent her tears while he'd been playing the piano...he just hadn't known what to do about them. He couldn't provide her with any succor or make any promises. He couldn't very well solve her problems when he knew he was their cause.

He made a loop of the room, looking at the books on the floor without touching them. Hachiro was right; they were all open to stories about, or images of, the sirens. He sat on his heels near the last pile, scanning it.

Why?

What possible interest could she have in the beasts?

He'd think she heard his ritual, but she'd wanted to know about them prior to when they were sitting at the table with the pie. So it seemed like something else had triggered this.

Out of all the bizarre, glorious, or baffling creatures in the bestiary to read about and then apparently do a deep dive on, why choose the one that he'd dedicated most of his life to stopping?

He'd taken out all the stories that were about him in his books. He just didn't want them out there was all. Not even in his own personal copies. He'd gone through them all and torn out the pages and folded them away, they were at the bottom of his altar. He couldn't bring himself to destroy them, they were still artifacts from his past, but he also didn't want to read them ever again, nor for anyone else to be able to.

Rax stood up and made his way to her bed again, breathing her cinnamon scent in deep.

He knew he'd be able to smell things underwater if he condemned himself to add his magic to his dragon's, but that in the vast darkness of the below he'd never scent her cinnamon again.

Nor would he be able to if he killed her, to save himself.

His hand found the glass knife Namir had given him in its case in his pocket. The glassmaker had provided a metal tube for it this time and he'd found a condescending note inside that warned him to "be careful" with it. The glassmaker was more affronted by him breaking a blade he'd made than by any damage Rax might cause with it.

Rax wondered if the glassmaker's opinion would change if he

knew how close it was going to have to come to a certain red-haired girl's throat.

Probably not.

After all, she was a plain, normal human. A disposable type of creature, easily replaced by one of the few billion or more of them in line.

But watching Samantha's chest rise and fall beneath the blankets, seeing her eyelids flutter in her sleep, and reading the hidden curves of her body, Rax found himself wishing more than anything else that he had some solution that would work for both of them. He hoped that the knife in his pocket—or one of the other two knives that he'd empowered—would work when she woke tonight.

Until then though, at least in sleep she looked untroubled.

Too bad she couldn't always look like that, and too bad he couldn't give that peace to her.

MR. JANVIER WAS NOT AS quiet as his fox, so she knew he was in her room with her.

Was this it?

The reason he couldn't really promise not to kill her? Because he was going to, right now?

Should she confront him—or hide and hope that everything would go away?

He watched her sleep for a moment. She could hear his thoughtful breathing and then she was alone again before she could decide. She opened her eyes and watched him walk up her stairs with his head bowed.

Why…because he felt bad for everything he was doing to her?

Project much, Sammy?

No…no, no, no, no.

Do not assume anything kind or good of him. Captives do that because they're tired of their captivity, exhausted by being scared, scrabbling for kindness to pin their hope on.

I have to be smarter than that.

She just had to keep figuring things out was all.

The scent of the oatmeal he'd made for her hung in the air. Sure he couldn't promise *not* to kill her, but he also wasn't *trying* to starve her to death. That was a fact. As was her current level of freedom—unchained, and no cameras had been installed—and he wasn't pretending that what he was doing *wasn't* hurting her anymore.

He was rational. She just didn't understand his *rationale* was all.

So that was what her next step had to be—feigning compliance—and understanding.

Earning his trust, no matter what.

Because if she could prove to him that they were on the same team, then maybe she could make him see her point of view, or figure out a way to exploit his in her favor.

Sammy waited a good half hour before going upstairs, using the bathroom, and changing into fresh clothes; gray fleece leggings and a cream-colored sweater that came down to mid-thigh, before joining him on the living level.

"Is it breakfast, brunch, or lunch?" she asked him, heading into the kitchen, trying to sound lighthearted.

"There's still pie in the fridge, so it's up to you, no judgment," he said from his position on a couch near where she'd written her name in blood on the wall the day prior. He'd been quietly doing something with a knife, she realized, as he turned toward her. "Not to frighten you," he said, raising it up. "It's a replacement for the one you broke."

"I didn't break it," she said, scooping out oatmeal into a bowl for herself, as he rose to come nearer. "Technically, that was your stomach's fault."

"Hmm," he said, taking a seat at the kitchen table, clearly expecting her to join him. He was already dressed in going-out clothes: dark slacks and a fitted burgundy dress shirt, which brought out the fire in his eyes. "Tell me, what was your plan, if it'd worked? If you'd strewn all my guts out, what then?"

"Well, after I'd stopped puking, then I would've tried to get out."

"Nice to know you don't casually go around disemboweling people," he said and then asked, "How?"

"Called 911, I guess. With my imaginary phone." She shrugged, sitting down. He set the knife down between them, the handle toward her. *This was where it began.* She took a bite of oatmeal before picking it up and sawing vigorously at her necklace's chain. She could feel the glass vibrating against the metal links as it grated, but the chain didn't break.

He watched her carefully, like he always did. The same way she watched the sharks or Comet, she thought. Like she was something curious that he didn't understand.

"So eager to be free?" he asked.

"Assuming if you get this thing off of me that I get to live? Yes." She pretended to contemplate her freedom. "What does it do, anyhow? Surely you can tell me, Mister Worst." She looked around the room. "I mean, it's not like I can leave here, right?"

Janvier put his hand out for the knife and she set it down on the table for him. He picked it up and flicked its tip up at her, indicating that she should come closer. She stood and walked over to his side of the table to stand in front of him, lifting and holding all her hair up with both hands. He picked up the stone like he always did, chastely, but there was no way for him not to touch her skin and she was right, his touch did burn.

He looped the chain in his hand, ran it over the blade he held and used a hundred times more force than she had, sawing. She knew because the sound of glass on metal was infinitely louder, even though his hand protected her from the pressure.

"May I?" he asked, without explaining himself, with her standing there like she was about to be strip-searched in a prison movie, before he leaned forward and did what he wanted to anyway, catching the dangling stone in his own mouth, as he tried to break the chain again. His breath was hot on her skin. She couldn't help but smell him; he was so close, and the stubble on his chin grazed her collarbone. She closed her eyes and froze until he stopped, first releasing the chain and then pulling away, letting her neck tug the stone out of his mouth, to fall back, hot and wet with his spit, against her chest.

She stepped back quickly and let her hair fall, blinking at him, torn between pissed off and turned on. His gaze was inscrutable, *of-fucking-course,* and she knew she needed to figure out some way to play this to her advantage, fast. She rushed back to her side of the table, glad that her sports bra/sweater combo was definitely hiding her peaked nipples from him.

But if she was turned on? All the better. Make it seem genuine.

USE THIS, she growled at herself.

She gave him a shy look across the table, the kind that she knew men liked, because it made you seem smaller and them feel bigger, the kind that said, *"I'm helpless, please, teach me."*

But the encounter seemed to have had no effect on him. He set the knife back on the table with obvious disappointment and considered her for a long moment. She could almost see him deciding to tell her the truth. "It's a part of a key."

She hadn't been expecting that and broke character with a pout. "To, like, what, a treasure chest?"

"Hmm. Not really."

"But...what it locks is really important, right?" she asked him. "I mean, I don't want to get killed for just any old reason," she teased, keeping her voice light. She let her lips part softly, and she let herself give him a look she might have given him if he'd sucked on any part of her under any other setting moments ago without death on the line.

"It is important," he confirmed, without seeming affected by her feminine wiles, and then he stood. "I've got to run errands before work, but I'll be back in a few hours. Behave."

She let her gaze slide off of him in apparent disappointment and caught a glimpse of a very firm erection straining against his slacks before he could turn away from her. She gave a shrug, more of a very intentional full-body wriggle, and promised, "I'll try."

"Why do I doubt that?" he complained, picking up his suit jacket off the back of his couch and heading for the door.

Sammy let herself unabashedly look at him on his way out,

following the line of his slacks down his ass and thighs.

Got you.

SAMMY INTENDED on spending the rest of her unattended evening—*or morning? or midafternoon?*—doing two things: creating a sheath for the paring knife that she was definitely stealing from Janvier and cross-referencing siren stories with a clearer head.

The fox had strong feelings about both of those things. It started growling at her in the kitchen, where she'd taken one of Janvier's shoes—he wouldn't notice he had so many—and began cutting the tongues out of a pair to stitch together with the shoelaces, so she'd have a flat, safe pouch to hold the knife.

She knew it wouldn't actually stop Janvier if he got up to anything, but it'd make her feel better to have it on her, especially now that she was playing with...fuck, she'd graduated from fire to lightning. Flirting with him was lava-level shit.

Especially because sometimes his eyes did look like coals.

The fox growled at her upstairs, in the living area, from across the room, from closer, and eventually, she just shouted at it. "Just say it!"

It glowered. Its eyes were copper pennies, lighter versions of its owner's.

If Janvier was its owner.... She glowered back at it and then started stabbing holes through the leather to sew atop his nice dining room table. "I can understand you now, you know. And you must be able to understand me. I've heard him speak to you."

"So you know I'm going to tell him you're cutting things up the second he gets home."

She hadn't thought about that bit. "So?" She pretended not to care.

"And a mere knife isn't going to hurt him anyhow."

"Double *so*," she told it. If it was coming at his eyes, he'd blink, or between his legs, he'd jump. *Probably.* "What are you, anyhow?" she asked it, as she worked, poking a waxed shoelace through the holes she'd just made in the leather. The fox stopped growling, at least.

"A fox."

"And how do you know him?" she asked, setting the leather down for a moment. "Are you trapped here, too?"

"Hardly!" the fox sniffed. "I'm his oldest friend."

"A friend who he keeps trapped in here, all the time?" She gave the creature an innocent look. "Are you sure you're not a prisoner?"

It gnashed its teeth at her. "I know what you're trying, and it won't work."

"What, he kidnaps lots of women who understand foxes who then try to get on their good side?" The fox kept showing her its teeth, but then it chuckled. A strange, throaty noise that she was utterly unfamiliar with, but was more friendly than any other sound the creature had ever made at her. "What do you do here when there are no strange women, then?"

"I sleep. A lot. I'm quite old." It ran its teeth through its fur as though chasing a flea before snapping them up at her for watching.

"Ahhh." She finished her sewing, set the paring knife inside its new case, and then tucked it into the top of her leggings, at the small of her back. "You sure I can't convince you to keep a secret?" she asked, standing up.

"Not in the least. Plus, I still want to bite you," the fox told her, trotting by her feet.

"Why?" She paused by the trash. If the fox was going to tattle on her, she might as well throw Janvier's shoes away where he could see.

"Because I haven't gotten to bite anybody in a very long time," it complained, before following her downstairs to the mess she'd made of Janvier's books.

RAX ADJUSTED himself in his garage before he got into his Jag. He didn't need to go into the casino for hours yet—it was only five o'clock—but he did need to get away from her.

She knew what she was doing, of course. She hadn't come over to stand helplessly in front of him, hands raised, the very image of submission, for nothing. *Quiet for once, too.* He snorted at the memory.

He'd known things would eventually come to this. Samantha was too smart not to play all her cards if she felt cornered, and there was no real way for him to make her feel safe anymore.

What he needed to decide was what he would do about it from here on out.

Take advantage of her, playing her as she hoped she played him? Or push her away and try to spend his last days above the ocean—or with her, alive—with honor?

He'd taken the key into his mouth, hoping that if it unlocked words for her maybe it could unlock her, for him. But then once he was there, so close to her neck and breasts, breathing her cinnamon in.... He reached down to shift his cock again, between changing gears. How cruel it was that his last experience with a woman before going to the bottom of the sea might be with one who now thought him loathsome.

But that night at Belissima's, she hadn't. Thinking back, once they'd started, once he'd warmed her up...it was like she'd been in heat, and he'd had no choice but to respond in turn.

Even if she was a human.

He growled at himself for being hard now and at his mind for betraying him with memories, rolling his side window down to help cool himself and make his thoughts blow away.

THE CASINO RAN as it almost always did—minus drowned ones and the occasional human who couldn't handle their liquor—smoothly and profitably, but not quite distractingly enough for Rax to forget his problems. He stepped behind the bar to mix himself a fresh drink, wishing that the alcohol had the same effect on him as it did on certain other patrons.

"Aw man, you get demoted?" asked a voice he hadn't heard in quite some time. Rax looked up and over to see a short wide woman with close-cropped black hair, her eyes almost as black, dressed much the same as Rax was, only with suspenders. At seeing her, Rax couldn't help but smile.

"Siku! What are you having?" Deepwater shifters were rare and what Siku was rarer still— an Akhlut, able to shift between orca or wolf, depending on her mood. They'd first met in the 1800s, teaming up when Rax had spent a portion of his time sabotaging whaling vessels from aboard them, while as an orca Siku had worked from below.

Siku gave him a toothy grin and then looked over her shoulder, pointing out a curvy young-looking woman in a skimpy red dress. "I am having ever-so-much of that," she said and gave Rax a leer. "A shot of Grey Goose for myself, and a vodka cranberry for her."

"Of course," Rax said, intercepting his bartender to pour his friend's drink himself. "What brings you here?"

"Eh, the selkies asked me to come to town to mediate some dispute."

Rax gave her a concerned look. "Did you mishear the word 'mercenary?'"

Siku chuckled. "I definitely did not. I'm too old for that shit. But I have history with several of them, on both sides. They asked, and I agreed."

Rax grunted. Perhaps Delphine did not need his help so desperately after all.

"And then, I thought," Siku continued, "where better to take my girl, while I was here, but the den of iniquity of an old friend?"

"Sounds like I should thank your girl then. What's it been…twenty years?" he asked, handing the drinks over.

"At least."

He looked between Siku and the second drink like he might withhold it. "Is she twenty?"

Siku chortled. "When did you start carding, old man?"

"Never," Rax said with a grin. "I just haven't gotten to give you shit in a long while, is all." He took a sip of his own drink. "How are the fisheries?" Siku worked for the National Marine Fisheries Service, trying to stop humanity from harvesting the ocean dry.

"Eh," Siku said before shaking her head. "You read the news. You know how it is. You're lucky you're mostly illegal. I have to play by rules and shit; it sucks. And even when we do the right thing, humans keep fucking it up."

"And yet you sleep with one," he taunted her.

Siku polished off her drink in a gulp and slammed the glass down. Rax beckoned his bartender to set her up with another one. "Look at that ass. Don't tell me you're so old you're immune."

"I'm not," he admitted because his time with Samantha had definitely illustrated otherwise. "It's just all the trouble those kinds of asses are attached to, is all." Humans had been nothing but—beginning with Seris and ending with Samantha.

Siku's brow furrowed and she barked a laugh at him. "That's half the fun, old man."

He made a disparaging sound. "You're just as old as I am."

"Yes, but I'm a bon vivant," she said, pointing at herself before looking at him. "Look at you," she said, then making a circle of the room with her eyes. "You're managing all of this, and you don't even enjoy it." Siku enjoyed the semi-stunned look on his face for a moment before continuing. "See? After two centuries, I can give you shit back. Probably the only person in a five hundred mile radius who can."

Rax gave her a rueful expression. Siku didn't know that another dragon, Damian, lived less than thirty miles away, but it would've been pedantic to mention anyhow because she was right. "It's a little hard to have fun when I'm running a small empire," he said, trying to defend himself.

"You know what would fix that?"

"You're going to tell me whether I want to know or not," he said dryly.

Siku gave him another toothy grin. "Blow jobs."

Rax laughed. "There was a time I would've agreed with you."

Siku's youthful girlfriend ran up, carrying a double handful of chips and beaming, as Siku held a drink out to her. "Look what I won!" the girl exclaimed.

"Oh baby, that's awesome. Dinner's on you," Siku teased, then took a chip from the pile to tuck it into Rax's unbuttoned shirt-collar, where it fell down to his waistline, rattling against his abs as it fell. "Buy yourself something pretty," she told him with a laugh, hauling her girl to her side.

Namir spotted him and made to rush up, assuming the worst of Siku who he hadn't met before, but Rax subtly shook his head, laughing and unbuttoning his shirt low enough to pull the chip out. Rax knew Siku could flatten the tiger-shifter like a living hammer, and what was more than that, she was a friend. "Do you remember my stories from that one night?" he asked her. They'd shattered a whaling ship between both their efforts and cruelly left the cold-hearted sailors in the ocean to die, while the two of them had climbed aboard an iceberg and watched the northern lights, talking until dawn, listening to the waves lap as the iceberg melted. He hoped that night had meant as much to her as it had to him. Not that they'd slept together or anything of the sort, Siku's interests had always been in women, but that he'd trusted her with his truth. All of it. She was one of the few people alive who knew...everything.

Her expression sobered. "I do. Of course." She leaned over and addressed the girl at her side. "Montclair, give us a moment, will you?" The girl gave Rax a look then made herself scarce.

"Montclair?" he asked after she'd departed.

"Her parents thought it sounded fancy," Siku said and shrugged, then jerked her chin at him. "Fess up."

He stared at the last fingerful of liquid in his glass. "My dragon's time is almost up."

"No shit, really?" Siku asked and glared at him. "What about the key-thing and the lock?"

"No luck on that front. Unless I'm willing to commit murder, and even then, it's not guaranteed."

Her thick lips pursed. "Do they have it coming?"

Rax snorted. "Unfortunately, no."

"Shit," Siku cursed, extending the 'sh' an unreasonable length of time. "Although, we killed enough people together it ain't like I'm going to tell anyone if you change your mind."

"I appreciate that," he said grimly.

She inspected him further and made a show of it, looking him up and down, taking a step to her left, and then to her right, and then looked around the room. "Rax, what the fuck are you doing here?"

He frowned deeply. "What do you mean?"

"If a clock is ticking for you, if you do decide to go below…is this really where you want to spend the end of it?" He inhaled rather than answer her as she punched him in his arm. He took the blow without rocking as she continued. "Are you dead?"

"Not yet," he said, twisting his arm. She'd hit him with enough force she would have killed a human.

"Then figure out a way to fix shit, old man. Or at least book yourself something fun—or someone fun—to do before your funeral." Her dark eyes traced him up and down. "I can't have you dying or disappearing. That shit makes me feel even older than I am, you know?"

"Yes." Rax knew all too well, having lost the friends he had over the years.

Siku gave him a glare, shook her head, and shuddered. "I'm going to have to sleep with two girls to make myself feel young again tonight, after seeing you."

Rax tossed back the end of his drink. "How's Montclair feel about that, eh?"

A slow grin spread across Siku's face. "If I let her pick the other one? Just fine."

HOURS LATER, after Sammy'd gotten hungry and had made herself a snack—Janvier had definitely stocked his fridge up for her—she felt like a rookie FBI agent on a TV show, with books scattered all across the floor of her room, stories about the sirens arranged in what she believed was chronological order.

She'd hoped that she'd been too worked up the prior night to understand things, but now that she had more lights on and wasn't crying, the result was the same.

The sirens were awful. They attacked things and then eventually they went away behind some kind of Gate, and then the endings had been torn out of all the stories, leaving her to wonder what'd happened in the missing pages.

Had the Gate opened up? And what the hell was up with the weird prayer he said every night?

The gaps at the end of the books didn't seem wide enough to accommodate the passage of much more time....

Maybe there'd been extra volumes of the tomes though, and Janvier hadn't paid for the whole set?

Well, who would, if they kept getting them and all of the important parts were missing?

Sammy groaned at her own stupid joke. All of this work had likely been for nothing because if she asked him anything he was going to want to know why, and her desire to relive the experience of her parents' death for him was even lower than experiencing her own—because it would require being vulnerable.

There was so much already about him and his house and her being here...she couldn't stand the thought of giving him any additional leverage against her. He didn't deserve to know their stories, and besides, what was more, was that asking him wouldn't really change things.

It definitely wouldn't bring them back.

And having read all these stories about the sirens and seeing their illustration in the bestiary, she already felt one million times saner. Shittier about her entire goddamned childhood, one hundred percent. But at least one good thing had come out of all this, she thought, brushing her hand over another lovingly drawn illustration...she'd get to die knowing she hadn't made everything up.

SHE CHANGED INTO HER PAJAMAS, tossing her old clothes into the corner. Eventually she was going to have to figure out a laundry situation, assuming she got to live that long. Then she went upstairs to brush her teeth. The fox was snoozing on Janvier's couch in the living room, she hadn't seen Comet since he'd drifted by hours ago, and the sharks didn't seem to care what she did. She stretched her wrists out —they were tired from holding heavy books up—and yawned, feeling like a very down-market fairytale princess, as she crawled over the back of a couch to get into her nest of a bed.

Before she could fall asleep though, she heard the door open up, just a level above. Mister Worst, coming home.

Had she stayed up late, or had he come home early?

Part of her wanted to go and ask him, but she knew it was a weakness. She only wanted to talk to him because she was lonely. *The fox wasn't much of a conversationalist.* She bit back a quiet snort.

She heard him go about what was clearly his usual nighttime, she thought, routine: opening and closing the refrigerator, probably eating, then definitely washing a plate off in the sink. Then he walked up to his level. She heard the bathroom door open and close as he showered off his day. She knew he'd see the washcloth that she'd used earlier, wrung out and hung on the edge of his sink, and find the wet spot where she'd dried her face off if he used the wrong towel.

Then he left his bathroom and must've eased himself into bed because she didn't hear his feet again…but a few minutes later, she did hear something else.

Sammy had had more than enough boyfriends and shameless male roommates to identify the sound of a man jacking off. His breathing was quiet, probably for her sake, but there was no misidentifying the sound of skin over skin.

Maybe this was a daily thing for him and she'd just never timed it right before? Or maybe, after what happened earlier between them, he needed to release some tension.

He could've had sex with *anyone* at the club though, even women who didn't know he was the Lynx's owner. He was too beautiful to refuse. If you were in a happily committed relationship and Janvier tapped on your shoulder, you'd figure out a way to get a hall pass.

So why here, and why now?

She listened as his hand sped up, his quiet breathing got rougher. It was so animal, so filthy, and so…human. It proved that he wasn't carved out of some cruel block of ice, moving through life robotically.

Draconically, she corrected herself, biting the tip of her tongue as she listened in.

What if that time at Belissima's was the last time she'd get to have sex?

Even if the whole reason for it happening had been bullshit, just thinking about it sent a thrill through her body, and listening to him now wasn't helping. Knowing he was just a few steps above her, fiercely stroking the same cock that'd fucked her right.... One of her hands crept between her legs without thinking, rubbing the seam of her pajamas against herself, remembering the adept way his fingers had touched her in the wine cellar. She knew she was unreasonably turned on, more so as she fumbled her hand beneath her pajamas and underwear both, finding herself wet as she touched herself quickly skin on skin.

She screwed her eyes shut tight, listening, echoing his motions with her fingertips, remembering their past, and feeling violently ashamed as she desperately stroked her clit to catch up with him.

What was wrong with her? Why was she like this? Wasn't this dangerous as hell?

Probably the three most common questions she'd gotten to ask herself over the course of her entire lifetime.

But right now, she knew the answers: there was nothing wrong with her, she was lonely, and it was only as dangerous as she'd let it be. She knew she was only touching herself because listening to him was like being on the moon and discovering that the only other person there desired his own company over hers.

She was painfully lonely, so she was going with him, whether he liked it or not.

She threw her other arm across her face and bit into her sleeve, listening to his soft crescendo overhead, feeling her body match it, tensing up, wishing it was his hand touching her instead, and more, so much more.

He gave a soft grunt, his breathing deepened, and she swallowed down a moan, finishing herself at the same time he did. She lay there, breathing quietly through her mouth, listening to her heartbeat in her ears, winding down.

She didn't know much except that something, she didn't know what, was going to have to change between them.

And soon.

RAX MANAGED to finish an entire night at the casino, probably the first since Samantha had woken up at his place. He'd spent more time with Siku, which had forced him to mingle with the rest of the patrons, and she'd given him another stern look before he left, telling him he'd better check in with her again within a month, or else. But it wasn't like she'd left him her phone number or anything. When you lived as long as they had, you trusted in time to bring you back together rather than intent.

And then he'd gotten home.

Normally, he'd eat dinner and play piano until his mind was calm enough to go to sleep. But he couldn't. She was sleeping downstairs and there were little touches of her everywhere. Small marks she'd made on his table for some reason. A little bit more of the pie he'd made her was missing. And everything was suffused with her smell, her spicy cinnamon aroma. He cleaned it off himself before he went into work each night, but that meant that his nose was entirely unprepared for it when he came home. It hit him like a wall, and it didn't matter what he did, what he ate, or how he washed—*because they shared a bathroom*—it was always there.

It'd been bad enough when it'd impregnated his sheets—*that he still hadn't changed*—earlier.

But now, it was unavoidable.

He ran through his ritual and went into his bathroom. Her washcloth was on the edge of his sink, still damp. Her purple toothbrush was on the same ledge where his razor was.

She was so close, just two floors away from him and still so far, in that she'd rather be literally anywhere else.

196

He brushed his own teeth, took off his clothes, and crawled naked into his bed like he always did. The sheet brushing up against him, the way his pillow still smelled like her hair, the way she'd stood in front of him earlier—and the memory of the way she'd looked at him when he'd pulled away from her...frightened but also *turned on*.

Within moments he was painfully, achingly, hard, and he didn't have it as easy as Siku seemed to. He didn't want just any human; they were not interchangeable to him, as he mostly loathed their kind.

No, he wanted the one he shouldn't have most, the one sleeping just twenty feet down, the one who was going to pretend to want him too until she realized she'd never be free.

Unless he could make her somehow understand.

Could he?

If he took her to the sea and told her everything?

Maybe, at the least, she wouldn't hate him as much.

He lay there, his blood rushing through his body, breathing her in, exhaling her out, and then he gave up and reached for himself, stroking his cock in time with his breath, sliding his soft foreskin up and down his hard shaft. She was asleep, it didn't matter to her, but if he didn't come, it felt like he might die. His hand sped up and he imagined it was her—her hand, wrapped around his girth, traveling his length, lightly twisting expertly—her mouth, her ocean blue eyes staring dizzily up at him, the guttural sounds she'd make as the head of him beat against her throat—and then her sex, him shoving himself inside of her and her wet, hot, channel, holding him like a glove, thrusting relentlessly until she cried out and shuddered, coming on her own and then taking him with her. He pulled his hand up his straining cock a final time and felt the release of his balls pulsing as his cock spasmed, shooting heavy ropes of cum up and across his stomach. He stroked himself until he was finished, his imagination tormenting him with the idea that he could smell her heady scent, too, but he knew that it was lying to him.

He wiped himself clean. Tomorrow he would change his sheets.

And tell her the truth.

He had to.

CHAPTER 13

"RED, WAKE UP."

Samantha blinked. She felt really rested for the first time in ages.

"Red," Janvier called to her again, from the landing up above.

"What?" she asked, sitting up.

"I have a surprise for you."

"Would you say it was good or bad if you were me?" she called up, and she heard him chuckle before answering.

"Get dressed. I'm taking you outside."

She went up on her knees in her nest. "Why?"

"Only good reasons. I swear."

"You already know my feelings about your promises," she said, but she had a leg over the couch's edge and was running for the pile of clothing she was working through. She ran back to grab the knife she'd made a sheath for from her nest and then took everything she might need upstairs, not looking at the living level or him as she raced up for his bathroom.

It occurred to her while she was getting dressed that there was a chance it was for her own funeral—but if so, fuck it. As long as it was outdoors—she'd take it.

She came back downstairs completely dressed and found him

standing by the door holding both boots and a coat for her, looking surprisingly gallant. She put her hand to her mouth, then danced up to take the boots from him, taking them back to tug onto her feet from a safe distance. They were nice new Frye's, black leather booties with motorcycle buckles on the side.

"I guessed at your size," he said, watching her. He was already dressed to go out, wearing a wool peacoat instead of a suit jacket. With the coat and his dramatic features, he looked like a perfume ad model ready to go on an expensive adventure.

"You did okay," she said with a half-shrug, even though they fit her perfectly. "Did you ask the saleswoman what styles were popular with kidnapping victims this year?"

He laughed—a sound she enjoyed—and shook the coat at her. "Come on."

He was pleased with himself. *Why?* "I know it's not winter," she said, stepping hesitantly closer.

"True, but it is windy where we're going." He held it open for her, and she realized it was one of his. She stepped close enough to put one arm into a sleeve and let him help her with the other. It was too big for her but warm. "Wait, did you want to eat first?" he asked as she turned around.

She looked between him and the door, feeling like a dog waiting to be walked. "No."

"All right," he said, opening the door like it was nothing, letting her into his garage, the first bit of freedom she'd had in days.

Sammy wanted to run to his car but then she saw hers, parked beside it. "What's my Subi doing here?"

"I didn't want you to get any tickets."

"Uh, more like you didn't want to get caught. If my car's gone, people will assume I left town rather than being abducted."

"Is that so?" he asked her. She caught him trying not to grin. *Bastard.*

She peered in through the windows. All of Eumie's bloodstains in the backseat were gone. "You had it detailed?"

"Yes. It looked like there was blood in the upholstery. It took them ages to get out, apparently. My guy charged me a premium."

"Oh, it didn't just look like blood, Mr. Worst," she said with a head-shake. "That was like my most violent period ever. Oceanic amounts of blood everywhere. Like a horror movie. Your sharks would've been crawling out of the tank to get to it if they'd been there."

He paused, amusement and disbelief warring for control of his expression until he snorted. "Good thing I bought you tampons for your next one then." He hit something on a keyfob, and she heard the doors of his Jag unlock. "Get in."

SAMMY SAT, perched in the passenger seat, wondering what else he'd updated on his vintage car from the seventies, but not wanting to let on she knew anything by asking questions. "Where are we going?" she asked instead, craning her neck for even the tiniest bit of light as his garage doors opened. They were someplace desolate, outside of town. She didn't recognize the road, and it was nighttime. "No sun," she whispered.

"No. But there's sky though," he said, pointing up.

"What about wind?" she asked, looking at her car door disappoint-edly. The usual hand-cranks for a car this old were gone, clearly replaced with more modern gear, but there were no buttons for her to try.

"Just as you don't trust me, I don't entirely trust you, alas. But…I was hoping," he began, glancing over at her. "Just wait a bit. You'll see."

She huddled back into his coat in frustration. It smelled like him. "Do you really think I'd try to throw myself out a window on the open road?"

He gave her another look as half his full lips curled into a grin. "Red, I wouldn't put anything past you."

IT SEEMED like they were going further away from civilization, and not toward, and she realized they were on one of the highways that paralleled the ocean when she saw a road sign not long after. What time was it? It was truly dark out and there wasn't much traffic. She leaned her head against the window glass, staring up at a sliver of moon, trying to remember what it'd been when she'd seen it last, but truth was she'd never paid attention and she wouldn't know whether it was waxing or waning besides. You needed to see a moon more than one night in a row to know which direction it was going about its business.

But with people, sometimes you could just guess right the first time out.

"What are you thinking?" he asked her, looking over.

The usual. How long we're going to play this game. How long I can stay sane while we play it? "The moon," she only half-lied. "I read about werewolves in your book. Do you know any?"

"Yes. Quite a few."

She turned toward him in the car. "You're...not teasing me?"

He shook his head roughly. "No. Not anymore."

She inhaled deeply and settled back, playing her tongue against her lips in thought.

"What?" he asked. "I thought you'd appreciate the honesty."

Not really. Because if you start telling me things now, it means something's changed. "I'm just surprised, is all."

"I could tell you about them, if you wanted. More than what the books say, at least."

Sammy snorted softly. Maybe she could pull a reverse Scheherazade and stay alive by asking the right questions. "Like what?"

He glanced over at her again, his eyes somehow bright in the night. "Like most of them drink too much. And they're very live-by-the-sword, die-by-the-sword types."

"And dragons aren't?" she asked him, trying to sound like she was teasing.

"We can be," he admitted. "Though I like to think we're better at long term planning."

"How many dragons do you know?" she asked him.

"How many dragons have I known, might be the better question."

She watched his strong hands tighten on the steering wheel as he took an exit toward the ocean. He was driving fast and she liked that, but only because he wasn't reckless; he was maintaining complete control. He changed gears, working the Jag's pedals fluidly. It made her jealous of the car, as she felt it respond to his touch. "There are more of us, back where I come from."

She tucked a lock of hair behind her ear, all the better to look at him. "The same place the books come from?"

"Yes."

"Where is that?" The books always called where they were from the Realms, which wasn't very helpful. It was like calling Earth, Earth.

"There's a particular Realm where I come from, but there's more than one of them. They're all magical, obviously. It's rather hard to explain."

But, she realized, he wanted to. She leaned closer to him in encouragement, desperate for even the smallest crumb. "Tell me about yours then."

He took his eyes off the road long enough to stare at her, and she realized how close they were in the car, trapped together beneath its small roof. "I'd actually really like that. Hold on."

He took another side road at speed, and then another, and Sammy realized they were driving right out onto the beach at night.

"Driving on sand's a magical prerogative," he said, as the car bounced up and down dunes until it was at the water's edge, in front of a receding tide.

Sammy stared out at the moonlit ocean in the dark. The closest she'd gotten to the ocean since her parents died was that childhood trip to the aquarium, another reason why she'd only sat in front of the octopus tank. "Why are we here, Mister Worst?" she whispered, feeling her throat close up.

"I wanted to talk to you was all. And I thought you'd want to get out of the house. I know it's not daylight, but if you truly wanted to feel the wind, we can get out and walk."

Sammy swiveled her head back and forth quickly. "I...I don't like beaches."

"Why not?"

"Because," she said, looking away, repeating the answer he'd so often given her.

But the truth was, she could tell him about her parents...if she wanted to. There would never be a better segue. *And maybe if he found out she was an orphan, he'd want to kill her slightly less.* She brought her hands to her face.

"Samantha?" he asked, with what sounded like genuine worry in his voice.

The car suddenly shook.

She screamed in terror, she couldn't help it, and he lunged over her, shielding her with his body. The shaking stopped, but her screaming didn't and then the rocking started again, the car shifting back and forth.

"It's okay—it's okay," he told her, carefully holding himself over her without touching her, but it felt like he took all the space in the car up. She felt his chin over her head, strands of her hair catching on his stubble, as she panted for air near his chest. She closed her eyes and tried to concentrate on his oiled-leather scent instead of her rising panic. "It's just an earthquake, is all," he said, sounding less thrilled about that.

"Are you sure?" she whispered with next to no sound.

"Yes," he reassured her, sinking back into his own seat, taking her in again, and totally misreading her fear. "I shouldn't have lunged at you—obviously, nothing's going to fall on us outside."

Sammy didn't know whether she wanted to look through the windows or not. What would she do if she did see a siren out there?

What would happen if she did and he didn't believe her?

She took long, deep breaths, trying to get ahold of herself. "There...was an earthquake the other day. Back when I was in my apartment. Whenever that was."

"Hmm." He made a thoughtful sound then looked outside the car himself. "I do want to have this talk, but I need to check on something first." He pulled himself out of his coat, and then his hands went for his collar. "You'll have to excuse me," he said, as he started unbuttoning his shirt.

Her eyes followed his hands down his chest in disbelief. "What?"

"I think I need to go out for a bit."

"Out there?" Her voice rose in pitch and volume as she looked at the blackness all around them.

"Just for a fast swim. I want to check on something," he said, pulling his shirt off. She saw him kicking his shoes off as his hands dropped for the belt of his slacks.

"No," she commanded him, watching him unzip his slacks in horror. "Why?"

"I spend most of my time in magical environments. I didn't know there'd been earthquakes recently."

"So?" She watched him rise up in his seat and tug his slacks off, kicking his way out of them.

"So, it's probably nothing. But I'm going to go out and check on something, I'll be right back. And then we can finish our conversation. I promise." He put his hand on his door, and she grabbed for his other one.

"I don't believe you," she told him.

He looked between her hand on his arm and her. "It's a real promise, Samantha."

"It's...not that, it's...," she began, but he was already pulling free of her, stepping outside faster than she could access the part of her that could say those words, that people died on the beach, in horrible ways, all the time, and please *don't leave her!* "Please," she said, and realized she was almost as unfamiliar saying it as he was, now. "Please, stay here," she pleaded. "I'll do anything—"

"It's not you, Samantha."

"Anything! Anything! *I'll be good!*" Her voice rose and broke.

But then he closed the door on her and looked in at her, standing outside in just his boxer briefs. The moonlight slid over all of his muscles like he was a statue, but he wasn't. He was about *to leave her.* Her stomach clenched and churned.

"I'll be back," he repeated and did a thing with his hand, waving in the car's direction before turning to walk into the ocean.

Sammy beat on the windows and started screaming at him not to go.

RAX WALKED AWAY from his car and Samantha inside of it, listening to her shout at him. *So panicked, all of the time.* It made him feel sorry for her, which was what she wanted, of course.

He looked over his shoulder and didn't see her, she must've ducked down inside his car for some reason.

She was so strange. Beautiful and compelling, but also broken. Too prideful to admit it, or perhaps she didn't think it true, but she had more sharp edges on her than all his knives put together. If she bunned her orange-red hair atop her head sometimes, just like a furling rose, well, the rest of her was wrapped in thorns.

He was up to his thighs in the freezing water now. He dove in and swam beneath the waves straight out, feeling in his element again.

Not that he enjoyed swimming in the open ocean as a man—it reminded him of everything he missed. The ocean's strength and power reminded him of when he'd been able to be his dragon, fully, how he'd been able to slice through the waves, utterly unstoppable, at home in his domain. Swimming in it as a man couldn't begin to compare.

The shore dove away from him into darkness and he followed it, dropping as it did, trying to feel for anything out of place. Earthquakes weren't improbable locally, but they were uncommon, and now that the Gate Below was sending drowned ones for the key—it hadn't occurred to him earlier, but Rolm's reanimated corpse had to have come from the oceans of his home.

But if so, how did it get to Earth to visit him?

There must have been some point of connection, and that's why the earthquakes made him worried. Shifting tectonic plates weren't the only things that could create pressure that needed to be released.

He swam deeper in the dark, relying on his other senses to answer him, feeling the profile of the seafloor below him as he swam over it in a way he couldn't have quantified on the ground. It was just that he knew where it was, the same way he could smell-taste-feel the salt-water around him and knew what else swam near.

A shoal of fish parted around him, he couldn't see them, but he could feel the rippling of their efforts to swim out of reach, their tiny currents reporting in all along his body, as the thing that was still predator in him told him of their heat. If he'd wanted to grab one he could have, easily. He surged forward, concentrating his power and pulsing it out in bursts, listening, feeling, intuiting anything that might be out of place around him—and then he heard it.

The low thrumming sensation of the siren's song. Underwater it was safe to hear, its maddening magic blunted by the medium it traveled through, but it was unmistakable.

How?

He followed his ears until light he didn't want to believe he was seeing began to brighten up the dark. The quality of the water changed around him, changing from the polluted sea of Earth to waters just as cold but far more pure. He was horrified but he couldn't stop himself; he kept going forward, threading himself along an ever brightening magic course, where the taste of the water was familiar, knowing what he was going to find.

A rift.

A temporary connection between Earth and the world of his home —in this case, between the bottom of the ocean here, and a space in the Below, inside the Gate. Arcane light radiated in all directions, almost painful for his eyes to see, and in the center of it, a cluster of madly angled wings, scrabbling claws, and shining eyes. Sirens, on the other side, desperate to break free, the magic from the Gate Below still managing to hold them back.

And beneath their cries and songs and whispers, Rax heard a resonant steady beat.

His own dragon's heartbeat, coming through?

No. His dragon's was much slower, in its currently suspended state.

But...he knew it was another dragon.

Rax swam as close to the rift as he dared and whispered, "Tarian?" to himself.

Oh, God.

He'd assumed when he'd locked the door on his brother—*when his brother had given him no choice but to, it was either shut the door or set the sirens free on the world*—that the sirens would've torn him apart eventually.

Not...that he'd imprisoned his brother in there, too.

Rax clutched his stomach and doubled over as the light from the rift dimmed, the connection between the worlds collapsed, and the Gate Below was Realms away, again.

WHEN SAMMY LOST sight of Janvier, she took off her seatbelt and put her head between her knees to breathe.

He'd just left her. Here. Alone. On the beach. In a car.

In the goddamned dark.

Of course she was panicked. There was no reason for her not to be. He'd abandoned her, and what if he didn't come back?

And that *thing* did?

When she rose up, she beat at all the windows of the car with her hands, then leveraged her seat back so that she could kick out at each window in turn, with all her strength, yelling out in anger, and doing nothing but exhausting herself.

After that, she caught her breath, laying down, staring up at the Jag's cream-colored ceiling upholstery, now dark gray in the night, wondering who or what god she'd pissed off for this to happen to her for a second time.

Then she pulled out her knife from the waistband of her leggings and tried to crack the seam of the window. If she could leverage it in there somehow, maybe make a gap, and send something down to pop the lock...this was an older car, it should've worked, but whatever he'd done with his hand before he left—*magic*—had sealed it off to her. She pressed and pulled so hard with her knife that it seemed like it might break before she gave up.

Where the fuck was he?

She could barely bring herself to look out at the water. It felt like at least half an hour had gone by. The moon had definitely moved in the sky. She stabbed the driver's seat in frustration, ready to make him regret leaving her here alone anyway she could—and then she felt the car rock.

Sammy whirled, looking in the direction the force had come from and didn't see anything. But the car rocked again.

Another earthquake?

She bit back a scream and dared to look toward the ocean, where a figure was resolving, coming out of the tide.

Janvier, back at last, and she was going to give him such a piece of her mind! *What the fuck had he been thinking?*

But whatever was walking toward her didn't have his steady stride. Instead, it lurched, looking like it was having a hard time pulling itself from the water. Sammy gasped as she spotted another one just like it, coming out of the next rolling wave, and behind that, a third, all of them lumbering for the car.

No.

A part of her mind started screaming and wouldn't stop. If she'd been back in her apartment, or at Janvier's house, or anywhere-the-fuck-else-but-here she maybe could've handled it better, but something inside her mind broke. She felt a rush of heat between her legs as she screamed helplessly and peed herself, right as the first creature put its hands on the other side of the window and shook the car again, looking in with its dead black-on-black eyes and dripping, puffy, skin.

One by one they surrounded the car, hands on the windows, repelled by the same magic—*she hoped*—that kept her trapped in. She screamed until her throat tore as the car rocked, and she scrabbled into the backseat. If she saved herself in a trunk once, she could do it again. She slashed the small chairs to pieces, looking for a latch, plunging her hands into the stuffing to pull chunks of it out, trying to climb through to freedom as if the leather interior was hiding a path to Narnia, but she couldn't find shit behind the wads of stuffing except a smooth metal panel.

She'd been focused on working despite their rocking the car, hammering their sickly fists against the window glass, ignoring the way everything around her smelled like piss and terror, but now as she was forced to give up, she looked over and saw all their horrible eyes staring in, blackness seeping from them, their jaws hanging open as more foulness poured out, gurgling things she couldn't understand with soft floppy tongues.

And they...were making progress.

Because every time they hit the car with their overly large hands, she saw something outside shimmer, until there were so many of them hitting it that it wouldn't stop shimmering, like the moonlight on ocean waves, and she knew exactly what was happening from the books she'd read.

It meant that Janvier's magic was about to break.

Then it would just be her alone, trapped in here, with them.

She threw up, dry heaving into the driver's side, just air and bile, because there was nothing in her stomach. When the drowned ones finally broke in, would she have a chance? They always made it look so easy in zombie movies but in real life, fuck no. If there were people around your car twenty feet deep, you weren't coming back.

But these weren't people, or zombies—and she'd read about them! According to his stupid books, drowned ones weren't strong individually. Their strength was in their numbers. And if she could just start popping them like the books said would work, before they got hold of her and held her down—or worse yet, took her out to sea to join them....

The shimmering on the passenger side increased until it shattered and there was nothing protecting that side of the car anymore. She screamed and scrambled over to the driver's seat as they pried the passenger window down from the outside and shoved it open a few inches— then she recovered herself enough to lunge over and stab at their fingers.

Just the slightest prick and the creatures outside exploded, blacking out the window with she didn't know what, but it smelled foul, and now she couldn't see out anymore. She kept stabbing anything that reached in by the light of the interior light up above, and she was screaming, she distantly heard herself like she wasn't *her* anymore, like she was just some creature made of anger and fear, then the window shattered, and now there were whole arms coming in, swatting at her, and she wasn't fast enough. She was never going to be fast enough, and the whole car was rocking like they were already out to sea.

She shrieked in terror and rage and her left shoulder hit the horn on the steering wheel, and suddenly she was a little girl again, utterly lost, completely forgotten, alone in the entire world. She sobbed, blindly swiping her right arm out with its knife because she was unable to see through her tears. This was it. *There were too many of them.* It was her time to die, just like she should've died the first time, with her Mum and Pop. The sirens were right, just like they'd told her —she wasn't worth dying for. They'd always been right, she'd never mattered to anyone, and now she never would.

She curled into a ball, leaning against the horn with all her might, waiting for the death that she'd always known was stalking her her entire life to finally catch up.

"SAMANTHA!" shouted a voice from the direction of the sea.

It wasn't real, she didn't hear it, and the arms didn't stop. It was just the fever dream of her overheated brain, granting her one last wish before she disappeared.

"SAMANTHA!" she heard shouted again.

She blinked her eyes open and looked up, snorting back tears, as the entire car rocked again, only this time with blue light, and the wall of drowned ones in front of her exploded and disappeared.

She could see through the empty space where the window had been, it showed her the waves of the ocean, and someone was running out of them, a man, not a drowned one, and he was screaming her name. "SAMANTHA!"

But other drowned ones clambered back in, blocking him from view, and the sound of the horn now felt like her own heartbeat, beating so fast it was just one continuous flat line. All she held was terror; there was no room for hope.

"SAMANTHA!" The voice was a growl now, and blue light hit the Jaguar over and over until all the drowned ones fell apart, and then the window framed Janvier again. He had an unholy glow about him, like he had harnessed the moon to his cause. His muscular chest was heaving and he'd slowed now, walking up to the side of the car with a hand out, approaching it like she was a beast caged inside.

But there was still *ocean* visible, all around him.

Anything could come out of it.

At any time.

She dove through the broken window, feeling the glass there cut against her hands and scrape against her coat until she was outside, and then she ran, not toward him, but away from the water, away, away, away, until he tackled her, catching her leg with one hand, making her fall down against the sand. The wind knocked out of her as she landed, leaving her gasping, just like she might if she'd drowned, but she made it up to her forearms and turned to look at him. He was getting to his knees behind her, his hand still locked around her ankle, his eyes alive with flame and his expression full of a humbling concern.

He cared about her.

A little.

Maybe the sirens were wrong.

"Samantha?" he asked, at a much more reasonable volume, and she double backed over herself to crawl into his arms and press herself against his naked chest, feeling sand and salt grind between her cheek and his hot skin. She clung to him, trying and failing not to cry. And then she reached down to grab hold of his wrist that held her ankle and pulled it up around her, and then his other arm, too, and he let her, stiffly, either unaccustomed to the motion of hugging another being or because he was afraid. She didn't care which was true, she fucking needed to be held, and as his arms finally cinched around her of their own accord, she started to feel safe again, which set off a whole new wave of tears.

It was okay. Everything was going to be okay. She knew she was whispering to herself and didn't care if he heard her.

For right now, as long as he was between her and the open ocean, it would be all right.

RAX SWAM back to the shore as quickly as he could, chased by his own horror, following the same path out as he'd taken in and when he breached the waves, the first thing he heard was his car's horn.

He cursed. He hadn't even thought of silencing it—*she was too smart for her own good*—of course, she was trying to get help.

But then, as he knocked the water from his face with a hand, he saw why. His Jaguar was surrounded by seventy drowned ones, picking up his car with their ineffectual fingers, trying to take his damn Jag out to sea.

With Samantha trapped inside of it.

He was not a dragon anymore but he felt flooded with power as though he were, and he'd never felt an urge so strong to change before while trapped as human, not even prior times he'd risked his life.

It was one thing for him to be attacked; it happened with surprising frequency, so much so that he was casual about it, but at the thought of one bad thing happening to *her,* magic leaped into his hands to cast as he tore his way up the sand, running as fast as he could while shouting her name so she'd know that he was coming for her.

"SAMANTHA!" *If they had hurt so much as one strand of hair on her head,* "SAMANTHA!" he shouted, the wind ripping her name from his mouth.

He couldn't see into his car past them. He cast out a magical wave ahead of him, wiping out all the drowned ones on his side, he watched his car rock with the force of it. He caught a glimpse of her inside the car through a broken window—*clearly terrified, but alive!*—as drowned ones from the other sides of the car mindlessly moved over to replace their brethren.

The Gate didn't care if he gave up his life for a fate worse than death in joining his dragon at the bottom of the sea, just like it didn't care if Samantha died underwater in the arms of a drowned one. All it cared about was being locked, and as long as Samantha still held a portion of the key, they would be relentless.

Her shrieks of terror pierced his soul.

"SAMANTHA!" he called for her with a growl and shoved wall after wall of magic forward until all of the drowned ones were obliterated, and he was nearly at his car's side.

She...hadn't stopped screaming. Or pressing the horn. Her hair was wild, as were her eyes, and he wasn't entirely sure she was *there* anymore. He slowed down so as not to scare her further, putting out a hand, willing her to remember who he was.

The man who'd left her alone on the beach like she had begged him not to.

And then, before he could react, she'd jumped through the open window. He could scent her blood in the air. *And what the fuck did it say about him that he knew what her blood smelled like?* As she ran around the front of the car and back toward the road he lunged after her, grabbing her ankle and catching himself on his knees, bringing her tumbling down with a dull thud in the muck covered sand.

He had to catch her, he couldn't let her go, it was for her own safety, surely now she'd get that—but he still expected her to kick him, or slip her foot out of the boot to escape. Then she looked back at him, breathless and terrified, and crawled into his arms, pressing her shivering form against him, the scent of her blood and cinnamon mixed equally with her tears.

He...froze.

He wanted to hold her with all his might, but if she didn't want that hadn't he already done enough to her? He grit his teeth and bowed his head and then her hands were finding his, wrapping his arms around her, making him hold her as though he were a human-sized doll. At that moment it felt like his heart stopped and when it restarted, several seconds later—he was a different man.

For the first time in eight hundred years, he felt whole.

Even without his dragon.

Like something long lost to him had been returned.

Some icy part of his soul cracked and thawed as he cinched his arms around her, pulling her to him, letting him feel the slight line of her body against his beneath her coat. He ran his cheek against her hair as she started whispering to herself, telling herself that it was going to be okay as she kept crying, which only made him hold her tighter. "It *is* going to be okay," he swore, echoing her. "I promise, and I mean it, I swear."

"Liar," she sobbed from the vicinity of his chest; he could feel her lips brush against his skin as she spoke. No matter how tough she was, she was still human, and he had almost broken her on accident. He dared to stroke his thumb where he held her in his arms, against wool, wishing it were skin.

"Not this time," he said, shaking his head, worrying his chin against her. "Samantha, I never would have left if I had known." How long had he been gone? He could see the path the drowned ones had dragged the car along, five hundred feet closer to the ocean than they'd been when he'd parked. No wonder she'd nearly lost her mind. "Please. Believe me."

She pulled her head away from his chest and sniffled. "I don't know if I can." And then she seemed to come to her senses, pushing away from him, and he let her go. "You left me to die, Worst."

"I did not," he refuted her. "Samantha, I..." he began, to, what, tell her everything he'd meant to when he'd first brought her out here? And what he'd just discovered below about his brother? When she was still breathing hard and halfway-shattered? *Now was not the fucking time.* "I would never," he repeated softly. "Please, believe me."

She shook her head and stood up, dusting herself off as she stared at the ground. "Thank you for rescuing me. Please take me home," she said, utterly devoid of emotion, and that hurt him almost as badly as her terrified screams had earlier or the scent of her fresh blood.

He stood and looked at her, illuminated by the door light behind her, watching her stare bleakly forward, thinking only the worst of him. Anything that he thought he'd crushed from her soul before—no, that'd all been for show. This was her at her lowest.

This was, through his carelessness and cruelty, the Samantha that he'd made of her.

The version of her that he'd earned.

He'd given so much of himself to his cold and sleeping dragon over the years that some nights he'd wondered how much of his human-heart was left. Now he knew its measure because he could feel it breaking on her behalf. And it was only the knowledge that him falling to his knees in the sand would be self-indulgent in the extreme that stopped him from doing it because he certainly fucking wanted to.

He hurt from hurting his brother, he knew, he'd swam back with that horrific knowledge, echoing in his soul. It was like his discovery had ripped off a scar on a very old wound. It was an awful, yet some-what familiar, ache.

But now, watching her, he hurt like someone had reached in with both hands to grasp his heart and were prying it apart at its folds with their thumbs. It was a crushing agony that made it hard to breathe.

Why?

"Get in the car, Red," he commanded her and then watched her do it without question.

JANVIER PULLED on his clothes and drove them away. He could only stand the first five miles in silence. After that, he wanted to know if "there was anything he could do," or "if she was okay," or "please Samantha...say something."

But she didn't honor any of his attempts at conversation with a response. Everything he did had the subtext of 'come back to life for me.' But she wasn't a child, nor was she his toy, and she didn't owe him a goddamned thing.

"Are you cut badly?" he pressed her.

She shrugged one shoulder and deigned to answer. "I've been cut worse."

He hauled the car over to the side of the road, Sammy heard its tires grind over gravel as he waved his fingers, and the cabin was illuminated with light. "Fucking show me," he demanded, even as she curled her hands into fists and shoved them in her pockets. "Why are you so stubborn?" he snapped.

"Probably for the same reason that you're an asshole; it's an innate state."

He growled at her. "Show me where you hurt," he enunciated slowly, like a threat.

Sammy stared at him blankly for a few moments, trying to actually quantify that with a response. When had she started hurting, and when the fuck would it end? Had it ever let up in the meantime? Or was there a part of her inside herself that was going to be screaming on a beach for the rest of her life?

She yanked her hands out of her pockets and grabbed the neckline of her sweater beneath her coat, hauling it down, not to flash him her chest but to show him the space filled by her broken heart. "I. Hurt. All. Over!" she screamed at him, biting back fresh sobs. "Are you fucking happy now?" She let go of her neckline and felt it rebound as she twisted away from him, staring out her broken window.

All she heard was the sound of the wind outside rushing by and the roughness of his breath.

"No," he said softly and pulled his car back on the road.

TWENTY MINUTES LATER, they were inside his garage. He'd pulled over on a side-road and then it was like they'd pierced a magic veil. She knew which direction the town was now, at least, if she ever got to leave here and not be chased by half-dead things.

He took a moment to survey all the destruction she'd caused inside his very expensive vehicle before turning to her, and she shrugged herself down, expecting him to yell. But instead, his voice was low and calm. "I know you're pissed at me, Samantha, and you have every right to be."

He didn't even know. He had no idea what he'd done to her. She'd been willing to tell him her truth if he'd only waited, but he couldn't be bothered, and now she was full of jagged pieces she'd have to put away again and it was all his fault.

"But for what it's worth, which I know right now is not much to you," he said, raising his hands to run them through his hair, "I'm sorry." He twisted toward her in his seat, and he still hadn't buttoned his shirt up, so she could see the outline of each and every one of his abdominal muscles because she had no interest in meeting his eyes. "If I could take all this back, undo it somehow, figure out a way to fix it— I would. You have no idea how badly I wish I possessed some ability to time travel, truly." He made a quiet noise then. "I only wish," he began, and then stopped himself. "No, what I wish is not worth troubling you with. Just know that I will never not listen to you again. From here on out."

Sammy hugged herself in his coat in the garage's dim light. Her throat hurt, her hands hurt, her heart hurt, but the worst thing was almost as bad as everything else she'd gone through tonight that a traitorous part of herself wanted to *believe him*. To cling to any shred of hope he dangled out.

Especially, she thought, as she raised her gaze to meet his and found his expression soft and open, *when he looked at her like that.*

Like for once he valued her, and not what was on her necklace's chain.

Tears she was ashamed of sprang to her eyes at the thought of his kindness, and she cursed herself for being weak. "Can you," she asked, waving him out of the car, asking for privacy, before putting her head in her hands to hide.

He inhaled, clearly worried about leaving her alone versus doing as she'd asked. "The garage is magically locked, so please don't waste your energy. Just, when you're ready...come in." She felt the car shift as he exited it, and the door close, as he left her alone to sob.

She curled up in a ball in the passenger seat, closed her eyes, and let herself cry until she was utterly exhausted and there were no more tears inside of her. She was so, so, tired. Of being in danger. Of trying to be in control and failing. Of fighting. Of not knowing if there was a way out. Of being alone and being lonely.

She stared down at the lines of cuts in her palms, feeling glass she knew she needed to take out grind.

That would be easy enough to do, but what about the glass inside the rest of her?

The glass that'd been lodged inside her soul since she was eight years old?

She bowed her hands into her face and sobbed.

She could put herself together again. She'd done it before; she was good at it, truly, she just needed time. She was strong. She could fight. It was the only reason she'd ever made it this far in her short, sad life.

Sometimes it felt like fighting was all she knew.

But...what if it wasn't serving her?

What if she did just...give up?

She swallowed to think on it.

It was clear Janvier wanted to be kind to her, at least for now. If he was offering, shouldn't she take him up on it? She pressed a sandy fist to her lips.

Because, God, how nice would it be to pretend that things were normal for just even one night?

So what if she knew it was pretend?

Who would care?

Who the hell was keeping score?

She could just go along with whatever he wanted instead of fighting on the inside all the time—because fighting and not winning was breaking her.

So what if she lost herself in doing it?

What was so great about being her, anyway?

Sammy put her head down between her knees again to breathe, trying to calm herself down so she could attempt to be logical. *But why? Logic hadn't done shit for her here yet!* She took a shuddering inhale and swallowed a fresh wave of panic down. First things first, she knew she was disgusting. So she'd take a shower and brush her teeth. It would make her more human. And then she could just go downstairs, and he could wait for a day or three until she had a little more resiliency.

But.

Then.

What?

"I don't know!" she howled, hammering her open hands on the Jaguar's dashboard.

She hissed in pain afterward, but at least the pain made her mind crisp, and she was eye level with the glove box. She reached for it without thinking, ready to pilfer anything that was there, just like when she'd once worked at the chop shop. Her hand paused on the lever.

Maybe that was why this was happening to her. Because once upon a time, she hadn't been a very good person. When she'd been working there with Danny, she'd figured she was in the clear—because her childhood sucked so bad, she thought the world owed her.

Maybe all of this now was proof that it did not.

Fuck it, now was not the time to start being good.

Especially not for him.

She wiped her running nose with the back of one hand, opened the glove box up—and found her phone inside.

Seeing it was like getting hit with lightning.

Her eyes flickered to the door and back; she really was alone. She turned it on and watched it boot up, her intent crystallizing around it, her prior panic shoved aside. It only had a smidge of battery left and absolutely no signal. She didn't know if that was because he lived in the boonies or due to magic, too—but she'd gotten texts! She went into her app instantly, praying to see that Andi was coming back, only to find that she'd 'sent' a text of her own to Andi not long ago.

I'm so sorry! I was busy, and then I lost my phone for days! I'm not mad, don't worry—we'll talk when you get back!

Janvier.

He'd written it, pretending to be her, throwing the only other person on the planet who currently cared if she lived or died off the trail.

I know we need to talk, Sammy. Andi had written back, twelve hours after she'd gotten the text from him. *Just know that I miss you, and I think about you every day, okay?*

And then Janvier hadn't texted back, nor had Andi texted her again.

She could still be in Italy for all Sammy knew.

Which meant Sammy was on her own.

Just like always.

No one else was getting her out of here but her.

Her eyes turned toward the door again, narrowed, and then she ever so quietly got out of his car.

JANVIER WAS WAITING for her when she eventually came inside. He stood as she entered, and he hadn't yet buttoned up his shirt. "Do you need help with your hands?" She shook her head silently as he looked at her with concern. "You should shower. Or take a bath if you like," he said, backing out of her route to the stairs.

"I don't know that I feel comfortable with that," she whispered. She did her best to sound frail, like it was hard to keep hold of herself.

"Understandable," he granted. "I can go. How much time would you like?"

She made a show of swallowing. "An hour? Two? It takes me a long time to blow dry my hair." He nodded and picked up his keys, making a wide arc around her for the door. "Mister Worst?" she called after him when he was half-way out.

"Yes, Red?" he asked her, pausing.

"Can you come back with vanilla ice cream? For what's left of the pie?" She darted a glance at him, like she could barely bring herself to look at him, and saw him sink back.

"Certainly," he said and turned.

"Actually?" she added, stopping him a second time. "Maybe you could come back with it fast? I'm not sure what I need more—a shower or pie."

"Of course," he said and then gave her another look of his own. Hesitant, as though he didn't want to trust himself to look at her with his eyes.

Probably scared to look at the mess she'd made of herself. *Because of him!*

Sammy nodded encouragement as she gave him a meek smile, and then he shut the door.

She waited until she heard his car leave. He would have to drive north into town, which would take him over several overpasses and she knew now how fast he drove, like a man who'd never been pulled over in his life. The tiny nicks she'd made on his brake lines were so infinitesimally small they wouldn't make a difference in the straight-aways. But the second he tried to turn and feather the brakes to shift, as he took one of the big swooping curves…she stared at the door, imagining his beautiful car flying off of one at speed.

Taking him down with it.

The image wasn't as satisfying as it had been a moment ago or the moment before that. In fact, now that he was gone, all she could really remember was the way he'd looked at her right before he'd left.

What if he wasn't scared to look at her for her sake, but for his?

Why would anything about her ever make him avert his eyes?

But it didn't matter now. It was too late, and he was getting what he deserved because it was his fault she was still *trapped **here.***

Smoke trotted up to her, made a show at growling, then sniffed her and sat back casually. "Rough night?" he asked her.

She looked down at him. "Oh, it's just starting."

CHAPTER 14

Rax extricated himself from the wreckage of his vehicle. It was easier than it might have otherwise been because he was slicked with his own blood. One of his legs was healing the most magnificent break he'd had in centuries, and it was a toss-up of what would've killed a normal man, the decapitation that had nearly missed him, or getting hit-slash-stabbed in the chest with the remnants of his steering column.

Luckily his phone was still in his pocket, intact. He texted Namir with one hand while casting magic out with his other to send the driver of the semi-truck his Jag had slid under to sleep.

"Oh my God, you're all—" the man started and collapsed.

Rax snapped his fingers and hid the wreckage from the road so that no one else would feel compelled to be a Good Samaritan.

Like he had been.

Trying to ignore thinking about his brother's fate—imprisonment amongst the sirens, for eight hundred years! —and off getting her *FUCKING ICE CREAM*.

The *depths* to that woman! He stood there panting, his free hand straining in and out of fists like it was imagining strangling her. His beautiful car, of which he was the original owner, had slid right beneath the Mack truck coming the other direction. His brakes had failed him during an emergency lane change when someone tried to cut him off.

At first, he'd been all too willing to believe it was caused by driving on sand or the drowned ones, but then he remembered her sending him off.

Urging him to speed.

And that the first job on her resume, because she'd skipped Belissima's, was at an auto shop. He assumed she'd worked the counter—and he'd assumed fucking wrong.

Namir pierced the veil of magic easily, driving in like a man possessed, stopping just before he hit the Mack himself.

"What the fuck?" the tiger-shifter asked, hopping out of his own truck's cab. "Jesus Christ, Rax. Did you make an enemy and forget to tell me?"

"You could say that," Rax said. He pointed at the sleeping driver. "Tell him he fell asleep on the road, but you pretend you were my car's driver, miraculously unscathed. Pay him for his silence, I don't care how much."

"Jesus," Namir repeated. "And...you're bleeding—"

"I'm healing," Rax corrected him. "Give me your keys. I need to go."

Namir reluctantly handed them over. "Do you need back-up?"

Rax laughed harshly. "No. I'm handling this alone."

RAX HIT the button to open Namir's truck up and hopped inside, driving back the way he'd come, seething with anger at having been taken advantage of.

He had been about to tell her everything, *if he hadn't fucked it up*, and then he had actually *felt bad* for her? Felt sorry?

Felt like he, himself, was to blame?

For his brother, yes, maybe, but not for anything about Samantha. She was wearing *his necklace!*

Fuck that!

And she had just tried to kill him. Same as she had that first night with the knife. Any moment of weakness she'd ever shown him since was untrue. If he was half-dragon—she was half-snake. He parked Namir's truck outside the garage lest she hear him coming, and then quietly entered his domain.

Any small doubt he might have had that his accident wasn't intentional was erased by the fact that she'd barricaded the stairs down to her level with his dining room table.

Fuck. Her.

"Red!" he bellowed, slamming the door behind him. "I survived!"

Smoke leaped to stand on the table's top edge. "She's down there with knives. She wouldn't tell me what she was doing."

He stormed over and Smoke jumped to the side as he kicked his dining room table in half, sending splinters raining down the stairs, where she'd pulled his dining room chairs to act as further barriers. He flung the first one down into his study below and heard her squeak at the violence. *Yes, well, she should see what she did to his Jag.* "Red," he snarled. "Come up and face your consequences."

"Fuck you!" she shouted at him.

Not apologetic in the least.

He growled and ran down the stairs, feeling her slash out from behind them at his ankles and only barely missing as he leaped into his study halfway down, whirling to corner her beneath the stairs, against the aquarium's glass. She'd upgraded from the small knife Smoke had told him she'd been keeping to a butcher knife and a carving knife, one in each hand, and he stopped in front of her, breathing hard.

"You're a little viper, and I should've treated you as such from the beginning," he said, his voice low and full of threat.

"You should have!" she shouted. "You should have just killed me! Because at least then, I would be free!"

"It's not too late," he said, reaching for her with both hands. She screamed and tried to defend herself, but he caught one blade in one hand, twisting it away from her without even cutting his skin, and the other lightly slashed the back of his arm before he batted it aside. And then he grabbed her, still screaming, hoisting her up over his shoulder, to carry her back up the stairs, fully considering just tossing her into his shark tank as he picked up one of the chairs he'd kicked with his free hand, hauling it upstairs with him. He ignored her blows and planted the chair in the middle of his living space, sitting her down upon it. She shut up as he pinned her there with his eyes, likely trying to figure out her next move.

If his brother was still alive, inside with the sirens, then in addition to saving his own dragon—he needed the *fucking key*.

"Beg me to save your life," he told her.

Her lips lifted in a snarl and the words coming out of her mouth dripped with sarcasm. "Please, oh, please don't kill me, Mister Worst."

He growled. "Say it like you mean it, Red."

"Fucking make me," she said and spat at the ground by his feet.

Evil things in him lurched forward. He'd already tolerated levels of insolence from her that would've made him slaughter any other living being. Whatever pain he thought he'd felt on her behalf earlier at the beach, her behavior now had burned away.

It didn't matter what hung around her neck when it was attached to the rest of her.

But he inhaled and caught the scent of bile. She'd gone straight from retching her guts out in his car to luring him in, using his kindness against him to plan his murder. He ran his eyes over her. One simple little human was the only thing that stood between him and a chance at freedom.

Why couldn't he just kill her?

He wanted to. And he'd already killed so many others! He'd spent centuries among their kind, unable to avoid them on this planet, trapped with them on sailing vessels, or moving alongside them across continents, before he'd built up his casino and shielded himself with shifters.

But somehow, she was different.

If he'd been sure he could anneal the pieces of the key and save himself—and now save his brother—maybe he could've, but he wasn't.

And if he killed her for nothing.... Her orange-red hair was wild and tangled, her breath was acidic, she smelled like the essence of terror, and she was still here.

Hating him with a raw fury that made her shine like the sun.

Over the course of his long life he'd met too many humans. He knew he'd never seen the likes of her before, nor would again.

He crouched on his heels to bring his head even with hers and even though her eyes were bloodshot from crying, the blue inside them still flashed.

No normal man could ever be her master.

And perhaps not even a dragon could manage it.

He rocked up. "Stay here," he commanded and went up to his level of his home. He walked around his bed and opened his altar. Smoke followed him, moving with alacrity.

"What are you doing?" the fox asked as he pulled his dragon bone knife out.

"Finding out what she's made of," he told the fox, loud enough for her to hear, coming back to her side with the knife and a bowl full of warm water.

She hadn't moved because she knew there was nowhere she could hide from him here. *Which didn't mean she'd given up.*

"How strong are you, Red?" he asked her.

Her eyes danced between his face and the knife, ignoring the bowl entirely. "As strong as I need to be. Forever."

"That's what I thought." He tossed the knife into her lap. "That's the only thing in this whole house that can kill me. Not a car accident, and not the sharks. You cut me with that, and I may as well be mortal."

"That's a sick fucking joke," she said, without touching it.

"Look in my eyes, Red. I promise you I'm not joking." She did and then quickly looked away. He knelt in front of her, setting the bowl to the side, and then pulled her chair closer so that his shoulders spread her legs. He grabbed her hand, wrapping it around the knife's hilt. "I mean it. You really want to kill me, now's your chance." He yanked the blade in her hand up to rest at his throat, feeling her pulse race beneath his fingers before he let her go. "But before you do, I want you to know—I acknowledge that everything I've put you through is bullshit." Her brow furrowed as she frowned, and the knife trembled against his throat as he went on. "We both have problems, Red. And we are the solutions to each other's problems, possibly. I know you're strong enough to fight me, but now I need you to be strong enough to fucking stop." He swallowed and felt the sharp edge of the knife ride the motion up and down. "I won't beg you for my life Samantha, but if you can't finally fucking behave, then you probably should take it because I don't want to have to hurt you. Truly."

He closed his eyes, same as she had with him not long ago. Only he knew he wasn't making peace with God, he was trying to make peace with her—the strangest, fiercest, strongest creature he'd ever met—or prepared to die trying.

Her hand steadied, and he wondered at the irony of him dying at a human's hands after all these centuries, *but better cleanly here than at the bottom of the sea!* Then she let the blade go. It dropped to the cement floor, clattering by his thigh, and he dared to look up.

She was gawking down at him, breathing hard, smeared with the green of his blood from where she'd cut him. There was sand in her hair, and she smelled like piss and fight and cinnamon, and fat salty tears rolled down her cheeks. He wondered what ocean they tasted like. He knew he'd already made her cry enough for him to swim in.

"If it makes you feel better, I couldn't kill you either," he said.

"I still hate you," she whispered.

"I know," he said. He went up to his knees and put the bowl of water in her lap. "Give me your hands." She did so, reluctantly, and he took them and dunked them, feeling her pulse bound, as he carefully stroked the flakes of glass out of her wounds with his thumbs, using magic. And when he was sure they were clean and they'd heal well, he set the bowl aside before grabbing hold of her knees to rock himself up to standing. He picked her up without comment, and she didn't fight as he carried her up the stairs to his own level, opening the bathroom door to take her to the empty tub and set her inside of it. "Take your time, Red," he told her and then left her there.

. . .

228

As she bathed, he cleaned things up. He went downstairs and removed the chunks of wood out of his study while leaving whatever strange things she'd done with his books intact, collecting clothing for her. He heard her splash away as he put a fresh outfit in the bathroom for her, cotton underwear, tube socks and all, laying them on the counter without looking. His knife he returned to his altar, said his ritual, and then reached into the bottom of the thing, pulling a thick sheaf of papers out.

It was everything he'd torn from the books below, anything any historian had written about him or his family. The stories they told were priceless to him, but at a certain point he realized priceless became worthless if no one else cared.

His bathroom door opened and he looked up. Her clean wet hair was in another of her braids, her color was better now, and he was oddly relieved.

"I know you're not currently happy with me." He moved to stand and held the papers out.

"That's an understatement," she said as she crossed her arms.

"It's just that...you like to read. So, here," he said, shaking the papers at her. "It's everything that's missing from the books." She licked her lips and looked at him, eyeing him for tricks. "I want you to know why you're here. It's only fair."

She took a quick step forward, grabbed them, and then took a quick step back as he inhaled, waiting. It was momentous for him, but just another strange thing on an already impossibly strange day for her.

"I'm not going to thank you or anything," she said.

"I didn't expect you would," he told her and closed his eyes. When he opened them again she was gone.

He went and took the longest shower of his life and then came out, half-expecting to catch the scent of burned things, seeing as he'd finally given her the chance to damage something of value to him, but no, all he heard was a distant hairdryer running.

He changed his sheets with a towel wrapped around his waist and afterward dropped the towel to get beneath them. He wasn't tired in the least, but this was where he belonged right now, not down a level closer to her, pacing or playing the piano, interrupting her as she read.

If she'd read anything at all.

He resisted the urge to ask Smoke or Hachiro to spy on her, although he knew Smoke would be doing so regardless, and eventually he wore himself down into a fitful slumber, which he woke from when he heard her socked feet below him on the stair.

"What is it, Red?" he called down to her.

"Is everything in these real?" she called up.

He put his hands behind his head and stared at the ceiling. "Unfortunately."

SAMANTHA LET the hairdryer run to cover her reading as she hurriedly flipped through the pages, looking for the reason she was here and how the hell she could escape.

But he hadn't been lying. Her necklace was a key...from a dead woman.

A dead human.

Who'd gotten Janvier's brother killed, apparently.

And if she couldn't get it off, and he wasn't willing to slip it off of her dead body, then he would have to choose between joining his dragon at the bottom of the sea or losing it forever as the Gate opened up.

At the back of all the papers she found a portrait of his beast, on torn out page four hundred seventy-four. It was a dark black monster that the artist had made occupy almost the entire page in an intricate knot of shadow. The dragon she didn't recognize of course, but the eyes she did—some gemstones had been crushed up in the paint to capture them. They were amber coals of red gold, staring out at her, just like they'd burned at her tonight when he'd come home.

And the reason half of him was at the bottom of the sea to begin with really was to stop the sirens—the same things that had killed her mom and dad....

But how had they gotten here when his dragon and the gate it guarded were at the bottom of a different ocean on another world?

Had he let them out? Was it his fault they'd escaped? Were his prayers to assuage a guilty conscience?

She'd gotten so good at hating him she didn't really want to stop, but as she reassembled the books he'd destroyed, going by page numbers and matched torn edges, she wasn't sure she still could.

But if he was innocent, why hadn't he just told her everything in the beginning?

If she was going to talk to him again, give him the benefit of any doubt—considering all he'd done to her—she had to be sure.

She cleared her head and went back to the beginning of the books.

OVER THE NEXT FEW DAYS, several things happened:

Janvier left for several hours in the morning and again at night. She didn't know where he went, but he made an extraordinary amount of noise when he did it; both so she'd know she was alone and that he was coming back in so she could hide.

A pumpkin pie appeared in the fridge and vanilla ice cream in the freezer. It turned out Smoke did like pie, but what he really liked were the pickles she'd made Janvier get her. He joined her for most of her meals on the kitchen counter, seeing as the dining table hadn't been replaced yet.

Janvier's knives appeared and disappeared on the kitchen counter too. Glass, gold, and rose petal along with a note that said: *Don't cut yourself ~ R.* She tried them out on the chain without comment every day.

And a television as wide as her outstretched arms appeared on his coffee table. She ran to this when she first realized it was there and turned it on—the remote control had been left out on his couch. It booted up and the time and a date appeared in the corner.

3 a.m.?

She'd thought it was noon.

And she'd been here for almost two weeks?

Wasn't Andi home yet?

The television wasn't connected to Wi-Fi, so she only had the few channels it could pick up out here. She imagined a TV antenna on top of the random hill outside with a snort. God, if only she could've gotten to Netflix, she and Andi still shared an account. There'd have been no surer way to tell her best friend she was in trouble than leaving some rom-com on the 'resume watching' screen. If Andi saw that, she would *know* Sammy'd been kidnapped— or possessed.

But there was nothing on except for infomercials right now... because it was 3 a.m. She looked at the 'lunch' she'd made herself and clicked the TV off as Smoke jumped up to the counter. "Are there any more pickles?" he asked her.

"Sure," Sammy said, opening up the jar.

SAMMY MOVED through those days otherwise unaccosted, albeit alone. She'd read the whole story of Janvier's tragic family after figuring out which sections belonged to which books, and probably could've made a decent map of his whole family tree.

So she understood what had happened to him, how he'd been imprisoned for a hundred years—if that wasn't an elaborate metaphor, meant to make him seem more macho—and where his dragon was now, at the bottom of an ocean on an entirely different planet.

And that his clock was slowly ticking.

She was certain he felt it too, but he never called for her, nor wrote other notes. Sometimes he'd play the piano and she wondered if it was for her, much the same as the food he cooked was. But that was that.

And every day she didn't talk to him the heavier her tongue felt in her mouth. Because if it wasn't his fault that her parents had died— which it didn't seem to be, although she knew she still needed to ask— then the only thing standing between him and his freedom was her.

If she'd never put the necklace on...he might've been able to lock the gate and free his dragon. Or if she could ever figure out how to get it off, but she couldn't. She tried, she really did, sawing at it with the knives he left her with all her might, but the chain never budged.

She looked at herself in the mirror one night—*day?*—that she was alone and felt like the red gemstone was an anchor.

Would she have to wear it for the rest of her life? If Janvier chose to rejoin his dragon and keep the sirens locked up—the choice she selfishly wanted him to make—would it sit around her neck, a morbid reminder of his imprisonment, for the rest of her days?

And what was it like for him to see her and be reminded that he was going to either lose his dragon or himself because ironically, of all things, he was too kind?

For all that, he had kidnapped her to begin with.

So maybe it was for the best they didn't talk now, seeing as they couldn't help one another. She couldn't free him, and he wouldn't let her be free.

Even if he did sometimes stare in.

She knew he was keeping an eye on her, and she supposed after cutting herself and stabbing him, she couldn't blame him. When he swam by, which he did once or twice a day, she was sure he looked in on her. And when he didn't Comet was there, drifting by occasionally, shifting colors in pleasing patterns. She always waved to the octopus.

And Smoke was almost always, very quietly, around.

"Why'd you have to tell him about the knives?" she asked the fox the first day when Janvier was out.

Smoke tilted his head to look at her like she was daft. "Because he's my friend."

"Yes, but it's not like I can actually hurt him," she said, frowning.

Smoke did a twisting shake that started at his nose and ended at his tail. "Trust me," he said afterward. "You have."

SAMMY WAS PERCHED in her nest between the couches the next day reading, with the stone in her mouth. She'd switched back to stories from Janvier's day to much, much older ones, fantastically courtly tales, when he swam by again, running the same wall to wall pattern

233

he always did. She'd noticed that he was always wearing swim trunks now. *A shame, really.* She watched him through her lashes, careful not to tilt her head and let him see.

And she knew what he'd do immediately after swimming; go take a shower, maybe play the piano some, and cook a meal before leaving, making sure he rattled the door for her.

He wouldn't let her go, but at least her being here made some small amount of sense now.

And then Comet drifted by, chasing after him. She did watch that because the octopus was moving with a sense of purpose....

CHAPTER 15

RAX WASN'T SURE WHAT ELSE TO DO WITHOUT TALKING TO HER. AT first, he'd relished the silence, to deal with the knowledge that his brother might not be dead. He'd wanted to be alone, laying on his bed or swimming endlessly, meditating on his tragic thoughts. Because if a hundred years of imprisonment had almost broken him, what would almost a thousand do to his brother, in the Below, listening to nothing but siren song? If he chose to rejoin his dragon rather than lose it, what would it be like to be trapped outside the Gate, knowing his brother was still inside?

And now he and the girl had a strange new routine. He would take the knives away, empower them up for hours at a time, and then leave them downstairs for her and go. Smoke said she was trying them, but other than his fox's testimony, for three days the only way he knew she was in the house were her dishes, her washcloth, and her scent.

He would go swimming to get it off of him, limiting himself to the areas of his tank that didn't look in on her level, swimming quickly below, or quickly above, any time he had to cross her possible line of sight.

If she ever saw him, she never let it on. Sometimes she was sleeping, but if not, she was always absorbed in a book, at the desk or on the couch. One time—the worst time—she had had her back against the tank, so it was like if he could just reach out far enough, he could touch her hair. She kept the stone tucked in her mouth, the golden chain hanging down like loose reins, eyes focused on a page.

Was she reading with intent? Just to pass the time?

To learn more about him, or forget him, entirely?

"And to think, all this time I thought you were a creature of air," Hachiro told him on the fourth day, on his second time in the tank.

Or was it his third?

"Swimming calms me," he told his friend.

"Ahh. Yes. Swimming in circles in a place you cannot get free from," Hachiro agreed with sarcasm.

Rax twisted himself to float in the mid-water column. *"You've never complained about it before."*

"Oh, no. I wasn't talking about me," Hachiro explained. *"I have lived a long life. I enjoy being someplace where the delicate ends of my tentacles do not get nibbled on. But you, however,"* the octopus said, billowing nearer. *"This is not your home. Not fully."*

"It feels like it is. Or perhaps like it should be." Maybe he was just getting himself ready, no matter his choice. He'd largely turned the Lynx over to Namir, choosing to drive aimlessly for hours when he was away from her, always ready to drive back. *"Can you read her mind?"* he asked.

"No. She would have to want to bridge the gap, and she doesn't. Although she also doesn't know that she can. But I can read her enough through the glass, dragon."

"And?"

"And I think telling you anything would be rude," Hachiro informed him.

"What? Why?" Rax frowned. *"Wait...do you really like her better?"* He snorted.

Hachiro laughed, sinking, and Rax swam after him. *"No. But I won't be a party to you hiding anymore."* Hachiro sent out a row of suckers winding it around Rax's arm.

"Hachiro?" Rax thought as another tentacle bound him up, and the

creature used its great strength to pull him further into the tank. *"What the fuck are you doing?"*

"What I, as a friend, should have done a long time ago. Stopping this nonsense," the octopus said, winding about him more.

Rax didn't know what to do. Hachiro had never attacked him before, and he didn't want to hurt the beast. He struggled with it, trying to detach himself, as Hachiro wound him further. *"See?"* he said, twisting Rax toward the glass where Samantha was now standing, looking at the two of them with her eyes wide and her jaw dropped. *"She cares."*

"No, she's horrified, that's different," Rax thought, but then she beat her hand against the glass as Hachiro slid a muscular tentacle around his throat. Rax pretended to try to get it off, catching her gaze with his, and saw her…laughing?

"She cheers for me," Hachiro chortled, and sure enough, Rax could hear the vibration of a faint 'Co-met! Co-met!' from outside the glass in time with her lips moving.

"Is that how it is?" he mouthed out at her, letting Hachiro momentarily win, letting him take him down further in the water column while she peered in, both of them play wrestling now for her benefit. He freed himself from Hachiro's arms and was kicking away when the octopus grabbed him again, hauling him back, and he heard her distant delighted squeal. Then he kicked both of them lower. *"Come here, and don't bite me,"* he said, grabbing Hachiro's mantle. *"Do you remember the Battle for Hageland?"*

"Like it was yesterday."

"Then let me shoot you like an arrow."

The creature laughed at that and let Rax mock draw him up and aim, shooting him to the tank's far side, where the octopus made a dramatic 'splat' shape for Samantha's benefit and then squirted out ink as an afterthought.

Rax laughed at the creature's poor comedic timing and then looked back at her and saw that she was laughing too. He swam up to her on his side of the glass. "Come up?" he asked, mouthing the words to her, pointing up to his level.

She gave him a soft nod and mouthed, "Okay."

SAMMY RAN up to wait for him, kneeling on the platform he dove in from, just a few inches above the water, in a dark sweater and warm leggings and three pairs of socks. When he resurfaced, he took a deep gulp of air, and so did she. She hadn't even realized how lonely she'd been until seeing him again. His eyes burned even hotter in real life, and it was like she could feel his gaze upon her.

"Samantha, about the beach, I'm sorry," he said, in time with his strokes, swimming toward the platform.

"I believe you now," she said. After reading all his books, she had to. "Thank you for giving me time." Her voice was thick with disuse.

"Thank you for not setting anything on fire." He tread water below her, knocking water off his face and pushing his hair back with a hand. "That I know of, at least," he added, with a grin.

She caught herself smiling back, unintentionally. "It was just the once," she defended herself. "And Comet put it out." He caught his fingers on the edge of the platform and held himself there. "Why didn't you just tell me all your stories? From the beginning?"

He blew air across the surface of the water. "Because I made the grave mistake of thinking you were normal."

"Far from it." Sammy hugged herself and rolled her eyes. "Was everything in the pages you gave me true?" Her gaze caught his again. "Were you really imprisoned for a century?"

He nodded his chin just above the water's level. "I was. You think I don't know about prisons, Red, but I do. Only I wasn't allowed to fight. If I fought, I'd set the magic off course, and what they were doing to me would've taken even longer. I had to let them torture me for my country's survival. So I didn't get to show half the ingenuity that you have shown."

"Ingenuity," she repeated his word, making quote-marks with her fingers.

"It's kinder than saying you have a propensity for chaos," he said, still smiling.

He'd missed her, too, she realized. It made her feel something warm inside her belly. A fire she should definitely put out. "What about the sirens?" she asked.

"Still locked away below. That's what I was checking the other night when we were at the ocean."

And he sounded so sure…. "When your family made their pact, did you trap all of them?"

"Yes," he answered quickly and then grimaced. "And then some."

She blinked. "What do you mean?"

Sammy could read him deciding whether or not he should tell her something. "I think my brother might still be alive, inside the Gate."

She gasped. "But the books say he died!"

"They thought he died. And so did I. But if he didn't—"

"You'd have to release all the sirens, and let your dragon die, to free him." She put a hand to her mouth in horror and watched him nod.

"Yes. You see my dilemma. I don't know what to do, Red." He took a stroke back in the tank.

"So murdering me's still on the table?" she asked, half-teasing, half-not.

He looked over sharply. "Of course not. No. It means I just wonder what I owe people who don't remember I exist. I've already paid a terrible price to keep them safe. Do I still owe them more? Or could I just let the sirens out along with my brother?" Janvier raked a hand through his wet hair. "Who's likely mad, by the way. Tarian was already insane with grief when he went down there. I can't imagine listening to sirens for eight hundred years has helped anything."

Sammy frowned. "Unleashing sirens on the countryside…that's not very princely of you."

He shrugged beneath the waves. "I'm hardly a prince anymore."

"No. Just a kidnapper." The words leaped out of her mouth before she had a chance to stop them. They were true, yes, but…she hadn't come up here to have her first conversation in days just to stab at him with words.

Janvier sighed and took another stroke back in the water, even further away from her. "For your own good, Red. You saw the drowned ones come after you on the beach and at your apartment."

"While I agree with you ninety-percent, I feel like there's a ten percent chance you're lying just to keep me here."

"I would protest my innocence, but I'm afraid we both know otherwise." He gave a rueful snort. "Have you really been trying the knives?"

"Smoke hasn't been reporting back my every move?" She doubted that. Apparently, she was the fox's only entertainment.

"He has," Janvier admitted. "But I want to hear you say the words."

"I have been trying them. Especially after what I read." It seemed safe enough to confess.

"Thank you," he said graciously.

Sammy bowed her head slightly in return. "You're welcome, Mister Worst."

He closed his eyes as though pained. "Call me Rax."

"Uh, uh." She shook her head. "We're not friends, Worst. I'm still trapped here."

"Yes. You are," he agreed with a sigh and kicked himself toward the platform. "Step back, or I might splash you," he warned.

"Are you getting out?" she asked, moving to stand without giving him room.

He looked between her and the water. "Unless you wanted to come in."

She contemplated it quickly. "That water's freezing...."

His eyes lit on hers. "So? You can take a tub afterward."

"And there's sharks in it, Worst," she protested.

He laughed. "I won't let them hurt you. Although knowing what I know about you now, I should be more concerned with protecting them."

She looked between him and the water below. How many times had she watched him through the glass, envying him his weightless freedom? "I can't believe even I'm considering this."

"Me either, honestly," he said. "But...how often do you get to swim with sharks, Red?" he asked, and his eyes traveled up her. Asking her for something; she didn't know what.

A second chance?

Her hands reached for the hem of her sweater. "I'm not skinny dipping," she said. "Don't get your hopes up."

"I would never," he swore and pushed back.

She could feel his eyes on her as she pulled the sweater up and off, folding it neatly before setting it down and taking out the small knife she carried to place on top of it. Then she stepped on her socks in turn to free her feet, and her hands went to her hips to help shimmy her leggings off, leaving her there in just a gray sports bra and dark green cotton underwear. She hadn't asked him for a razor and didn't want to try using his straight edge, so she knew there were little licks of orange-red hair at her armpits and the edges of her underwear and faint traces on her legs.

When she was done, she stood, already freezing, surveying the water and caught him staring up at her, rapt. She looked away and asked, "What's the least bad way to do this?"

"Like so many other things in life—all at once," he counseled, kicking further back.

She scrunched her face up, held herself tighter, then jumped in. It was like hitting a wall of ice. There was no part of her that wasn't instantly cold. She resurfaced seconds later, sputtering. "Oh my God, oh my God, oh my God," she said and flailed.

"Shhh," he said, swimming closer to grab her by her upper arms. "Just because I can control the sharks doesn't mean we should torture them. You can swim, right?"

"Yes, but, oh my *God*, Worst, this is freezing!" The only place where she was warm was where he touched her.

"You get used to it," he said, pulling them both further out into the water.

"No fucking way," she hissed, blinking, drops of water trapped in her eyelashes. She twisted free of his grasp and he didn't try to keep her. "Seriously. Are my lips blue?"

He seemed to take her request seriously as he inspected them. "Not yet."

"They will be!" she said and laughed, chattering. "This was such a bad idea."

"No—not in the least. Put your hand out," he said, even as he reached for her wrist to make her. She went with his movement and then one of the huge fish, half again as long as Janvier was tall, circled around. She fought the urge to flutter kick away. "Remember, you promised not to hurt it," he reminded her.

It was clear he was teasing, but as a sleek three hundred pound shark neared, her heart leaped into her throat. One bite from its broad mouth would kill her, making her bleed out, crushing her internal organs, and its flat black eyes said it wouldn't care.

It passed by at the last moment, but she could feel its skin beneath her fingertips. "It's rough! Like sandpaper!" she exclaimed softly.

"It is," Janvier agreed.

"I feel like I'm in *Jaws*," she said, turning to follow its path.

"These are bull sharks. Those were great whites."

Sammy looked over her shoulder at him. He was closer than she thought he'd been. "You know what the least attractive thing in the world is, Worst? Shark pedantry."

He looked affronted, and then he laughed. "Sorry," he apologized, and she grinned.

"What's his name?"

"Her name," he corrected her, "and they don't have ones."

"Why not?" she said, as the beast took another circle around them. The closer it got, the happier she was to be near Janvier.

"They're killing machines. They don't get names."

"Huh. You don't say."

"I know what my name is," he told her, giving her a look.

"I'm sure. But I suspect, much like the sharks, you don't come when you're called." The water made them both the same height, and it felt like they were on even ground for once, even though she was far colder.

"True," he said. "But, like the sharks here illustrate, not everything that can kill you wants to. At least not all the time."

"What about the sirens?" she asked.

He frowned lightly. "What about them?"

"They always want to kill, don't they?" There'd been no stories in his books about them ever showing mercy.

"They're malicious, yes."

"And you're willing to consider setting them free?"

He took a deep inhale and closed his eyes. "For my brother's sake, also, yes."

"Even if it meant losing your dragon?"

"Losing my dragon...more?" he asked. "You read the books, Red."

She nodded, thinking. "But...what if," she said, swimming nearer as he swam back, more to stay away from the shark than close to him, she told herself. "You were protecting someone you knew? Instead of all those people you don't?"

"Like whom?" he asked her, his brow crawling up his forehead at her hypothetical.

"Namir."

Janvier rolled his eyes. "Namir's a big boy, he'd be able to handle himself."

"Okay then, what if it was just some humans?" she pressed him.

"Just some humans, eh?" He tilted his head at that and took a stroke back in her direction, coming near. "I had no idea you were such a philosopher, Red."

"I'm not. Just—answer the question." She didn't think he'd gotten her parents killed, at least not on purpose, but she also didn't *know*. And if she just straight up asked, there was also no way for her to know if he was lying.

He watched her with his eyes narrowed as he swam closer still, and the sensation of dangerous mass nearby was not altogether different from when it'd been the shark.

"I suppose it would depend on the humans," he answered, and the corners of his lips quirked. "I mean, I've met many humans I would've fed to sirens personally," he went on.

She frowned and recoiled, but then his hands were at her waist, pulling her near. Before she could say anything, he pressed her against his body, and his lips were on hers. His tongue asked them for entrance, and her body moved entirely apart from her mind. Her head tilted to fit his, her own lips opened without thought, and the inside of her knee slid up the outside of his thigh until she came to her senses and pushed herself off of his muscular chest.

"If we're not friends, Worst, we're definitely not that," she sputtered, wiping his kiss off her lips with the back of one arm.

He surveyed her coolly. "It seemed like you were looking for something to be angry about. I thought I might save you the hassle of digging so hard." He swam past her for the platform and boosted himself out of the water easily, and stood, looking back. "Your lips are blue. You do need to get out," he said, offering her a hand.

She ignored him to grab hold of the edge and pull herself out much less gracefully.

CHAPTER 16

AFTER THAT, THINGS CHANGED.

He was worried she'd wind up hiding in his study again, but she didn't. She began to bring whatever books she was reading up and read them freely on the couches, leaving them all around the living room. He took initiative and moved one of the couches to be closer to his piano, where the dining room table used to be, and she sat and read on it without comment as he played, ignoring him as completely as he ignored her.

Except he wasn't, really. He knew where she was at all times with a ridiculous precision; listening to her soft socked steps, the flip of pages as she read, the quiet sounds she sometimes made at night as she dreamt—or by how close he was to her scent, the cinnamon that filled his house the same as she did. They acted like celestial beings, wandering the same sky, always within view of each other, always keeping an appropriate distance between them.

And it was starting to kill him.

He thought he knew what cold was, in the deep dark of the unforgiving sea, but it turned out that what was colder still was her disregard of him. When he was so close—when she was so close.

They were both *right here*.

And yet, while she'd eat the food he made, try cutting the chains with the knives he empowered, and listen to his music, she wouldn't do any *more*.

He couldn't have told anyone else what *more* was, but he was starved for it. And the longer he lived without it, the more he could feel its absence gnawing at his soul.

But there was no way to tell her that safely. Not when he still had to keep her here. He'd stolen a kiss in his tank because he'd wanted to, but what good would enflaming his passions do when he would never force himself on her, and when every day she made it clear that while physically present, she would rather be *anywhere* else?

It started to make giving himself over to his dragon seem preferable. At least at the bottom of the sea, he wouldn't suffer from hope.

SAMANTHA KNEW that freezing Janvier out wasn't going to get her free.

It was just that…things were easier when she could count on his disdain. When any advance on his part was just to taunt or scare her.

But his lips on hers, in the tank—it'd felt real. He'd recovered quickly, but when she'd first pushed back, she could see the heat in his eyes, and she remembered the growing outline of his hard-on against her stomach.

So she'd gone quiet again. Quiet was safer. But it was stagnant, too.

It was one thing out in the real world to play this game with a stupid boy where she could've had an exit in any direction; it was entirely another thing to try to play with a man, here, trapped in his lair. It would require Bond Girl levels of cool, which, frankly, Sammy knew she did not possess.

And part of the reason she couldn't fake it was him.

She…liked him? And she wasn't sure if that was because she'd read so much about him, which was vastly cheating, him giving her several hundred pages of stories about him, so she had no choice but to think of him as at least a partially fictional character who'd stepped off a page—or because she'd run out of options, mentally and physically.

Mentally...it seemed like if she wanted to get out of here, the only way out was through. And, when they did talk, she liked talking to him. They were the same level of sarcastic, which she enjoyed, and he thought she was smart enough to be worried about, which she enjoyed even more. She'd been taken for granted a lot in her life, it was nice to be treated like an equal.

Physically, it'd been one thing to be lonely in her apartment. It made sense there. But here? When he was so fucking gorgeous and so close? And apparently willing? She'd talked Smoke into sleeping with her at night. Each evening, he said he'd probably bite her in the morning, although he hadn't yet. But snuggling the fox was not enough.

Not when Janvier was *right there.*

Sammy set her book down the next time he was cooking and came over to the kitchen, picking up the magical knives from her side of the kitchen counter to try them out in front of him. He ignored her, chopping vegetables with his plain steel ones on the counter's other side.

"What are you making?" she asked him after none of the magical knives worked.

He paused in his chopping, said, "She speaks," then continued.

She put her elbows on the counter and her chin in her hands. "Oh, an ironic dinner, I can't wait. I've heard those are very filling."

The corners of his lips lifted, although he didn't look up. "If you must know, beef Bourguignon."

"Did I forget to tell you I'm vegan?"

He set the knife down, wiped his hands on a towel, and looked over at her. "It won't work."

She squinted at him. "What?"

"Being nice to me. There's nothing you can say to me that would induce me to free you, for as long as it's unsafe for you outside these walls."

Sammy rocked back. "I can't keep living down here like this, Worst. I'm not some kind of mushroom."

"No, you're not, but I have to treat you like one, alas." He took the knife back up and pointed at her with the tip. "Talk to me if you wish or don't. But don't expect it to have some result for you."

She pouted. "You took me out once, you could take me out again."

"That was before you tried to kill me."

"And failed," she said, defending herself slightly.

"All the same," he chuckled. "I wouldn't trust you for as far as I could throw you, Red."

"I don't know. You look like you hit arm day pretty hard," she muttered.

"Thank you. I think." He paused in chopping again. "How long have you been a vegan?"

She waited for him to look up at her. "About thirty seconds," she said, and he laughed.

IN MANY WAYS, compliant Samantha was worse than the version that hated him.

Rax knew she knew what she was doing. He should never have kissed her in the tank. At the time, it'd felt like it'd given him the upper hand—but in reality, it'd only given her a point of leverage against him, because he wanted her around, and all she wanted was out.

She'd stretch out on the couch he'd put by his piano and curve her body just so, licking the tip of a finger to stroke through a book's pages, watching him through half-lidded eyes, not even reading.

She'd ask him questions about his life during their now shared meals, and because she actually had read so many books about him, she knew what she was talking about, but he hardly ever got anything out of her. She wouldn't tell him about her childhood or her family, except for strange bursts sometimes. A fondly remembered meal. A trip once taken cross country. A teacher she particularly liked.

But nothing he could lace together into a past for her, nor anything that would explain why his necklace was still around her neck.

It didn't matter, though. When he woke up, she was the first thing he wanted to see and any time spent away from her felt wasted.

"Boss, there's someone here to see you," Namir told him via his intercom one evening as he was packing things up. Namir was basically running the Lynx these days, all the better to prepare for a possible eventuality.

"Tell them to come back," Rax growled, reaching for his suit jacket. He'd been thinking about Samantha for the last three hours. All his time here had felt perfunctory, like he was a ghost of himself, just going through the motions.

"He's not going to take no for an answer."

Rax paused. There were only a handful of men in the world who could impose on him, and only one locally was likely. He tossed his suit jacket across the back of his chair. "Send him in," he said as he sat back down.

Sure enough, Damian Blackwood filled his door moments later. The other dragon gave his office a contemptuous look before sitting down across from Rax roughly. "You've got five minutes to tell me what you've done with Samantha O'Connor before things go poorly."

Rax blinked, letting his genuine confusion work on his behalf. "Excuse me?"

"Sammy. She was working here. But I've already interrogated enough of your staff to know she hasn't been seen in weeks. Seeing as people have a penchant for disappearing from your premises, I'm going to need some answers, now."

Damian...knew Samantha? Rax recovered quickly and continued to look baffled. "The Lynx is a bar, a nightclub, and a casino," Rax said, rocking back to blow air through pursed lips. "You can only imagine the sketchy type of people it draws, both for leisure and employment. I have no interest in keeping track of my employees off-premises, nor would I be able to, unless I were willing to tag them like wildlife. So be reasonable—"

"I don't have to be," Damian cut him off. "We both know what I am and what I can do."

"Indeed. But that doesn't change anything, Damian, when I have no idea what's become of her." He steepled his fingers. "What's your interest in the girl?"

"She's supposed to be my fiancée's maid of honor at my wedding." Damian's voice fell into a low growl. "And if you think disappointing me might come with consequences, consider what I would do to stop from disappointing Andi."

"Ahhh," Rax said simply, with a deep nod. He'd had the bad luck to meet Andi not long ago when her brother Danny had killed a hunter inside his casino. *And Samantha knew her.* It explained so much. "While your plight is poignant, and congratulations on your upcoming nuptials by the way, I cannot produce what I do not have." He shrugged casually.

Damian's eyes met and measured his. "If I find out you have anything to do with her disappearance—"

"Didn't Andi's brother 'disappear' and then reappear?" Rax asked, cutting him off. "Perhaps this will be like that." Rax moved to standing. "I was on my way out the door when you barged in," he said, picking up his suit jacket and sliding it on. "I'll report anything back to you I hear, I promise. And I forgot to thank you for killing so many hunters recently. It's been excellent for business. Where are you registered? I'd love to get you a place setting or two." Rax gave the other man a placid smile that did not reach his eyes, like he might were he meeting any of the other distasteful individuals that usually came into his office.

Damian's eyes narrowed. "Fuck you, Rax."

"Likewise, Damian," Rax said, gesturing for the door with one arm. "After you."

Damian hesitated though, turning back to give Rax a piercing look near his collar. Rax's gaze followed his and saw a single strand of wavy red hair.

He'd done such a good job of erasing her scent every night he'd never noticed that he'd had anything of her still on him. "Well, how did that get there?" Rax pondered, as if he didn't know. Damian took a step up to him, everything about him threatening violence. It was all Rax could do not to roll his eyes. "Uh, uh. If you kill me, you'll never know where she is, and she'll starve to death alone." Damian's nostrils flared. "Maybe if you were to invite me to your wedding, I could see —" Rax began. Damian punched a hole into the wall beside his head. Rax didn't flinch though. "Three place settings? Four? You drive a hard bargain—"

"What the fuck, Rax," Damian growled.

"The fuck is that she's mine." Rax lost his cool and snarled. "I own her. I claim her. She belongs to me."

Once the words were out of his mouth, he heard the truth in them —and so did Damian.

Damian tried to read his eyes, breathing heavy. "Does she agree? Why hasn't she said as much to Andi?"

"None of your fucking business. You were gone. Having fun in Italy, right?" Rax pressed, with the illicit knowledge he'd gained from using Samantha's phone. "I'll pass on your woman's regards when I see her tonight, and see if Samantha deigns to contact her."

"I don't believe you," Damian said. "What would she see in you?"

Rax laughed in his face. "One could ask your woman that same thing."

Damian glowered. "Fine. But...what on earth would you see in her? I actually like humanity. You—you just like to steal from them."

"You don't actually know anything about me, dragon," Rax told him. In fact, Samantha was the only one that did.

Damian took his measure. "I'll follow you home and talk to her myself—"

"The fuck you will, Damian."

"I'm not leaving until I see her," Damian growled. "I know you're a dragon somehow, I sense it, but I don't feel it...I can, and I will over-power you."

"You think everything needs to be about brute strength?" Rax stared him down and summoned to himself the power of every magical object in his office, locked inside his desk and that decorated his walls, millions of dollars of artifacts drained dry in an instant. "Sleep," he commanded the other dragon.

Damian's eyes widened as Rax's hand went for his throat.

RAX SET Namir up with the unenviable task of returning Damian to his compound up in the Briars, after carrying him through the casino in a fireman's hold to deposit in the back of Namir's truck. He was fairly sure Damian wouldn't wake up until Namir was there, he'd just hit the other dragon with the equivalent of a nuclear blast's worth of magic, but even if he did, he felt certain he could count on Damian's inherent civility to not murder Namir.

Mostly.

He took another employee's car home, one Damian's people would not be looking for, and drove aimlessly for half an hour before turning the correct direction, making sure he was in no way or shape followed.

The driving gave him time to consider things. If Samantha knew Andi it explained so much. How she knew of magic, and why she wasn't that worried that he was a dragon. What it didn't explain is why she'd never told him. She must've thought she was protecting Andi, and her loyalty to her friend made him want her all the more.

But 'want' was quickly becoming an inadequate word. The longer he was around her, the stronger his urges and needs became. It'd started with the necklace, yes, but now, just like he'd told Damian, it was her. And the thought of another man touching her, taking her, made him want to destroy things on a level he'd never felt before.

If only Samantha were as loyal to him as she was to her friend, what a pair they would make. He allowed himself one second to dream of it, her by his side, leaning her body against his as she whispered something into his ear, them ruling his underground empire together, before reality intervened as he parked in his garage.

He wasn't an emperor, but a man who had lost half himself below the sea, who might yet lose his whole self, and she was still the irrepressibly fierce woman who hated him.

. . .

HE FORGOT to make his usual fanfare entering his own home to warn her, closing the door quietly behind himself, and he heard Smoke growling from below as Samantha sounded unhappy. He went for the stairs and trotted down them, finding Smoke standing on the edge of one of her couches, looking down at her. She was fighting with a sheet, clearly in the throes of a nightmare.

"She's been like this for a while. Should I bite her?" Smoke asked, sounding concerned. "Just a little? To wake her?"

"No, Smoke," he said, reaching in and hesitating. Her nest was surrounded by books all opened up to the sirens. He didn't understand why she was so obsessed with them, unless she was hoping they'd kill him. "Samantha," he whispered, shaking her shoulder gently.

She fought him back, shoving his hand away.

"Samantha," he said a little louder. Her eyes snapped open, and she was panting. Her hand scrabbled for something at her waist—her little knife, he realized. "You're okay. You were having a nightmare, but you're all right," he told her, watching her slowly remember where she was and who he was to her, putting the knife down.

She put a hand to her head, sitting up. "Not really, Worst. How can I be? I'm still here."

He was glad it was dim in the room so she couldn't see how badly her words hurt him. "I told you not to read these things. Especially not before bed," he said, reaching in to close the books one by one.

"You're not the boss of me," she muttered but didn't stop him.

"Don't I know it," he muttered back at her. She looked up at him then, her eyes still dark with dreams. There was something tortured there, more so than usual. "Goodnight, Samantha," he told her and stood straight to walk back up a level. He would ask her about Andi tomorrow, now was not the time.

"Can you...wait?" she called after him, so quietly he wasn't sure he'd heard it. "Maybe?"

He paused and swallowed. "That bad, eh?" he asked, turning.

She wiped a hand across her face and looked ashamed. "You have no idea."

He sat down on the stairs themselves, putting his elbows on his knees. "I can stay till you're asleep again."

She looked around her little nest and frowned. "I don't know if I can."

"Now, or ever?" he asked lightly.

"Heh." She gave him a sad smile and ran her hands through her hair, making it even wilder than it had been.

"What was your dream about?"

She shook her head. "You'll only make fun of me."

Sirens for sure then. "Come upstairs," he told her, putting out his hand.

She looked between him and it, and he wondered if she'd refuse him, but then she climbed over the back of a couch and padded over in her socks and flannel pajamas. "Why?" she asked, without taking his hand.

"I'll show you," he said, leading her up to his level. He turned toward his bed and then walked beyond it, to the clear space with his altar. He opened its wards and pulled out the chalice, the dish of salt, and the dragon bone knife. He knelt in front of it while she sat with her back against the side of his bed. "See?" he told her, watching her watch him intently as he performed his ritual in front of her. He knew that she'd heard him say the words so often by now she might also have them memorized, but she still gasped as he cut himself because she'd never seen that part before. "I've made this pact for almost a thousand years, Samantha. So I promise you, no sirens will get to you tonight." He looked at the dark concoction in the chalice and felt her presence nearby. "I won't let that happen to you. Not now, nor ever."

If there was anyone worth going to the bottom of the sea to protect....

She made a small, sad sound, and he looked over quickly. Her arms were wrapped around her knees, her head was bowed, and there was salt in the air that wasn't from his ritual or his shark tank. "Samantha? What's wrong?"

"What's wrong is you pretend to care, but you don't, Worst," she said and then sobbed.

"Samantha," he said, trying to soothe her without moving her direction. It was as if he could feel the thorns around her growing, like her tears watered them. There was a slight possibility she could be playing him, he knew, but he doubted it when she was crying like that. The scent of her tears in the air was too true. "You know I can't let you go." *And wasn't that a perverted form of caring?*

"It's not about that," she said, sniffling, rubbing her face against her knees. "I mean...it is...but..." she said, sounding lost.

"Then what?" he asked her.

"My parents, Worst. You let my parents die," she said, without looking up. "How am I supposed to believe you'd save me when you didn't save them?" Her voice went higher as she spoke until it broke, and her whole body shivered, holding back another sob.

"What on earth are you talking about, Samantha?" Unless her parents were secretly magical object dealers—which would make an awful amount of sense—he had no idea.

She took a deep breath, raised her head, and stared into his altar like it had answers for her. "A siren killed my parents." Her voice was flat, and it was like he could feel her drifting away, while he would increasingly give anything to keep her safe, right here. "It rose out of the ocean, Worst. I remember the water dripping from its wings. I was just a little girl."

"Samantha," he whispered. No wonder the creatures mesmerized her. And he had a sudden sinking feeling inside his soul, as though part of him were being anchored down to the bottom of the sea already; all her panic, that night at the ocean, even before she'd seen the drowned ones. "So it was on the beach?" he guessed, and she nodded violently. *Oh, Red.* "How did you survive?" he asked gently.

"I crawled into the trunk of our car and hid."

Which was why she'd practically dissected his poor Jaguar. "Smart, brave girl," he murmured, and she shook her head.

"Not smart enough to save them. Or brave enough to tell anyone the truth, after a while." She took another long inhale and he watched her pull herself back together like she was refolding an old map, falling back into herself. He wondered how often she had to do that and if it got harder and harder for her to find herself after each time she pulled away. "This is the first time I've talked about it in probably a decade." She set her chin on her knees and her tousled hair covered half her face. "I was little. Everyone told me it was some random act of violence, that I hadn't seen what I'd seen. They made me think that I was mad—when they weren't making fun of me."

And all this time, he thought he'd been the worst thing to ever happen to her. "You have no idea how strong they are—and they're nearly indestructible. I can't believe you survived."

"I couldn't either, for a very long time." She lifted her head high enough to give him a sad half-smile. "But if they're all trapped under the sea, held back by the lock and your dragon—how did one get out to attack my family? On Earth, no less?"

He raked a hand through his hair, considering. "I saw a rift down there the other night. A small portal, in between worlds. It's possible that in the past, one or two got through."

"More than one or two," she corrected him softly. "The Sandcastle Killer—because that's what they call them since no one knows what they truly are, except me and you—has killed seven people. And I'm the only one who's ever survived."

"Sandcastles…like the ones in your bedroom?" So there was something of her family there, after all.

She nodded. "Yeah. I'm not going to ask what you were doing in my room though." She held her knees to her chest more tightly, as he watched her curl up into a little ball.

"Whatever they told you was a lie, you know that, right?" he asked her and saw her nod into her knees.

"That's what your books tell me. But it doesn't feel like a lie though," she whispered to herself.

It killed him that he had no right to touch her. "I don't know what to say, Samantha."

He watched her take another gulp of air. "I don't think there's anything to say. You were trying, I know. It's just hard being here, is all. For so long I thought you were going to kill me, and then I figured things out, and I wanted to be mad at you, but then I couldn't even get that right, could I?"

He knew she was asking herself, not him, but he still said the next thing that came to his mind aloud. "No wonder you hate me"

She looked over at him and her shoulders fell. "You really are an idiot sometimes, Mr. Worst." He frowned at her in confusion, trying to trace her mercurial moods. "I don't hate you. You just make me hate myself is all. Because the longer I'm here...." she began and then looked at him, pushing a wave of red hair behind her shoulder. "Why do you think I'm nice to you now?"

He continued to frown. "Lack of better things to do. Or, you're trying to trick me."

She glared at him. "You really think that's why? That's all?"

"I can't risk hoping that it's not," he answered truthfully. But he did, he *so fucking did*. Only that well had been tainted. He'd kept her here too long. There was no way to extricate fiction from reality, or for him to believe anything she told him.

"What if I told you, you were wrong?" she asked him. "What if —"

"Don't," he said low and closed his eyes. "Go back downstairs, Samantha."

He didn't hear her move a millimeter. "Why?"

"Because."

"No," she protested. "You can't boss me around anymore. You don't get to. Tell me."

"Because," he snapped and finally looked at her. "You're not the only one being tortured here," he said, then took a deep breath in. "Not anymore."

She frowned, and she pouted, and he thought she might cry, but then she recovered and went to all fours, crawling over to him. He braced for whatever that would bring, but all she did was kneel at his side and lean against him. It was such a simple, quiet, human thing, and it unarmed him utterly; more than her kissing him or her offering herself might have. Because both of those things would've made sense, but this? As she nuzzled her face into his shoulder, using his shirt to blot her tears? He wanted to pull her to him, to unfurl wings he no longer had to shelter her and protect her from utterly everything else. Her past, his future—him now.

And then she pulled his hand into her lap with both of hers, lacing her fingers through it as her breathing trembled. "Don't be scared," he whispered and felt her nod. He twisted his hand in hers, and he could feel how delicate her fingers were in comparison to his as he brought the back of her hand up for him to kiss. She gasped lightly as he did so. He bowed his head and smoothed the soft skin of the back of her hand against his cheek, and she sniffled before giggling. "What?" he asked.

"Sandpaper," she said, freeing her hand from his, to touch him on her own, stroking fingers across the stubble on his chin and down his jaw. "Just like the sharks."

He smiled and closed his eyes under her ministrations as she traced the outline of his lips and the edge of his cheekbone, breathing slowly and deliberately, staying completely still, giving her any chance she wanted to feel safe or run away. But it was hard. He could have pinpointed the distance between them now with any part of his body. For the first time in his life, he felt like he was drowning, breathless in an ocean of want and desire, and she was the shore he needed to reach to survive.

Then she stopped touching him and pulled back. He opened his eyes and found her fathomless blue ones waiting. "Don't you want me?" she asked.

He growled something incoherent as he lunged for her.

CHAPTER 17

S<small>AMMY HAD NO IDEA HOW MUCH</small> J<small>ANVIER HAD BEEN HOLDING BACK</small> until he rushed at her like a tidal wave. His lips met hers and took the both of them down, and she was so surprised she would've hit her head on the floor if his hand hadn't already been behind her to catch her. And then it was like she was being submerged in him—his tongue surged into her mouth, again and again, and she let it, right now she'd rather kiss than breathe—as his body rose over hers and crashed down, covering her completely. She moaned beneath him, running her hands up into his hair as his hips arched into hers, letting her feel the hard length of him rocking between her legs. She wrapped her legs around him, despite the fact that they were both still clothed, all too willing to give him whatever he wanted.

And then he pulled back, staring down at her, breathing hard. "I was wrong, Red. You should be very, very scared of me."

She was already dizzy from his kisses, so it was all she could do not to laugh. "Have I given you the impression so far that I give a fuck about my safety?"

His amber eyes studied hers. "I don't want you to hate me more."

"What if I promise not to?" she asked while rocking her hips against him.

He made another sound then, half-tortured, half-triumphant, and kissed her again, hard, running his hands into her hair and pinning her down, forcing her to surrender even more than she already had, until it felt like he might know her better than she knew herself and *how was that even possible?* Her head was spinning when he next lifted up, and she could feel her lips begin to swell. She saw his eyes trace over her, felt his hot and bothered breathing, and longed to tear his shirt off him and feel his skin.

"Samantha," he began, a question, surely, and she already knew the answer to it.

"Yes," she said, reaching for the waistband of her pajamas. "Condom now, and yes again."

He bowed his head over hers and snarled near her ear, a raw animal sound, and she felt his teeth graze her shoulder, and then one of his hands was with hers, shoving the fabric down that hid her before reaching to rattle his own belt open, and she heard the unzipping of a fly. He flipped his wallet open expertly with one hand and thumbed a foil packet out before throwing the wallet aside. "I just need," he growled, opening it with his teeth, before sliding it down his shaft in one smooth motion.

"Me too," she agreed, doing her final shimmy to get free, wrapping her arms around his chest and neck, feeling the silk of his shirt glide against the muscles of his back. And then he was against her, hot and hard and hungry, and she fisted fabric in her hands as he shoved himself in.

She was so tight, too tight, and he pistoned himself in roughly once, twice, making her whimper, even as her hips urged him on, and then suddenly everything was just right as her wetness caught up with her desires. He made a deep sound of carnal pleasure at feeling her heat envelope him and began to thrust more completely, taking her in long, strong strokes, whispering, "Oh, Samantha," as he lifted up her shirt, exposing her breasts, to kiss and lick and nuzzle as she rolled back and moaned.

What even was this? What was happening right now? Sammy ran her hands through Janvier's hair, clawing at his scalp, before running down his body, pulling up his shirt too, so that she could touch his muscles and his scars.

Who was this happening to?

Surely not her.

Surely she wasn't on the ground being fucked by a dragon, listening to him moan her name, feeling the thick hot length of his desire plunge in and out of her, like—if she were honest with herself—she'd been dreaming about for weeks.

Everything had an element of the unreal to it, from the entire situation to being here; until it felt like the only thing that was real was the shared space where they joined.

She pushed her small hands at his shoulders, arching her hips up to catch his. "Fuck me like that," she whispered.

He made an acquiescing noise, and he pulled his torso up as her hands directed so that she could look down through the valley between her breasts and across the small hill of her stomach and see where he relentlessly slid into her.

His eyes followed hers, and then one of his hands curled into her wild hair, keeping her neck bent and her gaze locked. "This is me taking you, Samantha," he said in a low tone, in time with his thrusts. "Owning you. Claiming you. Your whole body belongs to me." He lowered himself back down above her, fucking her harder now, more urgently, twisting her head so she could hear his rough whisper in her ear. "And now that I know I can fuck you like this, I'll never let you go."

She tensed because some part of her knew it was true. She should've never given into him, not one whit; she'd been a fool, she'd played the game to the edge and then pushed them both over.

But then, too, some dark and dirty part of her didn't want to go anymore. *Go back to jobs she hated and men who didn't care?*

At least here, with him—this felt *right*.

She made a soft submissive whine that was utterly unlike her and she had no idea where on earth it'd come from. Because she knew she should've been terrified and she should've fought back—she knew what it was to be a woman, and she knew all the rules.

But something about being trapped, knowing she was helpless and defenseless and utterly reliant on him—for once in her life, there was nothing she could do. So, whatever happened, it wasn't really her fault —right?

His dark amber eyes glittered and his hand reached for her neck, catching her so quickly she froze and gasped as he held her chin up. "I feel you thinking, Red, and I know you're turned on," he said, making her look at him as he pinned her, mid-thrust. "Which is it that you like? Being trapped, or being scared?"

His grip was tight enough that she knew he could feel her throat move as she nervously swallowed. "Both," she admitted in a shameful whisper.

A wicked smile played over his features. "Good," he said, and she watched him lick his lips hungrily as he released her throat. "All this time, I've been worried about breaking you, and it never occurred to me that you wanted to be broken."

"Only by the right man," she said to defend herself, moving her hands up to her neck where his had been. "Anyone can break someone else. But not everyone can put them back together again."

His eyes narrowed on hers. "True. Hold your breasts up for me."

She cupped her breasts together at his command, offering them to him, and he sucked at her nipples like they were dark pink candies, licking the lines of her fingers too, the roughness of his beard's shadow scraping against the softness of her under-breast, and a fresh rush of slippery heat spilled between her legs as she moaned.

He echoed her with a purr and then trapped her with his arms, the muscles of his biceps bulging. "I'm going to keep you here forever, Red," he promised as he thrust, lacing his fingers together behind her head, bowing his forehead to hers. "You have known the man of me so far, but the dragon of me wants to make you golden chains of rubies and diamonds and string you to my bed with them." Sammy shuddered at the thought, at both its horror and its beauty, and felt a forbidden tension rising between her legs as he went on. "I want you trapped here, ready, and waiting, so I can claim you morning, noon, and night."

He balanced himself on one arm and licked his free hand's fingers, sending them between them as he kept thrusting. When they found her clit her head rolled back, and she gasped again. "I want you to an unholy degree, Samantha," he confessed to her, his tone dark, and she could feel how his cock, already so hard inside of her, was becoming like an arrow, and she knew he was ready to blow...and...and, and so was she, her eyes screwed shut, imagining herself draped in jewels and beholden to a monster, both deliciously afraid and also fucking *fearless*.

"Janvier," she said, just like she had at Belissima's, clutching her hands in the hair at the nape of his neck as his fingers rocked against her clit, rubbing its little nub, as his hot, hard cock pierced her. "Mr. Janvier. Oh...fuck, fuck, fuck," she hissed, and then she couldn't make words anymore, all she could do was writhe and moan because waves of pleasure were wracking her, like a rose suddenly unfurling from her core, making her scream and twitch and shudder with each fresh petal's brush. Parts of her were coming that an orgasm had never touched before, and the parts that had, had never come this hard. "Janvier," she howled his name with tears in her eyes before collapsing and finally looking up. He was staring down at her, his eyes intently following everything about her, breathing hard, as he pulled out, discarding the condom to start stroking himself, sheathing himself in his foreskin, again and again, making the dusky red tip of his cock play peek-a-boo.

"If I can't come in you, I want to come on you," he warned.

"Or," she said suggestively, then sat up quickly, only to lay back down, this time on her stomach, facing him, pressing up on both her arms like a Sphinx to wrap her lips around his head.

"Samantha," he snarled, but his hand didn't stop; it beat against her lips as she sucked at him, kissing her taste off of him, running the point of her tongue against the slit at his tip. One of his hands wound in her hair and dragged her forward, and she went with it, taking more of him inside her, feeling his cock bend down at the back of her throat as she gagged.

"Can you take it?" he asked her, sliding himself in and out of her beneath his foreskin, as she nodded helplessly, eyes watering, looking up as he looked down.

He was so serious, and he was completely in charge of her, and yet he still looked like he was...in awe. "Red," he warned, "Oh...my, Red," he said and then grunted as his hips spasmed again and again, a wild sound, as his cock bobbed and twitched in her mouth and his cum poured, thick and salty, down the back of her throat.

"Samantha," he whispered afterward, his jaw dropped, looking down like he was scared of something that'd just happened, and she had no idea why, because wasn't she helping him? Hadn't he wanted a girl like her all this time?

What was the point of having chains if you had no one to put them on?

She took her time sucking off of him, cleaning him dry of every drop, until his cock hung down between them in its sheath and she was staring up at him, her lips as heavy from kisses as she could tell his were with things he wanted to say.

"We shouldn't have done that," he said, moving back.

Sammy pushed herself up to kneeling, tugging her pajama shirt down. "Why not?"

"Because it's not real."

She blinked at him, gathering her pajama bottoms into her lap to feel slightly less half-naked. "It felt real to me."

Janvier shook his head. "Only because I've trapped you down here." He was pulling his slacks up and lassoing his belt. There were dark stripes of sweat down the front of his dress shirt, and she knew the back was ruined from her nails.

She gave a sharp laugh. "I still have some agency, Mr. Worst."

"Do you?" he asked and lunged for her, pressing her against the side of his bed by her throat. "I'm a hundred times as strong as you; even if I wasn't, I'd outweigh you, and I'm keeping you magically trapped."

She grit her teeth in frustration even as her nipples went hard. "You didn't shove your dick down my throat...well, until the part where you did, but I *liked* that."

"Still," he said, letting her go.

"There's just the one thing, really," she told him.

"What? That fantasies are fantasies and life is not?" he asked with a wry snort. "Just that one huge thing?"

"No," she said simply while frowning at him. "I don't like diamonds."

He was momentarily disarmed by her; she could see it in his eyes. She knew he was opening up. She knew they were insane and that this was insane, but maybe, just maybe…. "Samantha," he said, putting his hand out for her cheek, right before he gave her an apologetic look.

She pulled back. "Don't you dare!" she demanded, right as he commanded her to sleep.

CHAPTER 18

WHEN SHE WOKE UP NEXT, IT WAS DAYLIGHT.

She knew because the room she was in had a window. It was half-open and there was a light breeze coming through it. She sat up, finding herself in a large bed in an airy space with a somewhat familiar Siamese cat sitting at the end of the bed. It saw her wake up and disappeared before she could pet it.

Literally.

Disappeared.

"What the—" Sammy said, putting her hand to her head. She had a headache and the last thing she remembered….

The door on the far wall burst open and Andi raced in at full speed. "Sammy!" she shouted, and she didn't let the bed stop her, she jumped aboard and climbed on over. "Are you all right? Did he hurt you?"

"Wait, what…who?" Sammy blinked and moved the hand she'd been touching her head with to her mouth. It felt like she could still feel his lips there. Why was she here? What had happened?

"Oh my God, I was so worried about you!" Andi said, engulfing her in a hug. "If he did anything, I'll have Damian dismember him—"

"No, he didn't, I'm fine," Sammy said, hugging Andi at the same time as she tried to hold her off.

"He's had you for three weeks, Sammy!"

"I...I know," Sammy whispered.

"I'm so sorry! If I'd have known that was going to happen to you, I never would have left!" Andi cupped her chin in her hands and stared into her eyes. "Are you hungry? Thirsty? Where did he keep you? If you were in a cage, so help me God—"

"No," Sammy said, more definitively, catching Andi's hands in her own to bring them down to her lap and hopefully calm her down. Everything seemed so bright and loud. She'd grown accustomed to her dim solitude. "I love you, but can we take it down a notch?" she asked.

Andi nodded, her face crumpling as she tried to hold back tears before she hugged Sammy one more time and squeezed her hard. "I'm just so glad you're all right!"

Was she?

"Yeah," Sammy agreed because she knew she ought to, hugging her best friend. She caught a glimpse of green on her right hand. Janvier had given her both her freedom and her ring back. "Me too."

THE REST of that day Sammy didn't really feel like her feet touched the ground. Not in an 'I'm so happy, I'm floating away' kind of way. It was more of an 'I'm not entirely sure how to interact with the world anymore' situation.

She'd spent so much time with Janvier trying to get free, but now that she was she couldn't for the life of her remember why she'd wanted it so badly.

Apparently Janvier had shown up on Damian's doorstep, rung the bell, and passed her sleeping body over without comment, and then she'd slept for half a day before waking up. Andi had assaulted her with love, and then a few hours after that, she was in a fresh change of clothing and being introduced to everyone...*werewolves, a princess, and a witch!*...at length inside a conference room, while they quizzed her on just what had happened to her. Sammy only told them what she felt they needed to know though. The necklace, the key, the sirens, the Gate. She skipped as much as she could of Janvier's personal history, most of his time with her, and anything about her past.

"So you really believe he was trying to protect you?" Damian mused aloud. He sounded upset to not have a reason to go pound Janvier's head in.

"Yes," Sammy said, nodding strongly.

"A dragon protecting a human? Who would've ever believed," Ryana-the-princess scoffed, taunting her brother Damian. She herself was half-dragon, and she had wide green wings that arched behind her. Sammy was having a hard time not gawking.

Mills, who'd been introduced to her as a witch, made a thoughtful noise. She was a well put together woman in her late thirties, early forties, with what must've been floor-length salt and pepper hair in a huge bun. "Well, while I'm unfamiliar with the magic involved, I can see why he was concerned. You're radiating energy."

Jamison, a black man not much older than Sammy, made a timeout T shape in front of his chest with his one human hand and his other metal one that was attached to a metal arm that rose up to a socket at his shoulder. "Hold up. So we're saying rifts can happen under the sea? How the fuck are we supposed to stop those? We don't even have any sensors down there."

"But we have fought sirens before," Zach said, leaning back. He was a handsome but very serious looking werewolf wearing a black suit.

"And, we didn't know where they came from," Max said. He was tall and lean, with pale skin and paler hair, and Andi and said he was a polar bear sometimes. The goggles he had on covering his eyes made him hard to read. "Now we do."

"Wait," Sammy said, looking around the table at their group. "You've fought them? And survived?"

"Yeah," said Austin, another werewolf, with auburn hair, who was the most down-to-earth appearing of the group. If someone had told

Sammy that she'd been at a party with him before, she would've thought, *Yeah, seems likely.*

"I mean, they fucking suck, and I wouldn't want to take one on alone, but," he went on.

Sammy's brain did a double take. Andi's new friends...*really had fought sirens.*

"Sammy?" Andi asked, clocking the amazed look on her face.

Sammy centered on Mills as the brains of the operation, based on questions she'd raised so far. "I think you need to map times of earthquakes, all of you fighting sirens, and the Sandcastle Killer's victims. I think you'll find some overlap."

Mills's eyebrows rose, but she nodded. "Easy enough."

"Thanks," Sammy said and stood. "I, uh, really appreciate all this, and you've been very kind to me considering the odd circumstances around my arrival, but I'm ready to go home."

Mills looked to Andi and then looked back. "I'm sorry, Samantha, but you cannot leave our compound." She gestured to the necklace that was still at Sammy's throat. "I'm willing to experiment on removing that, of course, but until we do, leaving our grounds without protection would be like having a bulls-eye painted on you."

Sammy's hand rose to touch the red stone without thinking. *Everything she'd gone through, everything she'd lost, and she wasn't even truly free?*

"It's nice here, Sammy. You'll like it," Andi said, grabbing her free hand and then adding, "I'm so sorry."

Sammy sighed, sitting back down slowly. "I know."

THERE WAS a knock outside her door that evening. Sammy felt a stupid lurch of hope inside her heart. *As long as the door was closed, anyone could be behind it.* And then she heard Andi's soft, "Hey."

"Hey yourself," Sammy said. She'd just been staring out the window, missing sharks.

Andi came in and shut the door behind her, leaning against it. "I want to ask if you're okay, and I know that that's stupid, but also I can't help myself."

"I don't know, really," Sammy said. She sat up and pushed a group of pillows behind her against the wall. Andi'd remembered her appropriate pillow ratio, seven pillows to every Sammy. "Like, I know that I will be all right again, eventually, because I've done this kind of thing before? And that's good, I guess. But right now I'm just really tired and really sad."

Andi crossed the room and sat down on the ground, putting her chin in her hands and her elbows on the bed. "I wish I'd known what'd happened, Sammy. We would've dropped everything and come back right away."

Sammy shook her head. "I'm not sad about that part."

"What part are you sad about then?" Andi asked gently.

Sammy looked down at her best friend's beautiful, kind face. *The part where I was finally getting to know Janvier?*

Or the part where I was finally letting him know me?

"It's okay," Andi said, reaching over to pat Sammy's leg beneath her blanket. "There's no rush. We can just hang out here if you want. Or, in a room with a TV."

Sammy gave her a tight smile. Andi was just trying to help, and hanging out with other people was probably better for her soul.

Even if they weren't the right person.

"With popcorn?" she asked.

"Of course," Andi said, moving to stand and holding out a hand for her.

Two days later and Andi's mansion didn't feel like home, but it wasn't entirely strange anymore, just perpetually disappointing.

Everyone in it was nice enough to her, and Andi was awesome of course, but she couldn't shake the sense that she'd lost something profound. Her time with Janvier seemed to blot out everything before it. She couldn't find her way back to being the person she'd been before.

She wasn't sure she wanted to.

Being with Janvier had felt more real to her than any other relationship she'd ever had. But she couldn't disentangle the parts of that that'd come from her captivity—or technically worse, her *utility* to him—from all the maybes of her hopes and dreams.

Hopes and dreams that he didn't share, obviously, seeing as he'd abandoned her here.

She would spend hours feeling sad and then getting angry, but what caught her and kept her unable to move on was what she'd seen when he'd let her watch his ceremony, inside his altar, the place where he kept his most precious things locked up.

The pink triangle of her scarf from that first night.

She'd assumed it was lost at Belissima's, but he'd grabbed it and taken it home.

Maybe she had meant something to him. From the beginning, not just at the end after she'd worn him down.

"Sammy?" Andi asked her, and Sammy blinked to life. She'd been staring out another open window.

"Sorry," Sammy said. She was sitting at lunch and Andi had made her a sandwich.

"It's okay. You don't have to apologize to me. Except for the fact that you like pickles," Andi said, giving her turkey sandwich a glare as if it'd bitten her.

Sammy snorted and took a bite of her sandwich. It was crisp and sour and delicious. She jerked her chin at the window. "Hey, can I go out?"

"You don't have to ask me either," Andi said. "You just can't go past the gate, is all."

"Yeah, that's how gates work, they keep telling me," Sammy muttered to herself.

Andi gave her a strange look, but with love. "Want company?"

"Maybe on round two this afternoon," Sammy said, picking up her sandwich, putting it on a napkin to take with her.

She was already dressed in shorts and a t-shirt, and she put sneakers on before going outdoors. Damian's cage was a little prettier than Janvier's, if you liked sunlight and fresh air. Sammy was trying to get used to them again. Hard to think that she'd taken them for granted for so long, then had wanted daylight like she was starved, only now to find it much too bright all the time. *What was with all this light? How did anyone stand it?*

She walked to the perimeter behind Damian's castle and started making a big circle, past his garage, where his Pagani was parked—which now, thanks to the necklace, she couldn't take on any drives—and around the back of the castle, where there was only a narrow gap before a very substantial drop, and lastly through his garden. It was her favorite place outside so far, lush and wild, and she'd found a bench hidden inside of it yesterday. She sat down, listened to the water trickle in the fountain closer to the house, and tried to get back to normal.

There was a rustle in the underbrush behind her and she turned around, kicking her legs to the back of the bench as Damian's cat Grimalkin appeared. It seemed like he followed her a lot.

"Well, hello there," she told him, pulling a pickle out of her sandwich to offer him. He made a hairball sound to show his disgust. She popped it into her mouth instead and then spoke around it. "So rude!" she teased. "More for me then, I guess." She fished another one out of her sandwich to crunch on its own. "I used to know a nice fox who was addicted to them, I'll have you know. And unlike you, he had good taste."

"I'll tell Smoke. I'm sure he'll be charmed."

Janvier's voice from behind her made her shiver even before she turned around. "You," she said, going up on her knees on the bench, sandwich forgotten. It was the first time she hadn't seen him in a suit or swim trunks, he was just in a dark gray t-shirt and blue jeans, and he had a stack of books under one arm. His eyes traced over her hungrily as she dismounted the bench and stormed over. "You made another decision without talking to me!"

There was a bright green light behind Janvier and the sound of more than one weapon arming—the familiar *chuk-chuk* of someone sliding a shotgun shell into place and a more ominous high-pitched whine. Austin, Ryana, Jamison, and Mills ran out, and she heard Damian's voice boom, "Get the fuck off of my property," as he advanced. Suddenly the Siamese cat beside her was the size of a tiger.

"No!" Sammy figured out what was happening and ran to the front of the garden, where all of Damian's crew was pouring in, blocking them from Janvier bodily.

Damian...was frightening.

Like all those times Andi had told her he could be an asshole, she hadn't really wanted to believe, because he was Andi's boyfriend, and who could scare her anyway? But the way he looked walking up, cold, cruel, collected, and entirely capable of murder, Sammy finally got it.

She grit her teeth though and she stood her ground.

"Hiding behind women?" Damian addressed Janvier, he didn't even spare Sammy a glance.

"The view is marvelous. Can you blame me?" Janvier said, then stepped to the side. "I only wanted to talk to her," he said, and Sammy watched Damian clench his jaw. "I would do it elsewhere if I could, but I can't." Janvier held up both his hands, as much as he was able to with the books under one arm. "I merely brought books for her to read. Nothing else."

"Mills?" Damian asked.

"He's got at least one magical object on him," the witch said.

Sammy looked up and caught him frowning. "A gift, for her," Janvier said.

"You lied," Damian growled.

"Well, it was meant to be a surprise," Janvier said dryly.

Damian advanced and so did Sammy, to cut him off. "Look, I know you want to yell at him and all? But so do I! So can I get some privacy?"

Mills brought a hand to her mouth to hide her chuckle, whereas both Austin and Ryana straight up laughed, and Jamison tilted down the front of his gun with a smile. "Other than that, Damian, I think it's fine," Mills said, reaching for the dragon-shifter's arm. "We'll have Grimalkin keep watch, just in case?" Mills asked of Sammy.

Sammy nodded quickly. "That's fine."

Damian glowered at Janvier one last time. "You hurt her and—"

"I know," Janvier agreed. "I won't."

The others stepped back and Grimalkin went back to just being the size of a normal cat. He leaped up to the bench, sniffed at Samantha's sandwich again, and then batted it over the seat's edge with an affronted swipe.

Janvier turned toward her once they were alone, and the way he looked at her made her want to go easy on him. "I can see why you survived the sirens."

"You're still in trouble!" Sammy told him, staying strong. "You... you abandoned me!"

Janvier tilted his head and looked around. "No, I brought you here. To the sunny and apparently well-armed abode of your best friend."

"I didn't want to be here!"

"You wanted to be free."

"This isn't freedom!" Sammy shouted at him. "You just made another decision for me without asking! Without listening! Even though you promised not to!" She wanted to throw herself at his chest and hit him. He deserved it, and she knew she couldn't hurt him, and maybe that was the problem. It didn't matter how pained he looked right now; there was nothing she could ever really do to hurt him, ever, and oh so many things he could do to hurt her. "Why are you even here, Mister Worst?"

He reached into his pocket and pulled out something, another piece of red gemstone, and held it out to her. "It's my part of the key," he said. She looked between him and it and gingerly took it from him. It looked exactly like the stone around her neck, without the setting and the chain. She flipped her necklace over and matched it to her stone's back. It fit, but it didn't feel any different and it easily fell right off.

"Why didn't you show me this already?" she asked, handing it back to him.

He looked a little sheepish. "I was worried that it might get stuck to yours, magically, and then you would have two pieces of the key, rather than just one."

"And now?" she wondered.

"It's yours. If you want it."

She frowned at the bright red stone inside her palm, contemplating what that might mean. "Are you giving up on getting your dragon free?"

Janvier shook his head. "My brother still waits on the Gate's far side. I haven't decided."

"But if you've given me two pieces of the key…." she said, the new piece in her palm growing heavy.

"I'm not saying I have an amazing plan," Janvier said and laughed darkly as Sammy took him in.

What were they to one another, truly? She knew what she wanted them to be, but if he didn't want that or didn't feel capable of returning it—she dared to reach up to cup her hand along his jaw. "How long do you have to decide?"

He twisted his cheek into her palm and then gently pushed her wrist away. "A week or two."

Hearing that—it was like getting stabbed. It made her forget that he didn't want her to touch him for a second. "I don't want you to go," she told him.

His eyes lit on hers and looked like flames, but then he sighed, stepping back. "As enjoyable as that is to hear, Red, I don't truly believe you want me unleashing a flock of sirens on anyone, either."

Hot tears she was angry at sprang to her eyes. "But…Damian's people, they've fought them before!"

"They're not strong enough for this many. And if I go, I'm going where they can't follow."

"And where I can't follow either." She grabbed hold of the stone so tightly it hurt. "Take it back," she said, offering it out to him again. "I don't want it." The stone looked like a small pool of blood in her palm, like when she'd cut herself not long ago. "Take it back!" she demanded, stepping forward.

"I can't—"

"You can!" she said, clenching the stone in her fist and set to throw it at him. He caught her wrist before she could, cupping her fist with his other hand's palm so she couldn't drop it, either, pulling her to stand close to him.

"What would you have me do, Red?" he asked and bowed his head to look at her. "Trade my heart for yours, and take it to the bottom of the sea with me? How badly do you want this to hurt, Samantha? You've read all the stories in my books. You know these things never work."

She tried to blink back tears. "But...Damian and Andi—"

"They just don't know any better yet," Janvier said softly. "What trials have they ever been through, eh?"

And now there was no stopping it; tears were streaming down her face. "I don't care! I'm just asking you not to leave me. Again." Sammy closed her eyes and begged him softly, "Please."

He caught her face in both hands, gently stroking her tears off of her cheeks with his thumbs, and then chastely kissed her forehead.

"Please," she sobbed.

"Good-bye, Samantha," he whispered. She felt him step away, and by the time she opened up her eyes again, he was gone.

SAMMY BUCKLED to the bench behind her, put her fist with the stone she didn't want to her stomach, and sobbed. She didn't like crying outside, in semi-public, but if she went indoors, Andi would know she'd been crying. Andi would want to hear everything, and it would only make her feel worse.

She didn't know how long she'd been morosely staring at the ground when she heard someone gently clear their throat.

"Samantha?" asked a woman's voice.

The cat strode into the small clearing, followed by Mills, the witch, who looked much less put together currently in a death metal t-shirt and leggings, even if her hair was still bunned up.

"Present," Sammy said, defeatedly.

Mills walked over and sat down on the bench beside her, Grimalkin weaving through her feet. "You're *the* Samantha O'Connor, aren't you," she asked, and Sammy knew instantly what she meant. The Sandcastle Killer's only known survivor.

"Yeah."

"Then, while I suspect it is cold comfort, you should know that you were right. There has been an overlap between small earthquakes and mysterious deaths on the beach here. For centuries, but it's gotten worse lately."

Sammy nodded slowly. "I had a feeling."

"And...it's getting worse because?" Mills prompted her.

"If I had to guess," she said, setting her free hand on the books he'd left her—and after having read so many of them in her captivity, she thought she might know, "It's because his dragon's power's lessening. He'll have to go down and join it soon, or all the sirens in his Realm will get free."

"What a horrible fate," Mills murmured.

"Yes," Sammy agreed. "And what's even worse is that his brother is trapped inside the Gate with them. There's no way for him to win. Either he stops the sirens and traps his brother for eternity, along with himself inside his dragon, or loses his dragon and sets his brother free at the cost of who knows how many lives?" Sammy turned toward the witch. "I told him you all could stop them," she began, hoping that Mills would say the right thing. "But he thinks it's too dangerous, he won't even let you try."

"In my rudimentary studies between when you were first returned to us and now, Samantha, if he's from the Realm I think he is, he's not wrong." Mills winced. "We do death-defying things regularly here but I cannot recommend we go on suicide missions. We can't fight them underwater and fighting them on boats is untenable; there'd be nowhere to hide from them and escape opportunities would be impossibly scarce."

Sammy bit her tongue to not say what she was thinking loudly: *But Damian's a dragon!*

Somehow Mills seemed able to read her mind. "All of Rax's people were dragons too. And if this is the solution they came up with, Samantha, they had their reasons."

She sighed as Mills reached over to put her hand on hers. "I won't give up," the witch went on. "But I can only tell you the truth: whatever he decides, it doesn't look good."

Sammy flipped her hand over quickly. "Can you do something with this? Maybe?" she asked, offering Mills the free portion of the stone.

"Is it the same as the one around your neck?" Mills asked.

"Yes," she said with a nod.

"I can certainly try," Mills said, taking it and moving to stand again, resting a hand briefly on Sammy's shoulder. "And I won't give up. I mean it."

Sammy gave her a sad smile. "Hurry then."

SAMMY LEAFED through the books Janvier had left her after Mills left. They were ones she hadn't read yet, so they must have not mentioned sirens. She picked them up and walked in to find Andi waiting for her right inside the door. Andi took her in, hugged her tight, and then looked at the tomes.

"Did that fucker give you homework?" she asked.

Sammy gave a rueful laugh. "No. He just knows I like to read."

"Read?" came another female voice from somewhere upstairs, and then Ryana appeared, wings and everything, racing down them. "Books…from the Realms?" Her expression was a combination of delight and hunger. She was eyeing the books like they were edible gold.

"Yeah." Sammy hefted them up and divided the stack in two. "Here. We can share, as long as you promise not to hurt them."

"I would never," Ryana swore, taking the offered books gently. "Thank you so much!"

A woman with wings was thanking her. *This was her new normal now.* "You're welcome," Sammy said.

"What do you want to do now, Sammy?" Andi asked, lacing her fingers with Sammy's.

Sammy didn't give voice to the thought in her head: *What I want is for him to come back.*

GIVING Samantha up was the hardest thing Rax had ever done, up until he'd left her again in Damian's garden.

He'd managed to convince himself he was doing the right thing letting her go, back when she'd been asleep the first time beside him in Namir's truck. That he was somehow being noble, that she'd wake up, have a brief moment of appreciation, and then never think of him again.

What he hadn't counted on was how much doing so would kill him. Every mile he drove away from Damian's house that day it felt like a part of his soul was coming unstitched. It was the same feeling he'd had when they'd separated him from his dragon, and he knew he didn't have much soul left to spare. And then, coming back to his villa, full of her presence and her scent?

The lack of her had almost killed him.

He'd spent his hundred years of imprisonment meditating on what a fool his brother had been to let his grief at Seris's loss affect him so, and then two hundred after that cursing both of their names.

But his first steps into his empty villa, without Samantha there, he finally understood. Not fully, because Samantha was still alive, but Tarian's pain made sense to him at last.

He finally cared. Not about himself, or his tremendous burden, or the losses that he'd withstood. But about a singular woman he'd had to release for her own wellbeing.

He ate alone, like he always used to, only now he felt it for the first time. He played the piano, and it seemed pointless because there was no one listening. And at night, he heard the tap-tap-tap of Smoke's claws on the cement floors as he paced below. He snapped for the beast, and the fox jumped up on the bed to lay beside him.

"I never got to bite her," Smoke complained.

Rax ran a hand over the fox's wiry hair. "Me either."

So then of course he'd tried to move on. *Because that was an important thing to do before one made irreparable life choices.* Clean slate and all that. Choosing between freeing your brother or letting heinous beasts out and undoubtedly losing the respect of the woman you'd discovered that you loved.

Because that's what this was, wasn't it, this hollow emptiness and yearning, the shadow left in his life in the places she had been. Even if he was vastly unfamiliar with the concept, it seemed like there was nothing else that it could be.

He had loved her in his own strange, cruel way, and now it was too late.

Only he couldn't stop thinking about her. He couldn't bring himself to erase her scent from his home or thoughts of her from his mind.

And then, as he was cleaning his study and putting all of the books she disrupted away, taking apart the nest she'd created in the couches, he'd found the note she'd created for future historians and hidden in its stuffing, from back when she'd been so sure he was going to murder her.

Against his better judgment, he added to it and decided to see her one last time. To give her the final portion of the key on land. Hoping beyond hope that maybe once the stones touched, they'd heal, free her, and somehow grant him the ability to open the Gate. Then he could free his brother and close it again without losing himself or releasing the sirens.

But that hadn't happened, and now he was driving home with the scent of her tears on his fingers and pain more crushing than the deep below pressing on his chest.

CHAPTER 19

A FEW DAYS LATER, SAMMY AWOKE FROM AN EVENING NAP TO A knocking at her door. She still wasn't back to a normal sleep schedule yet, but that was okay because Damian's house seemed to be a twenty-four-seven situation.

"Sammy?" whoever was outside asked.

"Just a second!" Sammy shouted, grabbing clothes up off her floor. She didn't even bother with a bra as it was a girl's voice, she pulled a hoodie on over her t-shirt and tugged on a recently dropped skirt. "Come in," she said, and Mills opened the door. Sammy wiped her face to wake up, as Mills sat down on the purple couch Damian had bought Andi months ago. Andi had gone back by their old apartment and had brought back most of Sammy's belongings, her desk, their TV, and a dead houseplant, and so things in her room were homier here now, but still felt wrong. At Mills sitting though, Sammy moved to perch on the end of her bed. "Yes?" she asked with hope.

Mills opened her hand and showed Sammy an hourglass full of red sand.

"Is that...the key I gave you?" Sammy gasped.

"What's left of it," Mills said, twisting it lightly, without flipping it over. "It can shield your necklace from discovery for three hours, but only once."

Sammy blinked. "What good will that do?"

Mills set the object on her desk and gave her a look. "You tell me."

Sammy contemplated the hourglass and what the sand inside it meant. Three hours of freedom, true freedom—to do whatever she pleased. But the only person she wanted…. "He's left me twice now," she said aloud.

"True," the witch granted, with a nod. "But he's also taken on Damian twice now, for your sake."

A fresh knocking at her doorjamb interrupted their conversation, and Ryana stepped in through the open door, tucking her wings down to enter. "I found this in the back of a book," she said, handing a piece of paper out. Sammy took it and saw it was written in the looping script of the Realms.

"You can read ancient dialects?" Ryana squinted at her.

"With the necklace on," Sammy said, touching the stone around her neck as if for luck. At the bottom of the note she'd written was a post-script in someone else's handwriting.

My name is Rax Janvier, and my heart is being held against my will.
I think it's been three weeks.
My captor is a human.
And if you're reading this, Samantha…you may keep it for all time.

SHE SWALLOWED. Their relationship, strange and sharp and not-right as it was, wasn't just about the necklace. And her feelings weren't just hers. Sammy stood as if compelled and picked up the hourglass, her feet deciding for her yet again. "Thank you," she told Mills and meant it more than she'd meant almost anything else, before looking to Ryana. "Tell your brother I want the keys to his Pagani. He still owes me."

A slow grin spread across the other woman's face. "You really can read it!" she said and laughed and then Andi was in the doorway with keys in hand.

"Ryana told me what it said and Mills told me what she was working on." Andi tossed the keys to Sammy. "Just promise me you'll come back before you turn into a pumpkin?"

Sammy caught the keys with her free hand and grinned at her. "I'll do my best."

SAMMY TURNED the hourglass over the second she passed through the gates leaving Damian's compound in his two million dollar car. She tried not to watch the red sand fall down as she navigated the twists and turns to get down to the Lynx. She didn't know where Janvier's home was so she couldn't meet him there, but she knew this time of night the club would be open, and if he wasn't there surely Namir would know how to get a hold of him.

She raced into town, hardly able to appreciate the amazingness of Damian's frankly ridiculous vehicle until she double-parked in front of the nightclub and got out.

She was still in the clothes she'd picked up off her floor when Mills knocked. She hadn't brushed her hair—or her teeth.

But it didn't matter now. She held the hourglass in one hand as she approached the bouncer, cutting to the front of the line of fashionable looking people queuing to get in. She recognized the bouncer from working there, but it was clear he didn't remember her in her civilian outfit.

"Yo, Charles. I need you to pass something on to Mr. Janvier."

The man gave her an annoyingly blank look and then focused on the Pagani, slightly stunned. She snapped her fingers for his attention. "It's about a drug deal," she said, loud enough for the first five people in line to hear, which shut them up. Saying that seemed likely to explain her possession of that kind of vehicle and would make what-ever she said next worth passing on. "I need you to tell him this code phrase, precisely, okay? And he'll reward you, I swear. You hearing me?"

The man frowned but grunted. "Yeah. Go on."

"Tell him it's Red—I've never been in a relationship that worked, so why the fuck should this be any different—and that he's got two hours and thirty-seven minutes before this spell expires."

Charles looked between her and the car again, shrugged, and said, "Copy that," before repeating exactly what she said into his earpiece.

Sammy rocked back, holding the hourglass tightly in one hand, swearing she could feel the sand run out inside it.

Charles cupped a hand to his ear and gave her an appraising look. "He says to give him fifteen minutes and to step back."

Sammy closed her eyes. *Fifteen fucking minutes?* her very soul complained and then she heard the fire alarms go off. Women screamed, men shouted, and people came pouring out of the club. Sammy stayed plastered along an outside wall as the people who'd been lining up dispersed, and people running out hailed taxis and Ubers. Charles made a bored spinning motion with one arm, directing patrons out, muttering, "Come on, come on," and after the first rush seemed to have stopped Sammy stepped inside.

A few rogue employees were shuffling out drunken patrons and Namir was closing out the register behind the main bar. "Hey!" he said sharply, seeing her come in, and then he recognized her. One of his eyebrows crept up his forehead and then he jerked his chin toward the door in the back.

She fought upstream through the last of the stragglers, to the door that'd never opened for her before—she tried it and found it unlocked.

She stepped into a short dark hallway with another door. She would've paused to make herself more presentable, but the sand was still sifting. She closed her eyes briefly, willed herself to be brave, and opened it.

Inside was a massive room, full of card tables and booths, with a huge bar in back. People had *just* been here, there were cards and chips strewn about the tables, half-finished drinks on the felt, and Janvier was standing at the back of everything, in front of the bar, taking off his coat to drape over a nearby chair and then work on the buttons of his cuffs, as he gave her a sidelong glance with his fiery eyes.

"I need you to know, Samantha," he began, "that if you take one more step inside this room, I'm going to make you say my name."

Sammy set her hourglass down on the nearest table and ran for him.

SAMANTHA FLUNG herself at him and he caught her. She was *real*, he could figure out how she'd gotten free later, but for now his mouth found hers.

God, she was really here.

He felt immersed in her, smelling her, touching her, tasting her. Her arms were around his neck, her legs were around his waist, she was covering him in kisses, and for maybe the first time in his life and definitely hundreds of years, he felt adored.

Samantha didn't want anything else from him—she had no subterfuge, no angles, nothing to prove—she just wanted him.

Yes, he thought as something deep inside himself began to unknot. *This is what being loved is like.*

She pulled up to look down at him, crying happily for the first time since she'd met him.

"No tears," he told her.

Samantha pretended to pout. "Shut up, I'm a crier, you know that."

Rax did. He laughed, kissing her again, staring up at her, and trying to memorize everything about her. He wanted forever with her, but he knew he'd only have tonight. "I wish I could take my time with you," he whispered.

She shook her head sorrowfully, glancing back at whatever she'd set down. "Time's the one thing we don't have," she said. "Besides," she said with a swallow, "I'm not used to that."

He wanted to promise her that she would be, were she to stay with him, but he knew he couldn't. Nor did he want to make any promises on behalf of any men she might have in the future because thinking on that would kill him.

Before he could think of what to say instead though, she took his face in her hands. "Just give me your now?" she asked him.

"Yes," he agreed instantly, completely, from the bottom of his soul.

She stared into his eyes and then kissed him hesitantly after that, thoughtfully, like she was trying to learn everything about him, and he wished he had the patience to let her, but he did not. The longer he touched her, held her against him, her breasts against his chest, his hands around her waist and on her ass; he twisted his lips away from hers and growled against her neck. He shuddered with need for her. He wanted her like he'd never wanted any woman prior.

As a human, could she understand? Did she know what it meant to have a dragon love her and only her, from now until the end of time?

Even if that dragon was at the bottom of an ocean, trapped in blue darker than her eyes?

She made a relenting sound against him, burying herself into his chest, and his cock was heavy against his slacks. All he wanted to do was free it and shove it inside her, feel her walls wrapped around him again, and watch her beautiful face as he made her come.

He swept all the glassware that'd been on his wide bar aside with an arm, listening to the glasses fall and shatter, and then set her on its edge. Her legs circled him to keep him near even as he started kissing at her throat and neck while his hands pushed up her skirt.

She kept making small soft sounds, gasping as his lips kissed her, running her fingers through his hair and down his neck, kneading him closer to her, twining her ankles behind him, as his fingertips found the edges of her underwear. Her hands found his on the outside, and then raised her hips up off of his bar for long enough for him to pull them down, rocking back and forth, and then she unzipped her hoodie, letting it fall open so that he could bury his face between her breasts, pushing up the fabric there too as she grabbed the edge of her shirt and pulled everything off until she was sitting almost completely naked in front of him, her skirt hitched high and breathing hard.

"You're so beautiful, Samantha," he told her, and he saw her flush.

He caught one of her perfect freckled breasts and held it up for himself so that he could suck on its peak and hear her moan.

She stared down at him, her jaw dropped. "I want this. Truly," she whispered.

He closed his eyes and kept sucking at her, lifting her other breast to join the first, brushing his lips against its nipple before licking it with his tongue. "Which part?" he murmured against her, his dark eyes flashing up.

"All of it," she admitted. "With you."

Rax closed his eyes again and let the echo of her confession fill him up, finding all the dark and empty places in his divided soul and occupying them with what was surely his mate's love. He bit the side of her breast gently, so as not to speak, bowing his head against her, breathing in her cinnamon scent.

If this was to be their last time before he took his leave and went down to the bottom of the sea...then he needed everything of her.

Now.

"Pull your skirt up and lean back Samantha," he growled.

She instantly did as she was told, exposing all of herself to him as she rocked back against his bar, each of her feet precariously balanced on the barstools to either side of him. Her delicate pink pussy was surrounded by a soft halo of red hair, and he reached in to hold her hood up with his thumb, exposing her tiny clit to him. He descended on it with his mouth, breathing first, so he could smell her sex and tease her, before he kissed it with his lips, shifting it with his tongue, following it as he rubbed it with his tongue tip.

Her hands were in his hair in a moment, holding him right where he needed to be, pulling his mouth onto her as she arched her hips up to give him more.

"Oh my God," she whispered, as he reached up his free hand to pull at her nipples while he taunted her with his tongue. "Oh, oh please—right there—like that," she begged, writhing, making sounds more beautiful than any his piano had ever given up. He went from tongue tip to broad strokes with the flat of his tongue as she got more turned on, rolling her clit up and down, back and forth, sucking all of her in,

CASSIE ALEXANDER & KARA LOCKHARTE

feeling her wetness drip down his chin. As badly as he needed to fuck her—and he did, his cock was harder than it'd ever been, aching for release—it was imperative she come for him like this. If he was going to survive the dark alone, he needed to know exactly what she tasted like, he didn't want to have to wonder.

She made a high-pitched whine and clutched his hand against her breast as he pulled a nipple hard, as her ass wound and her thighs tightened, and he growled for her, urging her on. He trusted his tongue to find her swollen clit and let go of her hood, reaching for his cock; he couldn't help it, stroking its length beneath his slacks as he sucked her harder with his lips and rubbed her faster with his tongue, his face buried between her legs, begging her to ride him and give him, a dying man, one last drop. "Oh!" she shouted as her first wave hit. "Oh my God—oh...oh!"

She curled up around him, her calves tensing as her hips thrashed, and he followed her through, making an animalistic sound of pleasure on her behalf, savagely licking her clean until she finally collapsed.

He wiped his mouth and chin clean against the back of his hand. "Red, make room," he said, his voice rough.

She pushed herself up on her elbows and twisted to lay lengthwise in the space that he'd cleared as he rose up to join her. He moved to kneel between her legs, setting his hands to the buckle of his belt. Her dark blue eyes watched him work as her breath trembled with anticipation, and then she sat up and started undoing the buttons of his dress shirt for him. He paused what he was doing, both feeling and watching her slide her hands against his skin, wanting to trap the moment for an eternity, wishing he could live a life where she could undress him every night, while knowing that this, right here, was all they would ever have. He wanted her to touch him so badly. All he wanted was to be known by her, the woman that what little was left of his dragon in him wanted to name his mate.

He had to be inside her, all the way.

For real this time.

He ripped his shirt open then held himself over her with one hand, holding his cock with the other, pulling his foreskin back against his rock hard shaft, so she could see just how badly he needed her. Her eyes followed the line of his cock with a gasp, and he looked down to see what she did, the thick red head of his cock already dripping precum at the thought of being inside her.

"I don't want to use a condom, Samantha," he warned her. "And I don't want to pull out. I want to fucking come in you and make you mine."

He dared to look up at her and found her nodding, fast. "Yes," she whispered, reaching up to grab her own breasts and pull them. "I want that, too."

Rax growled freely, lowering himself, stroking the head of his cock against her sweet soft pussy, watching her lips unfurl for him, feeling the heat that he'd kissed into her lying just ahead. Samantha caught her heels on the back of his slacks, pushing them down further, trying to bring him in.

"Is this what you want?" he taunted her, shoving just half of his head inside, enough so that she could feel herself begin to spread and miss it when he was gone as he pulled himself back out.

She would miss him, right?

"Don't be a tease," she pouted, arching her hips up to catch him.

He let go of his cock and put his other hand beside her. "I won't," he promised. "Not for long."

He stared down at her. She was finally where she belonged—in his life, on his lips—*with him*. Even if he couldn't keep her, he wanted to tell her everything before words became impossible. The need to fully share himself with her felt as heavy as the desire loaded in his cock.

But before he could, she brought her hands up to frame his face. "Rax...I—" she began, and he froze above her, hearing her finally say his name.

"Shhh," he told her. "I know."

He kissed her hard and then plunged in deep.

THE LOOK he had given her before he'd—he'd—filled her—and was filling her still—*oh God*—it was like—he was a metronome—taking her again—and again—in his own time—shoving in—and pulling out —and she could—only barely—hold him. When he was inside of her, it was like there was no more space, and she could hardly breathe— but when he was out of her, she wanted to feel *just like she had* again. And again. The thick head of his cock—stretching her entrance—his hips pushing her legs wide—listening to him take her—feeling the slap of his balls against her ass—the grunts and groans and breaths he made—as her moans matched him—as he kept taking her—fucking her—pushing himself—deep inside—

Her nipples were hard, her ass was clenched, and everything felt so fucking right, him rocking on top of her, skin against skin, stroke after stroke. He kissed her ravenously and she gave herself over to it, making small sounds of submission, completely lost for words, as his tongue painted up her neck, one of his hands firmly holding her breast, the other hand wrapped in her hair, as he took what he wanted and gave her himself—unrelentingly—driving himself home in her— again, and again, and again. He mounted her like his life depended on his coming inside of her—and even though she was overwhelmed and had just come…. "Oh God," she whispered, as she started to get that building feeling deep inside, like each of his strokes was pushing kindling over coals. "Oh my God, oh my God, oh my God." Her stomach tensed and she rocked her hips against him, starting to take what she needed from him, and he noticed the change.

"Fuck yes," he growled in her ear, rocking in her time now. He kissed her jaw and swiped his cheek against hers. Her hands went under his shirt to find the muscles of his back—and the scars there too—to grab and hold him to her, pulling him closer, keeping him in, and he thudded into her with short sharp strokes, letting her feel the thick head of his cock hit the right spot deep inside. It was the kind of delicious torture she didn't want to end because it felt so good, and why couldn't it just last forever?

"Don't stop," she begged him.

"Not until you're mine." He grunted his satisfaction after another thrust. "Fuck," he growled. "I've never been this hard." His breathing in her ear was harsh.

She was matching him with her hips stroke for stroke and had one hand on his ass, and one hand wound in his hair and all of her felt spread wide, and owned, and taken by him, but she couldn't stop herself from asking, "Not in all eight hundred years?" with a laugh.

He rocked his hips forward, keeping her pinned on him, as he held his head up above her, his flame-like eyes dark. "No," he answered simply.

She thought she'd been open already but hearing him admit that broke some door she hadn't known she'd still had closed. "Rax," she whispered and swallowed, trying to come back into her own body enough to have enough sense for an actual conversation.

He put his hand over her mouth to stop her from asking any questions and slowly started thrusting again, bringing his lips to her ear to growl, "You're my mate. You're the woman I've waited eight hundred years to find."

She gasped beneath his hand, both at his confession and at the fact that he'd chosen that moment to shove himself inside her again.

"You feel how hard you make me?" he asked her, his hand still clapped against her mouth, and all she could do was nod. "You've made me this hard for weeks. Since Belissima's. I have been trying to do the right thing ever since then, Samantha, and I know I haven't always succeeded, but I have been trying to keep you safe. Even from myself." He bowed his head above hers, and she could see the torment in his eyes, even as he kept up a rhythmic rocking. "You have no business being with me, and I have no right to claim you, but I have to, Samantha. Just for tonight. I need to make you mine."

She nodded helplessly below his hand, and he moved it, kissing her hard before she could whisper any words, still thrusting as she threw her arms around his neck, giving herself over to everything in a whole new way, as the fire between her thighs reignited.

His mate. The thought was electrifying.

She'd read all his books, so she knew exactly what he was asking for, although it felt unreal. But as his lips moved from her mouth to her throat, as the rhythm of his hips sped up and felt more urgent, as she could tell how badly he needed her—him, a dragon, wanting her, desiring her, aching to fill her—she found herself believing that he'd never been with anyone else quite like this, like he was right now, with her.

And she was damn sure she'd never been with anyone else like him.

"Rax," she whispered, feeling his intense concentration, feeling the heat of the place where they joined. It felt like everything spun out from that point of contact, and she realized that if she really was his mate then he was hers too—which would explain why she needed him so badly. Because suddenly it felt like if she didn't find release, if she didn't get to come around him and feel him empty himself inside her, knowing that they'd shared these moments in each other's arms, she didn't know how she'd go on. "I really am yours."

He paused, holding himself above her, his eyes searching hers. "For tonight," he agreed and put his hand back across her mouth before she could correct him, lowering his head as he arced his body over hers and *fucked* her. Thick, hard, strokes—he grunted with each thrust, and she took it, feeling the length of him ram in again and again, until all she could make was a low wild muffled moan beneath his hand, feeling all the friction in the world build up inside of her, her stomach pulling tight, her ass tensing, her toes pointed, until she was coming, hips shuddering as she screamed his name into his palm, feeling his hips scoop against hers, writhing as he rode her, listening to him bellow, the force of his strokes lifting her up.

"Samantha," he growled in her ear, claiming her, and it was like she felt it, body and soul, as he poured himself out inside of her, filling her up even more than she thought was possible, making her his for all time. His breathing was rough, and his cock kept tugging inside her as he thrust through, until he was spent, and he groaned her name again slowly, letting go of her mouth as he covered her with his body. He left himself inside her and she clung to him, stroking her fingertips up and down his back, breathing both him and the scent of what they'd done in and reluctantly exhaling it out. "Samantha," he whispered, kissing her neck. "My precious and beloved Samantha."

"It's not just for tonight." Sammy held onto him as tightly as she could. "Don't say I'm your mate, and then leave me, Rax." She'd been left so many times before, she knew exactly what the moments before it felt like, like the change in pressure before a storm.

He raised himself up over her, stroking a sweaty lock of her hair off her face. "Too late."

CHAPTER 20

Before she could fight him, Rax willed Samantha to sleep again. Just for a short time. He believed her when she'd told his bouncer her spell had limits, and he didn't need long. He'd been preparing to leave ever since he'd dropped her off at Damian's house; once he'd finished cleaning his study, he'd moved onto finalizing his business arrangements, making Namir the Lynx's and his casino's heir, and leaving his home and vault of treasures for Samantha.

He'd left Namir detailed instructions and not only trusted the tiger-shifter to follow through, he'd cast enough wards that if Namir didn't either his tail or his dick would fall off, so he felt sure he had the man's cooperation.

He cleaned Samantha gently and pulled her clothes back on, arranging her on her side atop the bar, and then buttoned the last working buttons on his shirt out of habit, the ones he hadn't ripped. What luck for her to come to him tonight. *His beautiful mate.* She was breathtakingly gorgeous to him, even in rest, and he felt heat surge through his body; were she awake and all their circumstances different, he would have had no problem taking her again, and again. He knew he'd never tire of her. She was so smart, so strong, so fierce, and so lovely.

And loving.

Whether she'd said it or not, he knew she loved him.

Just as much as he loved her.

Which was why he had to go to the bottom of the sea.

No matter what she said in the heat of passion, he'd been there that night at the beach and when she'd cried over her parent's deaths. She felt for other people. And if he didn't go down and rejoin his dragon, there was no way she wouldn't think about all the other deaths the sirens caused, no matter the Realm they flew in. Knowing that he could've done something to stop them and didn't—because of her—would lodge in their relationship like a splinter, festering, becoming gangrenous over time. She wasn't selfish like he was. She did love him, but she was different than him. She could've loved anyone.

Whereas his devotion was for her alone.

He brushed another kiss across her lips, wishing she were a princess like in one of those stories children fancied here, that he could wake her up and set her free.

But all he could really hope was that she would understand his reasons, given time. He went and retrieved the item she'd put down when she ran in—*an hourglass, how ingenious*—and set it by her hand.

He stole a final kiss because he couldn't help himself, the kiss that he would take down with him forever, a kiss he hoped would bring him light in the darkness and warmth in the cold, then walked into his office where his mirror was waiting.

SAMANTHA WOKE up with a headache on the bar and it only took her a moment to recall what had happened. "Rax?" she called out, and when he didn't answer, she took in her clothed state and the half-finished hourglass. "Fuck. No!" she shouted and hopped off of the bar, her sneakers crunching on broken glass.

"Namir!" she shouted, running through the casino for the door she'd come in through. Hopefully, he was still here. "Namir!" She burst into the Lynx's bottom floor and found the man waiting right outside. "Where did he go?" she demanded.

Namir gave her a pitying look. "Where neither of us can follow."

"No! That's bullshit!"

"I agree, and I've spent the past week trying to talk him out of it but...," Namir said, looking her up and down. "He left instructions for you." He handed a set of folded papers over, and Sammy scanned them quickly, but they were all functional instructions, nothing personalized.

"His house? His...vault?" She looked between the papers and the man, willing him to have answers for her. "What the fuck, Namir!"

"He said he already released the sharks? But that Comet wanted to stay behind for you —"

"NO!" she shrieked at him like she hadn't gotten to shriek at Rax before he'd gone. "How dare he!"

Namir held both his hands up. "Again, we agree. But his mind was made up."

Sammy looked at the hourglass she held. She was down to her final hour out here, and then she'd have to go back to Andi's for her own safety.

But what was the point of being safe if she wasn't going to see Rax again? She shook her head, thinking hard. "What's in the vault? Anything I can use to free him there?"

"Uh," Namir began. "Are you secretly magical?"

"No-the-fuck-I-am-not," Sammy said.

"Then I can show it to you, but I don't think you're going to be able to use anything. Come on," he said, leading her back into the casino. She followed him, her hands and jaw both clenched. "We were going to have to work together with this, anyhow," he said, taking her into an office that had clearly been Janvier's. *He had just been here.* It smelled like him, which was like a slap to her face, and she wanted to cry, but she stayed focused. *No giving up. Not yet.*

Namir went to the far side of the office and picked up the massive, fogged mirror that hung along one wall. The thing must've weighed several hundred pounds.

"What are you?" Sammy asked him in awe.

"Tiger-shifter," Namir confessed, putting the mirror down. He dusted his hands on his slacks and gestured at the heavy-looking wooden door behind where the mirror had been. "This is your part."

"What do you mean?" she asked.

"His vault's just past it. Just like the nightclub's a front for the casino, the casino's just a front for everything past that door, and according to what he told me, everything inside of it is yours."

Her eyes ran over the apparently smooth wood. "How do I open it?"

"You just do. You're the key." He gave her a bemused look.

Sammy thought hard. "Like, all of me, or just a hand?"

His brow rose. "All of you, to my knowledge."

"Willingly, or could you trap me in a cage just outside?"

He blinked. "Jesus, you're dark. But...yeah, no. I don't think so. Rax wouldn't let anyone do that to you."

"So...I just...walk up?" Sammy asked, doing so and the door swung open. She stepped back, and it closed. "Huh." She stepped up to it again, couldn't see anything inside, but walked through it anyway.

It was another massive underground chamber, as big as the casino, but outfitted like a museum, with floor to ceiling shelves, full of random-looking things carefully curated on them: pillows, game pieces, ceramic cats, musical instruments, ornaments. It was like a very well-lit and lovingly displayed thrift shop of epic proportions. It would take her *forever* to go through, and even then, how would she know if she could use anything?

"Whoa," said Namir, following her inside.

"You've never been in here either?" she asked him.

"No," Namir said with a headshake, and then let out a low whistle as he scanned the room. "My God."

"What are all these things?" she asked, looking around, although from reading Janvier's books, she thought she knew.

"Magical objects. I knew he was hoarding pieces, that we were taking in more objects than he ever let go, but...Samantha—*you're rich now*. Think Siberian oil heiress. There's more money here than you could spend in a lifetime." He walked to a shelf and inspected the pieces on it. "I'll help you sell them, for a cut, of course."

She whirled on the man. "I don't want a lifetime, not without him," she growled.

Namir held his hands up, under the force of her tone. "You're sure you don't have magical abilities?" he said lightly.

Samantha turned back to survey her new treasures and hugged herself. "Other than being able to get into here? No." She couldn't believe he'd left all these things to her, especially when she would've thrown them all in the ocean if it'd meant getting to keep him. She walked down the first aisle, scanning desperately for something, *anything*.

"Hey," Namir said, pleased with himself. He picked up a glass orb and held it. "I knew he'd get this from Delphine."

Sammy looked back. Namir was holding up a clear globe, and she knew exactly what it was. People used them all the time in Rax's books. "A sea bubble?" she asked, coming up.

"You speak that old-timey shit too?" Namir asked her.

"Not fluently." Sammy took the globe from him and held it up to one of the shelf's lights, which reflected and refracted inside. But she read it well enough, and she knew she knew how to use the thing.

She ran for the door and leaped back into Rax's office. Namir ran after her, barely getting out before the vault door slammed shut behind her. "If you go do something stupid, I'll never be able to get back inside," he said, looking between her and the door.

"Namir, truly? I don't care," she said, already running for the office's door, then pausing. "Wait...do you have a really big bucket here somewhere?"

SAMMY HELD the hourglass wedged between her thighs as she drove the Pagani at breakneck speeds down to Rax's house, trusting in local police to recognize well-connected Damian's overclocked car and forgive him. She pulled off the road where Rax's note had said his home would be and watched the mileage tick by on the gauge, hoping that she'd find the right lonely hillside, when a garage door appeared out of nowhere as she neared.

Just for her.

It opened as she got closer and she parked the Pagani inside, grabbing the bucket Namir had given her.

"Smoke!" she shouted, running for the door. She'd left the hourglass on the dash, she was down to her last thirty minutes of freedom, if that. "Comet!"

She burst into Rax's living room and found Smoke waiting there, ears perked in utter surprise. "Samantha!" he said with a joyful bounce. "You returned!"

"I did!" she said, swooping down to pet the fox. She saw Comet rising in the aquarium in the background. "I'm about to go make a stunningly bad decision. Are you two with me?"

RAX PULLED off his clothing when he was on his mirror's far side in the waters of his home, and the pieces of fabric floated away like a forgotten skin. He wouldn't be needing them again.

He kicked himself forward, diving down, sensing the path, listening for the slow beat of his sleeping dragon's heart. The magicians hadn't been entirely clear on how he ought to join himself again but he knew once he was at his dragon's side he'd figure it out.

He found himself...scared. Some. It was an awkward and unfamiliar feeling. But who wouldn't be scared of living in the unrelenting darkness alone? He'd lived long enough already to understand a taste of eternity, he knew exactly what he was giving himself over to.

But it would be all right.

He'd live forever knowing that Samantha was safe.

And that knowledge would comfort him. Give him something to think about, now, and for all of his endless days and nights.

He pressed a hand to his lips as he surged on into darkness. Thank goodness she'd come to him. Thank goodness he still held her kiss. Thank goodness she'd called out his name.

Rax was meditating on everything that had happened with Samantha when a force buffeted him from the side, sending him spinning into the wall of the canyon he was diving in. He recovered quickly, illuminating the space around him as he sent his senses out. He was almost to the Gate, and he knew he still had time.

Another blow; this time, dodged. He caught the tail of the creature that'd swam for him and yanked it back. A seal?

In the waters of his home? *No. They didn't belong.*

The creature rebounded and came for him, teeth out, and he avoided it, as other creatures just like it came into viewing range. Delphine's people, the selkies, swimming below the surface as seals and humans both, a hundred of them. She swam into view and even though he'd never seen her as a seal, he knew it was her; she was massive, sleek, and strong, magically made for swimming at any depth. He spoke into her mind. *"Why are you here, Delphine? Your fight was back on Earth."*

"I saw a rift while swimming months ago, heard singing, and found truth." She bobbed in the water in front of him, matching his movements, not letting him proceed. *"They said we could have this whole ocean if only we opened up their Gate."* Rax hovered in the water with a sick feeling of horror as she went on. *"I always knew you wouldn't help us. And the peace the Akhlut brokered didn't last."*

He swam as fast as he could, dodging around her. The Gate came into view, looming and ominous, and his dragon's heartbeat was like a slowing drum. He could feel his time running out through the faint connection they still shared. Its time was coming quicker than he thought though, and he saw more of Delphine's people below, grabbing up fistfuls of sediment from the floor, covering the blackness of his scales.

"No!" his mind shouted at hers in panic as he raced lower. She swam after him, biting his ankle and hauling him back. He felt the bones of his foot grind and scented blood in the water before he kicked himself free. *"You don't understand, Delphine! Anything the sirens promised you were lies!*

"No!" she shouted back at him. *"They told me where the stone was and to give it to the girl! You could have stayed above the waves and been happy!"*

He growled at her and swam deeper. *"They'll kill countless people on the shore!"*

"So? When was the last time a human helped one of us?" She wove sinuously through the waters and bared her teeth at him. *"I know about your brother, Rax. The sirens sang his story. All you have to do to see him again is let them be free!"*

He turned to face her in the waters. *"I am a dragon,"* he warned her.

"No," she refuted him. *"Your dragon's down there. This part of you is slightly more man. Strong, yes, but invincible? Not entirely."*

He ignored her and swam as hard as he could. He had to reach his dragon in time before the other selkies finished covering it up, but Delphine moved more fluidly under the water than he did. She was born to it in her form and while he caught her and pushed her away, she snaked her teeth up his arm, cutting a deep gash.

"I don't want to hurt you!" he told her.

He caught her as she surged at him next, spinning around with the force of her impact, grabbing hold of her jaws as though he were going to step into them as her mind shouted at his. *"You already had your chance! You could've taken our side! The sirens will!"*

Rax shoved her back rather than rip her lower jaw off and sank as fast as he could, but more selkies advanced, a living wave of them. At the same time, a group of drowned ones emerged from the ocean floor, shaking off sediment and slime like so many worms emerging after a rainstorm.

Half of them started fighting with the selkies upon his dragon's form, and the other half began to march across the seafloor.

He was wrestling the selkie nearest him but it was impossible without leverage. The things were made for swimming. Others bit his back and thighs as he tried to watch below.

Where were the drowned ones going? And to do what?

Had Samantha not gotten back to Damian's in time?

He was blindsided again in his worry for her, and Delphine's teeth took a chunk out of his chest.

"You can't trust them! They lie!" he shouted out with his mind to any of them that would hear, and then he choked out the selkie he held onto.

It was dangerous, the creatures could move their head in all directions, and it didn't stop the others from attacking him, but he was able to use its limp form like a kind of club and shield, whipping it through the water to protect himself as he raced for his dragon's sleeping form.

"Don't let him go!" Delphine shouted after him.

He summoned magic from inside himself and shot it out with his free hand, a sizzling bolt of energy to stun anyone too close, and he did it again and again, holding them back until his feet found the unsteady ocean floor below. The fighting drowned ones were malformed, time had not done their bodies any kindnesses, and several of them had exploded, tainting the water with their funk.

In his mind when he'd done this, he been able to take his time and figure things out. To brace himself and prepare. But now there was no chance, just the knowledge that he had to do what was needed to seal the Gate—to make sure there were never any other crying little girls just like his Samantha. He plunged his hand forward through eight hundred years of particulate and dust, crushed and pressed near to rock on the ocean floor, and shattered it, feeling his dragon's side with his open palm, as Delphine screamed in his mind and a small army of drowned ones held her people at bay.

Everything narrowed to the point of contact between him and his dragon's scales.

It was like falling in, falling home, and his human form was subsumed inside his dragon's larger bulk. His soul felt...entwined. All the ripping tortures he'd endured as the magicians had pulled his dragon away, all the scars he carried inside and out, were undone.

What had he been afraid of all this time?

To be his dragon was to be free.

Even at the bottom of the ocean.

He was the beast he was meant to be, doing exactly what he was meant to do, and he tightened his grip around the Gate, biting harder onto his own tail, sealing the door fully.

Delphine's anguish still shrieked into his mind, but did it matter? No.

Nothing mattered anymore. And soon she would go away, and he would be left, at peace, finally whole, in the deep, all alone.

CHAPTER 21

"Hachiro tells me to tell you that this is a very, very bad idea," Smoke said, sitting on the passenger seat. Comet was in a bucket full of water in front of him and, the Sea Bubble was in with him, and Sammy was driving as fast as she could to the beach.

"Well, tell him that I did explain this plan to you both before you signed on board," she told the fox to tell him back. "And look, I know it's not a great idea. It's just that I don't have a better one." She'd hurled the hourglass out her window miles ago, hoping it would crack and save her time. Because she knew once she got to the ocean, the longer she had to wait, the worse it would be. She drove the Pagani over the curb once she got to the strip of asphalt that served as this beach's parking lot—but without any magic, it mired in the sand. "Is there anything else he wants to tell me?" she asked Smoke, unbuckling her seatbelt to get out.

The fox conferred with the octopus. "He says you should let me bite you."

A thin jet of water sprayed out of the bucket and hit them both as Comet conveyed his disapproval and Sammy laughed. She got out of the car, gave the waterline a nervous look, and raced around to the other side, opening the door to lug the very heavy bucket out. She should've brought Namir along for this part. There was barely any room for water inside the thing; she was just going to have to dump it out and let Comet climb to the sea.

Smoke put his paws on the bucket's rim and sniffed inside. "He actually says to tell you good luck."

"Thanks," Sammy said. She offered her hand out to the fox. "Now or never, mister."

Smoke lifted his lips, showed her his needle-sharp teeth, then shook his head. "I will bite you when you get back."

Sammy reached into the bucket and picked up the Sea Bubble. "I can't believe I'm saying this, but I hope so."

Just then, horrible mumbling sounds began at the waterline as the first of the drowned ones pulled themselves free—because the only way she could figure out to see Rax again was to let the drowned ones take her to the bottom of the ocean.

"Okay," she said, priming herself as well as Comet. She tilted his bucket over and he sloshed out, using his tentacles to start hauling himself over the sand to the water's edge while she held the bubble in her hands. "I just need to...," she told herself, trying to ignore the fact that she was at the ocean, on the beach, all alone, and monsters were coming for her again.

"Kiss it already!" Smoke shouted at her. "Hurry!"

She knew from reading all of Rax's books how the bubbles worked. They were for people who didn't have much magic to draw from so that they could travel safely beneath the waves. But she wasn't sure it would work until she tried it, and she couldn't try it until it was too late. She didn't think the drowned ones particularly cared if she was dead or alive judging by her prior beach night, but she didn't want to waste the magic when she didn't know how far she'd have to go. So she waited until the drowned ones were an arm's length away, closed her eyes, and brought the bubble to her lips.

Air from another time and another world enveloped her, and right before any of them could touch her, she ran for the waves.

Comet was waiting for her just beneath the water's surface, one of his tentacles wrapped around her wrist and he began pulling her down.

She wasn't...cold? And—she could totally breathe. Although she was still scared of breathing too much. It was like she was swimming, but she was definitely dry, and the magic of the bubble illuminated everything around her, making it easy for her to see, which was good and bad. Seeing Comet swim up close was amazing.

Watching drowned ones reach for her was not, and the seafloor seemed covered with them. *Where the hell had they all come from?* She tried not to hyperventilate—this was the plan. Get to the bottom of the ocean and somehow stop Rax.

And if she couldn't, because he had a head start, then she was going to fucking yell at him so hard one last time that he'd wish he was dead instead of just kind of being in purgatory for eternity.

She'd already lost so much she wasn't prepared to lose Rax, too, and she was willing to face the things that killed her parents and gave her nightmares to get him back.

THE DROWNED ONES seemed all too willing to let Comet take the lead as he hauled her below, following their trail until some crazy strange light shone out ahead of them, just like the kind of light she'd seen Comet flash the sharks. He pulled her through a ring of it, and while the ocean floor was still littered with drowned ones, she knew the sea had changed. It was a slightly different color and the water was clearer. Comet took a moment to look back at her, making sure she was all right, and then a massive seal came out of nowhere and swept him aside. Sammy screamed inside her bubble, spinning with the motion as Comet let her free, and then she was drifting and that was worse, it was like being stranded in space—until one of the drowned ones grabbed her ankle.

She went to kick herself loose but caught herself in time. *This was what she wanted! She needed their help!*

That drowned one passed her to another one, and then another, and their slippery disgusting hands were buffered from her body by the thin layer of air the bubble provided. She scanned for Comet as best she could, hoping that her foolishness hadn't cost him his life; and then another seal came, bowling up through the drowned ones, moving her, knocking them every which way and making some of them burst. She screamed again and started swimming, following the direction it'd seemed they'd been taking her, unable to see much in the now filthy water. As it cleared though, she could see more seals attacking other drowned ones; they were having some kind of fight in front of a wall...no—

It was the Gate Below.

She'd only seen it in illustrations, and none of them had ever gotten across how huge it was. "Oh my God," she whispered, looking up. She couldn't see where it ended; she could only feel the immensity of the structure, more ominous than the pressure of the ocean all around her. And then she looked down because she knew what she'd find there. "Rax?" she whispered, at seeing the sleeping dragon coiled around the Gate's base.

The illustrations in the books hadn't done a good job of conveying him, either. His form was sinuous and long, and his scales weren't shiny black—they were flat black, the kind of black you could fall into —but the only ones left that she could see were a smattering of sharp ridges down the line of his back.

She swam closer, feeling the water around her becoming colder, knowing if she looked up she'd realize how much ocean was above her and lose her mind, and if she looked from side to side she'd see the strange fighting going on between the drowned ones and the seals.

So all she did was keep her eyes on him.

Because it was him, wasn't it?

And...it wasn't too late?

Her feet reached the ground and she put her hands out for the outline of his face beneath layers and layers of sediment and silt, knowing his eyes would be the same from the pictures, and needing to see them more than anything else, more than breathing, more than life.

The edge of the bubble that embraced her brushed him and he

shivered bodily. All of him. Like she'd seen Smoke so often do, from nose to tail-tip. The world was suddenly made of silt, someone had shaken a finely ground snow globe and then two coals appeared in the midst of the dirty cloud to stare at her.

"Rax," she whispered, rushing in to envelop any part of him she could get to in a hug, feeling ineffectually small in comparison to his bulk. But he smoothed his cheek alongside hers with a gentleness his great size belied, and she knew that he knew she was there. "Come back to me," she begged him, hanging on. She didn't care how much air was left in her bubble anymore and she was smart enough to know that she'd die instantly at this depth if it popped.

He pushed her back with the tip of his nose and marveled at her.

"I love you," she told him, crying freely now inside the bubble. "And you didn't stay long enough for me to say it."

He closed his dark eyelids slowly, acknowledging her pain.

And then a seal came up and hit her.

It buffeted her from the side, knocking her away from Rax's face, sending her to her knees on the silty ground. She heard him make a warning growl behind her as the same seal came straight for her again.

She ducked quickly, barely missing it as it barreled down, and the sound Rax made became louder and more ominous. She could feel the threat of his warning reverberating in her chest.

And then another seal raced for her, and he let go of his tail to whip his head toward her, along with the first third of his body, smashing the seal down beneath a paw, as the door behind him shuddered.

CHAPTER 22

OF COURSE SAMANTHA HAD FIGURED OUT A WAY TO COME TO THE bottom of the sea for him.

When he'd first felt her touch on his brow, he hadn't wanted to believe; he'd thought he was already hallucinating—because what else would there be to do in the dark? The drowned ones and seals fighting around him felt insignificant. Nothing they could do would change his course.

But as he'd realized it was her and that she'd followed him...*she was truly magnificent.*

Quite possibly insane.

And utterly his mate. Whether she knew it or not, nothing else would explain this wild level of devotion, far beyond what any normal human would ever have to give.

Oh, Tarian. I understand you now.

Then the seals had begun attacking her, he had no idea why. They weren't her enemy. But if they hurt her....

Then they were his.

As another one came for Samantha, he released his coil on the door and swung out with his paw to catch the creature.

The Gate swung on its hinges, batting against the broken lock behind him, as Rax growled.

SAMANTHA SCREAMED as someone else came for her. Not a seal this time, nor a drowned one, but someone who was somehow down here just like she was, only they also had a knife. Rax swept them away from her and she shrank back against his side, tucking herself against his paw. All she'd wanted to do was to see him again and try to get him back, but it was clear he'd made his *fucking* choice, *without her,* the *asshole.* So why was there still so much chaos?

And if he was here already, as his dragon, why had the drowned ones still wanted her? She couldn't hear them anymore, but she could still see their mouths moving as they kept up their gurgling refrain. What did they need her for?

Another person with a weapon rushed for her and Rax snapped them in half with his mouth, spitting out the pieces. She tried to ignore the chum in the water, even as it made her want to puke. *No puking in the bubble!* she thought with a fast, manic laugh and dared to close her eyes to think hard, trusting in Rax to protect her.

There was still a piece of the key in the lock.

And she still wore a piece of it.

She opened her eyes and looked up. The lock was a good fifty feet straight up, but the Gate looked climbable, really. She freed herself from him and started pushing herself up, first onto his back, his scales rough against her hands, then higher. The seal attacks became wilder, but Rax snaked his giant head up to bring them down and used his wings to shove waves out at the creatures, batting them back, clouding the water. She screamed against the Gate and hung on, climbing blind. She didn't need to see. She only needed to go up.

THE SECOND she stepped onto his back Rax knew what she was doing. He rolled his eyes up at her, trapped where he was below, leaning against the door with all his might. When he'd let loose for a second earlier, he'd attracted the attention of all the things trapped on the Gate's other side and he'd be damned if he let a siren hurt his Samantha again.

The creatures on the far side battered against the door. They weren't coordinated, but they were relentless, pounding the length of it, looking for a way out, closer than they'd been in centuries, except for the lucky few who'd managed rifts.

And while that was happening, the selkies continued their assault. They'd shifted their anger from the drowned ones to Samantha, finally recognizing her for what she was—leverage to distract him. He was sweeping them out of the way with his head and one forepaw, but he couldn't sweep too violently lest he knock her loose. Soon she'd be higher than he could reach and still keep the door shut safely, and Rax didn't know what he was going to do.

He loved her enough to die for her, but he could never watch *her* die.

No matter how keen she'd always seemed on taking risks with her own life.

"Come back!" he howled at her with his mind, but she didn't hear him. *"MY LOVE, COME BACK!"*

SAMMY WAS JUST twenty feet away, she could make out the lock even in the blurry waters; it was huge compared to her. She focused all her strength on making it there, trusting in Rax to handle all the monsters behind her, the seals with their frightening teeth and men and women with their knives. The air inside her bubble was beginning to taste sour and she knew from all the books she'd read the bubbles went bad eventually—she didn't have much time.

She felt a horrible reverberation from behind her as Rax wheeled his body to snake directly up the Gate, leaning against it with all of his

CASSIE ALEXANDER & KARA LOCKHARTE

might. She could see his muscles bunching as he writhed, stretching this way and that to try to keep the seal-folk away. She felt the tension behind the Gate, like the door was a lid on a pot about to boil over, bouncing and shaking in its hinges.

She yanked herself up higher to the next carved ridge as Rax swung back to sweep a massive gray blur away from her; the door rattled, hard, straining the confines of the looped lock, and something horrible burped out.

Dark feathered wings that shuffled like a deck of cards going all directions and glowing eyes like cats at night—Sammy let go of the door without thinking because suddenly her fingers didn't work, but then an orange tentacle looped around her wrist and grabbed on.

Comet. Tugging her upwards, missing two tentacles, but his remaining ones grabbed hold of the lock and pulled her up to its level. She fumbled for the stone around her neck and shoved it into the small and narrow keyhole, praying that it'd do something, as the siren rounded on her and she could hear its horrible voice, same as the day when she was eight.

"You're not worth dying for," its mouths whispered, their susurrant voices somehow pushing through the water to her ears.

The same thing they'd told her when she was a child. The last words she'd heard right before she knew her parents were dead. She'd spent her whole life so sure they were right, that her parents had helped her save her life for nothing.

But then now, looking down at Rax, she knew that they were lying.

If him coming to the bottom of the ocean to stop the sirens wasn't a kind of death on her behalf—what else could be?

"Not worth dying, you're dying, for dying," they kept hissing in different iterations, all of their mouths opening and closing at different times.

She shoved her necklace into the lock again as she felt Rax bellow below her—*in fear? In pain?*—and once again, her necklace slipped out.

The air in her bubble was so bad now and she was so scared and the siren wouldn't stop, but it didn't matter because there was no place she'd rather be. And there was no other man alive who she'd have come to the seafloor for.

Rax was now her everything.

And she had become his.

It was just like the door to his vault, the door to his garage, and the door to his heart.

It was never about the necklace, all along.

"I'm the key," she whispered and stuck her arm inside the lock, all the way.

RAX HAD SPENT the past few weeks preparing to meet his personal nightmare, which he thought would merely be spending the rest of his life in the dark, not watching the woman he loved on a suicide mission after he let a fucking siren out. He snapped out at the thing as far as he could go, listening to it lie to her, wishing he could tell her not to listen.

"Rax?" asked a mind he hadn't heard in centuries.

He quickly angled his head down. The same violence against the door that'd let a siren emerge had also let a familiar human-shaped form stumble away from the base of the Gate like a drunk from Lynx at last call.

"Tarian?" he thought back.

His brother stared up at him. *"It worked. Oh my God, it worked,"* he thought, and then passed out.

AS SOMEONE who had stolen a lot of cars (and a few motorcycles, which were easier, really), Sammy was intimately familiar with how locks functioned. So she wasn't entirely surprised when she felt the pins inside clamp down on her arm, as she grabbed the fragment of the key that was still extant deep inside the cylinder with the tips of her fingers.

What she wasn't ready for was the fire-feeling.

She shrieked as pain seared through her, feeling like her entire arm was being skinned and bleeding and then after that, the salt of the sea hit all her nerves and stung, and for the first time of her life, she was on the verge of passing out. It was like when Garrett had put his cigarette lighter out on her, only *so much worse* because it was all over, and there was nothing she could do, but after the astounding pain came a certain clarity. It was like her circuits overloaded and then there was nothing left but sheer analytical functions.

Were her fingers still attached? Yes. *Surprisingly.*

Could she operate her hand? Barely.

She made a fist around the end of the key, said good-bye to her arm up to her shoulder, and twisted it in the lock.

RAX HELD Tarian in one protective paw, snapping out at any oncoming seals, which were lessening in number even as the drowned ones increased. As the scent of human blood blossomed in the water he looked up in panic, just in time to watch the dangling lock jump into place after Samantha shoved her arm inside the keyhole. A pressure he'd felt bodily as a dragon for almost a thousand years disappeared—he felt the reverberation of the Gate closing behind him and he knew that it was sealed.

He began to unwind without thinking as the worst of his nightmares came true—Samantha's body, drifting away from the lock, her arm freely bleeding. She spun down like a leaf in the wind, without any control, and he knew he was losing her.

He surged for her, catching her as Hachiro did. The octopus wound himself around her shoulder like a piece of armor, stopping her bleeding, which showed him where the lock had wounded her, biting her to the bone, and now Rax had a person he loved in both forepaws and he had to get to the surface with them. Samantha had been down here too long, and his brother even longer—he swam like a creature possessed—

And behind him, the siren howled.

"You can only save one! You'll have to choose! You'll have to choose!" A hundred different dark mouths sang at him discordantly, and he knew he couldn't stop it, too—he would be lucky to reach the surface in time as it was. "You'll have to choose! Choose, you'll have to, save one only, *choosechooseschoose*!"

"No!" he shouted back as he raced through the rift into the Earth's water, tasting the pollution and stronger salt. Drowned ones burst as he raced over their corpses with too much force, surging up with the siren right behind him.

"Choose!" it taunted him, the words echoing through his mind, and it felt like it was right, he could swim faster with just one. "CHOOSE!" it cackled maniacally, and he felt the weight of its temptation. How could he save both Tarian and Samantha from the sirens when he surfaced if both of them were helpless?

"HELP ME!" he shouted out with his mind to any creature that would hear. *"SIRENS!"* he warned.

"What the...we're almost there!" came a masculine presence back. *Damian.*

And from a further distance, *"Old man, you owe me!"*
Siku!

He saw the light of the moon on the surface and breeched, arching up above the water and almost taking flight, wheeling to land on his back, protecting Tarian and Samantha against his chest from being smashed as his body fell back against the waters below. Then he twisted, raising his wings, unused to air for centuries, as he heard the siren splash out of the waves behind him.

"Choose, choose, choose, you have to, only, choose," they sang in their horrible chorus as Rax pulled both of his paws and their precious contents closer, dragging his wings at the sky, trying to fly with wings that'd forgotten how.

"COME FOR THE SHORE!" shouted Damian in his mind and Rax wheeled, spotting small beings a distance away. He swung his wings up again, shifting his tail sharply beneath the waves to gain freedom, all the while listening to the siren's howls. His wings grabbed air again

and he hauled himself free of the water, finally beating gravity to hover and then soar.

He rushed for the distant beach where he could make out swinging lanterns and he'd never flown so fast before. Tarian he could feel but Samantha...*Samantha!*

"Choosechoosechoosechoose!" the siren howled behind him, an engine of sheer hate.

He dove into the shoreline, landing ungracefully on his back paws, each of his front legs held out, hitting the ground hard with his chest, but keeping the shock from his wards, using his wings to shield Tarian and Samantha from the siren's song. If the last thing she heard was it and not him—*no!*

Damian's people ran up like he was a crashed plane and they all had ear protection on. Smoke wove among their legs, a gray streak of concern. Rax caught a green light, someone's magic, and saw two of Damian's werewolves start shooting over his head, most certainly at the siren and then he saw one of them mouth, "Oh fuck!" over the rattling sound of their guns.

Rax ripped his head back just in time to see Siku breech. She was almost three times the size of a normal orca and with centuries more cunning—she caught the siren with her giant white teeth, in her massive crushing jaws—and took it back down to the sea.

He sagged in relief and whipped his attention back to the contents of his paws as more of Damian's people ran up. He saw the girl, Andi, who he knew was a nurse, run up at the same time as Smoke did.

"You have to...," he thought at her, proffering her Samantha with his hand, and then realized she was as human as Samantha was, she wouldn't be able to understand him.

"I love her too," Andi said by way of explanation as she ran up, completely unafraid, and one of the werewolves dropped their weapons to join her. Rax carefully shifted Samantha's body to the sand, then Tarian's, and changed back down to his human form.

"Is she all right? Did I miss my chance to bite her?" Smoke asked him, rushing up, nosing Samantha's swollen right hand.

"Please?" Rax asked Andi, begging her to tell him she would be okay. He wanted to throw himself across Samantha's chest, but he knew he'd only be in the way, and he needed to stay beside his brother, just in case. The last time he'd seen Tarian, the man hadn't been well, so he wasn't sure what to make of him now.

He loved him, but he knew a mad dragon would be even worse than a siren.

Andi ignored him, working over Samantha's body, feeling for pulses, and listening for breath. "What's—" she said, reaching for Hachiro and hesitating. Samantha's arm south of the octopus was white and swelling.

"He's a friend. Don't hurt him; he's helping her."

"Tourniquet!" the werewolf by Andi shouted, and one of the others ran off to get it.

"What happened?" Andi asked him. "She needs blood."

"Give her mine," Rax offered, pushing out his arm as he knelt on the sand.

Andi took his proffered arm and gently pushed it down. "That's not how it works."

The werewolf replaced Hachiro's grip with a strip of fabric, and the octopus slithered back into the water. *"Can they save her?"* he asked.

"I don't know."

"We've got to take her in right now," the werewolf went on to say. He lunged to pick her up, and Rax snarled at him, rushing forward, as Damian blocked his path.

"Do you want her to live or not?" the other dragon growled.

"Come with us," Andi said, offering out her hand.

Rax would have, but then he looked to Tarian.

There was a small element of truth in the siren's song. He had to make a choice.

But, he wasn't choosing between his brother and Samantha.

He was choosing to trust her with her friends.

"Go," he whispered hoarsely. Damian nodded, and the werewolf was already running off, Smoke racing after them.

The other dragon spoke into an earpiece. "Tell Max to meet us at the hospital. We'll get her care and then wipe all their minds." He looked between Rax and his brother. "We're taking her to General."

"Save her or else," Rax growled. Damian's eyes narrowed, then he raced down the path his woman and the wolf had taken, leaving Rax and his brother on the beach.

CHAPTER 23

"This ocean tastes wrong."

Rax turned to find his older brother touching the damp sand and then press his hand against his tongue. "Tarian," he whispered, as his brother looked over at him. "How did you survive? I cannot believe you're alive."

"No? So you thought you had killed me, then? And that was better?" Tarian stood slowly, looking around at his unfamiliar surroundings. He had a massive beard, but the rest of him was knife-thin now, where once upon a time he'd been bigger than Rax. That was why Rax had had to close the Gate—there was no way he was strong enough to win.

Memories of their awful fight flooded Rax. "You left me no choice, brother. I had to choose between the Gate and you. You were mad with grief; you broke the lock. I still bear your scars across my back. I was tortured—"

"As was I," Tarian said flatly, staring through him with dark eyes. "What Realm is this?"

Rax swallowed. "It is called Earth. It's non-magical in its base state, although certain magical creatures live here." He watched his brother inspect his surroundings, wondering at the wisdom of having brought a maddened dragon back here, even in his brother's weakened form. "Tarian, it's been centuries. And this world is vastly different than the one you have come from. It is not safe. There are those that would hunt you here, if they knew what you were."

Tarian shrugged. "If there are oceans here, they will not find me."

Rax shook his head gravely. "I don't need you to forgive me, Tarian, but let me help you."

"I do not need your help anymore, Rax, now that I am free." His brother took a step back to the water's edge. "My priority is finding Seris."

"Tarian," Rax said, his voice low.

His brother rushed him, and Rax let it happen; he fell backward rather than wrestling with the weaker man as Tarian put his bony forearm across his throat. He had fought his brother once and doomed him, he could not bring himself to do it again, especially not now, when it looked like he could snap his brother like a branch. "Do you know that your woman is yet alive?"

Rax...*did*. On some internal level, he couldn't begin to explain. He nodded.

"Then trust that I know mine is, as well," Tarian said, pushing back, coughing.

Rax stood up and offered his brother a hand. "If you're so sure of her, then let me help."

Tarian swung his hand away, standing on his own, looking unsteady. "You could have. Eight hundred years ago—"

"You were mad with grief!" Rax protested.

"I was looking for answers!" Tarian snarled. "How do you think the sirens know how to lie to you? With lies that are almost truths?"

"I don't know—magic?"

"No! They see everything! That has occurred, that can occur, that is occurring! All at once!"

Rax's eyes widened. "You sound like them."

"Because the stories I read were right!" his brother shouted, his voice currently stronger than he was. "I know the truth now! Seris is alive. I just have to find her!" Tarian took an unsteady step forward again and fell to his knees.

"Tarian, I saw them bury her," Rax said, trying to get through. "After the Gate closed, and we thought you lost."

"No. You saw one of her die. But it wasn't her, in her true form; my Seris was taken away from me." Tarian hit his chest with force as his body crumpled forward, crying or coughing, Rax couldn't tell which.

"You can hate me later, but I'm taking you home," Rax said, picking his brother up. He cast a veil spell around them both and walked to the road.

FOR ONCE, Sammy woke up in a somewhat familiar location—back in her room, at Damian's house. She recognized the ceiling, then her pillow, then the distant purple couch. "What the fuck?" she murmured, looking down, seeing her arm wound up in gauze and hitched in a sling. It throbbed.

Two paws dented the edge of the bed and then a gray snout looked over. "You're up!" Smoke exclaimed. Before she could respond, he pulled himself up on the bed and sat down to report, "There is a stupid cat here, and I don't like him very much."

Sammy grinned at him. "I know. He doesn't even like pickles." She picked up her other arm without complaint and rubbed her hand over his head. "Smoke, if you're here…." She blinked as her brain caught up with her. "Where's Rax? Is he okay? What happened to the siren? And Comet? How is he?"

Smoke's copper eyes went wide. "The siren got chomped by an orca!" The fox gnashed his teeth in midair in demonstration. "It was the most glorious thing I have ever seen!"

"Okay," Sammy said, bemused. "But…everyone else?"

"Everyone else is fine, I think," Andi said, coming into the room, back first, holding a glass in one hand and a medicine cup full of pills in the other. "How's your arm?"

"How's Rax?" Sammy asked, gritting her teeth as she pushed herself up.

Andi rolled her eyes. "You know how I told you being a nurse to rich people sucked? Your boyfriend takes the cake."

"My...boyfriend?" Sammy asked. Boyfriend didn't feel right. Rax wasn't technically a 'boy', he was a man and a dragon and besides that the word didn't feel strong enough.

"Well, I don't know what you want to call him, but if he's not your boyfriend, you'd better tell him before he sends another bouquet. We're running out of room for them, and you know how big this house is." Andi handed the medicine cup over and Sammy popped the pills into her mouth without even asking what they were, swallowing them with water from the glass Andi passed over next. "Although when you *do* talk to him, figure out where the hell he's ordering from because they're *definitely* doing the flowers for my wedding."

Sammy smiled cluelessly at her, then looked around. "How did I end up here?"

Her best friend sat down on the edge of the bed, nudging aside the fox, who grumbled. "There was an earthquake and Mills said we needed to get to the shoreline, just in case. And then Rax came out of the water with you. What happened down there?"

"There was a fight...no...more like a war, and then a door—and a lock—and a key." She looked at her arm, which was reporting in slightly less pain now. "How bad is it? And how long has it been?"

"Pretty bad, and almost two weeks. Your arm was broken in three places, and you almost bled out," Andi told her and winced. "Honestly, once you're done healing, you might want some plastic surgery. You're going to have some gnarly scars."

Sammy looked at her arm, still covered by bandages and velcroed up against her body. "Scars are how you know you escaped," she whispered.

"Well...that's being melodramatic, maybe? But also pretty accurate." Andi rested a hand on her leg. "You should go back to sleep now."

Sammy blinked again, finding it hard to resist the suggestion. "What did you give me?"

"Ten milligrams of oxycodone and one pill from Mills's lab. I didn't ask what was in hers. She just said the more you sleep right now, the faster you'll heal; she's been using some heavy magic on you. You're already a ton better, trust me."

Sammy nodded because she trusted Andi implicitly, snuggling back down into her nest of pillows. "But are you sure he's all right? Where is he?" she asked, well aware she was sounding like a lovesick teen and not caring.

Andi brushed a lock of hair off of her forehead. "I don't know, Sammy. He calls every hour of every day, but he hasn't been by."

Smoke stepped in, both verbally and with a paw, looking at her. "He's with Tarian."

Sammy fought sleep for a moment more, realizing all the things that meant. "Oh my gosh," she said, and the fox nodded deeply.

"What is it?" Andi asked, looking between the two of them and unable to understand the fox. But it was too late; sleep had come for her.

"I DON'T WANT to know how you got my personal phone number, Rax," Damian growled on the far end of the line.

"I would say hefty bribes, but the truth is your witch took pity on me after I got hers, and she suggested I talk to you directly, seeing as your woman stopped picking up."

"My *woman's* at work," Damian said, mocking his tone, and then slightly more kindly said, "and your woman's completely fine."

"How do you know? Are you in there watching her? Is there human medical equipment on her? If you've left her alone with that werewolf, I will kill him *and* you," Rax threatened, feeling impotent from so far away.

"We're not going to let anything happen to her, Rax. I'm hanging up now."

"Are you sure she's all right?" Rax demanded.

"Not in the least," Damian snapped. "She's in love with you, so clearly there's something wrong with her."

"That's not funny, Damian," Rax growled.

Damian growled back. "Just fucking come and see her. I'm not so much of an asshole that I won't let you see your mate."

Rax made a strangled sound. "I can't. My brother's a dragon, same as I am, and he's not well. I can't leave him alone, but now that she is awake…knowing I cannot see her is making me want to die," Rax confessed.

There was an extraordinarily long pause on the far end of the line. "I'm going to regret this, I'm sure, but where the fuck do you live?"

THE NEXT TIME Sammy blinked her eyes open it was dark inside her room as well as out, with bright moonlight coming through the window, making a large flower arrangement cast wild shadows on her wall. For a second she remembered the sirens and was frightened— and then remembered they were locked away for good this time, without a key. Because of her. Her broken arm hung heavy across her body as did—*wait, what?*

Sammy spun around in bed beneath someone else's arm and found Rax behind her, also waking up from sleep. "Andi called me on the way here and threatened my life if I woke you," he apologized, as she set her good hand on his cheek.

"You took her seriously?" she asked him with a spreading grin.

He opened his eyes and began to smile back. "Honestly? I needed to nap. I've been watching my brother twenty-four seven for two weeks." He bowed his head to hers, and she breathed his scent in deep.

"Who's watching him now?" she whispered. *He really was here, with her, above the sea.*

"Damian," he said. "I'm not sure I can ever repay him for helping you heal and keeping you safe. I'm so sorry for not being here the second you woke earlier. Andi told me you asked and—"

"Shhh," Sammy put a finger on his lips. "You're here now."

"I am," he said. "And I need to tell you if I thought you were my mate before…I'm hopelessly in love with you now, Red. I knew it before I went down to the Gate, but when I saw you join me there, I gave a piece of my heart to you that I will never recover."

Sammy tilted her head from side to side. "That's funny because the only reason I was going down there was to give you a piece of *my mind*. I was so fucking pissed at you, Rax, for deciding shit without me *again*."

She felt him tense beside her. "I was trying to make things better."

"By abandoning me for a third time?" she asked him archly.

"No," he said, sounding wounded. "By being good. I knew if I didn't stop the sirens, you would never respect me, Samantha."

"But you didn't ask me, did you?" she asked and then sighed. "Rax, I've done a lot of uncool things in my life that I haven't even told you about." She moved to sit up beside him. "I don't want a *good man*. I just want someone who's *good to me*. And that means asking me questions and having hard conversations and not just putting me to sleep because it's easier on you. I know you've done whatever the fuck you've wanted to for eight hundred years, but if we're in a relationship, you don't just get to be the sole decider."

He sat up as well. "Would you have wanted me to go down there then? Be honest."

"No, but if you'd decided to regardless, I would've been braced. And I would've had a chance to say good-bye. You just leaving me was fucked up."

He was frowning deeply at her. "You told me you loved me at the bottom of the sea."

"So? That doesn't mean I can't ever get mad again. And I'm really good at being mad, as you should very well know." She crossed her left arm under her sling.

"I don't like the way this is going," he said, giving her a stern look, which faded quickly. "And I'm afraid my usual solutions won't help me here, seeing as I can no longer make decisions for you, cast sleep spells, or boss you around."

She shrugged. "Not my fault if you don't have a deep bench."

"Hmm." He considered her, making a show of stroking his chin in thought, before grinning wickedly. "Well, you've left me with one tool still."

"What's that?" she asked, eyes narrowed.

"Physical coercion," he said, carefully picking her up and pulling her into his lap, her back against his chest, where he could wrap his arms around her. She didn't fight him; in fact, she chased his hand beneath her sling with her good one and wove her fingers with his. "How is your arm?" he asked her in a whisper at her cheek.

"I haven't seen it yet. Andi says it's getting better though. But maybe not so pretty anymore."

"I find that hard to believe," he told her, resting his chin on the divot of her collarbone. "All of you is perfect to me."

Sammy nuzzled back against him. *He really was here.* "How's your brother?"

He sighed and leaned his head against her. "Broken. Time will heal his body, but he is prone to fits and moods and keeps claiming untrue things."

"Like what?"

"That he's the person responsible for coordinating all of this. You, the necklace, and me. Which I could almost believe, if he didn't use the next breath to tell me Seris was still alive."

She made a sad sound and squeezed Rax's hand. "Do me a favor?" she asked.

"Anything, beloved."

"Grant him some grace," she said. "After all, people told me I was crazy for a long time too, about the sirens, and they were wrong."

He thought on this and then nodded against her. "I will try." His one arm held her tight as he smoothed his other hand down her leg, like he was touching her just because he could. "Samantha...when I think back to how I treated you...."

"Yeah," she agreed. "That was pretty fucked up."

He held her more tightly. "I'm sorry. I know that doesn't make up for it in the least, but I am. The thought that you were scared because of me torments me at night."

She leaned her head against his. "So it would've been okay if it'd been someone else?"

She could feel the tension in his arms as he admitted, "If they had given me what I wanted, yes." He inhaled deeply. "I hope you meant what you said about not wanting a good man because I am not one. I have lied, I have cheated, and I have killed, Red, and I cannot promise that that will change, with the exception of me spending the rest of my life making things up to you and only you."

Sammy bit her lips and laughed. "I'd say I'd forgive you, but I'm really looking forward to this ongoing groveling."

"No one said anything about groveling," he said, with a sinister chuckle, then held her tightly again. "I spent so long thinking Tarian's grief was melodramatic, how could anyone care so much for a mere human? Then when I saw you in the water, bleeding, it broke me. I would've sold my soul to save you."

"Hmm," she said, in intentional imitation of him. "How much is a dragon's soul worth?"

"You will have to tell me, as mine is now yours." She felt enveloped by him there, in the quiet dark, as good as if he had wings and they were wrapped around her.

RAX COULD'VE EASILY HELD her for the rest of his life, completely content. He never thought he was meant to find a mate and then when he had he knew he couldn't keep her. So the fact that she was here, beside him, above the waves—he had no idea who he should thank for such luck, but he felt deeply grateful.

And then she shifted in his arms. "You know, Mister Worst," she whispered, "only my arm is injured. The rest of me isn't damaged in the least."

He nodded softly and then his hands went for her waist, helping to turn her so that she faced him, straddling him in her tank top and underwear. He pulled off his shirt and threw it across the room, then moved to hold her against him, one of her arms wrapped around his neck, the other folded between them, feeling the rough fabric of its sling scrape against his chest, a reminder of all the things he'd almost lost to darkness.

"I love you, Samantha," he whispered, breathing hard. "Tell me you love me too."

"I do," she murmured near his neck. "I hate the ocean, and you're an asshole for making me go there, and yet, somehow, I still want to be around you more than anything."

"No," he said, shaking his head slightly. "I want to hear you say the words."

She pulled her head back to look up at him. "I love you," she said slowly.

He was too used to her moods now to not hear her hesitance. "But?" he asked her.

"I'm scared," she said, giving him a sad smile.

Rax tilted his head, inspecting her. "*The* Samantha O'Connor? Scared?"

"Don't make fun of me," she said, pushing lightly on his chest.

"I'm not," he said, catching her hand to hold it to his heart. "What on earth could my Samantha be afraid of? If it's a thing, I'll buy it and crush it. If it's a person, I'll kill them myself."

She snorted softly. "It's not that easy...because it's me." She freed her hand from his so that she could hug herself, still straddling his lap. He put his hands on her outer thighs and soothed her with his thumbs, letting her gather the strength to talk. "I've spent so long knowing I was going to die, ever since I was a kid, you know? I didn't care about myself. I've always been the tough one. I never dared to let myself matter because what was the point?" She pointed up underneath her sling to where he knew her small scars were hidden. "Those were from my high school boyfriend, Garrett, Rax. I let him hurt me, really badly, just because he could, and I thought it didn't matter, that I didn't matter, because nothing did."

His eyes narrowed. "Two Rs, two Ts?"

Sammy shook her head quickly. "Don't kill him, please. He friended me on Facebook a while ago, and his current life is punishment enough." She winced and let her shoulders drop. "The point I'm trying to make is that I'm messed up. I've been messed up for a long time now, and now that I know that my childhood wasn't a lie, I probably still need a shit ton of therapy."

Rax listened to his impossibly-strong-yet-still-delicate mate tell him that she was broken, and it hurt him so badly he leaped to her defense. "You're not messed up, the world is—"

She put a hand across his mouth to shut him up. "Shhh. I am. I know it. I don't regret anything. Because being reckless and ready to die is what gave me the strength to go and save you. But...I think I'm so used to thinking I'm going to die, it might take me a while to figure out what living feels like."

He wanted to tell her she was wrong, to swamp her fears away with his affection, and *to do* something, then he realized all of that was only meant to make him feel better and not do a goddamned thing for her. Rax set his hands at her waist and bowed his head, so it was on a level with hers. "How can I help you, my love?"

Samantha inhaled and exhaled deeply. "I think you already are." And then her hand went to the hem of the tank top she wore, tugging it up.

He stopped her. "I don't want to hurt you."

"Then you'd better help me take this off," she teased him, as his hand tightened on hers.

"You know what I mean, Samantha."

Her eyes flashed up at him. "Then you already know the truth, too. It's too fucking late for that."

He closed his eyes and bowed his head even further, feeling her words slide in between his ribs and pierce his heart like a knife. "Even though my dragon is back now, I have no more scales around you."

Rax felt her head meet his with a tiny thump and saw her red hair hanging between them when he opened his eyes. "I'd say I'm glad to know I can hurt you back, but I'm not."

"Samantha," he began, lifting up, ready to start an infinite number of apologies.

She leaned in and kissed him, her soft lips pressing his words back. "Do you promise to be careful with me? And that you won't break me more?"

He slid his hands up into her hair, tilting her face up. "I do."

The look she gave him then was utterly unfamiliar to him, out of all her many moods he'd witnessed. Her eyes wide, her lips parted with just the slightest intake of breath, and something almost magical radiating off of her—he realized it was hope.

Hope for herself—and hope for them.

She'd never had cause for it around him up until now, but now that he'd seen the way it looked on her, he never wanted to take it away from her again.

She closed her mouth and grinned and laughed, and he could see the wetness shimmering in her eyes. "Then can you help me take this stupid shirt off? I think it's Andi's, so I don't want to tear it, but I *really* want it gone."

"Fuck yes," he agreed and started helping.

It was harder than it seemed like it would be to get her free, especially because the both of them kept laughing, and it felt like there was some oppressive need to be quiet because this was neither of their houses, which made being loud seem wrong, which made both of them laugh more. But she was mostly naked in front of him shortly, and he could carefully nuzzle his face against her chest if she angled her sling away right and *fuck he loved her.* He wrapped his arms around her tightly, hauling her up and to him, and she played her good hand through his hair, kneeling over him, letting him kiss a careful line of kisses across her stomach and hip as she softly sighed.

"Can I go further, Red?"

"Yes, please," she whispered, and he reached for the seam of fabric between her legs, shifting it aside, and started rubbing her clit with his thumb. She slowly sank back down, his hand following her all the way, and her lips were on his neck, his shoulders, his chest. He froze and she noticed, looking up. "What's wrong?"

He was so used to taking what he wanted he'd forgotten how to receive a kindness that was given. "I'm not used to being kissed," he confessed.

"Then we should fix that, shouldn't we," she whispered, then added, "If you want to, that is."

He nodded, and so she kept going, closing her eyes as her tongue traced the muscles of his chest, and then she pulled his hand closer to her heat, and he knew what she desired. He parted her open and pushed his two middle fingers in. She rewarded him with a beautiful moan as he began to rub her with them from the inside. Her hips arched against him, fucking his hand, as her mouth trailed his collarbone, her good hand turning into a fist against his opposite pec. He pushed her hair back with his free hand and kissed the top of her head before running it down her body, cupping her ass, helping her hips thud into his hand. "Is this careful enough, Red?" he whispered and felt her nod her head into his chest with a small whine. He was so fucking hard inside his jeans but he could feel her winding and right now her happiness was his own. He needed to make his mate feel good just as badly as he needed her to need him.

Her breath skipped, she started to shudder, and her hips moved of their own accord. "Rax," she whispered. "Rax, I'm—" she warned, but he already knew, he could feel her pussy grab him tight like it was trying to pull him in. "Rax," she hissed, as she pulsed around him, moaning, lost in waves of pleasure. He kept rubbing her till her hand caught his wrist then he slowly pulled out. She sighed his name again and he wanted to hear her say it like that always, deeply satisfied and out of breath, then she collapsed against him, sling and all.

"Do you feel better now?" he asked her, tucking her head under his chin.

"Some," she confessed, with a sigh and a nod. "But what about you?"

"What about me?" he said, trying for innocence.

She snorted softly. "I'm not stupid, I know you're hard."

He pet his hands down her hair and back. "As much as I metaphorically do not want to hurt you right now, Red, I literally do not want to do so as well. I don't need to fuck you if it sets back your healing."

Samantha looked up at him. "You've read all the books in your library, right?" Rax felt his eyebrows rise as he nodded. "Then how do you have such little imagination?" she tsked, wriggling free of his arms. "Scoot over," she said, pressing him away from the wall, moving herself beside him, her injured arm tucked between them both. "This part, I might need help with," she said, reaching for his belt with her good hand, starting to undo its latch.

"Samantha," he began, ready to swat her hand aside.

She glared up at him. "Relationships are all about compromise and teamwork."

He gave her an intentionally baffled look before laughing—hard. "How would either of us know?"

"I've heard people say it on TV before!" she protested, snickering before beaming at him. "Come on, Mister Worst, do you want a hand job or not?" Then her grin took a wicked turn as she brought her hand to her mouth and licked a stripe down the center of her palm.

He groaned at the same time his cock thumped against his jeans. "When you put it that way," he grunted, unlooping his arm from around her to undo his buckle quickly, unbuttoning and unzipping his fly, and then shoving his jeans down.

"Just get out of them," she asked him. "Give me you. All of you."

He nodded helplessly and freed himself from his jeans entirely, fully naked around her for the first time. She played her good hand up the dark hair on his thigh, bringing it between his legs to cup his balls as both of them watched his cock strain up his stomach, begging to be touched.

"I've never been with anyone uncircumcised before," she said.

"Except for me, repeatedly," he teased. "I assume it's much the same, though," he said, pulling her hand up to touch him. Her fingers wrapped around his shaft as his hand covered hers, stroking it up and down, feeling his foreskin rock with the motion.

"Like that?" she whispered, going with it.

"Yes," he hissed lightly, setting her hand free. "Just like that."

336

She kept going, playing his foreskin along his shaft, watching herself work, her jaw a little dropped, so serious to learn him that it made him love her even more, a thing he hadn't thought was possible.

"Do you like that?" she asked him, looking up.

"Oh yes, Red," he whispered, reaching his hands for her, catching her face to kiss it, timing himself, a kiss for each stroke, nuzzling himself into her neck, pulsing one hand against her breast, anything he could do to let her know just how he felt. He was rocking into her hand now, her strokes more confident as they took the length of him, and it was his turn to moan.

"I want to make you come, Rax," she whispered.

"You will, my love, you will," he promised. He took her hand in his again and showed her how to finish him, fast and loose, let her go, and seconds later, his head rocked back as his body spasmed and the first rope of his cum splashed up against his chest.

She groaned as he did and worked without stopping, like she was stroking all the cum out of him, sliding his foreskin up and down again, sheathing him repeatedly until he was spent and softening, and he pushed her hand aside.

"I love you," he told her again.

"You're just saying that because I jerked you off," she said, teasing him with a smile.

"True. But I loved you before that, and I'll love you forever now too." He let his head fall to the side, staring at her beauty in the dim light, wishing he could stay. He didn't know how long he'd been asleep though, prior to her waking him. He knew Damian had some sort of sporadic Do-Gooder job. He reached out to touch her cheek. *At least the circumstances around him leaving this time were much less dire....* "I've got to go though. I can't impose on Damian much longer."

Samantha brought up a pillow to blot at his chest as he sat up. "I understand why, but...." She flung the pillow across the room.

"Well, I wouldn't want you to be too happy that I'm going," he chuckled, standing to retrieve his jeans from the bottom of the bed to pull on, getting dressed beneath her watchful gaze. "If I thought it was safe to bring you home right now, I would, Red—clothing optional."

She sank back on her heels. "Is that place really home?" she asked him and he remembered that while it was his home, it'd been her prison. He'd been a fool to mention it.

He sat back on the bed and pulled his shirt on as she crawled up to be even with him. "We can talk about it while Tarian finishes healing. I promise I won't make any more plans for you without your input and if you want to move, we can. A tank for Hachiro and enough space for Smoke are all I ask," he said, and then realized that even that was perhaps assuming. "And that's if you want to live with me, which I hope you do, but if you don't, we can make that work, too. As long as there's an *us*."

She rested her cheek against his shoulder and caught his hand. "How do you feel about small apartments over bakeries?" she asked him.

"If it makes you happy? Done."

"And how do you feel about Damian being your landlord?"

Rax took a moment to stare at her and caught her trying not to laugh. "No. *Fuck* no," he said, as she collapsed into giggles on the bed. "Brat." He slid a finger up underneath the elastic of her underwear and made it snap against her ass.

She only laughed harder, rolling on her back to stare up at him, her hair spilled across the bed. "How will I know you're not a dream if you're not here when I wake up, Rax?"

"Am I so forgettable?" he asked her, leaning over. She shook her head beneath him and then sighed into his kiss. "Good," he said when he was done. "I love you, Samantha. I hope you can feel how much I mean it when I say it. We can work the future out together."

She reached up and traced the line of his cheek with her fingertips. "Now that I have one."

He cradled her hand to his cheek and kissed her palm. "Yes."

CHAPTER 24

After that, Rax's phone conversations with Samantha were the highlights of his day. Damian's witch truly was magical because she'd sorted out some kind of shifter-aware therapist for Samantha, and she and Andi were apparently having fun planning Andi's wedding, even though it was still months off. He listened to all of her stories, rapt, and she finally started telling him older ones, so the pieces of her prior life started making sense. (He also found out that she'd once dated Andi's brother, and he regretted not killing the man back when he was his employee.)

Tarian's health came back to him slowly, if not his common sense. He still believed extraordinary things, but Rax didn't think he was a danger to himself anymore. He gained an interest in learning about the new world he lived in and in wanting to explore it, if only to find Seris. And Rax did as he had promised Samantha and turned all his means towards his brother's cause, doing his best to instruct him how to live life on this new planet—having a television certainly helped—promising to provide him with all the documents he normally gave other refugees from the Realms, and access to a good deal more cash.

His one new hobby that he indulged in when Tarian was asleep and Samantha was not callable, was sorting through real estate listings. He tried to guess what kind of place would best suit her. Would she want a view of the ocean or of the city? Would she rather live in a penthouse or on a farm?

He knew he could just ask her, but things seemed to be going so well he didn't want to impose, or hear that she couldn't bear to live with him at all.

The only time he broke down was when one of the mansions near to Damian's in the Briars went up for sale. He didn't like the thought of being within spitting distance of Damian but if it made her happy…. He mentioned it to her casually and she told him she knew about it already, because she and Andi walked by it every day, and she'd seen the for sale sign up. He didn't know what to make of that.

Some nights it hurt to be apart from her physically so badly it ached, but then others she'd fall asleep on the phone with him reading her a book, and while his life wasn't perfect, it was far better than it had any right to be.

And then Tarian told him he wanted to meet her.

He'd been keeping Samantha away for her own safety, and because part of him didn't feel right flaunting her in front of his brother. As sure as Tarian felt of finding Seris, Rax still was full of doubt.

"I don't think—" Rax began, but Tarian cut him off.

"I heard what the sirens sang to you when we rose. They told you you'd have to choose and you didn't. I promise I also will not make you."

Rax considered this, then picked up his phone.

IT WAS Sammy's idea to meet them at the beach near sunset. Rax pressed her to make sure he'd heard her right, but she insisted. They were both dragons, so if something went south, she knew it was far safer for them to be outside. And unlike her own relationship with the ocean, they were born to it. She suspected they would find it calming, whereas she…just wanted to try to be normal again.

To see what that might be like.

She knew the Gate was locked by her, and she knew that from here on out Damian's people would be on alert to any dangers through rifts in the sea.

So beaches might really be safe now.

Her therapist told her it was okay for her to test it as long as she had her and Andi on the phone as standby.

And she found as she drove she was more nervous and excited about seeing Rax again than anything to do with her past.

She pulled into the parking lot and got out of the Prius Jamison had loaned her—a sad, sad, automatic car, but her arm was still healing, alas—to find the two men already waiting, leaning against a new-to-her vintage E-type Jaguar's hood.

Sammy hadn't seen Rax in person in a month so seeing him now was breathtaking. She got out of her car and had to fight not to run.

He felt no such compunction, shouting her name and racing across the few parking spots between them to pick her up and twirl her around carefully before setting her down again and petting his hand gently down her sling. He took her free hand in his own.

"Tarian?" she asked as he pulled her over toward his brother. The family resemblance was obvious, in the color of their skin and the shapes of their nose and their jaw, though Tarian's cheekbones were more sloped, and he was just a little taller than Rax was, though still quite much more lean. Tarian nodded at her with almost black eyes that stared through her.

"I am sorry about your parents," he said. Sammy blinked and looked to Rax, who looked as surprised as she felt.

"Thanks," she told him, and he nodded again. "When you do find Seris, this belongs to her," she said, fishing inside her pocket for the key. She'd tried to take it off not long after she'd woken up and after her night with Rax. She'd asked Andi for help, and the other girl had been able to undo the latch easily, dropping the whole necklace into her lap.

Tarian took it. "Thank you," he said gravely.

"I wish you luck. I hope you find her. Even if I'll miss understanding Smoke," she said and grinned lightly.

Tarian focused his distant gaze on her and reached out with a hand and Sammy felt the wind knocked out of her, at the same time as Rax stepped up and sharply said, "Tarian, don't!"

"She expressed a desire to understand the fox," Tarian said.

"We *ask* people if they want to be spelled on this planet," Rax muttered, and then more loudly, "For the record, I don't think you leaving is a good idea."

"No," Tarian agreed. "But I do. You have your life to return to," he said, looking at Sammy. "I have imposed long enough, and I need to begin my search."

Sammy watched Rax consider how best to send his brother off, finally deciding on a handshake, which his brother stiffly returned. She watched the other dragon walk to the Jaguar and drive away.

"Wait...that's not yours?" she said, following the car with her eyes.

"No. I showed him a picture of mine in its glory days pre-meeting you, Red, and he said he wanted one, so," Rax said and shrugged.

"And that's all he had to say?" Her eyes followed the car until it took a turn behind some dunes. "Because here I was thinking maybe after my first two hundred blow jobs...."

Rax laughed, and she loved the sound of it. "I'll call my dealer, quality vintage ones can take a while to find. But we can investigate this new currency of blow jobs in the meantime, I'm very interested in figuring out their exchange rate."

"I bet you are," she said with a grin.

"It's important to be precise." One of his eyebrows rose. "I'd hate for you to undervalue your skills." He was so pleased with himself she couldn't help but smile back. She walked back to the Prius and climbed up on its hood. He followed her, sitting down beside her on her left side, so they could hold hands, and she wondered at seeing her small pale hand in his much larger, darker one. The same hands that she was once so sure would hurt her now made her feel safe.

"Are you sure you're okay being here?" he asked, looking at her tenderly.

She nodded quickly. "Working on it, yeah."

"You don't have to get over the ocean for my sake. Or, any of it really. As much as I want you, I don't want you to come to me until you feel right, because when you do, I don't want you to have any questions."

He'd told her as much on the phone, multiple times. Sammy gave him a soft smile. "I know."

The truth was, she'd been thinking a lot about things over the past few weeks at Andi's house. As hard as it was being away from him, it was good to be given enough space so that she could be sure she was making up her own mind, and that it wasn't just the way that they'd met or the circumstances that'd overwhelmed her.

"That said, though," he went on, "Hachiro misses you. As does Smoke."

She looped her legs over his and let him cradle her to his side as the sun started to drift down to the ocean's edge. "And you?"

"I more than miss you," he said, pulling her close. "I don't know that there's a word that I can use to describe it."

"Hmm," she said like he so often did. "I'm going to be an asshole and tell you to try."

He chuckled, she felt it rumble beneath her. "Fine. You know how I acquire rare magical objects?" Sammy nodded into his chest as he started stroking his hand up and down her side. "I feel like right now, there's this one I want that's just out of reach, and it's killing me. Because I want it more than I've ever wanted anything else before in my life, in my entire past, and I am not a man used to patience or to being told no."

Sammy laughed. "So in this metaphor am I like a pillow with a cat embroidered on it, or...." she teased. "I've been inside your vault, you forget."

"No," he said and snorted. "In this metaphor, you're my most valuable possession, Red." He nuzzled into her hair and whispered, "You're the woman I was ready to dream about for eternity."

She gasped softly and tears sprang to her eyes. She wiped them away savagely with her good hand as he held her tight.

"Whenever you're ready, Samantha—come home to me. Wherever

that winds up being," he told her. "I love you, and I want to be with you, above the waves."

She turned in his arms to face him and gave up on not crying. The sun touched the water behind him and Sammy realized she wasn't scared of the ocean anymore.

Or him.

Or forever.

"Now," she told him, feeling urgency suffuse her. She twisted toward him. She'd waited long enough and she couldn't stand to wait any longer. "I want to go home with you. Now."

"Are you sure?" he asked her, pulling her tight.

"Completely," she said, beaming up.

He caught her mouth with his, pulled her on top of him, and everything else melted away. They kissed as the wind rushed, as the waves crashed, and as the sun fell into the ocean and it turned night. By the time it was dark, when the only light was moonlight and the fire of his eyes, Sammy knew she'd made the right choice.

Then she looked around. "Wait...Rax? How the hell were you going to get home?"

He chuckled beneath her. "My beautiful girlfriend was going to give me a ride."

Sammy gave him a mock aghast look. "You mean to tell me mermaids can drive?"

He laughed. "Sorry, my beautiful *human* girlfriend. I should've been more specific."

"That's more like it," she said, nipping at his chin. "Take me home, Rax." She fished the Prius's keys out of her pocket and put them on his chest. "Your home. Our home."

"Do you mean it?" he asked her, his voice just a whisper, belaying his hope.

"I do," she whispered back. "I want to go home right now and possibly start working on earning an E-type Jaguar."

He laughed even harder and curled up, grabbing the keys before they started to slide off his chest, dismounting the car's hood and practically carrying her with him. "I do realize you're joking though," he said, placing her in the Prius's passenger seat. "I mean, I would buy you any car you ever wanted, Samantha—"

Sammy flashed him a look. "And here I thought you were a businessman."

Rax paused, reading her, then slid across the Prius's hood, getting into the driver's side, giving her a meaningful look back. "Then if you weren't injured, I'd say you could start earning it right now."

"I've been feeling ever so much better lately," she promised with a grin.

He gave a growl, hit the button to start the car, and started undoing his belt. "I can't believe I'm saying this, but for the first time in my life, I'm glad I'm in a Prius."

Sammy laughed, starting to lean over as he pulled the car out of the lot. "Why?"

"This thing has fucking airbags," he said, stroking her hair back and winding it around his hand. "The Jags don't, and I care about your safety."

"You just remember that," she whispered, looking up at him from the vicinity of his lap.

"Always, Red. Always."

EPILOGUE

SAMMY WOKE UP TO AN ACTUAL ALARM CLOCK, WHICH WAS A RARITY, even though she now had ways of keeping track of time. But today... was important...why?

"Andi's wedding," she whispered to herself, half-awake.

Rax made a sound beside her, wrapping her with a strong arm and pulling her close. "More sleeping," he commanded.

"Can't," she said, starting to extricate herself. "Too much to do. And I have too much hair. It's already going to take the stylist forever. I can't be late," she said, wriggling away from him. "I need to go, you can catch up—"

The possessive growling sounds coming from the direction of her boyfriend continued. "No."

"I'm not asking permission," she hissed at him.

"Good, because I'm not granting it," he grumbled, waking up. "We have to have sex on a wedding day, Red. It's tradition. It's why they always book weddings in the Realms for afternoons." He stroked his hand up her stomach and cupped her breast. "And the politest hosts book theirs for evenings. Gives single people a chance to figure their shit out and catch up." He pulled his thumb across her nipple and kissed her neck. "Everyone of age coming to a wedding has to have had sex that day. It's good luck."

He sounded completely sincere. She turned toward him, putting both hands on his chest to give him a baffled look. "I've never read anything about that."

"Some things don't make it into books, Red," he said, running a hand down her thigh, picking it up and placing it over his. "It's an important tradition."

"That you *literally* just made up," she said, shoving him lightly.

"Did not," he said and shook his head. "I *guarantee* you Damian is fucking Andi this morning."

Sammy paused at that. Andi hadn't mentioned spending the night apart from Damian, like people usually did on Earth, even though Sammy had asked her. "But, why would you have sex before your wedding?"

It was his turn to stare at her, baffled. "Why would you be getting married if you didn't want to have sex with the other person? And why would you have sex afterward, when you're too tired from all the dancing and playing host?"

Sammy laughed. "If I find out you're lying, Mister Worst," she threatened, as she rolled back, letting him pull himself on top of her.

"Don't worry, I'm not," he said, roughly kissing her neck, as she wrapped her legs around his hips, feeling his hard-on already nudging against her. "I won't make you too late. But I will make you feel good," he swore. He slid his hand down her smooth left arm, pulling it up over her head to pin it, and then his other hand down her right arm, across the scrolling scars the lock had given it, to trap it over her head, but not quite as far, because he knew her shoulder was still healing.

And that was what made all the difference, she thought, pretending to fight back, as she pretended to want to be free, knowing that she was completely uninterested in ever winning against him and that he had conquered her utterly.

"You're so wet, Red," he murmured against her ear. "You love being trapped."

Sammy kissed him—hard. "Only by you."

They rocked together after that, fantasies forgotten in the name of expedience, until she curled into his chest, crying his name, and he grunted hers not long after, spilling himself inside of her again. She lay there panting, then kissed his cheek. "Okay, you were right, that was good, but—"

"I know, I know," he said, pulling himself out with a smile. "Go take your shower. I'll get ready too."

Sammy took a rinse-off shower and sprayed perfume in her hair so she wouldn't have to dry it, but hopefully it wouldn't smell like sex, and then she shoved Rax into the bathroom. "Remember, your only job today is to be nice to Damian and don't start any fights!" she reminded him before closing the door. She was slightly comforted by the fact he'd found his tuxedo and a dress shirt for himself in the meantime and had thrown them on their bed.

Andi's wedding coordinator was doing most of the work at the venue but Sammy still wanted everything to go well. She pulled on jeans and a flannel she didn't care about getting make-up on while finishing wildly packing for ridiculous emergencies. She was prepared for anything from a dress tear to a heel break right up through a bomb threat.

"Where are you going?" Smoke asked, trotting up.

"To Andi's wedding," Sammy said, looking around for her shoes because she couldn't remember if she'd sent them ahead or if she was supposed to bring them with her right now. "You remember Andi?"

"Of course!" Smoke said, then casually asked. "Does the cat get to go?"

Sammy tore through all of her shoes to find another pair that would work with a cream-colored floor-length dress, just in case. "Uh...I'm not sure?" She knew Grimalkin was practically family for Damian. But still, *a cat at a wedding!* Then again Damian's sister *had wings*, so who cared?

Smoke sat down and gave her a shrewd look. "When you get married, will I get to go?"

349

She laughed. "Sure. Maybe? I mean, if and when, as a reward for not biting me all this time, I guess," she said with a grin.

Smoke leaned over and looked past her shoulder. "What about Hachiro?"

She looked back at the tank and saw Comet hovering there. *From a cat at a wedding to an octopus?*

But it would be different, wouldn't it? It would be her wedding. And she didn't have any family she needed to show pictures to, so why the fuck not? "Certainly," she told Smoke. "Although…why are you asking?"

"No reason." The fox shrugged, then pretended to chase a flea, snapping his teeth against his shoulder.

"Smoke…." she warned. The fox ran away as Rax emerged from the bathroom with a towel around his waist, water dripping down the muscles of his stomach. He ran a hand through his hair, taking her in, kneeling on the ground in the middle of ten different pairs of light-colored shoes.

"Why do I have to wear a tuxedo if you're not even in a dress?" he complained as she stood up.

"Because. My dress—is there. My make-up—is there. My hair-stylist—is there." Sammy pointed frantically in what she hoped was the direction of Andi's ballroom. "That's why I need to get *there*. I will explain more wedding customs from *Earth* in the car."

Rax's lips pursed, and his eyes narrowed in thought. He stood a little straighter, and Sammy took a step closer to him. She glanced toward the aquarium, where Comet had jetted himself away, and she knew Smoke had zipped off. She turned towards Rax with her hands on her hips. "Darling and beloved, did you have something important you wanted to say?"

Rax stared her down and she dared him to lie to her with her eyes. "Smoke told you, didn't he?"

"Oh my *God*, no! But I'm glad he let on!" Sammy brought her hands to her mouth, horrified that Rax had been thinking of proposing to her at Andi's wedding. "You can't!"

Rax frowned. "But…Damian said I could."

"Oh God bless," Sammy said, kneeling back to the ground to shove shoes into her bag wholesale; she'd figure shit out later and could cover anyone else who broke a heel and was a size eight. "Look, just like the Realms has customs," she said, standing up and shouldering the bag, "although I'm still pretty sure the sex thing was one you just made up, Earth does too. And you absolutely cannot ask me to marry you at Andi's wedding. It's rude. Really, really rude," she said, roughly zipping the bag up as everything sunk in.

He was going to ask...her?

"But it's a beautiful happy celebration," Rax said, holding up two empty hands and joining them, like combining joys made sense.

She stared at him for a second. *He really had been going to ask.* Then she started shaking her head and didn't stop. "They paid a lot of money for this, Rax, and Andi's so excited to be a bride I can't stand it. That's why we can't take any attention away from her on her special day."

He very nearly pouted. "I want you to be special, too."

Sammy blinked and laughed, leaning up on her toes to kiss him. "I promise, you make me feel special. Every day."

"Hmm. Not good enough." He snapped his fingers and started walking past her for the shark tank, where Comet swam up, holding chains from all his tentacles. Sammy gasped at the sight as Rax leaned in and swooped the jewelry out of the water to bring it back to her, his fist dripping with salt water, rubies, and gold.

"Rax," she said, taking a step back. "What are you doing?"

"I want to bind you in the old ways. Come here, Red," he said, kneeling down.

"Rax...I," she tried to protest, not wanting to be late, but her feet led her to stand in front of him of their own accord.

He pulled off two smaller circlets and clasped them around her ankles, one at a time, tugging up the cuff of her jeans so that they rested against her skin. "So that you will always walk beside me," he said. Then he took two bracelets and linked them around her wrists, first her left and then her right. "So that your hands will always reach for mine, even in the dark."

"Rax," she whispered, glad she wasn't wearing make-up yet because she was totally about to cry. He smiled up at her, brushing her hair off her shoulders to loop a chain around her neck, with a sizeable sparkling ruby dangling from it. "So that you can always feel my heart against you, even if I am not near," he said, setting the stone down where the key used to rest, between her breasts, atop her sternum. And then he hitched up the edges of her flannel shirt, circling a loose chain of gold dotted with rubies around her hips. "And this one is for me," he said, making a fist of it and pulling her close. "So that I can always use it to hold onto you, until I must open it, to share you with a child." He looked up at her expectantly. "What is your answer, Samantha?"

She looked down at the bracelets on her wrists, the stone hanging from her neck, the chain wrapped around his hand, and more precious to her than any of them, the fire of his eyes. The dragon who, to her at least, was no longer cold nor cruel, who wanted to spend the rest of his life above the waves at her side.

The man who'd risked eternity to soothe her broken soul.

"I do," she breathed and then started nodding deeply. "Yes," she said, from the bottom of her heart. He engulfed her hips with his arms and then hoisted her up, laughing against her and spinning her around, and she was completely enamored with him, even as she fought him to put her down. "We've got to go!" she said, laughing, as he finally let her feet touch the ground. She reached up, grabbed his head, and pulled it to hers to kiss him deeply. He wrapped his arms around her waist, and he kissed her just as hard back, making her swoon with a sigh. "I love you," she whispered when he'd righted her. "Get dressed now, or else."

Rax laughed, dropped his towel, and started quickly putting his tuxedo on. She watched him, feeling encircled by his love, as all of the promises he'd made echoed through her mind. "Wait a minute," she said aloud. "I'm not babyproofing a place with a shark tank, Rax."

He glanced over at her from where he was tying a bowtie without a mirror and gave her a rakish smile. "You're not pregnant yet," he said, expertly tugging the end of the tie through. "I'm willing to work on that with you though."

"Oh, that's so kind of you!" she said, playing it straight.

He pressed a hand to his dress shirt. "Well, you know I am the giving sort."

Sammy snickered. "I'd noticed, Mister Worst." She walked up to him and straightened his already perfect bowtie, then looked up at him through her eyelashes. "Tell me, is it double good luck if you have sex twice before a wedding?" she asked him, the embodiment of innocence.

He paused, looking at her for a moment, before swooping her up and throwing her on the bed. "Yes," he said definitively.

"I was teasing," she protested, squealing as he pinned her down. "Rax!"

"Don't worry," he told her, smiling above her, giving her a look she couldn't wait to get for the rest of her life. "I'll make sure you're there on time, Red, even if I have to fly you there myself."

IF YOU ENJOYED this Wardens of the Other Worlds novel, you'll love Austin and Ryana's standalone, Wolf's Princess! Check out the blurb and excerpt below!

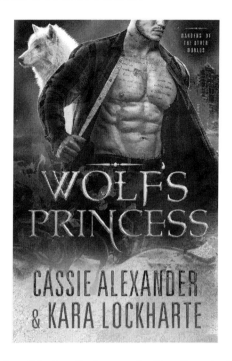

Rough-and-tumble Austin knows better than to flirt with his best friend's younger sister—she's a princess, part-dragon, and 100% off-limits—he just can't stop himself.

Ryana Blackwood, Princess of the Realms, is coming out of the worst break-up of all time and looking for a rebound. Luckily, her werewolf friend Austin checks all her boxes: he's hot, easy, and nearby.

So when Ryana asks him to pretend to show her what a real relationship is like...how on earth is he supposed to resist? But what is he supposed to do when she realizes she's too good for him? And how can she convince him when it's not a game to her anymore?

Wolf's Princess is a sweet yet incredibly sexy paranormal romance between two complicated people who are fated mates —they just don't know it yet.

Excerpt from Wolf's Princess:

Ryana sat in front of him and braced herself.

This was it.

She would graciously offer to sleep with him, he would graciously accept, and then it would be the beginning of her making new memories here on *this* planet, slowly scrubbing away the old. Eventually, nothing else that came before would matter, and even if she ever did go back to the Realms, no one *there* would ever worry that she'd come *here*, tonight.

Because Austin was a nobody, in a good way. Born on earth, he had no subterfuge, no secret allies, and no one to tell about their escapade—lest her brother kill him—so overall?

He was perfect.

And there was no reason on this world or any other for him not to agree.

She watched his eyes trace over her wings and saw him frown lightly. There was a pockmark on one of them, from when she'd deflected a bullet meant for him. She'd saved his life, although it'd punched a hole into her wing that'd left a scar.

He owed her. *Yet another reason he'll say yes.*

"Yeah, wings, I'd noticed you're not from around these parts," Austin said with a soft sigh, relaxing in his chair.

Time to be brave!

You are part-dragon!

She pictured herself sleeping through a night. Not waking up with a knot in her throat, crying, feeling horrified or ashamed. Finding rest, true rest, in someone else's arms, no matter how briefly.

The thought of it gave her strength. "Yes, well…different places do things on different schedules. So it seems that on Earth, of course, I'm woefully behind in some components important to my future well-being." She crossed her legs and set her hands in her lap, doing her best to seem as regal as possible.

Austin's head tilted and he gave her a befuddled look. "I can give you more movies to watch, Ryana…maybe even watch them with you, if you wanted?"

"No. That's charming, though," she said with a nervous laugh. *He is going to say yes. Absolutely.* "No, Austin, the reason I'm here is because I'd like you to sleep with me."

And then she watched Austin—suntanned, rough-and-tumble, never met a fight he didn't like, Austin—slowly go as white as the t-shirts that were for some reason littering his floor right now. "Excuse me?" he said, and blinked.

Yes. Immediately to terms. This was exactly how she'd hoped. She sat straighter and smiled winningly at him. "This is an experience I desire to have. And so I am here, requesting your assistance."

"No way," Austin muttered to himself. "Did Zach put you up to this? Because if so, it's really not funny."

It was Ryana's turn to blink—and for the first time since she'd walked into his room, she had a feeling things might not go as planned.

Which was stupid, right?

Because her plan was flawless.

His name was in her notebook!

He was him, she was her, and they'd get together and get it over with. He would be the first in her no doubt many future conquests, which would erase Baran from her memories.

Wouldn't he?

"No, I haven't told anyone else. I've just told you. Just now." She crossed her arms—and he rolled his chair back against the carpeting to be further way from her, a disconcerting maneuver. "Although I have to say, this isn't how I imagined that it would go." Her lips fell to a pout.

One of Austin's eyebrows crawled up to meet his golden hair. "And just what did you imagine, wings?"

She took him in with all her senses—his heart was beating a little fast, but it often did around her—all the more reason she'd assumed this would work! "I thought—I thought there'd be a little more enthusiasm. On your part. Not mine. I'm plenty enthused. It is time for me to be done with this." *And back on the path to sleeping without dreams.*

"You're serious?" he asked her.

"As certain as when Eloph made the sun."

It was an expression from the Realms, and he squinted, getting her gist even if he didn't understand the reference. "When?" he asked her.

"Now? I guess?" She looked around his unkempt room. It wasn't exactly like she'd pictured things, but, well, none of her experience on Earth really was. She'd always imagined her older brother Damian had gone off to a magical place to rule in peace and prosperity. The truth about Earth so far was much more prosaic—and violent. "So," she said, standing. Austin's bed was underneath that pile of clothing over there, surely. *Somewhere.* "Let's set to—"

Austin shook his head, with his tongue dug in beneath his lower lip. "I haven't said yes yet."

Ryana turned to fully look at him. "But you're going to." She hoped he heard the threat implicit in her tone.

He crossed his arms. "Am I? Does having wings give you the ability to read minds?"

"Austin," she said flatly. "I'm not going to beg you." Her pride had limits. Ryana lifted her chin haughtily and arched her wings out, occupying more space. "Do you not want me? Because if that's so, I'm sure I can find someone else."

He swung up out of his chair then. "You think you can waltz into my room and ask me to perform on command?"

Ryana frowned, feeling herself lose power over the situation. "Yes!" she snapped. "Why isn't this easy?" In all the variations she'd run through in her mind, not a one of them had ever ended like this.

"Because I'm not," Austin growled. He didn't need wings to loom in front of her. He had a good half-a-foot on her, and his shoulders were quite broad. "Despite what you may have heard."

Ryana squinted up at him. Clearly she'd pressed some button she didn't even know he had. "Fine." She folded her arms in on themselves and her wings back. Surely sleeping with one creature from Earth would be like sleeping with the next. "I'll find someone else. Forget I asked. Forget I was even here."

Austin groaned and rocked back. "That's not what I'm saying, Ryana."

She hugged herself. "Then what are you saying, hmmm? I'm listening—"

"Ryana," he complained at being pressed.

She took a step toward him, glaring up. She knew she was very good at it; it was a family trait. "Perhaps I've surprised you. And perhaps you're not interested. Perhaps you can't even make up your own mind? You are half-hound, after all," she sniffed, then put her finger out to tap on his chest above his heart. "You have three weeks to figure yourself out, Austin. And after that? I will be taking my interest elsewhere."

Ryana waited for him to say something, hoping he would. When he didn't, she whirled and left the room.

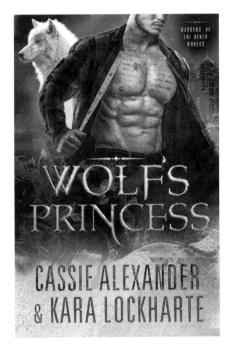

Check out Wolf's Princess and make sure to sign up to Cassie's newsletter!

ALSO BY CASSIE ALEXANDER

PRINCE OF THE OTHER WORLDS (co-written with Kara Lockharte)

(Andi & Damian's story)

Dragon Called

Dragon Destined

Dragon Fated

Dragon Mated

WARDENS OF THE OTHER WORLDS (co-written with Kara Lockharte)

(each book is a standalone)

Dragon's Captive (Sammy & Rax)

Wolf's Princess (Austin & Ryana)

Wolf's Rogue (Zach & Stella)

Dragon's Flame (Tarian & Seris)

…and don't forget to join Cassie's newsletter for access to an exclusive Andi and Damian prequel story, *Dragons Don't Date*, plus *Bewitched*, a Jamison and Mills novella!

THE DARK INK TATTOO SERIES

Blood of the Pack

Blood at Dusk

Blood by Moonlight

Blood by Midnight

Blood at Dawn

Cassie's Stand Alone Books

The House: Come Find Your Fantasy -- a choose your own adventure erotica

Rough Ghost Lover

Her Future Vampire Lover

Her Ex-boyfriend's Werewolf Lover

The Edie Spence Urban Fantasy Series

Nightshifted

Moonshifted

Shapeshifted

Deadshifted

Bloodshifted

Sign up for more news from Cassie here!

ALSO BY KARA LOCKHARTE

Dragon Lovers

Betrothed to the Dragon

Belonging to the Dragon

Bonded to the Dragon

Dragon Lovers Complete Vol. 1

The Space Shifter Chronicles

(Science Fiction Romances)

NOVELS

Wanted by the Werewolf Prince

Taken by the Tigerlord

Desired by the Dragon King (coming soon)

SHORT STORIES

The Boy Who Came Back a Wolf (free to newsletter subscribers)

The Lady and the Tigershifter

In Search of Skye

ABOUT THE AUTHOR

On her own, Cassie's a nurse by day and writer by night, living in the Bay Area with her husband, two cats, inside a massive succulent garden.

Whereas Kara's a California transplant by way of NYC and is still, to this day, searching for the perfect bagel (although the no-snow and strawberries out here help to make up for it.)

Follow Cassie's newsletter for a free book and bonus content! https://www.cassiealexander.com/newsletter

Follow Kara on Facebook, www.facebook.com/karalockharte or get a free book at her website, www.karalockharte.com/signup

Printed in Great Britain
by Amazon

17156967R00212